LETHAL BALANCE

Sons of the Survivalist: 2

CHERISE SINCLAIR

VanScoy Publishing Group

ABOUT LETHAL BALANCE

Sons of the Survivalist 2

Ms. Sinclair is a comfort read for me. She knows how to give me heroes who can take charge but in that protective, not possessive way that I love and heroines who may suffer but have that inner strength that makes them survivors. - After Dark Booklovers

His name means hunter.

Once the best assassin in black ops, Cazador is now the best at saving lives. His path has changed from seeking bloody vengeance to running a health clinic in Rescue, Alaska.

He will never again risk loving someone he can't protect.

His mother and sister were murdered in front of him, his fiancée slaughtered in a war zone. Despite his popularity with women, he's determined to remain unattached. His heart can bear no more loss.

Unfortunately, the universe isn't listening.

First, his brother hires JJ, a fiery-haired, tough cop who lives on the edge of danger and has the biggest heart of anyone he knows. And then, his disreputable past returns in the shape of an adorable, foul-mouthed nine-year-old daughter. Now he has two loved ones to protect. An impossible task, because...

Life is dangerous. Especially in Alaska.

ABOUT THE AUTHOR

Cherise Sinclair is a *New York Times* and *USA Today* bestselling author of emotional, suspenseful romance. She loves to match up devastatingly powerful males with heroines who can hold their own against the subtle—and not-so-subtle—alpha male pressure.

Fledglings having flown the nest, Cherise, her beloved husband, an eighty-pound lap-puppy, and one fussy feline live in the Pacific Northwest where nothing is cozier than a rainy day spent writing.

ACKNOWLEDGMENTS

As always and ever, so many thanks go to my critique partners, Fiona Archer and Monette Michaels.

Hugs and more hugs to my amazing beta readers: Barb Jack, Marian Shulman, Lisa White, and to my beloved psychology expert, Ruth Reid. Thank you!

My Alaska authorities, JJ Foster and Kathleen Cole, didn't let me get away with any cheechako goofs and have enlivened the story—and my life—with fun tidbits. (Any remaining mistakes are my very own). So many thanks go to JJ and Kathleen.

Ekatarina Sayanova and her Red Quill editors, Rebecca Cartee and Tracy Damron-Roelle, who do such a brilliant job of catching errors, worked long hours to help me get this book out before the holidays. Thank you so much!

Finally, I want to thank you, my readers, for your enthusiasm for the *Sons of the Survivalist* series. Y'all are the best!

PROLOGUE

T*wenty-three years ago*

In your darkest hour, when the demons come. Call on me, brother, and we will fight them together - Unknown

He was a crappy son. And brother.

Miguel Ramirez, now called Cazador, sat on a moss-covered log and dangled a stick in the stream. Tiny fish mouthed the bark before flitting away. Disappearing.

Like Mamá and Rosita had. Because they'd died.

His little sister's screams still filled his nightmares.

Caz hammered his fist on his thigh until his leg throbbed painfully. He *should* hurt. If he hadn't played soccer after school, maybe they'd be alive. Maybe he could've kept that man from shooting Mamá.

Maybe, maybe, maybe.

He'd told Rosita to lock doors. Told her and told her and told her. He'd told Mamá to make sure no one followed her home after she got off work from the bar. A breath of a sob shuddered through him. *I tried.*

His trying hadn't been enough.

That man had shot them. Mamá and Rosita died.

Before Papá left, he'd said Miguel was the man of the family. A tear dropped onto his jeans, a dark spot. He'd let Papá down, let them all down.

Now, Miguel had a new family. And a new name. Cazador. Just like Kana was now Bull, Derek was Hawk. Gabe was still Gabe because he was stubborn that way.

Mako had rescued them.

When the foster father had tried to make Hawk have sex—pulled Hawk's pants down and everything—Gabe and Bull and Cazador had attacked him. A big man—Mako—heard them yelling, walked in, and finished everything by punching the foster father. As Caz and the others started edging toward the door to escape to the streets, Mako asked if they wanted to go away with him. He said he'd raise them, if that's what they wanted.

Cazador looked around. All he could see were trees. All he could hear was the low gurgle of the river. No wonder Mako said social workers wouldn't find them. Not here in Alaska in the middle of nothing.

Caz didn't want to like the other guys or Mako. Not any of them. They'd probably die, too, cuz he couldn't protect them; he was the littlest. Hawk called him "the baby" since Cazador was only eight. Nine, today.

Stupidass nine-year-old Hawk wasn't all that cool, the way he cried at night. When Gabe tried to talk to him about it, the *pendejo* had hit him. Caz snorted. Gabe had knocked Hawk on his ass.

Gabe was all right. He was ten, and they all did what he said. Because he always seemed to know what to do.

Hawk was a stupidass. Well, maybe not. He'd jumped into the

river and saved a fawn that had its leg stuck. Caz would've, but he didn't know how to swim. His shoulders slumped. Hawk wasn't the only stupidass.

And unlike the rest of them, Hawk hoarded his treats, although he'd shared a candy bar with Caz last week. Yeah, sometimes, he was all right.

Bull was fun. Always laughing and telling jokes. Only, he had a temper too. He'd knocked Gabe into a tree when Gabe kept teasing him. And sometimes, his face got sad, and he just went and stared at the river.

Kinda like Caz was doing now.

Behind Caz, something snapped. He tensed and twisted to look.

Not a bear. It was Mako—who was almost as big as a bear. The sarge never made any noise in the woods. He must've busted a branch on purpose to let Caz know he was there. He carried a couple of fishing poles and a tackle box.

Caz scowled and turned his back. Yet...he kinda hoped Mako would stay.

Mako did.

The log sagged as the sarge settled next to Caz and made him feel even littler. Mako was tall and huge with muscles. His really short hair was going gray, and his skin was lined and tanned almost as dark as Caz's. His eyes were blue and scary, like he'd seen some bad shit. He'd been a soldier, like, forever, so he probably had.

"Your food's still on the table, boy."

Caz shrugged although his stomach rumbled.

"Gotta say, getting pissed off about birthday cake is new." Mako baited the fishing hook and dropped it into the river. "Did Gabe get the day wrong?"

"No." Caz scowled and picked up the other rod. Baited it. He'd just learned how. Too many things to learn. His English was still crappy, too, mostly when he tried to talk fast. "It's today."

"Did Bull misspell your name?"

Cazador. It meant hunter in Spanish. He'd chosen it when Mako told the boys they needed new names in case someone looked for them. Although Mako figured the foster father in Los Angeles would just say the kids ran away. "Bull spelled it right."

Bull was cool the way he liked feeding people. He'd made the cake and even decorated it.

Holding the fishing pole, Cazador frowned. It'd been rude to run out of the cabin. He eyed the sarge to see how mad he was. Cool or not, Mako didn't take any shit. Yesterday, Gabe mouthed off and got tossed in the river. And the water was like ice. "I just..."

He could feel when Mako turned to look at him. "Yeah?"

"*No quiero*...I do not want to like them. The boys. I do not want a family. I had a family, and they..."

"They died?" Mako didn't bullshit around saying they'd "passed" or "went to heaven". *Died*.

Caz nodded. "*Mi hermana*, she more little than me. I not protect her or Mamá."

"What happened to them?" Mako reeled in his line, sent it out again.

"Mamá and Rosita come home with groceries, and man come in. A druggie." The river seemed to turn red, dark, and ugly. "I come inside. Hear it. The gun." The gun fired, and Caz was running into the house, into the kitchen. Mamá lay on the floor, and her pink shirt, the one she liked, was all bloody. "He shoot Mamá."

"Shit, that's rough, kid." A big hand squeezed his shoulder, then Mako cast the line again. "It's not easy when crap like that happens out of the blue."

Caz saw it again, like in his nightmares, how he'd grabbed a knife off the counter and charged.

The words came out slow. "I take knife. And..." He shook his head when the words didn't line up. But Mako should know what a loser Caz was. If he sent Caz back to L.A., it would be what Caz deserved.

"Yeah? Knife versus pistol—the pistol usually wins."

The gun had made that noise again, like a sharp firecracker, and his head exploded with pain. "He shoot me." Caz touched the side of his head, the long scar from the bullet plowing through skin and hair. "I fall down, and he shoot Rosita."

Because Cazador had failed.

The grunt Mako gave sounded like pain.

Caz held very still and asked the question he'd never been able to ask anyone else. "Did he shoot her because me?" Was it his fault?

The scraping sound was Mako rubbing his chin. He shaved every morning, but his stubble showed up fast. He shook his head. "Doubt it, Caz. After he shot your mom, he couldn't leave witnesses behind. Not you or your sister. And a druggie? Most likely he was shootin' everything in sight."

"Oh." The dirty knot in his chest loosened a little. But if he'd moved faster, been better, maybe they'd be alive. He hadn't been...enough.

Mako recast toward quieter water under a tree. "Sounds like you left today because you don't want a family. At least not one you gotta protect."

"Sí."

"I get that." Mako turned his gaze up, watching something.

Caz looked. Wide black wings in the blue sky. White head. An eagle.

"Women and kids... A man does everything he can to protect them. They're our reason for being."

Caz nodded. It's what was in his heart. What he'd never been able to say.

"We got no women or children here," Mako said.

What were Hawk and Gabe and Bull? And Caz? "I am nine."

"You and the other boys aren't children—not any longer."

Es verdad. It was true. Living on the street changed a kid.

"By the time I get through with you, it'll take a fuck of a lot to kill you." Mako reeled in his hook and rose. "A man needs his team at his back. You could do worse than Hawk, Gabe, and Bull."

The other three boys. At his back. Guarding him as he guarded them. They'd already done it once with that perv in the foster home. Not a family—a team.

"Sí." No, he needed to use the English. "Okay." He looked up. "Is cake left?"

"Yep." Mako pulled him to his feet. "Let's go eat."

CHAPTER ONE

~ Twenty-three years later ~

Cutting his throat is only a momentary pleasure and is bound to get you talked about. ~ Robert Heinlein

After closing his medical clinic for the night, Cazador had settled down at his favorite corner table in his brother's roadhouse for a well-deserved beer. The big barroom was warm against the increasing chill of an Alaskan autumn, and the lingering aromas from the restaurant section made him wish he'd gotten here earlier. Bull and his chefs were great cooks.

Even nicer, Caz'd found a gorgeous woman to join him. He smiled at the pretty brunette sitting at his table. Conversation, a good beer, probably some fun to be had later. The perfect prescription for contentment. Fleeting, but that was the way Caz wanted it. No complications, no entanglements, no relationship.

"Please step out of my way." A young man's voice rose above the noise in the busy barroom.

Caz turned.

Felix, one of the waiters, was being harassed by two dumbasses. From the stink, they were probably fishermen.

"Look at the pretty boy. I think you should go back to San Francisco or whatever faggot place you came from." The big bald drunk gripped Felix's glittery purple shirt and gave him a shove.

Felix stumbled back a step.

The bearded, potbellied man followed and grabbed a beer off Felix's tray. "Thanks, pretty boy. Appreciate it."

Felix glanced at the bar, but Caz's brother Bull wasn't there. Probably in the back getting supplies for the bar.

Caz scowled. His shit list was short, but bigots and bullies were near the top. Besides, his brother considered his employees as extended family—which made them Caz's too.

Rising, he patted the hand of the lovely brunette. "Excuse me, please. I'll be back in a minute."

He didn't wait for her reply. Joining Felix, he smiled politely at the two bullies. "Leave the wait staff alone, please."

Baldy leaned forward, mud-brown eyes squinting in anger. "Butt out, beaner. What? Are we bothering your boyfriend?"

At a nearby table, Zappa from the gas station gave a loud snort. "Dude, what've you been smoking? The doc there goes through women like a bear through blueberries. You should be so lucky."

Unfortunately, dumb went hand-in-hand with prejudice, and the bigots weren't about to see reason.

He'd give it one more try. "Gentlemen, if you harass the wait staff, you'll get kicked out. Just a warning."

"I don't listen to spics. Get outta here." Baldy rammed his hand into Caz's shoulder, pushing him back a step.

There—Baldy'd made the first move. Having a brother who

8

was Chief of Police meant Caz usually made a token effort to behave.

He let himself stagger back a step. Then—accidentally, of course—he bumped Felix's tray hard enough to knock the drinks onto the bullies.

As they roared in wet outrage, Caz swung Felix out of the kill zone. "Go get Bull, sí?" That would get the young man out of danger.

"You fucker." Potbelly's beer-wet face was dark purple. High blood pressure. Should be on medication. He swung at Caz.

Caz ducked, stepped in, and punched. His fist sank nearly to the pendejo's backbone. Pitiful. "You should do sit-ups," Caz advised as the man folded in half, wheezing in pain.

"Fucking beaner!" Baldy yanked a long blade from his hip sheath and swung wildly.

Dancing back, Caz kicked a chair at Baldy, which knocked him back against the log wall.

Knives. They wanted to play with knives...

Delighted, Caz slid his own knife from the left wrist sheath and threw.

Thunk.

The blade pinned the asshole's sleeve to the wall. The man's screech was followed by a string of swear words.

Cheering came from the locals.

"Hey, the doc's playing with knives again!"

"More where that came from, asshole."

"Keep 'em coming, Doc!"

There were disadvantages to living in a small town.

Shaking his head at the bloodthirsty suggestions of where to put the next knife, Caz checked his six.

Potbelly had regained his feet. Head down, he charged.

Appearing suddenly, Bull clouted the man to the floor with one big hand.

At six-four and massive, Caz's brother had more than grown into his name...something Caz had envied when they were teens.

"Harassing the staff? *My* staff. What the fuck!" Bull's booming voice bounced off the ceiling and silenced the place. "Get out. Don't come back."

Still on the floor, Potbelly looked worried. As well he should. Bull's Moose Roadhouse was the only bar in Rescue.

"Sorry I was slow." Bull slapped Caz on the shoulder. "Thanks for stepping in."

"*De nada.*"

"Oh, hell, the cop's here," a customer muttered. "Funtime's over."

Caz glanced toward the door.

Yes, Gabe, their oldest brother, was crossing the room to join them. The shiny Chief of Police badge on his khaki uniform shirt glinted in the dim bar lights. "Another fight, Bull? Jesus, just one night of quiet out here would be nice."

"Nah, we'd get bored. The idiots are all yours, bro." After getting an *I'm-okay* sign from Felix, Bull headed for the bar, trading jokes and critiques on the brawl with everyone.

One customer yelled that Caz should've landed a blade in the bully's throat. Caz's gut tightened at the flood of memories. *Been there, done that, quit the business.*

"I really wanted a beer, not more paperwork." Scowling, Gabe walked over to Baldy and yanked the knife out of the wall.

With a high yelp, Baldy clutched his arm. "That damned—"

"Oh, shut up."

Baldy went silent.

At six-one and deadly, Gabe rarely got backtalk. He tossed the blade back to Caz.

Caz plucked it from the air and winced at the blood on the metal. "I cut him?"

"Looks like." With a quick yank, Gabe tore the injured man's shirtsleeve off to expose the bloody cut on the outside of the thick forearm. "Sorry, bro. You slice 'em; you stitch 'em."

"*No mames*." Truly, this sucked.

"Sorry about the extra work, but thanks, Caz," Felix called. The slender waiter was righting chairs and taking orders at the same time. The man had balls. Anchorage had a robust gay population. But the smaller Alaskan communities could be pretty intolerant.

Caz and his brothers hadn't been raised to tolerate intolerance. The sarge'd believed that a judiciously applied fist could activate neurons and set narrow-minded people to better ways of thinking.

There were days Caz missed Mako's straightforward approach to life.

Returning to his table, he smiled ruefully at the golden-tan brunette. She was a tourist from the ski resort up the mountain, and they'd been engaged in a flirtatious dance, both knowing what the oncoming night would hold. Tomorrow, she'd be on her way back to New Mexico, eliminating any awkward entanglements.

He did dislike entanglements.

"I'm sorry, *chiquita*," he murmured, caressing her soft cheek. He'd been looking forward to having his hands on other soft parts of her body. "I will have to leave you and take care of this man."

Her mouth turned down. "Why you? Can't someone else deal with him?"

"Alas, no. I run the health clinic." He was the one and only medical person in the tiny town of Rescue.

"C'mon, Caz." Having tied the torn sleeve around Baldy's wound, Gabe motioned to Potbelly. "You, too. Let's go."

"Why me, Chief? I didn't pull no knife." Potbelly rubbed his undoubtedly sore belly, scowled at his friend, then at Gabe.

"Because I said so. Now shut up." Gabe gave Baldy a shove.

Yes, the chief was in a piss-poor mood. Caz took a last drink from his almost-full glass and followed them out.

In the parking lot, Gabe eyed Caz. "Knife fights, bro? Aren't you ever going to grow up?"

The four of them had brawled their way through growing up, then the military, and actually, had never really stopped. Being the youngest, shortest, and lightest of his brothers, Caz'd often evened the odds with something sharp and pointy.

He gave Gabe a thin smile. "Even when I'm old and crippled, I'll have a blade in my walking stick."

"Bet you will." Gabe frowned. "Was there a reason for the fight?"

"They were harassing Felix. Bull wasn't around, so I told them to leave him alone. They didn't like taking orders from a beaner." The word tasted sour in his mouth. His white father had given him a few extra inches of height, but Mamá was Mexican, and he'd inherited her skin, dark hair, and eyes. Enough to make him a target for racists. He really did hate racists and bigots. "Baldy shoved me, and I lost my balance and hit Felix's tray. Spilled the beer on them. Potbelly tried to punch me."

"I see." Gabe's mouth twitched because he knew exactly how often Caz lost his balance.

Never.

Caz projected innocence. "Baldy tried to knife me. What could I do, eh, 'mano?"

"Self-defense, hmm?" Gabe's voice lost any iota of humor. "I guess I'm grateful they're still moving."

Caz looked away. His brothers knew how Caz had spent the year after his fiancée had been killed. Seeing his need for vengeance, a governmental black ops group had recruited him to eliminate high value targets. Quiet assassinations came far too easily to someone who liked knives.

He could've easily added two more bodies to his kill count tonight...and Gabe knew it.

As Gabe opened the back door of the patrol car, Caz pulled in a breath of the cold night air. Just a taste of frost. The snows would start soon, and the cold darkness of winter would close in. Odd that he was looking forward to spending it in this little town. But, his brothers would be here. After years of separation, first in the military, then just life, they were being drawn back together.

He'd missed them...more than he'd realized.

"Hey." Gabe brightened. "What with a knife wound, a hefty medical fee, and being banned from the only bar around, these assholes have been well punished. I won't need to lock them up or do a bunch of paperwork."

In the back seat, Potbelly looked up, his expression appalled. "Banned? The Bull was serious? We're here for another week."

The other sounded equally dismayed. "Medical fee?"

Oh, such a medical fee. Heading for his own car, Caz smiled. Emergency services and after-hours. Yes, he'd double his fee...even if the blade had been his own.

An hour later, Caz and Gabe returned to the roadhouse and found Hawk and Bull at a quiet back table.

"It's good to have all four of us here again." Dropping into a chair, Caz smiled at his three brothers. Bull was huge, Polynesian, shaved head, black eyes, and a black-and-gray goatee. Clean-shaven, Gabe had dark brown hair, blue eyes. Lean and ripped, Hawk was Gabe's height, with shaggy sand-colored hair and beard. He had blue-gray eyes and fair skin. In contrast, Caz wasn't quite six feet and had Latino coloring. They referred to themselves as brothers—because of Mako—but anyone seeing them side-by-side got confused.

It was good to have Hawk home, even if it was only for a couple of days. Unlike the other three, Hawk hadn't moved to Rescue. He still lived in the Lower 48—when not on a foreign assignment with whatever company he was working for these days.

"Here you go, guys." Felix brought over a beer for Gabe then one for Caz. "Thanks for the rescue earlier. It's really appreciated."

His flirtatious smile made Caz grin and give him a reproving look.

Felix laughed. "I have to try now and then, in case you change your mind."

As the waiter headed back to the bar, Gabe shook his head. "Takes balls to be open about sexual preferences in a place like this."

"Ah, but when someone looks like Caz," Bull said, "both sexes get tripped up with lust."

"Look who's talking. Give it a rest, cabrones." Caz lifted his beer and hesitated because his most taciturn brother was looking at him with...not hate, not quite, but anger? Interacting with Hawk was like white-water kayaking—dodging snags and eddies. The scars from his ugly past made for hazardous navigation.

Caz caught his gaze. "Hawk, a problem?"

Hawk blinked and shook his head. "Nope."

What was going on in his head? Well, if Hawk was around tomorrow, Caz would see if they couldn't have a talk. Not that Hawk talked much, but he shared more with Caz than the other two. Maybe because a hunter like Caz had more patience at stalking his prey. If his brother needed help, he'd get it.

Bull studied Hawk before looking at Gabe. "Thanks for dragging the bastards away. Any trouble with them?"

"Not really. Aside from their lack of personal hygiene." Gabe grinned. "Caz started swearing in Spanish about halfway through stitching up the guy."

"I should've hosed him down first." Caz lifted his glass and breathed in the fine aroma of malt. "He stank of dead fish and sweat. I don't think either of them'd had a bath in weeks."

"Well, you only have another few weeks of stink," Bull said. In mid-September, hunting, fishing, and tourism were grinding to a halt.

Gabe's face tightened. "Seems wrong to have had a fishing season without the sarge."

Mako had died a year ago. Even now, at sunrise when Caz stepped outside, he still expected to see the sarge doing PT on the lakeshore. The same grief came from Caz's brothers. One year or many—it wouldn't matter. Mako had begun calling them a team and ended up calling them brothers, and legal or not, he'd been their father.

The pain would never entirely fade.

Caz lifted his beer. "To the sarge. May the winds be soft and the fish biting wherever he is."

Gabe tapped his glass against Caz's. "May he always have a team at his back."

Bull tapped his glass against Gabe's. "May he always have good food and good beer."

Hawk lifted glass and muttered, "And may he remember how he saved four dumbass kids."

Caz nodded at Hawk's words. Yes, Mako had been proud of raising them. Trust Hawk to know it. He had the hardest shell—and a soft interior. Of course, let anyone say Hawk had a tender heart and the merc would mess them up.

Caz rather liked that about him.

"I left flowers on his grave when I was there this week," Bull said. No one was more loyal than the Bull. "There were a couple of other bouquets."

"Lillian," Gabe said. "Maybe even Dante."

Dante owned the grocery in town. He and Mako'd been friends since their Vietnam days. From what Lillian had let drop, she and the sarge had become very close after Mako'd moved from his wilderness cabin to the dying town of Rescue.

The town where he'd spent his savings buying up a shitload of failing businesses and properties then left everything—with a mission—to his four boys.

Death has been part of your lives.

Time to create something instead. Bring this town back to life.

That's an order.

Caz snorted under his breath and added a final blessing, "May the sarge look down on Rescue and laugh his ass off at the mess he left us to fix."

His brothers grinned, and three glasses clinked against his.

"How's it going?" Hawk's voice had always been a harsh rasp— Mako'd said it'd probably been damaged from screaming. "In Rescue?" Hawk's indifferent tone contradicted the interest in his steel-colored eyes.

"We're making progress." Bull glanced around his roadhouse with satisfaction. "Got this place running well. About half the empty buildings are filled now."

Bull was their financial go-to guy and handled the rentals and sales.

"Are you ever going to move back and help?" Gabe asked. He and Hawk had once been close, but something had come between them in the last year they'd served together as mercenaries. Hawk had pulled out of Gabe's unit before Gabe'd walked into an ambush and almost died.

Hawk's face tightened. "Not yet."

Gabe leaned forward. "You need to—"

"The health clinic is up and running." Caz cut him off. Gabe was their leader—always had been—but when Hawk shut down, he wouldn't take suggestions from anyone, let alone orders. "It's working well to share a receptionist with the police department."

All the municipal offices, including the police station and health clinic, were in one building.

Gabe backed off. "Audrey has the library running well, and it's damn popular." Gabe's woman had been a university librarian in

Chicago, but she jumped into small town living with such enthusiasm everyone adored her.

"You replace Officer Baumer yet?" Hawk didn't talk much, but he'd helped nail the bastard during a kidnapping attempt—which left Gabe the one and only law enforcement officer—LEO—in Rescue.

"Nope. Haven't found anyone I want to hire," Gabe answered.

"Seriously, hermano, you need someone." Caz scowled. "Yesterday, I patched up a hunter who almost shot his foot off, and his drunken friends kept starting fights in the clinic. Backup from the police department would've been useful."

Gabe scrubbed his hands over his face. "Yeah, I know. I'm sorry."

"Forget the sorry shit." Caz thumped his brother on the shoulder. Gabe's sense of responsibility for the entire world would give him ulcers. "Just hire someone."

"I've got three potentials coming in to interview next week. The off-season will give me time to bring someone up to speed before the ski resort's season starts." Gabe glanced at the door, and his expression lightened. "Ah, my woman's here."

Audrey walked across the room, smiling as half the bar called out greetings. She'd spent the summer waitressing in the roadhouse, starting up the library, and helping Dante in the grocery store. All of Rescue knew her.

She laughed when Gabe pulled her onto his lap for a hug and a kiss that left her flushed.

Gabe was more relaxed than Caz had seen him in years. Many, many years, if ever. Mako might have prepared his boys to be soldiers, but humans didn't adjust well to killing. Not with the devastating weapons of the modern age and certainly not for long periods. Caz and his brothers were damn good fighting machines —and they'd returned to civilian life with mental and physical scars. Gabe and Hawk were probably the most damaged since, after the military, they'd joined a mercenary outfit.

When Gabe had left the mercs and holed up in Mako's old wilderness cabin, Caz had wondered if he'd ever return to a normal life. But Audrey had pulled him out of the black hole. Her love had changed him.

Taking a chair beside Gabe, Audrey scooted close enough to snuggle against her man's side. Caz had to suppress envy. His Carmen had been like that affectionate, snuggly, and sweet... although he hadn't met her when she'd been carrying an M-16. So loving, and then she'd died, taking all his hopes with her. After losing her, he'd shut down his heart as quickly as Bull turned over his tavern sign from OPEN to CLOSED.

No, he didn't want another woman—not to love. *Dios*, what good was a man if he couldn't protect the people he loved? Mamá, Rosita, Carmen. No more women or children. He had his brothers who were tough enough to survive anything. They were enough family for him.

"Caz, hey, it's good to see you." A curvy redhead strutted up to the table, all assets on display. As he recalled, those assets were very nice when bare and a joy to touch. A second's thought brought her name. "Elliana, how are you?"

"Very good, thank you." She motioned toward the bar. "We drove over from Soldotna to celebrate my friend's birthday. Why don't you join us?"

Not a chance. He was very careful so no woman would get attached to him. He didn't return for seconds for that reason, no matter how fun a time he'd had. "I'm afraid not. My brother's not here long, and we have catching up to do." He motioned to Hawk.

She looked that way and grimaced slightly. "Well, pooh, Caz." After a pretty pout, she returned to her friends.

"Still breaking the hearts, bro?" Hawk asked, his mouth turning down.

"Our very own stud," Gabe agreed before asking Caz, "Didn't Grayson treat you to one of his infamous 'chats' about mending your ways?"

Caz snorted. The psychologist friend of Mako's had taken an interest in them years ago. He still showed up every year or so to check on them. To help when he could. "Zachary never lectures— he just asks questions."

Questions that had a man waking in the wee hours and pondering their meaning. Questioning the path he was on. Caz shook off those thoughts and grinned at his brothers. "Although he did mention he feared my habits would bite me in the ass one day."

"Jesus, sounds like a curse waiting to happen," Gabe muttered.

A chill ran over Caz's spine at the thought, then his attention was drawn to shouting at the door.

"Hey, Doc, need you at the clinic. Some hunter was splitting wood and axed his leg instead."

What kind of idiot would chop wood after dark? With a sigh, Caz rose. "Coming."

His brothers and Audrey gave him sympathetic looks. He'd been called away from enough gatherings that they weren't surprised.

"Text if you need extra hands on deck," Gabe said.

"Roger that." Caz trotted out of the bar, considering what would be needed at the clinic.

Although he didn't have a woman like Gabe's, he had a job he loved. One where he was needed and could make a difference.

Worked for him.

CHAPTER TWO

*I*t's not whether you get knocked down; it's whether you get up. - Vince Lombardi

In the Weiler, Nevada police station, Officer Jayden Jenner leaned against her locker and sighed. Damn, she hurt. Her gut and her shoulder throbbed painfully. A woman's juiced-up boyfriend had managed to get a couple of punches in. Dammit. Her stupid Taser hadn't worked on him. The darts had hit him but sure hadn't incapacitated him. Too drugged probably. Her stun gun had been effective—eventually—and she'd gotten the guy subdued and cuffed. The girlfriend and little boy were on the way to relatives. If JJ hurt a little, well, knowing the innocents were safe was worth it.

Her spirits were hurting worse than her body right now. When she'd realized how dangerous the guy was and called for help, no backup had arrived. That said a lot about her future here in Weiler.

It was time to make a decision.

After unloading her gear and duty belt into her locker, she felt immensely lighter, at least physically. She'd feel even better once she had a shower. Her own stink of fear was drowning out the sweaty stench of the locker room.

As she pulled on a loose over-shirt to hide her uniform, the flower she'd been gifted that morning fell out of her hair. It was surprising it'd stayed in during the fight. Smiling, she picked it up and tucked it into her pocket. Best reward ever for rescuing a child's escaped bunny.

The day hadn't been all bad.

Earlier, a woman's neighbors reported they hadn't seen her for a couple of days. JJ dreaded those types of calls where breaking in was usually followed by discovering a corpse. But this time, she'd found an elderly woman who was dehydrated and half-conscious, but alive. Joy swept through JJ because the hospital had reported the woman would be all right.

Like her father before her, JJ lived for those moments. There was a joy to serving. To knowing she'd made a difference in someone's life. To being part of the heartbeat of a community.

Her father had been beloved by the citizens where he patrolled.

He'd also been a vital member of the police brotherhood. Unfortunately, the important word there seemed to be "brotherhood". Females need not apply. As a rookie, with Gene as her training officer, she'd thought she was starting to belong. She'd been included in the social activities—the barbecues, the after-work drinks, football afternoons—and loved being part of the police fraternity.

Then it'd all gone to hell. Now her bad days outweighed the good, not because of her duties as a patrol officer. Weiler was a good place. Good people. No, her problems came from the police community.

Hearing the door to the locker room open, she tensed. After closing up her locker, she paused as two officers entered. Tall, desiccated-appearing, and bitter, Chapman had worked in the precinct a few years. Greene was newer. At one time, she'd thought they were comrades-in-arms. She'd been mistaken.

The two men ignored her, crossing behind her. At least they weren't coming on to her like too many of the others.

But she'd expected—deserved—more from fellow officers. Anger still burned inside her. And hurt. "I called for backup," she said in a tight voice. "Got no one."

Greene flushed slightly and kept going to his locker.

Sneering, Chapman shifted closer. "We were on break."

"Yeah. Apparently, *everyone* was on break." Why had she even tried? She picked up her keys.

"Hey, I'm off now. Wanna go get a beer?" Chapman made a kissy noise. "Have some fun afterward?"

Asshole. Even as an ugly feeling settled in the pit of her stomach, she gave him a scathing stare and tried to walk past.

He stepped into her. His bony shoulder hit hers and sent her stumbling sideways. Her hands closed into fists, but fighting would win her only a momentary satisfaction and would only net her a reprimand. *Been there, done that.* Instead, she edged away, almost tripped on a bench, and caught herself on the wall.

As footsteps sounded on the stairs, she looked up to see her ex-boyfriend Nash at the top.

Big, buff, and blond. Like a poster-boy for the ideal cop. She'd fallen for his gorgeous appearance only to discover it concealed an arrogant, selfish boy.

The smirk on his face told her he'd seen what his fellow officer had done. His expression dared her to complain.

Like that had ever worked for her before.

Not.

Anger tightened her muscles, her face. Her 5'4" to his 6-foot height meant she had to look up at him. Didn't that just bite? She kept her voice cold and polite. "Lieutenant Barlow."

"Officer Jenner." His gloating smile scraped her nerves. When she'd broken up with him, she'd foreseen some awkward moments. Instead, he'd gone after her with a maliciousness she'd never have anticipated. He wanted her destroyed, emotionally and professionally.

He took a step toward her. "I think you have—"

Before he could say anything nasty, she strode past him and out of the police station. As she crossed the parking lot, the dry mid-September wind whipped her loose hair around her face and tugged at her clothes. If only the wind could blow away her frustration, her anger...her sense that she was trapped.

"JJ! Hold up." The call came from behind her.

Turning, she forced a smile. Taking her frustration out on her old training officer would be wrong. God, she missed him. "Hey, Gene. What're you doing here?"

"Came to see you." He scowled at her. His gray hair was cut to an even quarter-inch length; his eyes were a bitter brown. On first sight four years ago, she'd figured him for a sexist jerk, but he'd given her a fair shake and ended up a friend. "Buy you a cup of coffee?"

All she wanted was to go home. But...his health had been bad. Heart going wonky. Maybe he needed help with something. "Sure. That'd be good."

The coffee shop was conveniently close to the station. They bought their coffee and settled at a corner table.

"So, what's up?" she asked, tensing for bad news. He was divorced and lived alone, although his three children lived close. Still, she worried.

He eyed her. "I heard you punched Hanson. Heard about the shit spray-painted on your locker, too. Those connected?"

"Oh. No, not connected. Just part of the general campaign to drive me out." Three times in the last month, her locker had been graffitied. That wasn't so bad. However, both physical shit and the lack of support could get dangerous fast. Like today where she'd gotten no backup, she could've been seriously injured. Would anyone have even come to look for her? "I punched Hanson for grabbing me. I'd've hauled him in for sexual assault, only...what would be the point? Any complaint from me would land in a wastebasket."

His rasping, exasperated grunt sounded like a garbage truck flattening cans. "Place has gone to hell since Barlow took over as Chief."

Her ex's uncle had been appointed Chief of Police about three years before, and he promoted his son—Nash's cousin—to captain. Then, Nash had been made Lieutenant right after she dumped him.

The Barlows had manipulation and charm down to a science. Their police skills were barely adequate. Their ethics? They had none.

Nash was doing his best to shred her reputation and drive her out of law enforcement. Since the Barlows and their buddies ran the station, her complaints went nowhere. She'd considered a sexual harassment suit, but lawyers cost money. And no other department in the country would be willing to hire her afterward.

Gene's concerned gaze met hers. "You need to get out of here, JJ. You know that, right?"

"I know. Unfortunately, the Barlow *clan* has let me know they won't give me a good reference. Ever."

His face hardened. "Bastards."

Yeah. They were. She stirred her coffee rather than flinging it across the room in frustration.

"I had an idea. Something that might work for you. Have you ever considered Alaska?"

"Alaska? Are you crazy?" She glanced out the window toward the foothills, the brown desert landscape. "It snows there, Gene."

"Yeah? Seems I heard that somewhere." He grinned for a second. "Just listen, girl. Got a couple of old 'Nam buddies, Mako and Dante, who ended up in Alaska. Mako's gone now, but Dante says Mako's son is the Chief of Police in Rescue, Alaska. My recommendation would carry more weight with him than all the Barlows' crap."

Alaska. Snow. Isolation. "Where's Rescue, Alaska?"

"Kenai Peninsula, close to Kenai Lake. Couple hours from Anchorage. It's a tiny town at the base of a fancy new ski resort, which means the place is growing, once again."

"A tiny town has a police department? Doesn't Alaska use state troopers for everything?" She'd seen that show on television.

"The place used to be bigger. Got incorporated, then the old resort went belly-up, and the town almost died. It's coming back now. With the state's budget cuts, the nearest trooper post is farther away than is comfortable. So the town council hired Gabe, and he's looking for an officer."

"It would be a two person department. The Chief—and me?" Her gut tightened. "What if he turns out to be an asshole? If the town's that small, I'd be screwed."

"You got a right to be cautious. But I'm damn sure Gabe's different."

She gave him a skeptical look.

He shook his head. "True, I only met him once—at Mako's funeral last year. But I knew Mako damn well. Back in the service, when a private groped an army nurse, Mako yelled at the idiot for a good five minutes. Dissected his manners, his appearance, his intelligence, and went on to ream out his ancestors as well. I doubt anyone the First Sergeant raised would be less than courteous to a woman. And I've talked to Gabe since. He's solid."

So. Maybe the guy would be all right.

Still, the job was being a patrol officer in a tiny town in the back of nowhere. Weiler was a small city. She knew her way around cities. Being a LEO in Alaska would be like working in a foreign country.

No, she couldn't. Just couldn't.

Trying to think of a way to turn Gene down politely, she picked up her coffee—and her bruised shoulder ached. No one had backed her up, so she'd been hurt. This time, it'd only been a shoulder. What about next time? Her throat tightened, and she set her cup down.

Dammit.

So, these were her choices: Go work in a strange wilderness, or stay here where her fellow officers would leave her out to hang, not caring if she was hurt or worse.

Really, what did she have to keep her here?

Not friends. Her social life had revolved around the force, which meant it was now kaput. Aside from Gene, she used to have three friends, fellow female officers, who'd taken jobs elsewhere. When Barlow had been made chief, they'd seen the writing on the wall and gotten out.

She was lonely. And rather than the previous comradery in the station, these days, she felt more like a cornered animal at times.

There was nothing to lose by leaving. If the job in Alaska didn't work out, she could always go serve fries in Anchorage.

Giving her time to think, Gene had been silent. Finished with his coffee, he set the cup down gently. "Rescue's very small. But I know what matters to you. There, you'd have a chance to get to know the people and be part of the community. You'd actually know who you were serving."

The words struck home like a low-toned bell. "All right, yes. Please, make the call."

CHAPTER THREE

W*hen you are a strong woman, you will attract trouble. When a man feels threatened, there is always trouble.* - Barbara Taylor Bradford

Almost a week later, JJ dragged herself and her suitcase into her hotel room. *Welcome to Alaska, woman.*

Why hadn't she realized the state was so damn far away? She'd spent the entire day traveling. Driving to Las Vegas, flying to Seattle, then to Anchorage had taken forever, because all the good flights had already been booked. After picking up her rental car, she'd driven another two-plus hours to the ski resort high above Rescue.

She'd been lucky to get a reservation, the desk clerk had told her before adding that the restaurant had already closed for the night. *Dammit.*

After the fastest shower known to man, she brushed her teeth, combed her hair, changed into clean clothes, and headed down to the bar—the only place she'd be able to get food. And since the bar would close in an hour, she needed to move. Apparently, Alaskan resorts didn't stay open late, especially on Sundays.

Walking into the lobby, she smiled at the desk clerk she'd met and nodded to the other two women behind the front desk.

The bar was on the other side of the lobby—a pleasant place with huge windows, giving a view of the last trace of twilight. She'd been able to complete her drive in daylight, thankfully. This far north, sunset was over an hour later here than at home.

And, oh, man, having daylight for the drive had been totally worth it. The scenery was jaw-dropping. Huge rugged mountains. Forests everywhere. Tiny remote towns. She'd had to keep stopping to take pictures.

Once in the bar, she stopped to look around. Exposed beams in a high ceiling, glossy dark wood flooring, square cranberry-red chairs at small tables. A loveseat and two high wingback chairs faced the chunky rock fireplace. That's where she'd go once she got some food.

The place wasn't busy. A group of men at a table. A few more here and there. Two couples at different tables. The bar had a man at one end and three women at the other. The women had dressed in city style—red dress, sequined black dress, slinky cocktail pants.

JJ might look out of place in her jeans and boots, but she wasn't going to sit at a table and wait for a server. The kitchen might close early. She settled at the small bar a few stools down from the women.

The bartender, an older brunette, looked up from the drink she was fixing to smile. "I'll be with you as soon as I get these drinks."

JJ smiled back and picked up the bar menu. Her stomach rumbled an urgent demand.

The women next to her were deciding on drinks. Having a good time.

Listening to them teasing each other, JJ had a flash of envy for their companionship.

"I'll have a Texas iced tea," the one named Kiki finally decided.

Huh. That sounded good. Mom, being from the south, had always kept iced tea in the fridge, and JJ rather missed it.

As the bartender mixed their drinks, the women chatted about striking out with a guy—someone who sounded like quite a man-ho. From Anchorage, the women enjoyed occasional weekends at the resort. The guy had spent a night with each of them at different times.

Tonight, Kiki had offered to buy the man a drink in hopes of another hookup. "He looked at me with those eyes—you know those dark eyes of his?"

"Oh, do I," the one in cocktail pants said.

The third—red dress—laughed and fanned herself.

"And Cazador says, 'Kimberly'." Kiki moaned. "Mmm, I love the way he says my name with that accent. But..."

"But what?" the one in the red dress asked.

"He says, 'Keem-bear-ly, I told you, did I not, that we would enjoy one night together and one night only?'" Kiki heaved a big sigh. "I wanted a lot *more* nights, for God's sake. I've never gotten off so hard in my life."

"Ma'am?" In front of JJ, the bartender was waiting for her order.

JJ grinned ruefully and dropped her voice. "Sorry. I was totally eavesdropping."

The bartender laughed, her voice equally low. "Cazador is worth hunting, but they're out of luck. He really holds to his one-night rule."

Worth hunting. No man was, especially a man-ho. Food, now. Food was totally worth hunting. JJ smiled and checked the menu again.

"You're interested in ordering some food?"

"More than anything in the world. If it's still possible, I'd love a double order of the chicken strips." The bland food wouldn't unsettle her stomach. She had an interview tomorrow. *Oh God.* "And a Texas iced tea, too, please."

"Coming right up."

JJ tuned out the women talking as squirrelly worries overcame her. The drive here had been amazing, yet had shown her how out of place she was. Forests with tangles of brush, everything so green. The mountains had taken her breath away. In more than one spot, she'd whizzed past a handful of stores and a gas station before realizing it was a town.

She hadn't been able to get an extra day off. What with the last-minute reservations, she'd taken a day to get here. She had tomorrow for the interview and looking around and would fly back to Nevada late tomorrow night on the red eye.

She'd simply have to scope out the place as best she could.

And maybe she'd be offered the job. *Maybe.*

In front of the resort lounge's fireplace, Cazador rolled his glass of beer between his palms. From the room behind him came the low hum of various conversations. As he watched the flames, his irritation slowly faded. At least the carpet had muted the sound of Giselle's stomping exit as the curvy blonde returned to the front desk. Damn woman. She thought if she kept trying—flirting and touching—that he'd change his mind and take her to bed.

The first few times, he'd politely explained he didn't "date" local women. Then he'd bluntly refused. Then he'd been rude. She only grew more determined.

He sighed and tipped his head back, listening to the cheerful crackle of the fire. A tinkling—forced—laugh sounded from one of the Anchorage women. Kimberly. At least she had taken a refusal politely. He'd enjoyed his night with her. Had enjoyed her friends on other nights. If he thought about it, he'd remember the other two names. He was good with names.

Good with women.

Not so good with being honest with himself. Because he'd told himself he was looking for a warm willing woman tonight, one who wanted conversation and enjoyable sex. That's why he'd driven up to the fancy resort bar. Yet, although there were women here he hadn't been with before, he was brooding by the fire.

He didn't approve of brooding.

Dammit. His mood had been *off* ever since Gabe had fallen for his pretty librarian.

The two were good together. Audrey soothed Gabe's spirit, and his brother supported her, helped her. He was needed. Years ago, with Carmen, Caz had known that feeling of being needed. Of partnering with a woman. Not shoulder-to-shoulder as he had with his brothers, but more...entwined. With Carmen, he'd felt as if their spirits merged in the same way their bodies had. Dios, he still felt the ache from losing her. He lifted his glass in a silent toast. May her spirit be happy wherever it had flown.

If only he'd been there to protect her.

Last summer, Mako's psychologist friend had asked Caz if he intended to move on with his own life. *No, Zachary, this is my life.* Grief was only a small part of the problem. What stopped him completely was the simple fact that he couldn't protect a woman. Women and children were just too fragile.

No, he'd never again get emotionally entangled.

Footsteps caught his attention, and to his annoyance, a woman set a glass and a plate of chicken strips onto the low table in front of the fireplace. She curled up onto the wide loveseat next to the chair where he sat. Eyes closed, she leaned her head against the back cushions.

His displeasure at the intrusion disappeared. He doubted she even realized he was there. His tall wingback chair concealed him from the rest of the room; it was why he'd chosen it.

Interesting appearance. Her hair was a mess of red-brown curls stopping a couple of inches above her shoulders. She had a strong face, narrow, with a pointed chin and a wide mouth. No makeup. Freckles were scattered across her cheeks and nose. Damn, he liked freckles.

Her brows were slightly darker than her hair. She wore a no-nonsense navy button-up shirt. Although loose cut, it fit well enough to show she had a sturdy body with straight shoulders and small, high breasts. Her cheekbones were sharp, her wrist bones slightly protruding; she was perhaps a bit underweight.

No fingernail polish. No rings. No jewelry at all, in fact. She wasn't the type who usually visited this expensive resort bar—although he wouldn't have been surprised to see her here with a husband for fishing.

Her eyes opened. A striking blue-green. Seeing him, she sat up and started to stand. "*Oh.* Excuse me, I didn't realize—"

"Relax. It's all right." She really was distressed, so he kept his voice to a soothing murmur. "I do not own the chairs or the location—and the fire is very pleasant. I would welcome the company."

Rather surprised at that truth, he motioned for her to resume her seat. And was pleased when she did.

"Well. Thank you." She leaned forward and picked up a chicken strip. "Would you like some chicken? I have more than I can eat."

A generous person. A sociable one. Worry lingered in her face, letting him know she would feel more comfortable if he joined her. "Thank you." He took a chicken strip and watched the tension slide out of her.

She finished her bite and took another piece with surprising enthusiasm for something so bland. Of course, the food here was excellent. Even Bull approved—and had wisely left McNally's, the high-end restaurant market, while his roadhouse concentrated on burgers and comfort foods.

"Are you here for a week of fishing or hunting or something?" she asked. He realized she was exerting herself to be polite. Not flirting—not even a little—but just making conversation. It was surprisingly...pleasant.

"No, I'm only here for tonight," Caz said.

"Me, too. I go back to Nevada tomorrow."

"You're a long way from home. Did you enjoy Alaska?" Caz took a drink of his beer.

"The mountains are spectacular—even more amazing up close than from the plane." She drank about half the liquid in the tall glass, choked slightly, and stared at the glass as if it had bitten her. "What did she put *in* this?"

"Is the drink not to your liking?"

"That is not *iced* tea." Her eyes narrowed. Firm jaw, eyebrows drawn together. The hint of toughness was interesting.

"May I?" Caz asked. The bartender was a sweetheart. He'd hate to see her in trouble with a tourist complaint.

The woman pushed the drink toward him.

He took a sip from the other side of the glass. "It tastes like a Long Island iced tea, but maybe with something added..."

Her eyes rounded. "A Long Island iced tea? That's...that's a cocktail."

"Yes. What did you order?"

"A Texas iced tea."

He pulled out his phone and checked. "Google says that's a Long Island iced tea with the addition of bourbon."

"Oh, just shoot me now." She rolled her eyes. "I'm an idiot. I thought I was getting a normal sweet tea—not something alcoholic."

From the amount she'd just sucked down, he'd bet she was getting a good buzz already. Long Islands were deadly, and the bartender made strong drinks. Nevada must've been thirsty. His lips twitched. "Have some more chicken."

She picked up a strip and frowned. "You're laughing."

"No, no, I would never be so rude."

Grinning, she pointed a piece of chicken at him. "You totally are."

After finishing the strip, she sampled the drink again. "It's really good. It doesn't taste that strong, but I can feel it."

He chuckled. If she'd been driving, he'd have asked for her keys.

Embarrassment stung as JJ looked at the man. First, she'd butted in on his secluded sitting area then slugged down a potent drink. Damn, she already felt the alcohol humming in her veins. The guy must think she was a real idiot.

Even worse, he was intimidatingly good-looking.

Not a fancy meat-market gorgeous though. His clothing was an understated casual—black jeans, black boots, long-sleeved, button-up shirt. He looked Latino. Fairly tall, closing in on six feet. And his build wasn't bulky like a power-lifter, but sheer streamlined muscles. The rolled-up sleeves on his hunter green shirt revealed corded forearms.

His black hair was short, with a few strands falling over his forehead, and his eyes, so dark a brown as to match his hair. His skin was a beautiful light brown, the tone she often longed for since her skin was all freckles. A dark beard shadow gave him a dangerous edgy look.

But handsome men reminded her of Nash. Sad as it was to admit, males, ugly or not, no longer interested her. Not after all the harassment of the last year.

Unconcerned at her perusal, he sipped his beer and looked her over in turn. "Do you have a name you would share, Nevada?"

She smiled at the polite phrasing. "Jayden. JJ."

"Jayden. A beautiful name."

"It sounds even better the way you say it." His Spanish accent softened the J, giving it an even more musical sound. Truly, he had an amazing voice. She didn't want a man, any man, but she'd be happy to listen to this guy read the phone book.

And then she blinked and glanced at the bar, remembering Kiki's comment about a man with an accent. *"Keem-bear-ly, I told you, did I not, that we would enjoy one night together and one night only."*

This was the notorious Cazador.

Following her gaze, he looked around the back of his chair and spotted the three women at the bar. His eyebrows lifted. "My name is Cazador—but, perhaps, you already know it?"

She had a feeling her cheeks had turned the dark red of the loveseat. "I...yes. I heard them talking about you."

He didn't appear offended. Or gratified. Simply slightly amused and somewhat indifferent. As if he didn't particularly care what others' opinions were.

Envy stabbed her. "They sounded as if they come here often?" He'd obviously been around this place before. Maybe she could learn something about the area so as not to sound like a total idiot at the interview tomorrow. She might even learn if she'd want to live here.

"McNally is close enough to Anchorage that women come to enjoy the mountains and be pampered. The spa is gaining a good reputation." He gestured toward the group of men at a table. "Not every fisherman wants to spend the night in a sleeping bag. Some prefer to be picked up in the lobby and driven to the boat. After a day of fishing they're brought back while their salmon is cleaned, iced, and packed to take home."

She studied the men. "I pretty much thought of fishing as a grungy tent or RV sort of activity, but the resort's method would be nice." Cazador was probably from Anchorage, too. A city guy, if Anchorage could be called a city. She settled into her chair, feeling more comfortable. Her hunger was assuaged, and her brain had a pleasant fizzing sensation going on, thanks to the drink.

Even better, she had someone to talk with. A man who wasn't putting moves on her but was interested in conversation.

He picked up his beer and took a sip. "What do you like about living in Nevada, JJ? I've never been there."

"Nevada's the only state with Area 51 and UFOs."

When he laughed, she grinned and continued. "Really, it's a state of contrasts." She told him about the quirks of Nevada—the gambling city of Las Vegas surrounded by gorgeous, wide-open land and wild horses. Desert, yet with snow-capped mountains and forested valleys. The Burning Man festival and Nevada Day. And, as she talked, homesickness swept over her. She loved her damn state. How could she move?

Turning her gaze away, she pulled in a hard breath.

"Ah, chica, you go home tomorrow." His voice was soft. Sympathetic. As if he could tell her throat had clogged with homesickness, he took over the conversation, offering intriguing Alaska tidbits, as well as comparisons to South America, the Mideast, and Europe.

Although the man had been everywhere, he wasn't all about his adventures but asked her questions. Listened. Was obviously interested in her opinions. When she asked him about dangerous Alaska wildlife, he took out his phone and moved to sit beside her on the loveseat. He had amazing pictures: a moose with a baby, a moose walking through a downtown area, a moose attacking a car —that one widened her eyes.

"What about other predators?" She flushed. "I mean, I know moose aren't technically predators, but—"

"But they're more liable to charge a person than our lazy brown bears."

She was holding his phone, and rather than taking it back, he closed his hand around hers to pull up a different set of photos.

"Oh, it's Hagrid." A second later, she realized he hadn't released her hand. Their knees bumped.

She tipped her head to look up at him, and they were too close, their faces only a few inches apart. Her gaze dropped to his mouth. His lips were sculptured, not puffy like a girl, but not thin. Just...perfect.

He leaned forward and brushed his lips against hers.

She jerked back. "No."

"No?" Heat simmered in his so-very-dark eyes.

Suddenly, she was far too conscious of how close he sat, how his shoulder brushed hers, the heat of his body. She pulled back. Dear God, she'd been staring at his mouth—of course, he'd thought she was flirting. "No."

"Ah, I misunderstood. Please forgive me." All the heat and sexuality disappeared, and he politely moved a few inches from her. His expression showed honest regret—without anger. He wasn't blaming her for giving mixed signals or himself for misreading her.

Instead, he motioned to the phone she was still holding. To the shaggy bear on the display. "You said the bear reminded you of Hagrid. Is he a relative?"

"Uh, no." She shook her head in mock horror. "You don't read Harry Potter?"

"I fear he's escaped my notice. Are those the books with a young wizard?"

"Movies, too, yes." She frowned. "You're not a flat-earther, right? Tell me you've seen *Star Wars*."

"And *Star Trek*, as well." When he grinned, she could see why numerous women had fallen for the man-ho. "So, who would you pick for your captain—Kirk, Picard, or Janeway?"

Now that was a question she could hash over forever. She drained her drink and set it down. "There's absolutely no question; the best one is Picard."

Their battles raged over starship captains, to white orcs that should have died the first time, to whether the Hulk could beat up Superman. She and her training officer, Gene, had enjoyed science fiction and fantasy discussions, but Cazador was even more fun. She pointed at him with a severe expression. "If Superman could—"

"Last call."

The voice made her jump. She looked up. "What?"

The bartender stood by the fireplace. "It's last call, people. Bar's closing shortly."

"Oh." Time to leave.

"Thank you for letting us know." Cazador turned to JJ, and his grin flashed. "Did you want another *sweet iced tea*?"

"Now that's just mean." She smiled at the bartender. "I'm through. Thank you."

"It was a pleasure, ma'am." The bartender hesitated, looked from her to Cazador, then left.

JJ frowned. "Did she seem...?" She shook her head, thinking how easy he was to talk with. As if they were friends rather than two people passing time in a bar.

"She wanted to warn you that I enjoy women. Which is true." He rose. "I need to be going. I hadn't realized we'd talked so long."

It really was late—and she'd had fun. "I need to head back to my room, too."

"Then, might I escort you to the elevator?" He held his hand out to help her to her feet.

"Sure." She let him pull her to her feet, and they walked out of the bar and across the hotel lobby. Only two front desk clerks remained. One smiled at her and nodded. The other one, a curvy blonde with big hair, frowned and turned her back.

As she got in the elevator, she smiled at Cazador. "Thanks for the escort—and the conversation."

"It was my pleasure. Good night, Nevada." With a smile and a nod, he walked toward the rear of the hotel.

She shook her head. That was one amazing man...although she still felt a bit embarrassed about the aborted kiss. Just as well she'd never see him again.

. . .

Caz rubbed his neck as he headed toward the back parking lot. A pang of regret ran through him. He hadn't wanted a woman tonight, and then JJ had arrived. Talking with her had been more fun than anything he'd enjoyed in a long, long time.

How he'd misread her body language enough to offer a kiss was a bit disconcerting.

Her lips had been soft...

No. She hadn't wanted anything other than someone to talk with, and he respected that...no matter his regret. He'd enjoyed getting to know her. Intriguing woman, the way she bounced from a tough confidence to hints of insecurity. She wasn't afraid to laugh at herself. Didn't trash talk other women. Looked him straight in the eyes.

Although women were enchanting when dressed to kill, he appreciated just as much a woman who was comfortable with who she was—without the façade of makeup, jewelry, and fancy clothing.

And one who liked science fiction and fantasy? A treasure.

He'd have to get Audrey to dig through her library and find him the first Harry Potter book.

CHAPTER FOUR

I f you're gonna fight, fight like you're the third monkey on the ramp to Noah's Ark...and brother, it's starting to rain. - Christopher Woods

Blinking gritty eyes, JJ drove down Rescue's Main Street. Although nerves—and two cups of coffee—had her well wired, her body felt the lack of sleep. After leaving Cazador and returning to her room, she'd been wide-awake and stayed up reading.

There was nothing like two cougar shifters courting a female Marine to settle a girl.

JJ parked her rental car in front of Rescue's municipal building and slid out. Standing beside the vehicle, she turned in a slow circle.

This was Rescue? Gene had been right when he called it tiny. From Anchorage, the Sterling and Seward Highways were paved, as was the Dall Road to the McNally Resort. But, once off the highways, the two blocks of downtown Rescue held the only other paving. The other streets were gravel.

Yet the town was charming. Looking freshly painted, the two-story clapboard buildings were an interesting meld of rustic and Victorian styles. The rich colors—gold and dark green, tan and mahogany, brick red and pale yellow, green and white—livened up the boxy buildings. To the south was a glint of a lake and forests rising to dark mountain peaks with the white streaks of glaciers. So beautiful.

Although she saw a few empty buildings, most businesses were open and showing the pride of ownership that was the hallmark of a good town.

Okay then. She glanced at her watch. Showtime.

She smoothed her dark blue pants and wiped off her clammy palms before twitching her dark blue jacket straight. Beneath the blazer, she wore a khaki-colored button-up shirt, because a clever applicant would wear the clothing colors of the job she wanted. The internet had provided a picture of the Chief of Police, Gabriel MacNair, in a khaki uniform shirt with dark blue jeans. Thus, her color scheme.

Job interviews. Talk about torture. Even worse than getting a starting hand of two and seven in Texas Hold 'em. Or being on the receiving end...so to speak...of an alien rectal probe.

She snorted. Those weren't comparisons she'd share with her interviewer.

After slinging her conservative black satchel over her shoulder, she walked briskly up the steps and through the glass-fronted doors into the big municipal building.

In the wide lobby, an older blonde woman in her late forties sat behind a semi-circular receptionist desk. The nameplate on the desk said Regina Schroeder. The woman looked up with a polite smile. "Good morning. How can I help you?"

"I'm Jayden Jenner, and I have an appointment with Chief MacNair."

The woman's gaze sparked with interest, although she merely said, "Of course. If you'll go through those doors to the police station, I'll let the chief know you're here." She pointed to the door to JJ's left.

RESCUE POLICE DEPARTMENT.

"Thank you." As JJ walked through the door, her heart rate increased. Maybe, maybe, she could escape the degrading atmosphere of the Weiler police station. Please, let that happen.

She glanced around. The police station's portion of the building wasn't huge, but more than adequate for tiny Rescue. The lobby door opened into a bullpen with a center conference table and several smaller desks against the walls. The far wall held offices.

A man emerged from the Chief of Police's office. Solidly muscular. Six-one. Rough-hewn and clean-shaven. Short brown hair. Dark blue eyes.

"Officer Jenner. I'm Chief MacNair." He held his hand out.

As she shook hands with him, noting his grip was strong without being overpowering, her hopes rose. He'd called her *officer*, as he would with any male applicant, acknowledging she was a professional. His gaze held no leer, but a nonsexual assessment of her build and whether she was capable of doing the job.

He motioned to the office behind him. "Let's talk."

As he settled behind the desk, she took the chair in front.

The interview was straightforward and his questions similar to those she'd answered upon getting hired in Weiler. Experience, strengths, weaknesses.

"Did you have any questions about the information I sent—the salary, benefits, and cost of living in Alaska?" Chief MacNair had a good smile, one she bet was very effective at gaining civilian cooperation.

"No. It was all clear." She smiled back, hoping he was done with questions.

No such luck.

"I'd be interested to know what drew you to law enforcement." He pushed the notepad away and leaned back in his chair.

"My father was a patrol officer and loved the job. I'd planned to follow in his footsteps."

She was going to leave it at that, but the chief frowned. "Planned. You changed your mind at some point?"

So much for avoiding her past. Not that it was a secret, but still... "He died when I was twelve. We were managing to make ends meet"—barely—"but when I was sixteen, my mom had a stroke. She needed me. Attending the police academy was out of the question, let alone taking a job with irregular and long hours."

"I see. You're an officer now. Did she get better?"

"No." The loss was still an aching hole in her heart. She could feel her shoulders curve inward with sorrow. "When I was twenty, she was walking home and got hit by a car. She died."

His gaze held sympathy. "I'm sorry. That couldn't have been easy for you."

It'd been devastating. "I was heading home too, and I saw the lights, saw her." Pain swept over her, and she pulled in a breath. "With the first responders were two police officers. The male was"—an asshole—"callous. Indifferent. The female officer made sure I was going to be all right, even as she processed the scene. Instant role model. I wanted to be the kind of person she was."

"Ah. Thank you. That's what I wanted to know." The chief studied her. "Now let's talk about why you want to change locations."

Dread rose inside her, and she shifted in the chair in a tell as loud as a shout.

His eyes narrowed.

Oh damn. MacNair might not have a problem hiring a woman, but he wasn't any pushover when it came to whom he wanted to hire. "Although my first years with the Weiler police force were challenging, they were also rewarding. I felt as if I was contributing to the community and was valued for my skills."

He held up a finger. "What skills are those?"

"I'm good at problem-solving. In fact, I was working toward

detective status. I'm an excellent negotiator, can defuse a lot of ugly situations. People seem to like me." At least the ones who could see past the end of their dicks. "Children trust me. I'm a skilled interviewer."

He nodded, face unreadable. "Very good. But now you're leaving Weiler? Why?"

Her muscles went tight again. "I'm ready for a new challenge. For—"

"For a station where you won't be harassed for being female?" he asked mildly.

He *knew*. Her stomach twisted, but she didn't move. "Ah..."

"You're the only female officer in that precinct. It appears you've been having some problems." He tapped a finger on the folder. "A friend of mine is skilled at research, including checking social media."

Nash—and later, just about everyone—had trashed her on Facebook. Posting things implying she was the slut of the department. Going after married men, after guys with girlfriends. Fucking her way to the top. And, more recently, there'd been accusations of her being aggressive and out of control.

The chief moved her resume to one side. "How many fights did you start?"

"None."

At his level look, she sighed. "My opinion is if someone grabs my breasts or ass, then they started the fight. I *finished* three."

His eyebrow quirked up. "Does finished mean you won?"

"Yes, sir. I did." She'd spent the year after her mother's death getting stronger and learning to fight and shoot. She hadn't eased up in the years since the academy.

"Good for you." He rested his forearms on the desktop. "Officer, I don't judge performance by gender. However, the Alaskan population can be sexist. In fact, we have a white religious fundamentalist militia group outside town."

She sat back, a whole inch, and stared at him. He was serious.

A militia group? Her shoulders slumped. Dammit, she was tired of being judged by her gender first and her abilities second. But, she'd liked the looks of the town, liked—

Shouting came from the street. "You fucking city boy, get your stinkass back to the—"

Chief MacNair glanced out the window overlooking the street. "Hell." He rose. "Excuse me. I'll be back shortly."

He was gone before she could respond.

The shouting increased. Sounded like several people were yelling at City Boy.

No, this wouldn't do. The chief against a bunch of people?

A chill ran through her. If she got the job, there'd still be only two of them, which meant she'd be without anyone to back her up most of the time.

Nonetheless, she was here now. Shoving her satchel under the desk, she yanked off her jacket, tossed it on the chair, and ran out to the street. The lack of her firearm on her belt nagged at her.

Once on the street, she frowned.

Ignoring Chief MacNair's order to step back, five men were shoving and punching a skinny, just-past-twenty, clean-shaven young man. The bullies were all bearded, and she labeled them according to hair color or style. Ginger Top, Stringy, Sandy, Buzzer, Brownie.

Five to one? Assholes. Anger flooded her system.

Scowling, the chief punched Sandy, dropping him onto his ass. The chief dodged Ginger Top's swing, then delivered a couple of hard blows to the man's gut. After that, Ginger Top was too busy puking his guts out to have any fight left.

JJ nodded approval. The chief had some serious skills.

He stepped in front of the buzz cut one and, with a hard sternum shove, knocked him away from the city boy. Regaining his balance, Buzzer charged MacNair.

Unfortunately, Stringy and Brownie headed in to join the fight.

No, I don't think so. Pulse speeding, JJ stepped in front of them.

She set her hands on her hips. "Back off, or you'll be hauled in on charges." Not that she was legal in this state, but still.

"The fuck you say, bitch," Stringy snapped. "Get the hell out of the way."

When she didn't move, he tried to slap her. Talk about insult.

She blocked and slammed her fist into his beer belly. The nice thing about being small was that her fist actually hurt her opponent more than a bigger hand would. His breath whuffed out. As he swung a big hand at her head, she did a quick foot sweep and took his legs out from under him.

His head hit the pavement—and he was out of the fight.

Never stopping, she sidestepped Brownie's punch, slid closer, and slammed her knuckles into his low back—his kidney.

Even as he made a gut-wrenching sound, Sandy charged her.

She dodged his rush and kicked Brownie in the ass, sending him headfirst into pile of sidewalk construction. She spun to face Sandy.

He yelled something that sounded profane, but was so angry he garbled the words.

Dropping low, she avoided his fist, straightened, and delivered a one-two punch to his gut and chin. There was a noise to her right.

Something slammed into her head. As her skull exploded in pain, her knees buckled, and the world went hazy.

"Fuck." That was the chief's growl, and then a man let out a high scream.

Brownie landed on the concrete beside a car, a 2 by 4 falling from his hand. He was out cold.

Eyes blurry, she heard a yell, sounds of fists. She tried to push to her feet and failed.

Sandy grabbed the 2 by 4 and charged the chief. JJ kicked her leg out, and the bastard tripped, landing on top of Brownie, his head hitting the side of the car. He went limp.

That was that.

JJ blinked, realizing something warm was running down her face. She swiped at it. Was it raining? Her hand came back covered in blood. Her blood. The side of her head pounded as if she'd gotten hit with a hefty piece of wood.

Oh, right. She had.

"Whoa, Chief. Need help there?"

"Dante. A hand would be helpful." The chief rolled Brownie over, handcuffed him, and did the same with Sandy. "Can you babysit the assholes while I take the officer in to the clinic?"

"You got it, Gabe." The man had a twangy drawl that brightened as he said, "Officer, huh? You finally got us another cop?"

MacNair squatted down beside JJ. "You're bleeding, Officer. Let's get that looked at."

Everything was going in and out of focus. When he lifted her to her feet, her balance tilted as if she was standing in a canoe rather than on hard ground, and he slung an arm around her waist.

"Sorry, sorry." She concentrated on putting one foot in front of the other. The world went dark...and she almost panicked until she realized they were inside the building. The lobby.

"Oh, hell, Gabe. That's not the way to conduct an interview." The scolding voice was familiar. The receptionist.

The Chief chuckled. "My bad. Is the Doc in?"

"Yep. Go on in."

MacNair steered her to the right and through a door.

"Doc, got a patient for you." The chief's loud voice echoed in the room. Somewhere a child was crying. A couple of people were talking. "She got thumped by a 2 by 4 and is pretty woozy."

"I'm fine." She tried to draw herself up.

"Nope, you're not." The chief sounded more amused than upset.

"Put her in room two, 'mano." The Spanish-accented voice was smooth, warmly masculine, and all too familiar.

No. This couldn't be happening.

Her knees buckled, and the chief's grip tightened. "Room two. Only a few more steps, Officer."

A murmur of voices came from another room. "Bring Niko back in ten days, and I'll take the stitches out. Remember what I told you about watching for infection."

"Will do. Thanks, Doc."

"Here, Officer." The chief took her into a small exam room and helped her up onto the table.

The man she'd met the previous night entered the room. Saw her. Stopped.

JJ put her hand up to her aching head and felt the warmth of blood. Her gaze went double, back to single.

Cazador. It really was him. He wore black jeans, black sneakers, and a white lab coat over a black T-shirt. Maybe she was concussed, but he was still the most intimidatingly handsome man she'd ever seen.

"*Ay, pobrecita,*" he murmured. Warm fingers under her chin, he tilted her head up. "Officer, hmm?"

"Um..." Whatever she'd planned to say faded from her thoughts under the impact of his dark, dark eyes.

"Let's get that bleeding stopped." After gloving up, the doc used gauze to put enough pressure on the wound that she squeaked.

"Sorry." He held her head firmly, not easing up. As she inhaled, she could smell his aftershave—the green of vetiver and lime. Like last night. A good memory of companionship. Along with a touch of embarrassment.

She tried to shake her head, but he didn't let her move.

"Stay still—"

"Her name's Jayden. Jayden Jenner," the chief said. "Officer Jenner, this is Caz or Cazador or Doc."

"Officer Jenner," Cazador murmured politely.

"If you're stitching me up, I'd just as soon you call me JJ."

Laughter lit Cazador's eyes. "JJ." He took the gauze off and eyed her wound. "Bleeding is stopped." He glanced at the chief. "What was she doing intercepting a 2 by 4?"

"Street fight. Five of the Patriot Zealots were picking on a tourist." The chief huffed a laugh. "Oddest end to an interview I've experienced."

"She's here to interview, and you pulled her into a fight?" The doctor opened a sterile dressing pack on the rolling stand before shooting the chief a disapproving stare. "In medical interviews, we ask questions, look at resumes. We don't slap a scalpel into their hands before they're hired and say *have at it*. What the hell, Gabe?"

"She stepped in on her own to back me up—and she took out two and a half of them on her own. She's almost as fast as you are." The chief's voice warmed. "Nice job, Officer."

"Except for getting caught out by the 2 by 4," she grumbled.

"Live and learn. You'll guard your six more carefully next time," the chief said.

Next time? Did he—

"Look up at me, JJ." The nasty penlight flashed in her eyes as the doctor asked the standard questions to see if she was concussed. If she had any allergies. Any other pain.

It was a bit comforting that she'd met him last night. And it was rather awkward, too.

"Let's get you lying flat. I don't want you swaying while I attack you with a needle." Hand behind her shoulders, Cazador laid her back on the exam table.

"Doctor." As her head spun, she pushed his hand away and tried to sit back up. "No needles."

"Yes, needles. Foreheads have too much tension for gluing." His hand closed on her shoulder and held her still. "And it's Caz or Cazador, please. I'm a nurse practitioner, not a doctor."

"People call you Doc."

When he leaned over her with a tiny needle and she tried to turn away, she got a tsking sound and a firm, "Lie still, Officer

Jenner." When she gave up, he continued, "A number of people have felt the need to call me doc, including the pendejo here."

Pendejo. Had he just called the chief an asshole?

MacNair chuckled. "You stuck me with the chief title. I get to call you Doc."

Cazador snorted, then warned her, "Tiny stick."

She closed her eyes and tensed. But he was good at his craft. There was only a small sting, then another and another.

"Done with numbing. You did very well." His deep, velvety soft voice compelled trust.

As shouting and cursing drifted in from the street, the chief grunted. "I need to deal with those idiots. Can you keep her here until she's back on her feet, Caz?"

The doc's dark eyes looked into hers. "It would be my pleasure."

JJ would have rolled her eyes if her head hadn't ached so badly. "Yeah, you just love having to babysit woozy officers, I'm sure."

The doc smiled at her. "We can argue about the impact of anti-super-heroes on the next generation while you're here."

The lure was more compelling than being offered a candy bar.

"Officer Jenner." The chief pulled her attention away. "That was a nice job of backup."

A compliment. How awesome was that?

"The position's yours, if you want it."

She stared. Closed her mouth. She could work here in this small town, a place that obviously needed her. One that might welcome her. The man on the street, Dante, had sounded happy that the chief might hire her. She could fit in here. Have a community to serve and a place to belong. Longing swelled within her.

Remembering the chief's compliment, she was sold. She could work with this man, Chief MacNair, and learn from him, too. "I'll take it."

"Excellent. Take some time and recover while I stuff those idiots into our token jail cell."

"Token?"

"Yeah, it's a reinforced room to stash miscreants until the state troopers take them off my hands. We don't have the staff to deal with housing anyone long term. The troopers also take dispatch calls when we're off duty. Rescue can't afford 24/7 police staffing."

"Oh. That makes sense."

The Chief smiled. "Come back to the station when Caz lets you go, and we'll start on the paperwork."

He wasn't treating her like a fragile bunny that needed to be sent home and pampered. Yes, this would work out. "Will do, Chief."

"Make it Gabe."

As he left the room, the doc made a disapproving sound under his breath. His brows were drawn together.

"What?" she asked.

"You haven't even started, and you're already bleeding."

She scowled. "Would you say that to a man?"

"Men aren't..." He said something under his breath, an exasperated sound. "Forgive me, you're right. I was out of line."

"Don't worry. I'll hose the blood off before I visit your clinic. Next time." Next time—because she had a job. Despite her aching head, her lips curved.

He made a grumbling, unhappy sound and then simply stitched her up.

A job. Her thoughts drifted to a vision of walking into the Weiler police station and slapping down her resignation. But... lovely as the thought was, she really should think a bit more about this decision. Be rational.

Well...the salary was high enough to compensate for the increased cost of living in Alaska. Benefits were the standard ones.

Working with Gabe—definite plus. Regina, the reception person, had been nice. The small Alaska town would probably be a mix of good and bad. Most of the people had seemed friendly. The cult was an ugly minus.

Then there was this man...

His fingers under her chin lifted her head. "All done. I'll give you something mild for the headache, and you'll stay here until the dizziness passes." His eyes were the warm color of dark chocolate...and unyielding as stone. He might be even more stubborn than she was.

He certainly was overprotective. And she didn't want his concern, heartwarming as it was.

She'd met him in a bar. They'd had an amazing discussion. He'd made a pass at her. She'd turned him down. That was that. She couldn't afford to lose this job, and after Weiler, she knew how disastrous gossip could be. A small town would be even worse. She wasn't ever going to chance that he wanted more than a doctor/patient relationship.

She gave him a nod and a polite, "Yes, Doc."

His mouth tightened, and then he nodded back. "Comprendo." *I understand.*

Good enough.

New job, new town. She was going to concentrate on her career and stay away from men.

With a sigh of relief, Caz finished the day's charting in his office. The usual colds and flu and cancer and infections, drunken brawls, and children tripping over every sharp object to be found. Add in hunting accidents and idiot fishermen filleting themselves rather than their catch, and it made for a long day.

Leaning back, he stretched and savored the silence. His health clinic was up and running. He even had almost all the equipment he needed. In another month or so, he'd see about hiring a full-time medical assistant. For now, part-time aides would do.

Sharing the receptionist with the police station was working better than he'd anticipated. Eventually, maybe, the population would increase enough he could hire more staff and use the clinic's own waiting room and reception desk.

After a bit of remodeling, the clinic now had an efficient layout. Behind the currently unused reception desk was the front office with computer, fax, and printer. A hall led to his office, the three exam rooms, and the procedure room.

Conveniently, a door in the front office also opened into his office, so when he was here alone, he'd leave the door open to see anyone entering.

Like now. He smiled as his brother walked in.

Gabe speared him with a dour look.

"Problem, 'mano?"

"Could be." Gabe dropped into the other chair in the room and stretched his long legs out. "JJ said she stayed up at the resort last night. Your stomping grounds." Unfortunately, Gabe's years as a cop granted the ability to see what was right in front of his nose, and Caz's interest in JJ had probably been more than obvious.

"Ah, the guilt. It stabs my heart." Caz clutched his chest. "This feels like the day Mako discovered our stash of *Playboys* in the loft." Mako had made them do a pushup for every page. The damn magazines were way too long.

"My arm muscles were so sore the next day that I couldn't even comb my hair." Gabe grinned. "Actually, he was right. Hell, you were only twelve. And you're changing the subject."

"No, mi hermano, I am not." Caz powered down his laptop. "I'm saying that males are interested in females. You and Mako might disapprove, but biology will not halt at your request."

Gabe's mouth flattened. "Listen—"

"No. We met. There was interest. She said she was from Nevada, didn't mention she was interviewing here. However, I did not fuck her." Although he had definitely wanted to. "We simply talked."

"Oh. Well. Sorry." Gabe rubbed his neck. "Still. It's like this, bro... Female cops have it rough. Even in this decade, too many guys think they're easy. And with JJ—well, I don't know if you met him, but one of Mako's old buddies referred her to me. Name of Gene. It seems *she's* had it especially rough. What I'm saying is you've a reputation and being seen with you might be a problem."

Caz's rep would rub off on her? The taste of that was bitter. It didn't matter, though. She'd indicated her choice. He would, of course, honor that. "I agree."

Gabe looked surprised.

"There are other women. There are always more women. I will stay away from your officer, 'mano." Although in simply talking, she'd given him the most pleasant evening he'd had in a long time. He liked her, dammit.

With a grunt of exasperation, he rose and walked down the hall, shutting off lights.

"Okay then." Gabe didn't sound totally convinced. "Appreciate it."

Lights off, Caz walked back toward the front office. "Bueno. That means you're buying the beer tonight."

CHAPTER FIVE

A diamond is merely a lump of coal that did well under pressure. - Henry Kissinger

Two weeks later, Caz walked across the grounds of what his family called "the Hermitage" or "the compound" on the southern bank of Lynx Lake. Today, the lake was a calm, glassy sheet reflecting the mountains rising to the south. The tips of the peaks were white with termination dust—the first high-altitude snow, signaling the end of summer. At least the cold had held off until October; there'd been years the first snow had arrived in August.

He walked over to the square wooden smoker on the far side of their compound. After checking the outside firebox, which was burning well, he opened the door of the tall box. The sweet scent of alder enveloped him. Inside, the salmon strips lay on racks. A glance at the thermometer showed the temperature was holding steady. He grinned, remembering the sarge's fit when they'd offered to buy him an electric one. He'd smoked salmon the old-fashioned way for years and wasn't about to change.

Mako also canned or jerked most of his fishing and hunting,

certain the next war or disaster was just around the corner, and he wanted to be prepared. He'd probably been annoyed as hell the apocalypse hadn't yet occurred before he went on to the next world.

Look, Sarge, we're still doing it your way. In fact, the three of them would can this last batch of cold-smoked silvers tomorrow.

The tug of grief eased slowly.

Over at the patio, Bull was building a fire in the big brick grill.

Caz joined him. "I'm tired of game and fish." They'd just finished off the last of what was in the various freezers and had been fishing, hunting, and trapping to refill them. He and Gabe had each shot a moose last week, providing more than enough for all of them with ample to share with the non-hunters or those like Mako's old friend, Dante, who hadn't been able to get out this year.

Bull grinned. "No worries. We're having plain old chicken today to welcome Gabe's officer."

"Good choice." Caz tipped his head, listening for a car. JJ was due to arrive today—and would be living here in the Hermitage.

That was going to be uncomfortable. For him, at least. Because he hadn't been able to get her out of his thoughts. She had all that curly, red-brown hair the color of maple leaves in the fall. Her eyes were a mesmerizing blue-green color. Freckles dotted her light skin, running over her cheeks, up her arms. So damn kissable. Did freckles dance across her skin elsewhere?

No. He wasn't going to think about her in this way. She was off-limits. *Stick to the tourists, estúpido.*

"Need me to make anything?"

Bull shook his head. "Got it covered. I brought a bunch of side dishes from the restaurant."

Having a brother who owned a restaurant had some perks.

Caz glanced around the compound, wondering what JJ would think of it. He still found it beautiful the way the five houses curved in a protective half-circle of the lakefront acreage.

Years ago, with all four of his boys in the military, the isolation of his off-the-grid cabin had aggravated the sarge's PTSD and paranoia. In response, they'd all built two-story cabins and gotten him to move to Rescue where Dante could check in with him. Mako, a survivalist before it'd been popular, turned the place into something that could hold off World War III.

To keep two-legged or four-legged predators out of the inner compound, electrified fencing ran between each house, as well as extended from the end houses down to the lake. The attic of each house was designed for a shooter, and the road-facing rear of the houses had small, defensible windows. The huge windows facing the lake could be shuttered—another battle the first sergeant had won.

Mako had been a bit crazy.

Yet, when Caz woke from nightmares of combat, the grinding crunch of a knife penetrating the base of the skull, the feeling of life draining out of a target...on those nights, the impregnable nature of the Hermitage was a comfort.

Mako's cabin had stood empty since he died last year. Now, JJ would be there. Caz laughed under his breath. So much for staying away from Rescue's new police officer. Gabe'd made that all but impossible.

Caz took the beer Bull handed him. "Did Gabe say how long the officer will be staying out here with us?"

"Until one of Dante's rentals is free. About a month, maybe." Bull glanced at the cabins. Gabe had the cabin on the western arm near the lake. Bull's, Hawk's, and Caz's cabins formed an arc. Mako's house anchored the east end of the U, again close to the lake. "Feels almost wrong to have someone in the sarge's place."

"Sí." Caz breathed out against the fresh burst of grief and the illogical resentment of a stranger in the sarge's house—as if leaving it empty would bring Mako back. It was good Hawk wasn't home, or there'd be hell to pay. He was even more antisocial and territorial than the sarge had been. "But if lending

Jayden a house means Gabe gets backup, Mako would be all for it."

"True enough." Bull held his hand over the fire. They had charcoal, but Bull preferred "real" wood, even if it took longer to get the coals right. "If nothing else, having her taking over his cabin forced us to finally deal with his stuff."

It hadn't been easy to go through the sarge's belongings, even though Mako hadn't accumulated much other than weapons and books. After protest, Gabe had taken the sarge's medals. Bull, his recipes—although they'd all learned most of them. But holding the cards, seeing the sarge's rough scrawl, had sent Bull out of the room for a few minutes.

Caz had taken Mako's blades. He still had the first one Sarge had given him. Now he had others. If he could see to use them.

They'd set a few things aside for Hawk when he came home. If he came home.

Caz rubbed his neck. "JJ should be here soon. Where's Gabe?"

"He's helping Audrey make up the bed, turn on the fridge, and get out towels." Bull gave Caz a wry look. "I didn't even think of that shit."

Caz smiled. "It's nice having Audrey here." It was difficult to overcome the habit of isolation the sarge had fostered, but when Gabe fell for Audrey, things had changed.

Love could apparently overcome anything.

Bull snorted. "First Audrey, now the officer. You met her—what's she like?"

Adorable. Tough. Vulnerable. Determined. He heard a car on the drive and smiled. "She's punctual."

He headed toward Mako's house.

JJ barely managed to spot the dirt road. Dirt—seriously? Thank God, she'd taken Gabe's advice to get a car suited for Alaska. He was right. Her little city car would've had heart failure by now. So she'd sold her Camry in Nevada and bought a used Toyota 4Runner in Anchorage.

It was a tough car—and a pretty blue. Score.

She braked, her tires skidding in the gravel, and turned onto the tiny dirt road. Honestly, the roads in this state were insane. *We pave our roads in Nevada, for God's sake.*

Gabe had told her, "*You'll see a lake on the left. Once past it, ignore the first two dirt roads on the left—they dead-end a few yards in. Turn left onto the third road. It'll look as if it dead-ends also, but it actually veers left before it terminates. Follow the road back to the lake and park at the last cabin on the east end.*"

This was a total wilderness. The so-called road was about as wide as a dirt footpath. As she drove down it, suddenly the thick forest opened up into a lakeside meadow, and the road curved around the back of five almost identical two-story cabins. Solar panels glinted from the top of each roof. A large outbuilding sat just past the westmost cabin.

After staring for a moment, she drew up to the house at the east end. Hers for a month. As part of Rescue's growing pains, there were very few rentals—and all were booked. When she'd told Gabe, he'd said he knew of a place she could live in for a month until a rental became available.

She'd accepted gratefully. But...boy, this was sure isolated.

The garage door was up, so she pulled in. After shutting off the engine, she sat for a moment. *Well.* She was here. In Alaska. Excitement vied with a sense of disorientation. Of loss. She'd never planned to leave Nevada.

But, aside from Gene, she had no real friends left there. This was good. Here, she had a chance to prove herself, to make a home. Make friends. Be a good police officer.

To help people the way she'd always wanted.

Sliding out, she opened the trunk and hesitated. Should she take in her luggage? She didn't have much. Being prudent, she'd left almost everything stored in Nevada, bringing and shipping only enough clothing, grooming items, and essentials like her eReader, flute, favorite pillow, to last her a month. By then she and Chief MacNair would know if she would work out.

"Welcome to Rescue, JJ." The warm masculine voice broke into her thoughts. It was Cazador. The doctor—no, the nurse practitioner who might as well be a doctor.

She turned, and—dammit—he still looked like any woman's favorite fantasy. No man should be allowed to be that sexy. A stabilizing breath helped. Thankfully, she wasn't affected by him. No, she wasn't. Absolutely not.

"Good to see you, Doc." Although she didn't know why he was here.

"I saw you standing there, just staring at your luggage. Are you having second thoughts?" He walked down the two steps into the garage and reached into the trunk to pull out a suitcase.

"Um. No. I wasn't sure what to do next."

"Ah. What comes next is getting everything inside, joining us for lunch—Bull is grilling—and then taking the evening to settle in." He wasn't as tall as the chief, but still way taller than her five-four. He smiled down at her with a warm gaze.

"I can get that." She reached for her suitcase.

He chuckled. "You have enough for both of us and a few more." He turned and shouted toward the door. "Viejo, your officer is here, and she has luggage."

An answering shout came back.

It seemed she would be assisted, which was actually rather nice. After Nash had trashed her reputation, she'd had no backup, whether in lifting things or to police calls that went bad. She'd gotten used to doing everything without help.

The doc's cheerful insistence was heartening. "Thank you," she said. "I do appreciate the help, Doc."

"*No problemo.* And it's Cazador as I'm sure you remember." Although his expression was reproving, his eyes held heat—and then the heat disappeared. He stepped back with a rueful smile.

"JJ, you're here."

She jumped at the chief's cheerful voice.

As Gabe and a woman walked across the garage, Cazador started pulling her boxes and suitcases from the trunk, setting them on the floor for easy carrying.

"I see you made it in one piece." The chief's brisk slap on the shoulder—just like he'd have done for any guy—made her feel more welcome than any handshake.

"I did. You have a beautiful location here." Crazy hard to find, but lovely.

"Thank you." He motioned to the golden-blonde woman who was all curves and an inch shorter than JJ. "JJ, Audrey Hamilton, my girlfriend. Audrey, this is our new officer, Jayden Jenner."

With a smile, Audrey held out her hand. "Welcome to Rescue, JJ."

JJ shook her hand, feeling a little wary. In Weiler, her fellow officers' women had thought JJ was man hunting. Threatening their relationships. Of course, with the way the misogynistic officers talked about her, maybe the women had cause to think that way.

Yet she was the furthest thing from a man-hunter. Nash had been the only guy she'd been with in Weiler. After him, she'd been disgusted with the entire male gender.

"Thank you, Audrey." She could only hope the woman didn't feel threatened about having only JJ and Gabe in the station. "It's good to be here."

The chief turned to the pile of suitcases and boxes. "Audrey, if you'll show JJ where everything is and explain the odd living arrangement, Caz and I will haul luggage."

"Sounds good." Audrey smiled. "We'll leave it to you manly men."

"Manly men?" Caz snorted. "That leaves you out, viejo."

The chief's shoulder knocked him back a pace, and JJ hesitated, wondering if there'd be a fight. But, no, they were both laughing.

"Brothers." Audrey snorted under her breath, leading the way up the two steps and into the house.

"Brothers?" JJ glanced back. Black-haired, brown-eyed Latino male. Brown-haired, blue-eyed white guy. No shared characteristics at all. "Seriously?"

"Not by birth. They were in a foster home together, and Mako saw them and decided to take on raising four boys."

"Four boys, all at once?"

"He'd spent time as a drill instructor during his twenty-some years in the military." Audrey snorted. "Four kids were probably easy as pie."

"Okay, so Gabe, Cazador, and...?"

"Bull, who is outside grilling right now. And Hawk, who's off doing secret military stuff. No one knows when he'll be back."

JJ heard an uneasy note in Audrey's voice. Perhaps Hawk wasn't as likable as the rest of the brothers. There was always one, right?

The entry from the garage opened into a long hallway. A door on the right revealed a huge exercise room with weightlifting equipment on the left and a martial arts training area with mats and mirrors and punching bags on the right. Farther down the hall, a bathroom was tucked under the stairs. The hallway opened into the main part of the house—a huge open arrangement beneath a high vaulted ceiling.

A brick-backed wood-burning stove stood between tall front windows that looked out onto the lake. The left wall held a massive flat-screen television surrounded by the biggest sectional she'd ever seen.

On the right front, under the windows was the dining area with a long oak table. The back on the right held a big kitchen, enclosed by two bar islands.

She turned to look behind her. Over the hallway, the staircase climbed to a second-floor loft that took up about a half of the house. Privacy to that area was achieved with rustic wood doors. "The chief said something about an odd living arrangement?"

"Yes." Audrey motioned toward the stairs. "The second floor is a complete apartment—and that's all yours. The first floor is considered the Hermitage's common area where anyone feeling sociable can hang out. You're welcome to use the space—just know someone might join you to watch TV or cook."

"Got it. You know, I never asked who this house belongs to." JJ followed Audrey up the stairs.

"It was their father's. Mako died about a year ago in a car accident." The loft had a long walkway with the railing on the left and a door in the center. Audrey pushed open the door and entered.

JJ followed her in.

A small living room was just big enough for a long leather couch, a recliner, a woodstove, and a carved wood bookcase. An archway on the left divided the room from a little kitchen with a two-person round dining table. Everything was in browns and blues, the furniture solid and comfortable. "This is, wonderful. Really cozy."

"It is. Although when I called it cute-and-cozy rustic, the guys almost disowned me." Audrey smiled slightly. "Mako raised the boys in an off-the-grid cabin in the middle of nowhere. I imagine he felt more at home up here in this little space than downstairs. Although when all four of the guys are home, even downstairs feels awfully crowded. Wait till you meet Bull, and you'll understand what I mean."

Four guys. One cabin apiece. JJ's stomach tightened. She'd be living here, surrounded by four men? None of whom she knew well?

No choice. It would be all right. Gabe and Caz were okay guys.

"There's a balcony off the kitchen for when you want to have your coffee out there." Audrey opened a door on the right. "This is your bedroom and bath."

JJ did a quick survey. A queen-size bed with dark wood nightstands and dresser. A tiny closet. A bright red, blue, and white patchwork quilt and blue rugs livened up the room.

The bathroom, with a big shower, a soaking tub, and a granite-topped counter, was perfect. A cupboard held towels and toilet paper. Everything was clean to the point of sparkling.

"Gabe and I made up the bed and put out towels. All clean."

"I thought I'd have to make a quick trip to town for bedding and towels. This is amazing. Thank you."

The guys came in then, filling the living room with her suitcases as well as the boxes she'd picked up from the post office in Anchorage. She'd mailed those a couple days after resigning.

The memory of Chief Barlow's furious expression when she'd handed in her two-week notice still made her smile.

Although she'd found smiles were rare that week. Her emotions had been all over the place. After all, the Weiler police station had hired her and sent her to the academy where she'd made good on her dreams and found comradeship. Made friends. And then their sexism and Nash's spiteful behavior had crushed those dreams and sense of belonging.

How could she feel vindicated and like a failure at the same time?

Hearing she was leaving, Nash and his friends had harassed her enough that she'd simply called in sick the final week and used the time to get the rest of her belongings into storage.

Although she could have driven here on the Alcan Highway, flying had been so much easier. She sighed. Now she had belongings in both Nevada and Alaska.

"Yo, people. Lunch is served." The booming voice came from outside.

Audrey smiled. "That's Bull. He owns the Bull's Moose Roadhouse and is a great cook. Let's go eat."

JJ glanced at all the boxes and stuff. So much to unpack. "I should—"

"Should get some food in you and have a chance to unwind," Caz's voice was authoritative—like a doctor. Yet the friendly concern was nice. "You have time to look around the place and to meet Bull. Gabe won't put you to work this minute." He shot an admonishing look at his brother.

Yes, total doctor. Although...hmm...if all the brothers lived here, he must live in one of the houses? That could be a bit awkward. No, she wouldn't let it be.

Tucking an arm around Audrey, Gabe chuckled. "Relax, bro." He smiled at JJ. "I'm a nice boss. You have today and all of tomorrow to settle in and check out the town. But that's it. After that, I expect you at work. Deal?"

"Deal." Delight rose in her. Because he needed her. The town needed her.

She followed everyone downstairs, out the door by the dining area, and across the deck.

"This is the inner compound of the Hermitage," Caz said.

It was a huge grassy enclosure with the lake on one side and the half-circle of cabins on the other side. This sure wasn't an elegant waterfront property with a pool and hot tub. No, their compound held an extensive vegetable garden, an orchard with dwarf fruit trees, and a small greenhouse.

There was a red brick patio with a massive stone grill, and at the edge stood a black-iron pole with a hanging bell. An adorable screened gazebo sat close to the lakeshore.

"This is great," JJ murmured. They had a wilderness mini-farm. A farmlet?

Caz's smile was warm. "We like it."

"You even have chickens." JJ stopped to look at the enclosed chicken yard and coop. The black and white chickens ran over to line up at the fence and cluck hopefully.

"They love scraps like watermelon rinds, lettuce ends, and apple cores," Caz told her.

"Got it." How pitiful was it that she couldn't wait to feed the chickens?

The sunlines at the edges of his eyes crinkled slightly. "You can toss them your leftovers anytime you want."

On the patio, a massively built man was removing food from the grill. He set a platter of grilled chicken onto the long glossy oak table and smiled at her. "I hope you're hungry, Officer. I'm Bull, by the way."

"I'm starving. And it's good to meet you, Bull. I'm JJ."

He had black eyes, a shaved head, a gray-flecked black goatee, and stood a good six-four. Perhaps Polynesian ancestry?

Caz motioned to the long bench beside the table. "Come and sit. Let's eat."

With brotherly insults and teasing, the men settled around the table with Audrey between Gabe and Bull. Caz joined JJ on the other side and passed her the platter of chicken. Food was served family style. The men had good manners—better, in fact, than most of the officers at the Weiler station.

After relieving a bit of her hunger—Bull was a great cook— she asked, "Can I ask where the name the Hermitage came from?" Because it sounded like a monastery.

"Bull called it that when we were building our houses." Gabe motioned to the cabins with his glass of iced tea. "Since the compound housed Mako—a born hermit if there ever was one— he dubbed it the Hermitage."

"The sarge didn't see the joke," Bull said with a snort. "He stuck me with helping the contractor put in the septic system."

"At least he didn't have you running laps until you puked like when we were kids," Gabe said. The three exchanged grins.

Damn, their adopted father must've been a real hardass. Yet their expressions held grief as well as love. She studied the guys—

the chief, the doc, and the restaurant owner. Mako had done a fine job of raising them to be men.

When they finished eating, the guys started cleaning up, and JJ rose to help.

Caz shook his head. "Not this time. You're worn out and still need to unpack. Audrey, why don't you sit with her and do girl-talk, yes? Later, if you have a moment, I could use help with a spreadsheet."

"Ooo, spreadsheets. I'm your girl." Grinning, Audrey handed him her plate. As he walked away, she turned to JJ. "So, what do you think of the place?"

JJ ignored the question. In an email, Gabe had mentioned Audrey had researched JJ's background.

Okay, let's tackle this head-on. JJ pulled in a breath. "I know you ran the background check on me, which means you probably also saw the stuff written about me on social media. I just wanted you to know, I had a relationship with a fellow police officer and learned the hard way that work and pleasure don't mix. To me, Gabe is off-limits. He's my boss—and isn't and never will be anything more. I just wanted you to know. Um, I also know that the man's head-over-heels in love with you, and it's not as if he was interested anyway, but I wanted that...clear, I guess?"

At Audrey's startled expression, JJ sighed. *And I told the chief I was good with people?*

"Sorry, I guess that was a bit too blunt and—"

"I like honesty. Yes, I saw what people wrote about you, but Gabe said that female cops have trouble like that—which sucks." Audrey's face softened. "When it comes right down to it, I trust Gabe's judgment—and I trust him."

Really? The worry that had simmered in a spot right under JJ's sternum dissipated, leaving warmth behind. She swallowed. "Thank you."

"No thanks needed. We women have to stick together."

Over by the grill, Cazador's laugh rang out as he teased his brother about something. God, he had the Mexican version of Sean Connery's voice. Every time he spoke, women's ovaries probably melted.

Huffing in exasperation, JJ shook the spell off.

Audrey followed her gaze. "That man. Although Gabe makes my heart stop when I look at him, I have to admit Cazador is incredibly hot. Plus, he has all that Spanish charm to go with it."

He walked across the yard, moving like a cat—all lithe, graceful muscles.

Hot was an understatement. "Yes, he's very good-looking."

"Too good-looking." Audrey shifted on the bench, obviously uncomfortable. "He has a bit of a...rep?"

JJ felt her jaw go hard. "What kind of rep?"

"No, no, nothing that would make you put on a cop face."

"Sorry." It was the downside of being in law enforcement—seeing the worst in people. But Cazador had women asking for a night with him rather than the reverse. And she knew from experience he took *no* for an answer.

"Actually, Caz is one of the most caring and honest people I know. It's just...well, Gabe says he goes through women like most people go through potato chips, one after another."

"Oh, *that*." JJ shrugged. She'd already known he was a man-ho.

"I don't want to make you think he's a creep—he's not. He doesn't lie or mislead the women. He tells them upfront he doesn't do relationships. It's when women don't believe him that there's trouble." Audrey was blushing. Embarrassed.

"Thanks, Audrey." Women looking out for each other. The same kind of sentiment had set JJ on the path to the police academy. "But...no warning needed. I'm not looking for a relationship, or a man, or sex, or anything."

Not after Nash and Weiler. Maybe she'd change her mind in a couple of years. Or five. Five sounded good. "I'm done."

Audrey blinked in confusion.

Gabe and Caz walked back, side-by-side. As they gathered up

the last of the condiments and dishes onto large trays, the chief eyed Audrey. "You're all pink, Goldilocks. Are you too hot? Or are you talking about something that makes you blush, in which case, I want to know."

His teasing made Audrey turn even redder—and glance at Caz.

JJ muffled a laugh. The woman had better avoid a poker table. Long before JJ was a teen, she'd learned to avoid giving away her thoughts. When Mom practiced dealing for her casino job, they'd both point out each other's tells—the expressions or body language giving away information about the cards in their hand or their plans.

As the two men carried their loads away, Gabe nudged Caz. "Bet she warned my officer about your dastardly reputation, stud."

"I am ruined." Caz's easy-going laugh was like a brush from a warm breeze. "It wouldn't matter. I consider our Rescue women off-limits."

"Especially ones who carry firearms?"

"Mako didn't raise any fools, mi hermano."

JJ grinned...and felt a pang of regret. Someday, maybe, she'd find a man who didn't care if she was a tough, firearm-wearing female. Yeah, in about five years she'd start looking.

CHAPTER SIX

I think women are foolish to pretend they are equal to men, they are far superior and always have been. - William Golding

It was her first morning in Rescue.

JJ had spent Monday evening unpacking and puttering around, locating where things were. Apparently, Mako had been compulsively neat. Then again, maybe he had a need to have things always ready for inspection. He'd been a sergeant, after all.

However, the sarge must not have approved of modern conveniences. There were no fancy kitchen appliances, just the basics—stove, fridge, toaster, coffee pot. No dishwasher. The can opener was crank-handled.

Yet she already loved the little apartment, and the location was astounding. No traffic, no sirens, no industrial noise. Just the lapping of the lake against the shore, the call of birds she had yet to identify, and the clucking of the chickens. She'd slept like a rock.

Tuesday morning, in the twilight before dawn, she stepped onto the balcony. The air was cold and crisp, and so still the lake looked like gray-blue ice. The chickens hadn't ventured out of their coop. Everything was silent.

Beautiful.

She caught her breath as something moved outside of the fence by the lake. A huge animal with a heavy rack. A moose. Oh, wow. She watched for a while until the cold drove her indoors.

Inside, she puttered around, unpacking the last few things and storing the empty boxes and suitcases under the bed since she'd be moving again in a month.

Time for the next item on her to-do list: check out Rescue and buy groceries. Coffee was first on the list.

She drove down the narrow road and out onto Swan Avenue, then past the narrow end of the lake. On the other side was a well-graveled road with a sign: Lake Road. Just for fun, she turned right and checked out the lake on the side closest to town. This was a much more developed area.

Gabe and his brothers had gone for the wild side. They had no neighbors; the tiny road ended at the Hermitage.

She passed a sign pointing to Dante's rental cabins. That would be where she'd be living in a month. Farther down was a small town park. At the end of the lake, the road dead-ended onto Dall Road. A right would take her to McNally Resort.

On the left at the intersection was Bull's Moose Roadhouse. She grinned. *I know the owner.* It almost made her feel at home.

She found her way into Rescue, parked in front of Dante's Market, and strolled down Main Street. Gabe had said the big tourist season was essentially over, although there were always some fishermen around. She saw three unshaven, flannel-shirted guys arguing about trout and lures. A young couple in spotless jeans and hoodies strolled hand-in-hand. An older man carried a chainsaw into the hardware store.

An elderly couple stood in front of a big display window. JJ slowed to look. It was an art gallery and a craft store combined. How cool was that?

One corner of the display was filled with enough gorgeous yarns to make a person yearn. She'd learned to crochet as a kid. Hmm. She'd need a warm scarf, and from what the guys had said, she'd need stuff to do during the winter.

A while later, after a pleasant chat with the storeowner, she was back out on the street with a crochet hook, yarn, and patterns.

As the aroma of coffee and freshly baked pastries caught her, she followed the scent right down the street to the coffee shop. Sugar and caffeine—what more could a girl want? Even better, the place was located across from the police station.

The day of her interview, JJ'd learned the chief liked his coffee past dark and approaching tar. Ugh. This looked like a far more palatable option.

Behind the counter, a short brunette in her thirties smiled. "Welcome. What can I get you?"

JJ studied the goodies in the glass display. "I'd like an apple strudel and a latte, please."

"Coming right up." As the woman worked the machine, she gave JJ a keen look. "Would you happen to be our new police officer?"

"I am." JJ glanced down. Had she strapped on her weapons belt? No, she was in her usual jeans, boots, and jean jacket over a flannel shirt over a tank top. "How did you know?"

"Caz was in this morning and gave me a description. Welcome to Rescue. I'm Sarah."

Now how would Cazador have described her? The officer who bled all over his exam table? "Thanks. I'm looking forward to starting tomorrow."

"You'll find Rescue an interesting place to work." Sarah placed her hand on her pregnant belly. "Alaska has some of the nicest people in the world—and a fair amount of drunks, fighting, and sexism."

"Ah, well, that's nothing new." Smiling, JJ accepted her drink and pastry and paid. Alaska definitely had some nice people.

Before she reached a table, a car horn blared—followed by a metallic crash. From the sound of the impact, it was more than a fender-bender.

I'm off today, darn it. She handed her coffee and pastry to Sarah. "I'll be back. Can you give the chief a ring?"

"On it," Sarah said.

JJ stepped outside. In front of the grocery, a pickup had rear-ended a parked SUV. Thankfully, there were no dead or squashed bodies. Relief washed through her.

A man stormed out of the grocery store and stopped at the sight of what was obviously his SUV. "What the fucking hell!" His face turned red.

And here we go. JJ moved forward...because an intervention was all too liable to be necessary.

The door of the pickup opened, and the driver slid out, hanging onto the door for balance. "Fuck me." As he swayed, a bottle of alcohol—gin—rolled off his seat and broke into fragments on the pavement. He was flushed. Drunk.

Lovely.

"You dumb redneck," the SUV owner shouted.

The drunk turned, leaned into his cab, and reached for the shotgun mounted inside over the rear window.

Oh, hell. Talk about escalating a conflict.

"Police!" JJ strode forward and grabbed the SUV's owner. "Sir, get into the store and wait for me. Now!" She shoved him in that direction.

Not waiting to see if he obeyed, she headed for the drunk. He'd gotten one clip released when she spoke.

"Hey there, mister." She drew every ounce of sweet female to the forefront until her voice sounded like sugar. "That crunch sounded bad. Are you hurt?"

Abandoning the shotgun, he pulled his head back out of the

cab. His face changed as his anger faded. The SUV owner was gone; instead, there was a woman asking about his health.

When he turned, JJ got a full blast of alcohol-laden breath in her face.

"Hi." He swayed.

Unfortunately, she couldn't assume his lack of focus and balance was entirely due to the drink. He might be hurt and not even realize it, considering the amount of anesthetic in his system. "Sir, did you hit your head? Was your seatbelt on?"

"Nah, the belt's busted."

"How about your head?"

He frowned and prodded at his forehead. "Maybe?"

There was a definitive answer. She bit back a laugh. "Tell you what, let's go over to the clinic across the street and have the doc make sure you're all right." She'd stall him over there until Gabe arrived. Since she wasn't really a legal hire yet.

"I dunno." He looked between the damaged SUV and his pickup, as if wondering if he could simply drive away.

"C'mon." She linked her arm in his. "If you hit your head, all sorts of bad stuff could happen. We should—"

Her words dried up.

Because Cazador was leaning against a streetlight. Simply watching. Laughter glinted in his eyes as he tilted his head toward the clinic in a wordless: *continue.*

He hadn't stepped forward to take over. Was treating her as he would any officer—trusting her to deal with the drunk.

The knowledge was as heady as a glass of champagne.

Smiling, she led her giant lamby-pie across the street and into the clinic.

Caz finished checking over the drunk, who would certainly be feeling the bruising when he sobered up, and handed him off to Gabe.

As Gabe escorted the guy out, Caz leaned against the exam table and studied JJ, who'd perched on a stool in the corner. "I thought you were starting tomorrow, not today."

"So did I." She wrinkled her nose, bunching the freckles together. So cute and yet the officer had been cool and competent during the incident.

She shrugged. "After the SUV owner got this guy riled up enough to go for the shotgun in his pickup, it seemed like a good plan to step in."

"You did a nice job of calming the situation. That feminine syrup is more effective than a tranq."

"I've learned to use the tools I was given."

If she turned that seductively husky voice on him, he would follow her just about anywhere. *No, Ramirez.* Not going there.

Turning away, he washed his hands. "You came out of the coffee shop—did you get a chance to enjoy your coffee?"

"No, not even a sip. It'll be cold now." Her look of annoyance made him laugh.

"Come, Officer Jenner. I'll buy you another."

She frowned at him.

"He wouldn't have cooperated with me if you hadn't stayed. You saved me work—and I have a craving for a cherry empanada." Caz pulled off his lab coat, hung it on the hook, and held the door for her.

He knew better than to spend time with her. But seeing her facing down the drunk had dried up all the spit in his mouth. He had a visceral need to know she was all right.

In the lobby, Regina said, "Way to start early, Officer," and gave JJ an approving smile.

Caz could see the pleasure in JJ's expression as she answered, "Thank you."

A look around the lobby showed no one was waiting for him. Perfect. "I'm taking half an hour for lunch, Regina."

"Got it, Doc. Enjoy."

In the coffee shop, Sarah didn't even ask what they wanted— she handed over their pastries before narrowing her eyes at Caz. "I was surprised you didn't step in to help her, Doc." Her frown indicated what she thought of that.

It'd been harder than hell not to. "Officer Jenner had it under control."

"Oh." Sarah's frown deepened, then she snorted. "And I accuse *Uriah* of being sexist? Sorry, Officer. Caz is right—you certainly didn't need help. You handled that idiot perfectly."

JJ's eyes lit.

As they looked for seating, Caz noticed she chose a table near the back where she could watch everyone in the shop. Typical cop. He moved his chair to the side so he could do the same thing. Old habits never died.

Leaning back, she studied him, "I appreciate that you didn't come charging in."

"If you'd needed me, I would have." He took a sip of his *café de olla*, enjoying how the sweet cinnamon flavor enhanced the coffee. After Sarah and Uriah had learned his liking for Mexican coffee, they kept him supplied. "Did you want someone to help out?"

"No." JJ's gaze met his. "I'd have been annoyed if you had. At the same time, it was nice to know I had backup if I needed it."

"Always." As she devoted herself to her strudel, he considered her. A puzzle, that's what she was. Tough, yes, with the self-confidence of someone who knew she could do the job. Yet she didn't have a hard-ass, macho attitude. Her skill at talking the drunk down had been excellent, and considering the amount of alcohol Alaskans tended to imbibe, the talent would prove useful. He could see why Gabe had hired her.

Why had she come to Alaska? "Gabe said you'd had a hard time where you'd worked before."

"Law enforcement is still a nontraditional career for a woman. Some guys will never accept a woman working beside them." She huffed out a breath. "When they stopped responding to my *officer needs backup* calls, I knew I had to leave."

Caz's hand closed in a fist at the pain and frustrated anger in her voice. Gabe considered the police to be a kind of family. To be on the outside of that would leave an officer completely alone. "Well, you'll probably have trouble with some of our set-in-their-ways Alaskans and the Patriot Zealots. But if you need help, you'll get it, not only from Gabe, but from a lot of the rest of us as well."

"Thank you."

Although suppressed immediately, the faint quiver of her chin broke his heart. Yes, she'd experienced a hard time of it in her Nevada city.

Gabe was right about something else, too. JJ didn't need Caz's reputation rubbing off on her. The best thing he could do for her would be to enjoy her friendship and keep it to that.

The bell over the door jingled, and several people entered. JJ gave them a quick glance, but when Caz stiffened, she took a closer look. *Hmm.*

Two men in their forties led the way, talking to each other. One was rake-thin and six feet. Black hair. Short, thick beard. Brown eyes. The other was five-eleven and lanky. Light brown hair. Clean-shaven. Both wore work shirts, jeans, boots and—dear God—were armed with semi-automatics in holsters.

The two women silently following the men were dressed in ankle-length dark skirts and long-sleeved, button-up blouses as if they'd stepped out of some Amish romance.

Not that JJ would admit to having read such romances.

The men glanced at Cazador with disgusted expressions. JJ

received a slow perusal, their gazes lingering on her chest. She'd been slotted into the sexual object category.

Lowering her voice, she told Caz, "Although I'm in law enforcement, I admit I'd enjoy shooting their little dicks off."

The doc broke out laughing. "I'm sure Gabe would ask that you not add to the violence in our community."

His smile faded slightly. "Those are Patriot Zealots—the PZs as we call them. The brown-haired one is *Reverend* Parrish, the leader. Black beard is his second-in-command, *Captain* Nabera." The twist of his mouth as he gave their titles showed a cynicism she rather enjoyed.

She kept an eye on the men—and their weapons. Although, this winter, she'd attend the academy session for out-of-state LEO transfers, she'd already read up on Alaska rules and regs. The open-carry rules here were very liberal. "Not a real reverend or a captain?"

"When researching, Audrey didn't find any indication they'd earned either title." He moved his shoulders. "That said, an organization can award any label they want."

"True." She ran her finger through the condensation left by her cup. "Did Audrey's research on their backgrounds turn up anything...interesting?"

The corners of Cazador's eyes crinkled. "You like gossip? You're a person after my own heart."

She drew herself up in token affront. "It's not gossip. It's essential information for a law enforcement officer."

"Yes, yes, of course it is." The laughter in his dark eyes didn't fade one bit. "The good Reverend Parrish comes from Texas. Was a college dropout, worked as a store clerk in Houston. Has been married three times. Got restraining orders on him by two of those wives. He crewed for a televangelist where he probably got the idea for this scam. After starting the PZs in Texas, he moved them here with a core group a few years ago."

"I see." Or maybe she didn't. She'd never understand people like this. "Where is their money coming from?"

"Apparently, new members turn over everything to the organization. They also get donations. They have a website advocating a return to the days when men were men and women were property." The doc looked as if even the words tasted bad.

"Isn't that precious."

"As an officer, you'll be a visible counter to those ideas. I like that; however..." The doc's troubled gaze met hers. "It also makes you a target for these rabid idiots. Be very careful, Officer Jenner."

He cared. After Weiler, it felt strange to have someone worry about her. Strange...and wonderful.

CHAPTER SEVEN

A sharp knife cuts the quickest and hurts the least. ~ Katharine Hepburn

At a back table in the roadhouse, Caz was talking with Gabe and Audrey about Bull's plans for Alaska Day. A holiday for many people, October 18th would be an interesting time at the Bull's Moose. Not that his police chief brother would get the day off.

"Isn't that JJ?" Audrey asked, pointing toward the door.

"So, it is." Gabe waved his officer over.

Dammit. For the last week, Caz had avoided the pretty officer, as he'd told Gabe he would. It helped that she worked long hours, learning the ins and outs of Alaska small-town police work. Gabe was damn happy with how she'd taken hold, and from the comments around town, most of the residents were pleased.

However, having her living right next door was a test of his willpower.

She got to him. He admitted it. The big eyes, the freckles, the way she moved that spoke of martial arts training. The way her jeans cupped her ass.

He'd never before had a problem ignoring a woman's physical appeal. But she got to him on an emotional level as well.

When she fed scraps to the chickens, her face would light up as the hens gathered around her feet. In the evenings, she would play the flutesad music that spoke of a lonely heart and made him want to hold her. Sometimes she'd simply sit in the gazebo to watch the sun going down over the snow-covered mountain peaks.

She liked the simple things in life...and he liked her.

It would be easier if he didn't.

He and Gabe rose as she walked to the table. Her duty belt was gone, and she'd changed her khaki uniform shirt for a blue-green sweater, which brought out the turquoise color of her eyes.

"Sit, guys." She smiled at Audrey. "I didn't mean to disturb your evening. I just popped in here to get one of Bull's burgers to take home."

"You're not disturbing us. Join us." Audrey motioned to a chair.

Pleasure swept over JJ's face at the invitation.

And Caz felt again that uncomfortable desire to simply hold her. Instead, he pulled the chair out for her. "Sit, JJ."

Her gaze met his, and a light flush appeared on her cheeks as she let him seat her.

Sitting back down, he glanced at the clock. Ten at night. She'd worked the noon-to-eight shift and was just finishing? "It's unhealthy to work too much overtime or skip meals, Officer Jenner."

She grimaced. "I know, but that's police work. Why did I think a small town would be quieter than a city?"

"Small towns are quieter...in a way." Gabe grinned. "No gang warfare, few murders. But two LEOs aren't many for a growing populace. It'll quiet down soon. Some. I do want you to take your breaks and leave on time if at all possible."

"Of course, sir," she said politely." The quirk of her lips showed Gabe was being optimistic.

Gabe lifted his drink in rueful agreement.

Yes, she was working out well for the chief.

Felix trotted over and took her order for a Coke, burger, and fries. The waiter patted her shoulder, obviously liking the officer. "Anyone else?"

"We're good, thanks," Gabe said.

"So very good, yes." Felix grinned at Caz before heading back to the bar.

JJ shook her head. "Everyone just falls at your feet, don't they, Doc."

"Sadly, not everyone, no." He heaved a desolate sigh.

Her lips tipped up.

It seemed he wasn't the only one who remembered how she'd turned him down. He met her gaze, letting her see his regret, and found an answering spark in her eyes. "Actually, when it comes to appeal, Bull leaves me in the dust."

Behind the bar, Bull was enjoying his work, mixing drinks, talking with his customers. His laugh rang out as he traded jokes with one man, puns with an older woman, and sternly told a younger man that he wouldn't get another drink unless he handed over his car keys. A quartet of young women were giggling at whatever he said, pulling necklines down to show off cleavage, and flipping their hair. They paid for their drinks in a way that their hands would touch Bull's.

Poor Bull.

"You're treated to about the same amount of attention, Caz," Audrey said. "The difference is you don't really mind, and you're extremely skilled at diverting interested women. Although he hides it, Bull hates being lusted over, and he's not as good at escaping."

Caz tilted his head, surprised at her insight. "True enough. It's nice that most women do take a hint." Most, not all. Some went after a man like avid fishermen would go after a king salmon.

"Poor guys," JJ said in mock commiseration.

He understood, actually. No female would be very sympathetic to a male whining about attracting female attention. He and Bull might grow tired of being importuned, but they'd never been fearful of being assaulted. "It's a tough job, bartending," he said lightly.

Gabe grinned then asked his officer, "By the way, JJ, did you find out who set out the illegal bear bait?"

"It was one of EmmaJean's renters, Chief." She glanced at Caz and Audrey. "The guy set up a bear bait station near the new B&B off Swan. He wanted to sit on his balcony and shoot a bear."

Caz straightened. "That's crazy." There were laws against putting bait stations close to habitation.

"Hunters." JJ shrugged. "I transferred the problem to Fish and Game."

Gabe snorted. "The dumbass thought he'd catch bear in October? Well, the brown hats'll be happy to deal with him."

A phone rang. Caz's cell. He frowned as he pulled it out. The clinic was closed, and emergencies would go to the borough dispatcher and on-call staff at the Soldotna Hospital.

The display was for a social services department. Now? Someone was putting in overtime. "This is Ramirez," he said.

"Cazador Ramirez?"

"Yes. Forgive me, but I'm in a noisy area. Can you speak up, please?"

"Of course." The woman's voice wasn't young. "I can't believe I located you."

"I didn't know I was missing." Caz realized he had the attention of everyone at the table now.

"Well, you weren't, not exactly, but, this is going to be difficult to explain. I'm Mrs. Townsend with the Sacramento County

Department of Child, Family, and Adult Services." There was a rustling of papers before she continued. "Back when you were in the military, apparently you had...well, intimate relations...with a woman by the name of Crystal Hodge."

The name was vaguely familiar. "Ma'am, I was discharged from the military"—he had to think—"over six years ago. Is there a point to this?"

Across the table from him, Gabe frowned.

JJ's head was tilted.

"It would have been about a decade ago," the woman said.

Ten years ago. That was the year his fiancée had been killed by an insurgent. He realized Mrs. Townsend was still talking. Clearing the thickness from his throat, he said, "I'm sorry, I missed what you said. Can you repeat that?"

"I said Crystal Hodge listed you as the father on her daughter's birth certificate."

Everything in Caz froze.

"¿Perdóname? Daughter?"

"Yes, Crystal had a daughter. Regan Ramirez."

"That isn't possible. I never—I always use protection."

As a health professional, he'd heard that protest before and said exactly what Mrs. Townsend now stated, "Mr. Ramirez, we all know that no birth control method is one hundred percent effective."

"This Crystal Hodge thinks it's a good time to tell me this now?" How old would this so-called daughter be? Panic welled up inside him. A child? Caz rose to his feet. "I want to talk with her."

"She's dead, Mr. Ramirez. Apparently, she believed you'd been killed in combat, which was why you weren't told." Mrs. Townsend sighed. "From what I can piece together, when she became persistent in trying to find you, someone in the Special Forces offices gave her the impression you'd been killed in action. A military friend of mine says you might have been in a covert operation where your bosses might have discouraged a woman from raising a stink."

Dios. Caz rubbed his neck, trying to think.

After Carmen died, he'd buried himself in a bottle first, then pulled himself together enough to seek vengeance instead. Black ops. Assassinations. "No, she wouldn't have been allowed to contact me. Not back then," he admitted. It'd taken a while to realize that more deaths wouldn't bring Carmen back, wouldn't heal the hole in his heart. More blood wasn't an answer to anything.

He met his brother's gaze. With Gabe's dislike of secrets, he'd wormed the story out of Caz a few years ago. "A daughter?"

Caz ignored him and said into the phone, "Crystal thought I was the father?" During that drunken time, he'd been with... honestly, he had no idea how many women. They'd been tag chasers—women targeting military guys for sex.

"Yes. Enough to put you down on the birth certificate." Mrs. Townsend sighed. "I'd suggest a paternity test."

"Sí, that would be the first step." Caz stared at the table. As the trap closed around him, anger flared. "Even so, I...I cannot... will not...have a daughter. It is impossible."

He rose and strode out of the roadhouse.

After Caz left, JJ talked for a while with Gabe and Audrey about the problems in Rescue. Then they'd taken her around the bar to introduce her to more of the town residents. She ended up in a great discussion of cozy mysteries. Denise, a schoolteacher, and Regina, the municipal building's receptionist preferred the classics like Miss Marple. JJ and the postmaster, Irene, a dour woman in her 60s, liked animal-centered mysteries. Who wouldn't like Yum Yum and Koko?

Alcohol and books. She stayed longer than she should've. Way longer.

Finally, she headed out and...dammit. Hours ago, she'd needed to clear her head and had walked to the roadhouse from the station. And now, she had to hike back downtown to get her car.

Way to think ahead, JJ. Not.

At least it wasn't raining. When she reached the intersection of Grebe and Main, she paused. A red GMC pickup was parked in front of the municipal building. Problems?

As she headed over, Bull was getting out of the vehicle. One of the most easy-going people she'd ever met, he had a frown on his face.

"What's wrong, Bull?"

He nodded toward the municipal building. "Gabe called to tell me about the news—and that Caz isn't at the Hermitage. Then Dante called to say the clinic lights are on."

JJ looked at the building. The lights in the right side. The clinic was closed. "Cazador didn't take the news well."

"Seems not. I figured I'd better check on him."

"Don't you have to close down the roadhouse?"

"Brothers come first." His resolute tone said this was a life principle that was buried deep.

Before she could respond, his cell rang. "Yo."

Felix's voice came over the cell: "Bull, those two big hunters—they won't leave. They say Alaska bars stay open all night."

"Fuck." Bull eyed the municipal building.

The roadhouse owner was a good guy. "Tell you what—I'll check on your brother. You go take care of your roadhouse. Felix shouldn't have to be a bouncer."

He eyed her. "True enough. You sure you're up to Caz in a bad mood—possibly drunk?"

"Seriously?" She laughed. Gabe would be tough to handle in a fight, Bull impossible. But Cazador wasn't huge. He didn't exude ready-to-brawl vibes like Gabe. "I think I can handle the doc."

Bull lifted an eyebrow the way her karate instructor had when she'd flubbed a block. "I better take this. You can help out at the roadhouse."

"I'm missing something, aren't I?" She thought back to what she'd heard of the conversation in the roadhouse. The social worker had been speaking loudly enough for them all to hear.

Caz didn't seem all that dangerous, but...duh, a medical practitioner would probably strive to appear harmless. "He was in Special Forces, I got that." The US Army Special Forces had once been called Green Berets. "The social worker said something about covert operations?"

Maybe he was more lethal than he seemed.

"Yeah. He spent a year as an assass—" Bull stopped. Eyed her. "I mean, he was sent after high-value targets."

Sent after as in killed? An assassin? Her jaw dropped. "You're joking."

Bull's flat expression said not.

Ooookay. So much for thinking the doc was a nice, sweet guy. Then again, he'd already shaken his "nice" impression with the way he reacted to having a daughter. She'd expected surprise, then joy. Something other than complete dismay.

Whatever he was, she could deal with him. JJ crossed her arms over her chest. "Bull, I've got this. Go, deal with your drunks. I'll handle the grumpy doc."

Once inside the municipal building, she used her master key on the clinic door and walked in. And stopped.

Thudding sounds came from a room past the front office. She headed toward the noise. What was he doing—kicking a chair?

No. He was throwing *knives.*

She stood, frozen, in the doorway of the office. Talk about lethal.

He even looked lethal. Dark hair, dark eyes, black clothing. He was spitting a stream of curses in Spanish. After taking a gulp from a bottle of clear liquid, he picked up a black knife from a stack on the desk and threw without aiming. The blade struck a bulletin board on the other side of the long room. The rest of the knives followed, *thump, thump, thump, thump,* to create a perfectly round circle on the board.

He crossed the room. She'd noticed his walk before, as perfectly balanced as a leopard, but...she hadn't realized he also moved in complete silence.

After removing the knives from the board, he turned to look at her, his expression cold. The laughter that usually lurked in his eyes was gone—and she missed it.

"Cazador."

"I am not good company tonight, señorita. Another time, perhaps." Polite. Dismissive.

She entered the room and tried to ignore the knives he dumped onto the desk. They looked very sharp. "Are you upset about your daughter?"

Duh. But she had to start the conversation somewhere.

His mouth set into a line. "I cannot care for a daughter."

What was she missing here, dammit? "You make enough money. You can—"

He waved his hand. "Money is nothing. She can have everything I own. If I'd known, I could have helped before."

"If it's not money, why are you so upset?"

"I do not want to... This is impossible. *No!*" And he forcefully shoved the knives off the desk.

JJ jumped at the loud clatter. "Caz."

"I will not care for her. I will *not*."

Care. He didn't mean physically caring for a child, but rejected *loving* the girl. "You love your brothers. Why not a child? A little girl who needs you."

"No." The stream of Spanish was too fast to follow. "Mi hermanos can protect themselves. A child, she cannot. I can't protect the women, the children."

His statement was simply not true. From what Bull had said, from what she'd just seen, the doc was as deadly as his brothers were. Maybe more so.

Why was there such pain in his voice, in his eyes?

Taking his hand, she drew him over to the chairs against the wall and down to sit beside her. "I don't understand."

"You don't need—"

"Who died?" It was a guess, but such anger spoke of trauma.

His expression darkened.

"Caz. Talk to me." She squeezed his hand.

His slow sigh spoke of surrender. "My mother and sister." He shook his head. "I should have been faster. Better. But the man shot before I could save them."

Shot? He'd seen his mom and sister murdered? The thought stabbed her heart. When had they died? Mako had gotten the boys from a foster home, right? "How old were you?"

Caz felt his muscles tense at the question. JJ's hand was around his, her warmth seeping into his cold fingers. Sympathy shone in her eyes. "I was seven."

"*Seven.*" She huffed like an annoyed brown bear. "Doc, you were too young to do anything. You know that."

That's what Mako had said. It didn't matter. Caz had been the man of the house. And years later, when he saw Carmen's body... He rubbed his aching head. The pain wasn't from the alcohol, but from the past.

Where were the words to make her understand why he couldn't have a daughter? "I didn't save them, and then, when I was a man, my Carmen died. I didn't go with her. I was setting up for a mission, but I should have been there to protect her. Should have..."

His heart squeezed.

JJ's quiet, level voice broke into his misery. "How did she die?"

He slumped, leaning his head back against the hard wall. How many walls had he punched after they'd told him? After he'd gone to the base hospital and seen the horror of the savage wounds. "An RPG struck her vehicle. In Afghanistan."

"You were in the military together?"

"Si. She was regular Army. I was Special Forces." Carmen had teased him about being a Green Beret *meat-eater*. "We were to marry the next month."

Tears filled JJ's eyes. "I'm so sorry. I can't even imagine how that must have hurt."

It had. The emotions had been overwhelming—pain, fury, helplessness. Guilt that he hadn't been with her to keep her safe. He'd tried everything to bury his feelings.

Releasing JJ's hand, he scrubbed his face with his palms. "Back in the States, I went crazy, tried to find the bottom of a bottle. That was when..."

She took his hand again, as if to keep him safely moored. "When you might have made a baby?"

"I can't remember her—Crystal. Dios, I could see this child who they say is mine, and I wouldn't even know her."

Did he really have a daughter he'd never met? What had she looked like as a baby? A toddler? If he'd been with Crystal a decade ago...and if he added in nine months of gestation, then the girl would be nine or ten.

The social worker had sent him information and pictures of... Regan. His daughter. No, no he couldn't have a daughter.

"The social worker thought Crystal couldn't find you because you went into something covert?"

He grunted. "I pulled myself out of the bottle and went looking for vengeance instead." He moved his chair away from her. She was a good woman; he was a killer. "The insurgents had been targeting the base with RPGs, IEDs, even suicide bombs. But they were just stupid peons following orders. I wanted the leaders to pay for Carmen. An SF officer heard me ranting—and I got recruited."

"Into going after the insurgent higher-ups and killing them?"

He nodded.

The memories of that year had never left him. The ghastly feel of his knife penetrating skin and cartilage. The stench of loosened bowels. The shudder and spasm and last heaving breath, even after the spirit had fled.

The first few kills had held a gruesome satisfaction. The bastards were paying for Carmen's death. Then...

"It didn't take long before I knew I'd made a mistake. Nothing I did would bring Carmen back. With each death, I lost a part of my soul. If I'd continued, there would not be a *me* any longer."

"Ah." She took his hands between hers, and he almost pulled away. His hands were drenched in blood. But, no, that was just another of those images that would impose itself on reality, a ghost photo from the past.

"So, you went from being an assassin to being a medic?"

He shrugged. "It does sound odd, doesn't it? But a...friend... knew I'd planned to be a medic before. He pushed me into returning to that plan."

"You're doing good here. It's where you belong."

Simple words. Ones that affirmed how he felt. Pulled him back to being...rational. How long had he been here in the clinic, raging against risking his heart again? Throwing knives at fate?

"What are you going to do about your daughter?"

"That is the question, no?" Caz glanced at the papers he'd printed from the documents Mrs. Townsend had emailed. "If the paternity test is positive, then..." Yet he knew the child was his.

He rose and handed JJ the girl's photo. Thick dark hair, eyes the same shape and color as his. His chin and cheekbones in a delicate, feminine face.

JJ ran her finger over the surface of the picture. The lips that matched his own. "She's like a mini-you."

Looking at the photo, he knew he was doomed. The girl's eyes held pain. Grief. Loss. The stubborn jut of the jaw was his when he was fighting back emotion. She was like him in more than appearance.

Even if she wasn't his, he'd want to help her. To see what he could do. "I fly out early tomorrow and will work on finding her the place that will be best for her."

"With her father, surely?"

His memory persisted in pulling up the past: Mamá's sightless eyes. His little sister's screams. Carmen's bloody, torn body.

His own death didn't worry him, but he couldn't bear to lose someone so vulnerable and innocent. Not again.

Nonetheless, this was his duty. His shoulders straightened as he accepted the responsibility. "Perhaps. Probably." It appeared that young Regan had no one else. Tomorrow or the next day, he would meet her.

After glancing at the wall clock, he frowned. "What are you doing here, Officer? It is very late."

"Bull was going to check on you, but he got dragged back to the roadhouse to kick out some obstinate drunks. I came instead."

"Ah. I do appreciate it." He studied her. Still in the black jeans and boots she wore for her cop duty. Short hair braided back tightly. But the sweater she wore was the blue-green of her beautiful eyes and looked soft. Touchable.

"Since you are off-duty, would you like a drink?" He motioned to the mescal.

"Sure, why not." Before he could move, she rose and fetched the bottle.

He tried not to notice how the jeans curved over her ass, how the sweater rounded over her small breasts. She was a friend. A friend.

Bottle in hand, she dropped down beside Caz and took a hefty slug. Blinked. "That's not scotch." She examined the bottle, mispronouncing, "*El Jolgorio Tepeztate.* It's not bad, whatever it is."

"Mescal." She did amuse him. "It's like tequila, only better."

To be sociable, he accepted the bottle but only sipped. Although he'd burned off much of the alcohol in his anger and blade tossing, the buzz still hummed in his bloodstream. "I'm sorry I have no glasses or mix."

"I can handle shots." After another swallow, she shrugged. "It was one of the things I learned how to do when I was trying to fit in. To be one of the guys in Nevada."

They drank for a while in companionable silence, passing the bottle back and forth. The comforting sounds wrapped around Caz. The hum of the equipment and florescent lights. The occasional car on Main Street.

The knot in his gut started to unwind.

Looking over, he could see a flush rising in JJ's cheeks and how her muscles were relaxing. He had to appreciate how she'd joined him. Hadn't made a fuss over drinking from the bottle or drinking undiluted mescal. She was damned amazing. "What other things did you do to be one of the guys?"

A corner of her mouth tipped up. "I took martial arts classes, went to the shooting range, ran, and lifted weights."

"That is a lot of work." He tilted his head. People said he was good with women, and occasionally, he thought he understood them. Mostly, he admitted, he didn't have a clue. "Why?"

Her gaze dropped.

Cupping her cheek, he turned her head toward him. "I do not try to make you embarrassed, chiquita, but to hear why you went into such a rough profession. Why?"

"It's foolish. I wanted to save lives. Protect people. Be a hero."

If she were his, he'd memorize lines just to make her turn the pretty color of red that was now flooding her cheeks.

"Not foolish. You are much like Gabe, and to be in law enforcement—to be good at it—that's a calling, not just a job."

She nodded—and smiled at him.

He'd noticed she didn't smile often, didn't laugh often, or perhaps it was just when he was around that she was subdued. The thought was annoying, saddening. Because she was something special. Her sense of compassion had brought her in here to talk with him, despite him throwing knives. She'd held his hand. Had grieved with him. She'd been drawn to police work by her need to help. To protect. He had the same sense of duty.

They were much alike, weren't they?

Unfortunately for him, she was also female. Chemistry and attraction couldn't be reasoned with...and Dios, he'd tried.

"Well." She rose. "If you're all right, I need to get home. You should go home, too."

He stood up, realized they were far too close to one another. Her cheeks were flushed a rosy pink. Her blue-green eyes were gentle, and her mouth...

Tipping her chin up, he took a taste of those lips. So soft and enticing. When she made a tiny entreating sound, he gathered her into his arms and took the kiss deeper, feeling her warmth, her curves against him, yielding and arousing.

She went up on tiptoes and put her arms around his neck.

His cock surged to hardness, and he cupped her ass with one hand, holding her against him. Her tongue fenced with his, her mouth hot and needy.

But when he pulled back, planning to uncover her breasts so he could enjoy them, sanity surfaced.

"Estúpido." He took another step back and captured her hands. "We were not going to do this. We will not."

Her gaze met his, desire giving way to dismay. "I'm sorry. Really. I didn't come in here planning to...to do anything other than talk."

He touched her cheek. The urge to pull her back, to lay her out on the desk, to hear her moan, scream. *No.* That urge must be throttled.

He could and would protect her in this way.

"I know you didn't, *princesa*. I'm sorry too." He glanced at his blades, tucked some away in his belt and boot sheaths, and waved her toward the door. "Let me walk you to your car."

She gave him a rueful smile. "Actually, I think we should call Bull and ask him for a ride."

CHAPTER EIGHT

A *person's a person, no matter how small.* - Horton the elephant

It had been a long—and far-too-fast—few days.

The expedited paternity test had shown Caz was a father.

Since then, he'd been trying to hasten getting Regan released to him. Because the other foster children were picking on her. His little girl.

He'd called Dr. Zachary Grayson. The respected children's psychologist was an old friend of Mako's and had known Caz for a couple of decades now. Grayson agreed that the less time Regan spent in foster care, the better, and had lent his influence to move things along.

Today, Caz would take his daughter home to Alaska. "Congratulations, *pinche culero*, you're a father."

He didn't feel like one. From Regan's withdrawn response upon meeting him, she wasn't impressed either.

Meeting her had rendered him speechless. Their meetings with either Mrs. Townsend or the foster mother nearby were awkward. As a health professional, he was skilled with drawing people out, with interacting. With a daughter he should have known about, should have been there for her first laugh, her first word, her first steps. Have taught her to use a spoon, to brush her teeth. Have dried her tears. The weight of those missed years had rendered him speechless. Clumsy.

Now, Regan would be dependent on a person she barely knew. He remembered all too well what that'd been like.

Caz pulled the rental car up to the door of the foster home where Regan was stationed. Housed. Whatever. He glanced up at the sky. "If you're keeping an eye on us, Sarge, I could use some help here."

He knew what Mako would say. "Cowards never start. The weak never finish. Winners never quit." And that was that. He'd do his best by his daughter. He could offer her no less.

He got out of the car, squared his shoulders, and marched up to the house.

Mrs. Townsend waited in the open doorway. She was a small woman, gray hair left natural, glasses perched on her nose and kinder than a first impression might convey. She smiled. "Good morning, Mr. Ramirez. Regan should be here in a—"

At a noise, she glanced over her shoulder. Her eyes widened.

He followed her gaze. "Well."

His daughter had a bloody graze on one cheek, a swollen lip, hair in a tangle. Blood on a skinned knee.

As Regan crossed the living room, her face hurt, and so did her knee where she'd landed on the concrete. Tears stung her eyes, so she screwed her face into a fierce look. That stinkface Haley couldn't make her cry. No one could make her cry. She was—

"How badly are you hurt, Regan?" A man's voice made her look up and take a step back.

It was the guy who Mrs. Townsend said was for sure her

father. Only Mom'd said he was dead. How could someone make a mistake about being dead?

He crouched down in front of her. His eyebrows, just as dark as hers, went up. "Regan?"

The question, the...almost worry...in his face made something inside her feel weird, like she'd eaten too much ice cream or something.

Her chin rose. "I'm fine."

"Ah, of course you are, chiquita," he said, not shouting or anything. He talked to her like she talked to the cat from next door—all soft and careful.

"Let's get your scrapes cleaned up and bandaged before we leave, yes?" He moved forward and put his hand on her shoulder. "Mrs. Townsend, could you round up some first-aid supplies, please?"

To Regan's shock, he scooped her up, took her in the bathroom, and set her on the counter. Her words got stuck in her throat as he gently washed the blood and dirt from her leg.

"It doesn't bother you to see blood, does it?"

"Uh-uh."

He picked up the goo stuff, and she tensed. Instead of rubbing it into her scrape like the foster mom did, he squirted some on the Band-Aid. "Good. You're a tough child."

As he applied the Band-Aid, his nod said he liked her being tough. That he thought she was brave.

Her chest got that squishy feeling again, until she remembered she really wasn't brave.

He wouldn't like her once he really knew her. What would she do then?

Caz settled into the plane seat with a sigh of relief and forced his hands to stay still as Regan fastened her own seatbelt.

Successfully. When she looked up at him, he smiled. "Very good."

Damn airports always left him on edge. But today, it'd been worse. He'd read too many headlines of lost children, kidnapped children, children hurt in terrorist attacks. He was okay with getting hurt himself, but no one—*no one*—was going to mess with his girl. Just the thought made him clench his teeth and growl.

When she shot him a worried glance, he wanted to kick himself. He was an idiot. Keeping her safe needed to start with him.

"Sorry, Regan." A portion of the truth might help. "I was in the military for a while, and now I don't like places with too many people."

Her little brows drew together. "Because guys might have guns and shoot at you?"

Or shoot at the child he'd vowed to protect. That was far worse. "That's it exactly."

"Oh. You can hold my hand if you need to."

Everything inside his chest melted into one big puddle.

"Thank you, mija." Her heart was a generous one. An empathetic one.

She curled her tiny hand around his and looked around. Listened intently as the flight attendant delivered the inevitable safety lecture.

"Is this the first time you've been on a plane?" Caz asked her.

"Uh-huh. I've only been places in California."

He wasn't surprised.

Mrs. Townsend had put together Regan's history. When Regan was a baby, Crystal had stayed with her mother until the woman's death. Then Crystal worked as a hairdresser, not keeping a job for long. The woman had lived with a series of men, and they'd apparently grown less honest. Less decent. She and one boyfriend had been arrested for dealing. That had been Regan's first stay in the foster care system. Unfortunately, no one had questioned Crystal's statement that Regan's father was dead. Mrs. Townsend hadn't either, actually. She'd simply been looking for possible relatives of his who might take Regan. With no current reason to hide his existence, the military had been forthcoming, and the social worker discovered Caz was alive and well.

Crystal's last boyfriend had talked her into robbing a mini-mart—and the bastard had shot the cashier. Crystal went to jail and died of a subdural hematoma after brawling with another inmate.

Mrs. Townsend hadn't been able to tell him much about Regan's relationship with her mother. During interviews, Crystal spent the time raging about her conviction and the boyfriend instead of discussing her daughter. Regan hadn't been forthcoming, either. He'd been the same—answering questions if prodded, but not offering any extra information.

Hopefully, Caz could learn more if he used a more subtle approach. "Did you and your mother ever go camping or visit the forests?"

"No. Mom didn't like dirt much." She hesitated. "Is that bad?"

Caz chuckled. "No, chiquita. It just means Alaska will be as full of surprises for you as it was when I first arrived there. I was younger than you are when I lost my family—my mamá and my sister. I went into foster care"—her eyes went wide—"and ended up in Alaska with Mako, who raised me."

"Your mom died?"

"When I was seven." Then he'd been in foster care off and on for a year. All too often, he'd been placed in negligent—or terrifying—homes and would run away and attempt to survive on the streets. He was small, but fast, and that was where he'd first discovered the silent equalizer—a blade.

Regan stared at their entwined fingers in her lap before turning her big brown eyes up again. "You lost your family, but you said you got brothers. How?"

"Mako took me and three other boys to Alaska. We ended up calling ourselves brothers."

"Huh."

He needed to talk about something less worrying.

In fact, he had an assignment from his shopping team at home. Last night, he'd called and asked Audrey if she'd do some shopping. Audrey had not only agreed but also asked him if she could take Lillian and JJ. It was a great idea. He had a feeling JJ's career and the mess in Weiler had left the officer bereft of female friends. Perhaps even a little wary. He'd approved and asked Audrey to push JJ if needed. Dios, he hoped he hadn't stepped in it.

Meantime, he'd like to give Audrey and crew some suggestions before they left for Kenai.

He looked down at his daughter. His daughter. How long before he became used to that word? "Now and then, I like to play a get-to-know-you game." He'd used questions like these as icebreakers with women, then adapted them for anxious pediatric patients. "It's a good way to kill time. You in?"

Her wary expression broke his heart, but she nodded.

"Good enough. What's your favorite color?"

She blinked as if she'd expected an uncomfortable question. Then she smiled. Dios, she was beautiful. "Red. I like red."

Answering her expectant look, he told her, "Mine is blue. Favorite food?"

"Pizza."

"Can't argue with that. Mine, too." That netted him a delighted grin. "Although ice cream might come in second."

She nodded enthusiastically.

"Favorite thing to wear."

"Uh, jeans and T-shirts." She gave him a worried little-girl frown. "I don't like dresses."

"I don't wear dresses either."

She giggled, lightening his heart.

Okay, she wasn't a girly-girl, then—and wasn't that a relief? "I like jeans and T-shirts, too. Favorite things to do when you're not in school?"

More comfortable now, she wiggled into a cross-legged position in the designed-for-dwarves airline seat. "I like soccer. Reading stuff. Watching TV."

Reading was good. TV—well, he could see battles ahead. Soccer might work.

"What about you?"

He paused, at a loss. Was he ever not at work? Recently the clinic had taken most of his hours aside from the time he'd put in to fill the freezers with meat. His tendency to spend evenings at the clinic was going to have to change, wasn't it? "I hang out with my brothers—your uncles. We grill food. Go fishing."

"Fishing?" The look on her face was priceless, as if she couldn't decide whether to look enthusiastic or wrinkle her nose.

"Sí. I'll take you a time or two, and you can see if you enjoy it."

The wariness was back, but she nodded.

"I read, watch movies"—find a woman to enjoy—"go out to eat, work in the garden, and play music. Drums."

"That's a lot."

"What did you and your mamá do together for fun?"

The silence simply broke his heart. Nothing?

Regan blinked hard. "I helped her get dressed sometimes. Before she went out at night. But...not much."

He nodded. "Every family is different. Because we grew up in a little cabin with no electricity—no TV, right?—my brothers and I got used to doing everything together."

"No TV. For real?"

He almost grinned at her appalled expression.

"Do you have TV *now*? And the internet?"

"Yes, chica. We have the internet. And a television."

"Oh." She slumped in obvious relief. "Okay."

"What would you two like to drink?" The flight attendant stopped the cart.

Caz waited for Regan and was pleased with her forthright answer. "A 7-Up?" She looked at him for approval.

"Good choice. I'll have the same, please." He showed her how to use the tray table.

As she settled in with her drink, he considered what to do next. Because he still had questions. So many questions. Like... she'd evaded the questions about the cause of her fight in the foster home.

He frowned at the seat in front of them. Mako wasn't a shining example of fatherhood, although he'd done his best. Heart-to-hearts hadn't been his strength. Then again, Caz did have fair people skills. He'd spent years as a combat medic, then a nurse practitioner. And he'd learned that talking face-to-face and direct questions could inhibit conversation with nervous people, especially children.

Pulling out his phone, he started to type out a text. "I'm going to let your uncles, Gabe and Bull, know when to expect us."

She nodded.

After that, he worked on a group text (him, Lillian, Audrey, and JJ) with Regan's favorite colors, styles, and interests and sent it off on the plane's Wi-Fi.

As Regan watched the flight attendants push the cart down the aisle, Caz said idly, "Back when I was your age, my brothers and I used to fight quite a bit."

"You did?"

"Mmmhmm. Sometimes for fun, sometimes because one of us got mad. Lots of reasons." He grinned. "So, at the foster home, what was your fight about?"

From the corner of his eye, he saw her glance at him, but he kept his attention on the cell phone.

"Um." Her little fingers were making pleats in her shirt. "Snowball lives next door, but she comes over to visit me. Haley was picking on her. Pulling her tail and was going to burn off her whiskers. An' she wouldn't stop, so I hit her."

Snowball must be a cat. "In that case, I'm glad you hit her."

"For real?"

"Sí." Regan's astonished expression almost made him laugh. "I'm proud of you for protecting an animal from a bully."

Her look of surprise, of relief, was saddening.

She stared at her hands, a crease between her brows. This child was a thinker, and one who usually thought before speaking. He remembered how he'd also learned to think first—from being backhanded by foster parents.

His daughter was so young, so small, so fragile. How the hell was he going to keep her safe?

A montage of memories swept over him. Mamá, Carmen. All his comrades in arms who'd died, bleeding out on a battlefield. Everyone he'd not protected, not been able to save. Probably every combat medic in the world felt the same.

He realized she was watching him. Still frowning.

"We're going to do fine, Regan. You'll like Alaska." He ruffled her hair.

Maybe he could keep her indoors, away from everything. The inner compound was safe. She could stay there until...oh, until maybe she was fifty or so?

Smiling, JJ followed Audrey and Lillian into the Kenai Walmart. Cazador's text about Regan's preferences had arrived, and they had shopping to do.

JJ had met Lillian last night when the older woman—a retired English actress—had invited her, Gabe and Audrey, Bull, and Dante, the grocery-store owner over for supper.

Lillian was an excellent cook, a fantastic gardener, somehow both diplomatic and blunt. She considered Audrey "her girl".

Envy touched JJ's heart. Although her mother's stroke had messed with how her brain processed things, she'd still been... Mom. JJ would always miss her. Miss the love, the support, the simple you can-do-whatever-you-think-you-can belief.

Lillian's support of Audrey was like that—and made JJ's eyes sting. Audrey'd said once that her mother had been more of a tutor than a mom. Even if late, it was nice Audrey had someone now.

While everyone was at Lillian's, Caz had called from his Sacramento hotel room to give an update on his daughter, saying that they'd be on the plane today. Friday.

Yes, he was bringing his little girl home. He'd been worried if the move would be too much for her, worried about getting her into school. JJ smiled. He'd sounded like every new father she'd ever met—even if his baby was already nine. She knew he'd be a natural.

Then he'd said his daughter's scant amount of warm-weather clothing was in pretty sad shape, and she had nothing for Alaska temperatures. And had no other possessions.

To top it off, her bedroom in Caz's house had no furniture.

When he said he didn't want Regan to come home to a bare room, JJ had gotten teary-eyed. He didn't want to love that little girl—but he was falling fast.

Yeah, she knew he would.

Today's shopping trip had been arranged quickly. Since Gabe had appointments at the station he couldn't postpone, Bull took charge of getting furniture. Audrey had asked Lillian to go to Kenai with her to get clothes, bedding, and whatever else, and had asked JJ to come as well. Had almost demanded that JJ join them, actually.

It was nice to be wanted. And wonderful to be here today.

"Are we ready?" Audrey stopped just inside the store.

"We are." Lillian pushed a shopping cart to JJ and took one for herself. Lillian had opted for the bed and bath portion of the shopping trip, stating JJ and Audrey would do better at buying clothing a little girl would wear. "As Dante would say, you two have your mission. I have mine. We'll rendezvous at checkout one in twenty minutes."

"The children's clothing section is that way." Audrey pointed toward the middle of the store. "This would be easier if I had little sisters or nieces and nephews or something. Do you have any experience at this?"

"Not at all. I don't have any family left." She'd thought she'd answered casually enough, but Audrey's sympathetic look showed her loneliness had slipped through. "Anyway, I've always been too busy with work and school."

"I know the feeling. Well, we'll manage the best we can." Audrey stopped at a rack and held up an adorable shirt.

More and more clothing landed in the cart.

JJ found a winter jacket in a dark red and a hoodie in a vibrant green. The colors would look good on Caz, and he'd said Regan had his coloring. "How about pajamas?"

"Definitely. Warm ones."

Socks, underwear, sneakers. "More shoes?"

"We'll wait to get boots until we see if the sneakers fit." Audrey added colorful socks. "We can bring her next time. But, it's kind of fun to play godmother, don't you think?"

"It really is."

By the time they had the cart almost filled with garments, Lillian appeared. Her cart was piled high with bedding and towels, pillows and rugs. She smiled at the clothing in their cart. "Those look lovely, my dears."

"We did well," Audrey agreed.

JJ looked at all the bedding and envisioned how the bare room would look once filled with furniture. The French country floral quilt in dark reds and teals was gorgeous. Lillian had added two fluffy teal rugs.

Audrey pulled out her phone and snapped a picture of the

bedspread and rugs. "I'm going to tell Gabe he has to paint one of the walls to match the teal. If he does it at lunch, it'll have time to dry before she gets there."

"Poor Gabe." The bedroom was all white paneling. An accent wall would be lovely.

But...the little girl would still be alone without her mama in a houseful of strangers.

JJ shook her head, remembering her first week in Alaska. Even as an adult, she'd felt displaced. It hadn't been her home; she hadn't known anyone. Even the land had looked different. What else could they do to help little Regan? "She needs personal things. Maybe a hairbrush, toothbrush, and shampoo for a child? And toys."

The other two stared at her.

Then Audrey rolled her eyes. "Duh. We got focused on rooms and clothes and forgot the fun stuff."

Lillian turned her cart. "I'll swing by the care products and meet you in the toy section."

The toy section was huge.

Audrey blew out a breath. "Isn't it weird that I'd like to buy some of these toys for myself? I call dibs on the crafty stuff."

"I'll see what else there is." JJ planted the cart at the end of one aisle. "Meet you back here in ten."

It took her closer to fifteen minutes. By the time JJ returned, Lillian was waiting with Audrey.

Audrey held up her finds. "The basics: crayons and coloring books, rubber stamps. A Lego Hogwarts."

JJ burst out laughing. "Great minds think alike." She set the first Harry Potter movie into the cart and added *The Princess Diaries* and *Frozen*.

Lillian nodded her approval. "Do plan on inviting me over for the girls' movie night."

After dropping in the board games, *Labyrinth* and *Carcassonne*, JJ flushed. "I also picked up this." The stuffed animal—a white cat—was just the right size to cuddle in bed, super-soft and plush, with big appealing eyes. "To, uh, welcome her since Caz texted she got in a fight to help the neighbor's kitty."

Regan's mom was gone and everyone should have something to hug.

"Perfect choice, love." Lillian gave the cat's soft fur a stroke and smiled at JJ. "I'm very pleased you came with us today."

The sentiment was so unexpected. So sweet.

Audrey laughed. "Caz told us not to let you wiggle out of joining us. That you would make a good friend."

Caz said that? Even as JJ's mouth dropped open, Audrey leaned forward and gave her a solid hug. "Caz was right."

JJ managed a choked "thank you" as she turned away, frantically blinking away the unwelcome tears.

There was silence that Lillian broke with a cheerful, "Well, let's queue up at a checkout stand."

Audrey grinned. "Two carts worth. It looks as if we almost bought out the store. I hope poor Cazador's savings account is healthy."

"Tsk." Lillian shook her head. "He doesn't spend his money on anything other than running around, the brazen-faced varlet."

JJ stared. "The...what?"

"I think that would be"—Audrey considered and grinned at Lillian—"an unapologetic man-ho. And isn't it fun to label a man with the sticker of shame?"

Lillian smiled smugly.

Emotions on a rollercoaster, JJ felt her face get tight. She knew all too well what that sticker of shame felt like and wouldn't wish it on anyone. Even a guy. She cleared the thickness from her throat. "Looks like the last checkout is the emptiest one."

Lillian tucked her white hair behind her ear as she studied JJ. "Audrey told me your former colleagues gave you labels, ones similar to varlet. How did that come about?"

"I...I"— JJ stared. "I thought the British were polite. And you—"

Lillian was dignified, almost regal. "In my younger days, I was most polite, young Jayden, I was. Then I spent time with two appallingly blunt Yanks who'd been in the military."

Audrey let out a snort. "Mako and Dante?"

"Indeed. Mako had no tolerance for what he termed bullshitting. Dante, being a bit more couth, calls it 'beating about the bush'. I find, as I age, I'm inclined to dispense with superficial courtesy and ask what I want to know."

The woman was simply awesome. "Can I be you when I grow up?"

Lillian laughed. "Tell us the story, Officer Jenner."

Here? In the toy section of Walmart?

Audrey leaned on her cart. Lillian folded her arms. Both were obviously prepared to wait forever. For the story. For JJ's nightmare.

Fine. "I was twenty-one when the Weiler Police force hired me. I graduated from the academy, got off probation, was a real officer." She shook her head. "I was so happy."

"No problems with being a woman on the force?" Audrey asked.

JJ shrugged. "There were a few sexist officers and some harassment. I was the only female officer. But my training officer, although he started off being annoyed about teaching a newbie who was female, ended up solidly on my side." Where would she have been without Gene? She'd call him tonight, catch up, and try to explain how much his support had meant.

Lillian frowned. "But something happened?"

"A fellow officer happened. Nash is a couple of years older than I am. I thought he was amazing. We started dating—and I fell for him. So hard. And, God, I was such an idiot."

Audrey narrowed her eyes. "Not much experience?"

"Very little. I missed out during the early dating years. No time." Her mom had been sick. JJ'd had to work and attend high school. Then there was the police academy and striving to be the best officer ever. "Nash turned controlling and disparaging and... just plain mean. I wasn't sure if it was him or me, not until he tried to push me off the force."

"Why?" Audrey asked. "I mean, it seems like he'd welcome being a two-income family."

JJ rubbed her face. Boasting wasn't something she did. "I...uh, was trying to improve all the time. Studying and working out and—"

Lillian studied her with keen eyes. "You were better than the sodding fool, weren't you? He couldn't accept it, so, rather than improve himself, he wanted to remove you from direct competition."

Cheeks hot, JJ nodded. "It took me awhile to realize how I was being manipulated."

"When did you figure it out? How?" Audrey asked.

"The DEA asked us to assist with a takedown of a drug distribution gang. At the warehouse, we were waiting for everyone to arrive and get into position. Nash got impatient and rushed in, hoping for glory. I saw him go through the window, and I yelled out orders to cover the exits. I took the rear exit."

She'd been so furious at how he'd risked all their lives. They hadn't had enough people there. And then the rear door burst open, and she was alone with no backup.

"JJ," Audrey said softly. "What happened?"

"We managed to take them down, although a few escaped from side windows." Her mouth set. "Nash's entry had warned the gang. I got two that tried to escape out the rear. Barely. I tased the first, caught a bullet from the second—on my vest—and shot him."

"How badly were you hurt?" Audrey asked. "Gabe says you still feel the impact even with body armor."

"It broke a rib." She'd had nightmares for weeks, dreaming she hadn't worn the vest, or that the bullet had been higher—blown out her brains, or she'd hear the sound of her bullet hitting the man.

She pulled in a breath and finished the story. "I avoided Nash that night. The next night, I dropped in at the local bar we all liked. People congratulated me, asked how I was. Nash was furious. When I left, he followed and yelled at me for making him look bad. I wanted to beat the hell out of him, but I just told him we were done and walked away."

Lillian eyed her. "I can see that. You're quite controlled. I assume he didn't take the news well?"

"That's when he started openly criticizing my performance as an officer. Saying I couldn't handle the job. Spreading rumors that I'd slept with my instructors to get through the academy. That I was always coming on to other officers and he'd broken up with me because of it. And then he got promoted to Lieutenant."

"A screw-up like him?" Audrey looked outraged.

"His cousin is the captain. His uncle is chief of police." JJ grimaced. "It puts a whole new meaning on the good-old-boys' system."

"A complaint would go nowhere." Lillian's grim expression showed she understood. "I'm surprised they gave you a reference."

"They didn't. My old training officer knows Gabe, a little, and sent me here." JJ smiled at Audrey. "Gabe is the boss I always wanted to have. I can learn a lot from him—and I'll do my best never to let him down."

"I know that." Audrey squeezed her hand. "Gabe's needed a good officer since he got here. I'm glad he has you."

Seriously? The compliment took JJ's breath away.

"Yes, Rescue will do better with you here." Lillian smiled. "All right, my girls, let's get out of here. I want to stop at Sweeney's in Soldotna. I doubt either of you have the right gear for winter. We can get Regan some things there, too."

As they walked toward checkout, Lillian patted the stuffed cat in JJ's cart. "You have the right instincts to make an excellent mother."

JJ blinked. "Um. I actually never gave that much thought."

"You're young yet. But really, it's best to be married a few years before the first baby, so you don't want to procrastinate too long." Lillian tapped her lips. "We have a few likely lads in Rescue. I'll see that you're introduced."

"Wait..." JJ shot Audrey a helpless look, a plea for help, but the blonde was cracking up with laughter. Easy for her, she had Gabe. JJ gathered her resources. A good LEO should never be at a loss for words. "I appreciate your interest, but since I'm new to the police force, that's where my focus must be. I don't have the time"—or the interest—"for dating."

She gave the Brit a very firm look.

Lillian patted her arm. "Of course. But you'll see—there's always time for love. Your man will have to be quite secure in his masculinity. I'll have to make a list."

Dear God. Everyone in town loved Mayor Lillian, and JJ was rapidly falling for her, as well. Nonetheless...

Would Rescue notice if their mayor went missing?

CHAPTER NINE

Sometimes the best we can do is to remind each other that we're related for better or for worse and try to keep the maiming and killing to a minimum. - Rick Riordan

Regan felt more like a little kid than a nine-year-old, and she wanted to crawl into the bedroom closet and hide behind all the boxes. Only she didn't have a closet or a bedroom or boxes. Or a mom either.

She didn't have anything. Just a stranger who said he was her dad.

He walked partway across the living room and turned. His brows pulled together. Angry? Or...or worried? Returning to her, he put his hand on her shoulder, but didn't ask her anything. Just stood with her.

Beside her.

Pulling in a shaky breath, she looked around. There were humongous windows all up one wall with a lake right outside. The ceiling was way far up. On one side was a big TV. Chairs with flowery material. A big tan couch and a littler one sat on a fancy rug with reds, tans, and black colors. The kitchen and dining table and stuff were on the other side.

How could it be so big and still feel kinda snuggly? "This is Bull and Gabe and Hawk's and your house?"

His eyebrows rose. "No, your uncles have their own cabins." He motioned toward the side windows toward the other houses. "All five houses belong to us."

He owned a whole big house. Beside a lake. "And I-I'll live here?"

"That's the plan." He smiled at her. "Let me show you your bedroom. You can wash up and then meet your uncles. And we can eat."

She put her hand on her stomach. Food sounded good—and bad—cuz her stomach was all weird and quivery. She had uncles here. What if they didn't like her? What if she did something, said something stupid? "Okay."

When he squeezed her shoulder, the funny feeling eased up. "My bedroom is in the loft." He pointed toward the railing upstairs. "I'll show you that later. Your bedroom's this way."

He went back down the hallway toward the garage, under the loft part, and opened a door.

Behind him, she stopped and stared. "For real?"

"Yes, this is yours."

"Fuck," she breathed, winced, and looked up.

He blinked. Then he chuckled. "I take it you like it."

"Uh-huh." She watched him carefully. Teachers usually yelled at her for swearing, but he'd laughed. What did that mean? Still, if he got upset, he might throw her out. Put her back in foster care. *Don't say fuck. Ever.*

As he moved out of her way, she took a step into the room. The bed was really dope, a fancy white metal that made pretty swirls, and there was a bedspread on top, with squares of flowers. She just wanted to sit and look at the room. The blue in the flowers was the same color as the wall behind the bed. And there were all sorts of pretty pillows in reds and blacks, enough to bury herself underneath.

Across the room, bookshelves as tall as she was, stood on each side of a big window. Between them was a long bench with a black cushion and soft red pillows. She could read and look out the window.

A smaller window beside the bed faced the road where they'd come in. A huge black beanbag chair sat in that corner with a fluffy red and black blanket.

A white desk had a bulletin board over it. And it had a cute rolling chair...with a stuffed white cat. Unable to help herself, she walked over and picked up the cat. So soft and fluffy and nice. "For me?" she whispered.

He touched her hair, and his smile made her want to cry. Made her want a hug and... She was such a baby.

"Everything in here is for you, *mija*."

For me. She squeezed the cat tighter and swallowed hard. "What's *mee-ha* mean?"

"My little girl," he said softly.

Oh. She looked down, unable to look at him longer. "Um. What...what do I call you? Cazador or..."

"No, I don't think so. Even if I wasn't there for you, I'm your father." He squeezed her shoulder and stepped back. "You have choices, though. Daddy, dad, father, padre, papá."

"Oh."

After a second, he said, "I called my father Papá."

Papá. *PaPA.* It sounded chill. But...she couldn't say it. Not right now. "Okay."

A corner of his mouth tipped up, like maybe he understood, like it didn't bother him. He waved toward the doors across from the bed. "Come and see."

"Your closet is here." He opened the first door.

She had a closet. With dark corners where she could hide when he got drunk and mean.

115

Hangers held clothing, but not grownup clothing. The coat and hoodie were her size. For her? She couldn't ask.

He opened the next door. "This is your bathroom."

White walls—a long counter of swirly white stone. Sink and tub with a shower curtain—with smiling cats on it. The towels and rugs were all a dark red.

She looked at the cat in her arms, the ones on the shower curtain. "Did you know I liked cats before you came to get me?"

"Not until you let me know about saving Snowball. I texted your uncles and JJ and Audrey, who went shopping." He walked out of the bathroom. "This room was bare. We needed to get you furniture, or you'd have been sleeping on the couch."

She took a step back. "You got all this just for me?"

"Yes. Let's walk over to Mako's house so you can meet everyone. Gabe and Bull are here. Audrey is Gabe's girlfriend. JJ works for Gabe and is staying upstairs in Mako's house until she can rent a place."

Regan counted on her fingers. Four. Okay, she could handle four people. Maybe.

But it was really hard to put the cat on the bed and leave her room.

Her very own room.

Arm curled around his tiny daughter's shoulders, Caz guided her out of the house and chatted about the chickens as they crossed to Mako's house. Rain drizzled down, more of a fine mist than a drenching. He was used to trotting around in the cold, but he probably should've grabbed her a jacket. She was a California girl. He'd have to be more aware.

Of the weather. Of her worries.

Her too-slender body was trembling lightly. Dios, how could he make her feel comfortable? Settled? He couldn't. Not all at once. No matter how his instincts screamed at him to try.

"Mija, if you want, we can just say hello to everyone, then if you want to go back to the house... How about you squeeze my fingers twice if you want to leave? We don't have to stay to eat." He considered. So many new things coming at her in the next month or so. "Whenever you need to escape something, you can use squeezing fingers method to let me know. Does that make sense?"

"If I want to go back to my room, then I squeeze your fingers. Two times." Her tense shoulders relaxed. "Okay."

They walked across Mako's deck and into the dining area. Caz sniffed. "Smells like fried chicken."

When her stomach rumbled, he grinned.

The open arrangement of the big cabin let him see that everyone was seated on the massive wraparound sectional. As Caz and Regan crossed the room, everyone rose—and Regan stopped dead.

"We're here, as you can see," Caz nodded at his brothers and at Audrey who stood beside Gabe. Her gray T-shirt was the color of her eyes and the quote on the shirt said: *Never trust an atom. They make up everything.* The woman was a nerd and proud of it.

JJ stood near the end of the sectional. With her autumn-colored hair and wearing a golden thermal under a blue and brown flannel shirt, she seemed to warm the entire room. Warm him.

Her expression as she watched him was unreadable—something she did when she was feeling uncertain. She still didn't know what to think or do about him.

That made two of them.

Her gaze softened when she looked at Regan.

Under his arm, he felt Regan stiffen with obvious anxiety. Yes, they were all staring at her.

Tucking her closer, he bent and started pointing out people. "That's your Uncle Gabe—he's a police chief—and that's his woman, Audrey, who runs the library."

Sensitive to Regan's worry, Gabe sat on the old barn wood

coffee table Mako had built. "We're glad you're here, Regan. Caz needs someone to keep him in line."

Caz played along with an indignant "Bro, *please*," back.

It took his daughter a second, and then she giggled.

Trust Gabe to know how to lighten the mood. Even in combat zones, he'd managed to coax smiles out of his men.

Audrey smiled. "It's nice to meet you, Regan."

Biting her lip, Regan nodded.

Continuing the introductions, Caz motioned toward his other brother. "That's your Uncle Bull. When he was your age, he chose the name, because he wanted to grow up to be as big as a moose. A male moose is called a bull."

Bull rubbed his shaved scalp and gave her a grin. "It worked, right? You think I got big enough?"

She nodded solemnly before frowning up at Caz. "How come he got to pick his name?"

Hmm. This wasn't the time to explain how Mako had stolen them from the foster home—with the boys' consent. "Ah, Mako spent his life in the military, so he let us pick soldier names."

"Oh." She considered. "I like my name."

"That's what I told Mako. I kept my own name," Gabe said. "You don't have to change yours. Regan is a great name."

Her happy smile turned every adult in the room to putty.

Caz turned to JJ. "Mija, that's JJ. She's a police officer and works for Gabe."

"Hi, Regan," JJ said in her husky voice. "Welcome home. You had an awfully long trip. Are you getting a little hungry yet?"

Regan's stomach growled in answer.

Or maybe it was his. "If she's not, I am. Tell me it's fried chicken I'm smelling."

"You got the nose, bro," Bull rumbled. He grinned at Regan. "We used to make it for him on his birthdays. He'd come running from wherever in the forest he was."

When Bull moved forward, like a grizzly lumbering through the woods, Regan retreated behind Caz.

Ah well, it was going to take time. Especially since no one, including him, knew exactly what she'd endured. They'd have to move carefully. The first couple of times Caz had touched her—ruffling her hair or touching her shoulder—she'd winced away. His guess was she'd learned to be wary—perhaps Crystal hadn't been careful about her men—but hadn't suffered systematic abuse.

The thought of anyone hurting this girl—his girl—made him want to reach for his knives.

Gabe rose and put an arm around Audrey. "C'mon, people. Let's start getting some food on the table."

As everyone moved, Regan stood frozen until JJ held her hand out. "Hey, how about you help me get silverware on the table."

After a second, Regan took her hand. "Okay."

As the two walked into the dining area, hand-in-hand, Caz glanced at the window. Still raining. Odd, because it felt as if the sun had come out.

An hour later, dinner finished, kitchen clean, everyone returned to the living room for drinks, for talk, and for music. JJ ran upstairs to her part of the house to grab a plate of cookies she'd baked. In her limited experience with children, she'd never met a child who didn't like chocolate chip cookies.

Music greeted her as she walked into the living room.

Of course, music. Since her arrival nearly two weeks ago, she'd heard the guys singing together nearly every day. She'd never met anyone like them. It seemed growing up in a cabin with no electricity and long dark winters meant they'd learned to entertain themselves. Since Mako had loved music, his boys learned to sing and play various instruments.

With Regan beside him, Caz sat at the near end of the

sectional, playing a djembe—a skin-covered goblet drum. He'd told JJ he liked the sound of a handcrafted drum.

Beside Audrey, Gabe strummed a guitar. Bull had a bass guitar that suited him well. Bass voice, bass guitar.

As the guys started playing "Lonely People" by America, JJ had the urge to run back upstairs and fetch her flute, to join in. But, although she'd started on the flute at Regan's age and played in quartets in high school, this kind of living room jamming was far more...intimate.

She'd stick to playing just for herself. It was her way of coping with loneliness. With stress...and even anger. Hadn't Mom said how thankful she was that JJ played the flute instead of walloping other children?

Her mom had known her well.

Maybe someday she'd try jamming with the guys. Meantime, she set the cookies where Caz and Regan could reach them then sat down on the other side of the girl.

As the men sailed into the chorus, Audrey winked at Regan and joined in for the finish. She had a beautiful soprano.

"Wow," Regan said under her breath.

Caz smiled at his girl. "I bet you've watched *The Jungle Book*, haven't you?"

Regan nodded.

"Perfect." He grinned at Bull who put on a fake scowl.

Gabe laughed and told Regan, "Caz and I learned this song so we could give Bull a hard time after he'd busted an ankle and was just sitting around at home." With a few quick strums, he started singing "The Bare Necessities."

Audrey burst into giggles.

To JJ's delight, Regan was whispering the words under her breath. JJ manned-up and whispered, "It's one of my favorite movies. C'mon, we can do this."

Smiling at the little girl, JJ added her voice to the singing, and a second later, a high little voice joined them.

Caz shot JJ a grateful look that made warmth rise in her cheeks, and then he winked at his daughter.

JJ's heart simply melted.

After the music, Caz had taken his exhausted daughter home and fumbled through what would someday be a bedtime routine. Regan had managed her shower and shampooing her own long hair. The women had stocked her bathroom with everything a girl might want, bless them, including shampoo with conditioner in it. And a wide-tooth comb.

They'd also gotten her soft flannel pajamas. One set with kittens. The other had snowflakes and featured some female from a Disney movie he'd not seen. *Frozen?*

She'd chosen the kitten jammies and pulled on fluffy slippers. Those women hadn't missed a thing.

In the living room, as he combed the tangles out of her hair, he read to her from the library book Audrey had left on the coffee table. *Harry Potter.* When he talked Regan into taking turns, each of them reading a page, she did damned well.

After she'd climbed into her bed—with the stuffed white cat —he reminded her he was just upstairs and to yell if she needed him. Such big eyes. So lost.

"Sleep tight, mija," he murmured, kissed the top of her head, and tucked the covers tighter around her.

There was a nightlight in the bathroom, he'd noticed, and as he turned the light out, he saw there was another one in the bedroom. A prancing unicorn glowed a soft white.

As he pulled the door not quite shut, he heard a whispered, "Night, Papá."

Papá. He walked into the living room, rubbing away the burning in his eyes.

Unsettled, he took a beer from the fridge and walked

outside onto his deck. The rain had stopped, and the air held a bite, warning that snow would arrive in a week or so. The shoulder he'd busted rock-climbing as a kid agreed with the forecast.

Not yet, though. Above, the clear dark sky showed only wispy clouds flitting past the quarter moon. Over the lake, the misty fog glowed in the thin moonlight.

Leaning an arm on the railing, he breathed in, trying to pull the silence of the night inside him. To soothe the storm of emotions in his heart.

He had a daughter.

He'd thought he'd accepted the fact. But bringing her home, seeing her with his brothers, and tucking her into bed had turned knowledge into living reality.

Dios, he didn't know *how* to raise a little girl. He rubbed his neck. Better him than his brothers. They'd be more at a loss than he was.

Then again, they wouldn't have gotten their asses into a fix like this.

A fix.

A gift.

Both.

He heard soft footsteps and turned.

Someone walked across the compound, up from the dock on the lake. Too short for Gabe or Bull. He tensed, preparing to charge the trespasser, then remembered Gabe and Bull weren't the only people living at the Hermitage these days. Which woman?

The curly hair identified her—and his fingers itched to run through the soft strands.

"JJ. You are out late," he said, knowing his voice would carry to her in the quiet air.

Halfway to Mako's house, she looked around.

He'd be invisible against the darkness of the log wall behind him, so he walked down the steps and across the damp grass. "Forgive me for startling you."

"It's all right." Her face was a pale shape in the darkness. "How's Regan doing? The first night in a strange house must be rough."

"She's a real trouper." He could hear the pride in his voice. Already. "Thank you—all of you—for making her room so special. There was much I wouldn't have known to get. She was delighted with everything."

"We had a wonderful time shopping for her." JJ smiled. "Next time, we'll take her so she can pick out what she actually likes."

"She took the stuffed cat to bed with her. Audrey said you picked it out...so she'd have something to cuddle in a strange place."

He had a feeling this woman had a heart that understood loneliness.

"I'm glad it helped." Her wide smile pulled at him. "You know, she'll soon have you talked into getting a real cat."

"I don't think so." Although a pet wasn't a bad idea. Perhaps one to help keep her safe. "Maybe I'll get her a big dog though." Big enough to take on a brown bear, a cougar, a—

"Poor Cazador. You're going to have a time of it." Her laugh was adorable. Low and husky, like her singing voice.

"I liked hearing you sing today." It had been the first time—and they all knew she'd joined them simply to get Regan over her worries.

"It was fun." She looked up at him, eyes sparkling in the moonlight.

"Sí, it was." Unable to resist, he put an arm around her and pulled her closer. Lowered his head, giving her time to object.

She didn't. Her lips softened under his, and he pulled her tightly against him, taking her mouth in a slow, seductive kiss. One that made the world fade away. When she melted against him, he stroked down her spine, over the sweet curve of her ass, and back up. Her small breasts against his chest begged for his attention. He licked her lips, tasted chocolate—no wonder women liked it so much—and went for another kiss.

Then, before being tempted past reason, he pulled back. Studied her face and found desire. He wasn't the only one tempted.

There was also confusion. Match again.

He saw the rueful quirk of her lips as she said, "Thank you. More would be a...bad idea."

"Unfortunately, yes." He had a child to protect from the world, as if anyone could. He absolutely could not add another string to his heart—especially not a law officer. The career was as risky as that of a soldier.

With regret, he ran a finger down her cheek. Her skin was damp from the mist, fragrant from a shower. "Sleep well, princesa."

"You, too, Doc."

Unable to help himself, he watched until she was safely inside Mako's cabin.

CHAPTER TEN

I f you are short of everything but the enemy, you are in the combat zone. - Murphy's Laws of Combat Operations

This wasn't like any school she'd ever seen. Monday morning, Regan followed her father toward the school building from where he'd parked his car in the round drive. The school grounds were a couple of blocks from downtown—and not even on a real street. The road was gravel.

"Are you sure this is a school?" She motioned to the four tiny buildings and one slightly bigger one. "What are those?"

"The smaller ones hold the classrooms. The big one has the multipurpose room and administration." Papá eyed the buildings. "They're portable rooms and pretty old. What with the growing population, the town council needs to find options for a better school."

The buildings circled an open area—what must be the play-ground—since there sure wasn't any place to play in the surrounding forest. The grounds were the only flat spot in the area. To the right, the land went uphill fast. On the left, it was really steep going downhill.

"Doc, it's good to see you." The man waiting by one door was a bit taller than Papá, and his short brown hair was going gray. He looked friendly enough.

"And you." Papá shook his hand. "Principal Jones, this is my daughter, Regan."

My daughter. That still made her feel funny. Bubbly-like, inside.

"It's good to meet you, Regan." The principal had a nice smile. Like he meant it. "Let's get some paperwork done, and we'll go to your classroom."

The boring stuff didn't take too long—less than she'd had to go through whenever she and Mom moved.

But...fuck. When she followed Papá into her new classroom, the place felt weird. In the corner, four older kids were sitting at computers, and she thought she was in the wrong room. Only there were kids her age doing something around a table near the front. But there were littler kids—maybe in third grade—at desks lined up between the two small windows.

Principal Jones was over talking to the woman who must be the teacher. The teacher wasn't pretty and was older than Papá. Still, she didn't look mean. Her brown hair was even curlier than JJ's, kinda squiggly, and her nose was pointed. She wasn't all dressed up, just wearing black jeans and a blue shirt with buttons.

The teacher and the principal stopped talking and looked at Regan.

She inched back, wanting to hide behind Papá, but the kids would think she was a scaredy-cat. She could feel their eyes.

Papá put his hand on her shoulder, the way he did, not to push her around or anything, but like holding her hand only it was her shoulder. She was too old to hold hands, really, but this was okay. Nice.

She looked up. "Why are there older kids?"

"Since this is such a small school, there are only three teachers for kindergarten to eighth grade. Children from different grades share the room. Your room has third, fourth, and fifth graders in it." He shrugged. "Even with three grades together, there are only about twelve to fourteen children in each classroom."

The woman came over, and Papá shook her hand. "Regan, this is Mrs. Wilner, your teacher. She's been an instructor for a while and knows how to keep things interesting."

Regan started to nod and then remembered what Audrey had said. How she'd said it. "It's nice to meet you, Mrs. Wilner."

"Thank you, Regan. I look forward to getting to know you."

Papá went down on one knee and took Regan's hands in his. "I'm working in the clinic today, but one of us—me, Gabe, or Bull will pick you up when school lets out. Then you can do your homework in the clinic until it closes."

She saw two girls exchange glances and recognized their expressions: *The new girl can't even walk by herself for two blocks.*

Today it was true—she wasn't quite sure which building held the clinic. He should've showed her. Should've walked with her so she knew. Her voice came out ugly. "Yeah, okay. But I'll walk tomorrow. By myself."

His jaw got all hard, then he nodded. "We will compromise. This week, you will put up with one of us picking you up. Next week you may walk on your own, yes?"

A week. Relief swept through her that she'd have time to learn her way. She nodded.

He touched her cheek, rose, and kissed the top of her head. "Have a good day, today, mija."

As he walked out, leaving her there with strangers, her stomach quivered, and she wanted to run after him, have him hold her. *Don't cry like a baby.*

"Come with me, Regan, and I'll introduce you to your class-mates." Mrs. Wilner walked with her over to the group at the table.

The morning hadn't been too awful, Regan decided as she followed her classmates outside after lunch. The so-called playground had swings and a small field to play soccer and a paved basketball area.

Not that she was playing. The soccer field was wet. The two boys in her class were shooting hoops—something Regan sucked at. Too short. No practice. Regular kids usually had hoops at home to practice on.

She pulled her coat closer as a gust of cold air made her shiver. But her coat was warm, and hey, her new clothes were as nice as everybody else's, and that slayed. No rips or holes or stains. Her jeans and shirt even fit. In the foster home, her wrists had stuck out of her sleeves, and her ankles out of her jeans.

If Papá—Cazador—got tired of her, would he let her take the clothes?

Her stomach felt icky as she thought about leaving. Going back to the dirty foster home, sharing a room with mean girls.

As the kids on the playground shouted and played, Regan sighed. Trying to look like she didn't care that she stood alone, she stuck her hands in the pockets of her new jacket and found something in there under the glove. She pulled it out.

A bag of M&Ms—a big one—with a note taped to it. *Have a great day, Regan! JJ*

Her whole world got brighter.

"All right!" Laughing, Regan ripped a corner off the bag and saw the other girl in her fourth-grade class look over. "Want some M&Ms? Um, Dela-a-"

"It's Delaney. Sure." The girl pushed her light red hair out of her eyes and moved closer. She was a little taller than Regan and heavier. One of the bigger kids had called her fat. She'd been standing alone.

Regan poured some M&Ms into Delaney's hand.

"I love the green ones." Delaney popped a candy in her mouth.

"Are you new here too?"

"Sorta." Delaney ate another M&M. "We used to live in Anchorage, but Mom got a job at the resort, and we moved here last month." She rolled her eyes. "Mom grew up here, and my grandparents are here, and Mom used to say she'd never come back to Rescue."

"But you did." Regan frowned. "Do you like it here?"

"Sometimes." Delaney shook her head. "I get to do more cuz it's not a city—like I can walk to where Grams works at the post office. But I don't know many kids and some are—"

"Hey, new kid." The big boy had short yellow hair and stood beside a really pretty girl with long hair that was even lighter. Fifth-graders. "If you got candy, you share—and that fatty doesn't need more food."

Delaney's shoulders rolled in, and she started to hand the candy back.

Regan pushed her hand back. "You're not fat. He's a stupidhead."

"What did you call me?" As the boy stomped over, the littler kids scurried out of his way like mice. The girl beside him was laughing.

Regan shoved the M&Ms back into her pocket because he'd try to grab her food. She'd learned that way back in kindergarten. Her hands curled into fists. Slapping didn't work as well as fists.

No. She shouldn't fight. The grownups would get mad. Papá would get mad.

She retreated a few steps. She wouldn't fight if she didn't have to. Maybe the teacher would do something? "Get away from me," she shouted. "You can't steal from me."

The boy looked shocked and took a step back. He kept his voice low. "I didn't steal anything, you dumb spic. Why don't you go back to Mexico where you belong?"

Regan rolled her eyes—and didn't stop shouting. "I was born in California, Mr. Stupidhead."

"Brayden, let's go." The blonde girl pulled at his arm, and he wrenched it out of her grasp.

"No, this beaner-bitch—"

"Fucking asshole, get lost," Regan yelled, and at Delaney's gasp, she realized what she'd said.

Oh, shit.

"That's not language we use." Mrs. Wilner pointed toward the building. "Let's go inside. All of you."

A wave of fear swept over Regan. How mad would Papá get? Would he send her back?

JJ had used the kitchen downstairs to bake banana bread from the browning bananas that she hadn't managed to eat. Considering the cost of produce in Alaska, she sure wasn't going to waste them. She felt a twinge of guilt—the chickens would have enjoyed the treat.

Up in her second-floor rooms, she heard the timer go off and trotted downstairs, only to realize that Caz was there with Regan and delivering a lecture.

Not good. Should she go back upstairs until they were gone? No, the bread had to come out now. JJ eased down the steps and tried to tiptoe into the kitchen area although that wouldn't do much good since the entire downstairs was one giant room.

Thankfully, they ignored her as she pulled the bread out and turned off the oven.

And listened. *Snoopy much? You're a bad girl, Jayden Linnea Jenner.*

"It's not easy being the new person in a school, but you're going to have to make an effort to get along," Caz was saying in that resonant voice that sent shivers through her every time she heard him speak. "And there are certain words that aren't allowed.

Fuck in all its variations. *Asshole.* Those are two of them. You are not to use those words."

Regan stood, head down. But from the side, JJ could see that her expression was more pissed-off than apologetic.

Then Caz went on to say little girls shouldn't even know those words and—

"Seriously?" JJ leaned forward on the counter. "I'm sure I've heard you and your brothers use those words."

Caz turned, his jaw tightening. "This is not your—"

"Oh, but it is. Because I'm female." She glared at him. "Go ahead and tell her there are places where swearing is inappropriate. It's the truth. But telling a child she's too young to say certain words when the adults around her do? Isn't that a form of age discrimination?"

Caz rubbed his hand over his neck. "JJ, that is—"

"And telling her that *girls* don't get to swear and *boys* do? Not on my watch, you don't."

Caz frowned and then shook his head. "I did say that, didn't I?"

To JJ's surprise, he went down on one knee and took Regan's hands. "JJ is right, and I apologize."

Regan's shocked expression was priceless. The child hadn't been bothered by a scolding, but an adult apologizing left her stunned.

JJ pulled in a breath, because he'd admitted she was right and he was wrong. A simple statement without excuses or hedging.

He continued talking to Regan. "However, that said, there *are* places where swearing is considered very impolite. As a rule of thumb, if there are more people than just family around, it's best to avoid swearing. That applies to all of us, male or female, young or old. And, as you can tell, whether it's right or not, people react more strongly to a child cursing than an adult. You might take that into consideration."

Regan frowned. "But...he was going to take my candy."

When Caz's smile appeared, JJ's heart simply turned over.

"Mija, I'm proud of you for standing up for yourself. There are ways to do so that might work better and keep you out of trouble, so we'll talk about them. In fact, we'll clean the living room together, since we both messed up, and you can tell me more about that *pende*— Ah, that *boy* and about what happened."

Unable to watch longer, JJ turned away, because she'd give anything to have Cazador look at her with that tender expression. She turned the loaves out onto two plates, picked one up, and left the other on the counter.

"The cleaning crew gets banana bread," she said. "Take it home with you when you're done, okay?"

Caz ran a hand down Regan's hair, then smiled at JJ. "We accept with thanks...but only if you join us for supper tonight."

Her breath caught. The warm look in his eyes made the floor beneath her feet feel uneven. "What?"

"Please, JJ?" Regan bounced up and down on her toes. "Please come?"

She shouldn't. She shouldn't. "I'd love to join you."

CHAPTER ELEVEN

W*hen life closes a door, breach the wall and walk in like a boss.* -
Unknown

On Saturday night, almost at the end of October, JJ was beginning to feel as if she was settling in. She'd been in Rescue almost
three weeks now.

Sitting back in her chair, she looked around. Lillian's home
was filled with stunning antiques and beautiful Oriental carpets.
The green felt poker-table topper that covered the dining room
table looked quite out of place.

The Brit didn't seem to care.

Then again, Lillian was full of surprises. Look at the guests
she'd invited to her poker night. Both of Rescue's police officers
were there, as well as Bull and Caz. Bull had taken the evening off
from his roadhouse. The market owner, Dante. Tucker and
Guzman were both gray-haired, bearded, and scruffy back-
woodsmen who lived outside town in neighboring, off-the-grid
cabins.

As the break ended and everyone returned to the table, Caz

walked across the living room, talking on the phone with Regan. This was the first night Caz hadn't been home with his daughter.

His dark red V-neck sweater over a black turtleneck clung to his broad shoulders and muscular chest in a way that kept drawing her gaze. She knew better and still couldn't keep from looking at him.

His voice was a smooth croon as he said, "You go to sleep now, mija. Audrey will stay with you until I get home."

Every child should have a father like him.

As he pocketed his phone, he looked up...and caught her watching. His dark brown eyes held hers, and a crease appeared in his cheek.

Warmth heating her face, she cleared her throat. "Is Regan all right?"

"She is. It sounds as if they had fun." He picked up his cards and eyed the pile of fudge sitting on a plate beside his chips.

"Is she doing all right in class? Our tiny school must be a huge change," Lillian said.

"She doesn't look...eager...to go to school in the mornings. But her teacher says she's doing all right. Participates. Might be making some friends." Caz's jaw tightened. "She's pretty quick to jump into a fight."

Gabe snorted. "Like father, like daughter."

Really? As the play started, JJ considered the doc. Tried to imagine him in a fight. Starting a fight. Cazador always seemed to possess an almost infinite amount of patience. Although he did have those knives...

Smiling slightly, she examined her cards, then the other players and their faces. It looked like—

Around them, the building seemed to groan, and it *moved*. She felt as if she was in a boat on choppy water. Was her chair broken? Only, no, her drink was sloshing in the glass, the donut holes were rolling over the table. Glassware clinked in the kitchen. Even as

Lillian and the men pushed away from the table, everything stopped.

"Nice and short. I'm just as glad not to have to crawl under the table." Gabe scooted his chair back in. "Maybe a 3.7 or so."

"Nah, it was bigger than that. Didn't you see the donut holes rolling around? I got five that says it was a 4.2." Dante tugged at his white beard. "Maybe a fifty miler deep out in the Gulf."

"I'll take that bet." With a laugh, Guzman held up a five-dollar bill. "I'm going for 4.0 and central Alaska."

As wagers were taken, JJ stared at the crazy people. "That was an earthquake, and you're betting on it?" And now they were just going to go back to playing?

Picking up his cards, Guzman laughed, showing off a mouthful of silver fillings. "Yep. Your first quake?"

"Mmmhmm." She set a hand on her stomach. "It felt pretty weird."

"Alaska gets a few thousand a month, usually so small we don't feel them. But some we do." Bull gave her a reassuring smile. "Might as well get used to them. When you're decorating, keep in mind that things might go flying. Or falling."

"Seriously?"

Everyone around the table nodded.

Well, okay then. She blew out a breath and picked up her cards. "I'll raise two fudge pieces."

Since Tucker and Guzman lived mostly off the land, Lillian had provided pastry stakes to give them a home-cooked treat. Tucker—who was no slouch at poker—had won the last hand, and his gloating over his winnings of donut holes had been adorable.

Now, the man gave her fudge a sad look and tossed his cards in. "Fold."

Next to Tucker, Bull stroked his goatee—a lovely tell that said he had nothing.

JJ nibbled on a piece of fudge she'd pulled out of the pile in front of her. She could afford to eat one piece, right?

"Chiquita," Caz murmured from her right, "You shouldn't eat your stakes." The way he looked at her, the same tender way he looked at Regan these days, simply melted her heart.

She tried to erect a defense, find distance, and couldn't. "I love chocolate," she admitted. Her father had kept a supply of M&Ms to offer along with his hugs for easing bad times: playground fights, scraped knees, broken toys. She took another nibble. "Hey, I was just in an earthquake, and this is one of my comfort foods."

"Ah, that is good to know." With a tiny wink, he set one of his own pieces of fudge in her stack.

She felt as if she'd gotten a hug.

"I have nothing," Bull announced and folded. The others jeered, and the play went to Lillian, Dante, Gabe, and Guzman.

Finally, Caz pushed a mixture of fudge and donut holes forward. "Call. Let's see what you have, Officer Cardsharp."

She grinned and showed her hand. A full house.

Tucker scowled at her. "Missy, you're even better than Mayor Lillian. Your daddy teach you that?"

She laughed, pulled in the pot, and pushed him a piece of fudge, making his eyes light up. "My mom. We lived in Las Vegas, and she dealt cards for years before she got sick. She taught me."

"No wonder you're cleanin' up." Guzman tugged on his gray-white beard.

Bull frowned in concern. "Your mom got sick?"

JJ'd discovered the huge guy hid a soft heart. "A stroke left her partly disabled. I came home from school and found paramedics in our apartment." She tried to laugh lightly. "It was a shock."

"School? How old were you?" Twisting around in his chair, Caz studied her.

"Sixteen."

"Damn, that's rough, girl," Dante said. "Strokes are nasty. How bad did it hit her?"

"One side was paralyzed. And her"—JJ considered how to say it—"her emotions and thought processes were messed up. She was determined to overcome it. And she recovered enough to get around, but her mind didn't track as well as before. She couldn't deal cards, but the casino was nice enough to keep her on in the stockroom."

"Quite a pay cut, I bet," Bull observed. Having an MBA, of course, he'd know that. When Mako left his sons a bunch of Rescue properties, Bull was drafted to handle the business in addition to owning a restaurant and brewery in Anchorage and a restaurant in Homer.

He frowned at JJ. "Surviving on minimum wage isn't easy. How did you two get by?"

"We managed. I helped out with an after-school job at a small market."

"Working, taking care of your mother—not the usual high school experience." Caz's eyes were warm. Understanding.

She felt her cheeks heat. "After nearly losing her, I was grateful for the extra time I had with her. She was a great mom."

"I'm surprised you didn't go into dealing cards when you turned twenty-one," Gabe said. "Easier and probably pays better than being a patrol officer."

"Not at first. Dealers start out at minimum wage—although tips make a difference. The money you earn depends on experience and the table limit and all that."

Caz swept up the cards and shuffled them, his lean fingers graceful. Skilled. "You said *was*. How did you lose your mamá?"

As the cards whisked across the table, she picked up her hand and glanced around, expecting one of the others to shut down the questions, to want to play, but everyone was waiting. "She got hit by a car when she was walking home from the casino. Two drunk drivers playing chase downtown went right through the red light. A couple of other pedestrians were hurt, but the car got Mom straight on." She glanced at Gabe, wondering how much he'd shared.

He shook his head slightly. Nothing.

She pulled in a breath. "I'd been on my way home, too—I kept my hours synced with hers so I could cook... I saw..."

Caz plucked the cards from her hand and held it in his. Her fingers were cold; his hand was warm. Steadying. Strong. "How old were you then, JJ?"

"Twenty." She shook her head. "One of the responding officers was a total jerk, but the female patrol officer was great. Compassionate and efficient and competent. The contrast was incredible, and"—she laughed—"I applied to every police station within a hundred or so miles."

Having heard much of that during her interview, Gabe smiled at her. "And Rescue is glad you did."

Her boss knew how to make her day.

And that was enough about her. She pulled her hand from Caz's, wishing she didn't have to, and smiled at the others. "Let's play, people. The best solution for sadness is chocolate, and, oh look, there's a nice pile over there." She pointed to the pieces of fudge in front of Dante. He gave her a chiding look.

Caz's resonant chuckle filled the hollow inside her, and she couldn't help but smile at him.

When she looked up, Bull frowned slightly, his gaze moving from his brother to her. And back. Gabe was looking at her and Caz the same way.

Major oops. She needed to remember to keep her distance from Cazador, mentally and physically and every other way.

At midnight as she'd warned them, Lillian called the evening to a halt. Tucker and Guzman disappeared to start the trip back to their backwoods cabins. Bull and Dante were straightening up the dining room—and JJ got the distinct impression that Dante would be spending the night. The Okie and the Brit were so very different, yet watching them together was simply lovely.

As JJ helped carry dishes out to the kitchen, she smiled at her hostess. "Thank you so much for inviting me tonight. I had a great time."

"It was wonderful to have you—and how fun that another woman enjoys poker nights. I tried to get Audrey to join us, but she said absolutely not." Expression filled with laughter, Lillian stacked the dishes in the sink. "She was delighted to stay home with Regan instead."

Gabe handed over his glass. "When I left, they were deciding which chick flick to watch."

JJ felt a stab of envy. Her time of movie watching with other kids had ended when she had to work after school and evenings.

"Look at that face—she wants to watch chick flicks, too." Caz covered the appetizer tray and tucked it into the fridge, obviously knowing his way around Lillian's kitchen. "Don't worry. With you living at the Hermitage, there'll be other opportunities."

Gabe's keen eyes narrowed, then he smiled. "Actually, Audrey doesn't like being alone in the cabin when I'm working late. She'll love having someone to hang with."

Someone to hang with. A female friend. Because Audrey was coming to be that. JJ couldn't keep from smiling.

"Yo, Gabe, let's go, bro," Bull called from the dining room. "Lillian, you do excellent poker nights—thank you. See you in a month."

Gabe kissed Lillian's cheek, raised his hand to Caz, JJ, and Dante and strode out after Bull since the two had come together.

"Is there anything I can help with?" JJ asked.

"No, love. Everything is tidy." Lillian motioned to Dante. "Can you see her to her car, dear?"

JJ shook her head. "I don't need—"

"I'll take her, Dante. I parked near her car," Caz said. "Thanks, Lillian, for the night—and the fudge."

JJ frowned as she picked up her coat. "Thanks, again, Lillian. Bye, you two." She headed out the door, not waiting for the doc. Being near him wasn't the best of ideas. Besides, she didn't need an escort—she was the law, for heaven's sake—and certainly not from the man who'd won most of her fudge with the last hand.

She'd been looking forward to indulging.

As she stepped off the porch, something cold brushed against her cheek, so she stopped. Looked up. Fat flakes of snow were spiraling down, white against the dark night sky. A light film of white already covered the grass and the gravel road in front of Lillian's house. So beautiful.

"It's pretty, isn't it? We might even get enough to make the roads slick." Caz trotted down the steps and stopped beside her. "You got your snow tires on just in time."

"Because you and Gabe made sure I did." They watched out for her so carefully. And she loved it. She smiled up at the sky. *Snow.* "Weiler didn't get more than a couple of tiny snowfalls a year. What happens when you get a lot? Who clears the roads?"

As they strolled along the side of the gravel road, he put a hand behind her back, not in a controlling way, not like Nash, but simply keeping her close. "The borough hires local contractors for the highways, but they don't bother to plow until there's, maybe, half-a-foot of snow on the road. The town handles snow removal within the city limits, so Lillian's street will be plowed. I think Chevy and Knox picked up a contract to shovel the downtown sidewalks. They used to work winters on the North Slope ice roads, but this year, they have enough work to stick around."

Chevy and Knox were the local handymen. "Don't they live outside of town? How will they get in?"

"Snow machines. You call them snowmobiles in the Lower 48. In winter, our transportation here shifts to ski planes, snow machines, and snowshoes."

"Oh." She walked beside him, her hip brushing his. His hand created a small circle of warmth on her back under her jacket. "How about the Hermitage?"

"Our road is private, but we keep a small tractor to clear

enough snow that we can get out. We have snow machines, too. You'll be able to get to town."

"Oh, good. I guess I should keep more food in the house. You guys seem awfully well prepared for the winter."

"You have no idea, chica."

At her curious glance, he grinned. "Mako was a survivalist and paranoid, always expecting a war or disaster. We have solar panels to supplement the electric power, and there's enough food stored we won't starve for...mmm, maybe a year or so, even without hunting or fishing."

"That's actually pretty cool." Then she stopped. "Wait. Social services let a paranoid survivalist adopt four boys? How old were you?"

"I was eight." The corners of his eyes crinkled. "He didn't exactly ask the government for permission to take us."

"He didn't ask...he *stole* you from a foster home?"

"Mmmhmm. We were willing participants though."

"That's just wrong." Her law-abiding heart was outraged, but she went for the bottom line. "Was he a good father?"

"He was." Reaching her Toyota, Caz leaned against it. "He had PTSD with some bad spells of paranoia. Years in the military made him hard as nails and expecting one hundred percent from his"—he grinned—"soldiers, no matter how young."

She could hear the grief in his voice. "But you loved him."

"He expected a lot but gave as much or more. We never doubted we were wanted, that we belonged, and that he'd die to keep us safe." As Caz looked up at the falling snow, a nearby porch light illuminated his lean face, the jaw shadowed with a day's growth of beard. His expression had softened at the memories.

A hard childhood, a hard father, yet this man remembered the best parts. He didn't whine—in fact, she'd never heard him whine. Even at the card table where behavior often deteriorated, he'd lost with a laugh, won with a grin, obviously there more for the company than the competition. Had she ever met anyone so completely confident in himself?

Why the heck did she have to like him so much?

His gaze met hers. Setting his fingers under her chin, he kept her face turned up toward his. "Such a frown. What's the matter, mamita?"

She didn't want to answer that. "What's mamita mean?"

"Ah, it's short for mamacita—little mama."

Patronizing, condescending term...yet, when he called her that in a voice like melted chocolate, she melted, too.

"Tell me what is bothering you." His smile was slow. "Mamita."

The words slid from her. "I don't want to like you this much." Even worse, she was sliding into more than like, and the knowledge scared her spitless.

His grin was white in the darkness, then his voice dropped, so smooth and masculine. "I feel the same."

His fingers on her skin were slightly rough...and so warm. She remembered the touch of his hand, the way his lips had felt, brushing against hers as if each sensory detail had been sewn into her soul. Her gaze dropped to his mouth, and her voice came out way too husky. "It seems we have a problem."

His lips curved up. Then he slid his fingers into her hair, cupping the back of her head as he kissed her forehead, her temple, her cheek. His lips were so warm.

Slowly, his grip on her hair tightened enough to tilt her head back. His mouth came down on hers.

This...this was what she'd wanted, hoped for, craved, from the moment the evening had begun. Need pooled low in her stomach.

"More," he murmured, lifting her arms to his neck, and pulling her firmly against him. His lips were firm, teasing over hers, coaxing her to open. He took her mouth with devastating control, leaving her thoughts scattered in fragments around her.

. . .

Dios, her lips were soft. The way she responded was turning a simple kiss into something so erotic that every resolution he'd made to leave her alone was driven right out of his head.

When he tried to pull back, her arms tightened around his neck. She pressed against him, her lower belly rubbing on his throbbing erection.

Maybe one more minute... Or more.

He cupped her ass—so very female despite the hard muscle—and pulled her tighter against him. Her small breasts flattened against his chest, tantalizing him. Begging him to touch.

When he started thinking about where they could go to finish this, he remembered he had a daughter. Audrey was babysitting Regan in his cabin. And he shouldn't, couldn't, mess around with Gabe's officer.

"JJ, we must stop." With an unhappy sigh, he gripped her wrists and pulled her arms down between them. The backs of his fingers brushed over her hard pointed nipples and made them both inhale sharply.

Had he ever wanted a woman this much? Not even Carmen had tested his control like this.

"Cazador." JJ shook her head, as if to regain her senses. Her voice had turned even more beautifully contralto. "I forgot what—"

"Now who could that be out there, making out like teenagers?" The woman's sharp voice split the quiet night like jagged lightning in a dark sky.

"Looks like our new police officer, doesn't it?" Another woman answered.

Caz turned and saw two women on the lighted porch across the street.

"*A la verga*," he cursed under his breath. One was Brooke, a woman he'd been with years before, who now worked up at McNally's Resort. Next to her was Giselle, also from McNally's, who'd been after him since she arrived in Rescue a couple of months ago.

Tipping his head down, he gave the woman in his arms a rueful smile. "Sorry. This is, perhaps, a bit too public."

JJ's laugh huffed out. "It is. Even if it wasn't, it's still not a good idea."

Rather than answer, he opened her door for her, touched her cheek, and brushed away the snowflakes glinting in her curly hair. "Drive carefully, princesa."

"You, too, Doc."

As he walked to his car, he watched the tail lights of her car disappear in the falling snow. No, being with her wasn't a good idea. Nevertheless, the attraction between them kept growing.

CHAPTER TWELVE

F*lank your adversary when possible; protect your own.* ~ Marine
Corps Rules for Gunfighting

In the exam room of the health clinic, JJ leaned against the wall
and texted Gabe that she was back in town. Just in time, too,
since the Wednesday night Halloween activities were starting.

Intent on his job, Cazador cleaned away the blood from the
ugly gash in Guzman's shoulder as the woodsman talked.

She couldn't keep from watching his lean, tanned hands, so
capable and careful. His white lab coat sleeves were rolled up, and
the scattering of dark hair couldn't conceal the hard musculature
of his arms. She remembered how those arms had felt around her.
How thoroughly he'd kissed her—and God, now she was staring
at his mouth.

Lethally attractive men like him should be outlawed. Well, no,
maybe that was a bit drastic. Maybe make them available only by
prescription. Like narcotics. Because, damn, he was totally
addictive.

Just watching him tend to his patient was heating her blood.

"Yeah, it was lucky for me our new cop showed up." Guzman stroked his chest-long beard and gave her a grin, snapping her back to reality. "Even if she is a card shark."

She grinned at him.

During the poker game last weekend, Tucker and Guzman had told her where their cabins were. Today, she'd been familiarizing herself with that area when she'd almost driven right into a tree that'd fallen across the road.

Slamming on the brakes, she'd seen something move and spotted Guzman lying on the ground and bleeding like a stuck pig. He *had* been lucky. If she hadn't slapped a pressure dressing on the wound and brought him in, he might've bled out.

"What happened, anyway?" the doc asked.

"Eh, I was cutting up a tree that'd fallen across our dirt road, and the damn trunk rolled. I jumped back—far enough it didn't flatten me, but one of the branch stubs ripped right into my shoulder. I went down—and hit my fucking head on a fucking boulder. Went a bit fuzzy after that." Guzman lifted his chin in her direction. "Thanks, Officer."

"You're very welcome."

Her phone dinged. Gabe had texted her to join him at the end of Main.

Dammit. She wanted to stay, to watch Caz work, to just...be around him. Oh, admit it, she totally wanted to ignore good sense and drag him into bed. She couldn't. After those two women had seen her kissing him—clinging to him—doing more would be the stupidest thing she could think of.

She held up her phone. "I have to go provide a police presence at the Halloween carnival. Are you two all right?"

Caz gave her a glance from dark eyes. "We're fine. If you see Regan, tell her I'll be out in a bit."

"I will. Guzman, you said you had a ride home?"

The old logger nodded. "Tucker's coming in. We'll have a beer, enjoy the kiddie parade, and he'll take me home."

"Have fun, then." She headed out of the clinic and paused at the lobby desk.

Pointed teeth on full display, vampire Regina grinned. "Officer JJ, are you ready for the insanity?"

"Absolutely." Through the windows, the twinkling white lights along Main Street were coming on, brightening the twilight. "I can't believe it's already getting dark. It's barely past six."

"This is nothing. Wait till December. You'll get out of bed in the dark, go to work in the dark, and come home in the dark." Regina waved at the street. "The short days are why the street—and a lot of houses—put their Christmas lights up now and leave 'em up until spring. Life's just too dark, otherwise."

"I should have looked for jobs in Florida."

Regina laughed at her. "Girl, we all know you're loving it here."

Once out of the station, JJ found Gabe at one end of the paved section of Main Street, helping Knox position sawhorses to keep cars out of downtown. Rescue was having a costume parade —all of two blocks worth of parade. "Are the other streets blocked off?"

The lanky handyman shoved a lock of his bushy red hair out of his face. "Should be. Chevy's getting the other end of Main. We've already blocked off Grebe."

"What's with the blanket?" JJ motioned to a blanket spread out on the ground.

He grinned. "For the ones who want to parade without being bundled up. I'm the coat pile guard."

JJ laughed, knowing Regan's coat would be tossed there. The girl was very proud of her costume and dying to show it off.

"Here they come." She pointed to the line of children walking from Queen's Rest, the Victorian B&B on the corner of Sweetgale and Swan.

"Damn, they're cutting it close. Can you tell Lillian to announce them?"

"Got it." JJ set off at a fast pace back to the center of town. A token stage with sound equipment had been built in the middle of Grebe and Main, and that's where she found Mayor Lillian, chatting with Sarah from the coffee shop.

"Jayden, my dear."

"Happy Halloween, Lillian. The kids are on the way from Queen's Rest. Can you announce them?"

"Indeed, I can." Lillian climbed the two steps onto the stage and leaned into the mic. "Attention, please. The costume parade is going to begin in just a minute. The children will parade up Main Street and stop here. Be prepared to vote for your favorites. After that, do take a tour of Main Street. Each shop has a Halloween booth inside—there is fortune telling and face painting, a bean-bag-toss, guessing games. So much fun. Down on Swan, the Queen's Rest B&B is celebrating their opening with our first annual Haunted House."

A spatter of cheering was the response.

As people began to gather on the sidewalks, Lillian stepped away from the mic and sat down on the edge of the stage beside Sarah.

JJ smiled at the older woman who could make black jeans and a dark red jacket look like the height of fashion.

Sarah was bundled up in a long purple coat that couldn't hide her pregnancy. A matching purple stocking hat covered her dark hair.

"This should be fun. We have lots more children. And doesn't the town look magnificent?" Lillian gave the street a pleased survey.

Each store had a themed display in the window or on the sidewalk. The art gallery's skeleton stood at an easel, paintbrush clasped in bony fingers. In front of Dante's Market, two skeletons sat on a blanket with a picnic basket between them. One held a sandwich with a desiccated lizard carcass between the slices. The post office had a ghost with a bag of mail at its feet. The sport-outfitting store window showed a witch fishing with a black cat at her feet.

"Those two are my favorites." Sarah pointed to the municipal building where straw-stuffed figures sat on each side of the door, one in a police uniform with a gorilla mask, the other in a white lab coat with a plastic stethoscope...and wearing a vampire mask. A sign at its feet announced, "*I vill drink your blood.*"

"The doc's sense of humor is quite nicely warped," Lillian agreed.

"He's not the only one." JJ motioned toward the pharmacy. A zombie stood in the window, arms outstretched, and rather than the drawn-out *BRAIIINS*, the cartoon cloud over its head said *DRUUUGS*. "I'm a little surprised there wasn't a pumpkin carving contest. Or any jack-o-lanterns at all."

"I think that was our first tragedy here in Alaska." Sarah shook her head sadly. "Uriah and I had made awesome pumpkin carvings—and set them out for the neighbors to admire."

JJ eyed her. "And?"

"We heard something and looked out." Sarah extended her arms wide. "One *huge*, hungry moose. *Chomp, chomp, chomp.*"

"He ate your pumpkins?" JJ stared. "That's so wrong."

Lillian smiled. "No one argues with a moose who feels a bit peckish and wants a pumpkin snack."

"I bet." Not with an animal that was bigger than a car. Uh-uh.

As Sarah and Lillian chatted, JJ leaned a hip on the stage and enjoyed the town. People were gathering and lining up along the street. Three men talked about their hunting successes. An older couple. Two younger women walked past...whispering and casting glances at her.

An uncomfortable sensation ran over JJ. But they were followed by several people, who gave her friendly nods and greetings. It seemed "Officer Jenner" had been abandoned for the friendlier-sounding "Officer JJ."

She didn't mind at all.

Music came from the far end of Main Street where speakers had been set up. Was that Michael Jackson's "Thriller"?

Applause greeted the appearance of the children's parade. The grand marshal was gray-haired Zappa who owned the gas station. He was dressed in a Victorian costume, complete with top hat and tails. Darned if he didn't look authentic.

The first child following him was a strutting five-year-old dressed as a brown bear.

More children followed. Lots more. "Did every single child from the school show up?"

"Most of them." Sarah rested her hand on her belly with a smile. "More than you see attending the school. A lot of the homeschoolers are marching."

"Ah." JJ frowned, remembering remote cabins and narrow gravel roads. "I can see where getting to school in the winter might be difficult."

"But they come in for these events," Lillian said. "Home-schooled or not, they're still part of Rescue."

Wasn't it wonderful how Rescue appreciated its children? "What about the Patriot Zealots?"

"Homeschooled," Sarah said. "The children won't be here. Parrish doesn't approve."

Before JJ could say anything, the music changed to the *Ghost-busters* movie's theme music, and cheering broke out.

The children in the parade were almost dancing down the street.

There was Regan, dressed as Wonder Woman, long brown hair held back from her face by a gold tiara. JJ smiled, because in the dim light, the long-sleeved, dark brown fleece shirt and double pair of leggings that Caz had insisted on for warmth couldn't be seen beneath the bright red corset-like top and short blue skirt.

Each night for the last week, JJ, Lillian, and Audrey had helped Regan with her costume. They'd wrapped her knee-high boots with red aluminum foil and created aluminum-foil bracers. "Regan looks adorable, doesn't she?"

"Oh, isn't she cute!" Sarah grinned. "Trust Caz to give her a sharp, pointy weapon, hmm?"

"The man's blade-crazy." Thankfully, the sword was rubber. If he started arming his daughter with steel, they were going to have words. "Look, there's your Rachel. She's the cutest mermaid I've ever seen."

The kindergartner was dressed as Ariel from *Little Mermaid*. Sarah rolled her eyes. "She insisted on wearing it to supper every day this week...and singing "Under the Sea" constantly. Disney has a lot to answer for."

JJ snickered then patted Lillian's shoulder. "I'm off to do foot patrol. Good luck with choosing winners."

"Oh bugger! I volunteered for this? My wit is bankrupt." Lillian shook her head—and JJ knew why.

Because every single child was simply precious.

As Regan walked down the street, she couldn't stop smiling, cuz people were cheering and some were pointing to her and saying she was cute, and they loved her costume.

It was even more dope how Delaney had gone for a Captain Marvel costume, and both of them were in the superheroes group of the parade. Delaney had light hair just like Captain Marvel, and Regan had dark hair like Wonder Woman.

Seeing the people, Delaney'd gotten all shy and grabbed Regan's hand. But it was okay, cuz they were girl superheroes and supposed to stick together.

Like Regan, to stay warm, Delaney wore a blue leotard top and tights. Regan had told her how JJ, Audrey, and Miss Lillian had figured out stuff, like how to make her boots shiny and do the arm things—bracers. Yesterday, Regan had taken Delaney up to the library after school, and JJ and Audrey had sewed shiny red fabric and yellow ribbons on the leotard to make it look even more like Captain Marvel's superhero suit.

"They're cheering for us." Delaney's eyes got big.

Regan grinned cuz she could hear Uncle Bull—he could be really loud—and it didn't even scare her any more. The screechy whistle was JJ, who was going to teach her how to do that. She saw Papá standing by Uncle Gabe, and they were both watching her and clapping.

Inside her chest, she felt all fuzzy and happy. She didn't even feel the cold, even though there was still snow on the street.

Delaney squeezed her fingers. "Did your dad say you could trick-or-treat with me after the parade?"

"Yeah. But we have to stay together and can't leave the blocked off area."

Delaney's face fell. "Oh. But what about the haunted house? Gram and Gramps won't take us—they're kinda weird about Halloween stuff."

The haunted house was where they'd lined up for the parade—and was a block past the sawhorses. Even from outside, it'd looked super-scary. "Papá has to stay in town in case some idiot gets hurt."

"*Some idiot*" is what Uncle Gabe had said when he asked Papá to have the clinic open.

"Oh."

Regan grinned. "But Papá asked Niko's father to take the three of us. After the parade, Niko's dad'll take us through the house with him an' Niko. And we can go trick-or-treating downtown, and then he'll drop you off at your grandparents' place."

Delaney's eyes rounded, and she grinned *huge*.

Regan and Delaney had gotten prizes for their costumes—bright mini-flashlights. Regan couldn't believe it—she'd won a prize!

After Niko's dad, who was called Chevy, found them, they collected their coats and headed for the haunted house.

On the walk, Mr. Chevy scared them worse than any ghost, telling about a grizzly bear—a brown bear—that'd attacked him. He had scars and everything. The bear had chased Niko so far into the woods people had to search for him.

Regan was shaking even before they entered the haunted house.

There were ghosts and skeletons. She screamed when something grabbed her from behind, and Niko laughed at her, and she laughed too. Delaney squeaked and squeezed her hand so hard that her fingers went numb.

Then they were done and out. She and Delaney had to pee so bad they ran for the bathroom in the B&B lobby, leaving Chevy and Niko laughing behind them. In the stalls, Delaney let out a big sigh as she peed, and Regan giggled so hard she couldn't stop. Then Delaney was laughing, too.

It was the *best* night.

After getting their coats, she and Delaney walked out together and down off the big porch. Chevy stood off in a group of grownups. Crouching on the gravel sidewalk, Niko was shining his flashlight on the stones.

"Did you lose something?" Delaney asked him

"Uh-uh. We need rocks for school, remember?" He bent to pick one up.

"Oh, wow, we do." Regan pulled out her own flashlight. Mrs. Wilner had said to bring in rocks for some science thing.

"Check this out." Niko held up a rock, pushing his brown hair out of his eyes. He needed a haircut, and his jeans had a hole in the knee. Shelby, the blonde fifth-grader, had cast shade about him being poor white trash.

Regan had managed not to call Shelby a bitch—barely—cuz Papá said the word would get her in trouble. But Niko wasn't trash; he was nice. When he read stuff out loud during reading time, he acted it out and made everybody laugh.

Regan took the rock and lit it up with her flashlight. It was clear with gold lines running through it. "That's pretty." She showed it to Delaney.

"I want Dad to take me to Cook Inlet cuz he says we might find agates." Niko grinned and took his rock back. "Only last time we were at the beach, my dog, Einstein, rolled in a dead fish. I had to wash him, like three times, and he still stunk."

Regan laughed. "I wish I had a dog—only I want a cat."

"Maybe you'll find one, and the doc'll let you keep it." Niko pocketed his rock. "That's how I got Einstein. I found him under a car, all skinny and starving, an' Chief Gabe helped me catch him. And Dad let me keep him."

"You're lucky." She bit her lip and started walking down the path. "Papá might not like it."

"So, your mom might talk him into it?"

Mom. Regan looked away, remembering the last time she'd seen her mother. Talking all excited and kind of scared, Mom'd gone off with her new creeper boyfriend to rob a store, only she was caught and sent to jail. And then...she hadn't said goodbye or anything. "My mom's dead."

The sound of her voice was ugly. Mean. Like she was mad at Niko, only she wasn't. She couldn't even be mad at Mom—cuz Mom was dead and that wasn't right. Swallowing hard, she bent and grabbed a rock from the ground.

"Oh." Niko stared at her. "That sucks, yeah."

Delaney took her hand "Is that why you moved here? To live with your dad?"

Her throat was all funny. She nodded.

"That's hard." Delaney moved closer. "My daddy left us. He liked his admin better than Mom and didn't want to be with us anymore."

"Oh, look, it's New Girl and Fat Girl and Trash Boy." Brayden's hard shove pushed Regan off the sidewalk and into the piled-up snow.

"Stop blocking the path, moron." Sneering, Shelby tossed her braided blonde hair over her shoulder. She was dressed as Princess Elsa and even wore makeup.

As Regan regained her feet and brushed off the snow, Brayden laughed. "Definitely a moron. And ugly and brown."

The words hurt. Brown, okay, yeah. Her half-Latina, California-tan skin was darker than theirs. Only, she liked having Papá's skin and brown eyes and hair. But she sure wasn't ugly or a moron.

Her fingers hurt. Right. Fighting would be bad. Slowly, she unclenched her hands. Papá might not want a kid who got into fights.

Laughing, the two bigger kids walked toward the street.

"You okay?" Niko asked. He picked up the rock she'd dropped and handed it to her. "Ignore them—they're resort rejects."

"Resort?"

"Yeah, McNally's Resort. Big ol' fancy place for skiing in the winter and vacation stuff in the summer. It's bringing all sorts of tourists and new people here. Dad hates it cuz of that."

Niko had been the first person to smile at her in class. Did he think she was bad because she was new? "Do you hate the resort? New people?"

"Nah. I like new stuff." He grinned. "When I'm older, I bet I can get a job there. Teach people how to snowboard or ski, maybe. Delaney'll help, right?"

Delaney nodded and told Regan, "Mom works there."

"That's chill." Snowboarding and skiing sounded like fun. Maybe she could work there, too. Would she still be here when she was older?

"Niko, come here a minute," Chevy called.

Niko ran over.

"Let's find some rocks while we're here," Regan said.

155

Delaney pulled out her flashlight, and they knelt to look for glittery stones.

Regan had found one when two sets of shoes stopped in front of her. She looked up.

The two fifth-graders had come back and were staring down at her.

Brayden shoved his knee into Regan's shoulder, did it again, then stuck his hand out, fingers waggling. "Gimme the flashlight."

She stared at him. *Don't curse. Don't fight.* Papá hadn't said anything about just saying no. She stood up. "No."

Even in the dim light, she could see the big kid's face turn dark. His lips rose into a snarl like a dog's would. "You don't say no to me, spic."

"Just did."

He shoved her and tried to grab her flashlight.

Even as she put it in her pocket, out of reach, Shelby took hold of Delaney's hood. "It's dark, Fat Girl. I want your flashlight."

Standing up, Delaney tightened her grip on the light and shook her head. "No. Leave me alone."

"Give it over." Shelby slapped Delaney and grabbed the flashlight.

Delaney fell—and Shelby kicked her.

"Leave her alone!" Rage like a fire in her veins, Regan charged, ramming into Shelby.

Yelling, Shelby hit at Regan.

Then, somehow, Regan had her hands in Shelby's long hair and was yanking it. Slapping her face. They landed on the ground, and Shelby's fingernails clawed down Regan's face.

"Ow!" Regan hit her right in the eye. Really hard.

Shelby shrieked.

Something struck Regan's back so hard she screamed with the pain. Shelby was trying to scratch again and Regan grabbed her arm.

Brayden was yelling, "Get off me, Trash Boy!"

"Enough. That. Is. *Enough*." A woman's voice. JJ's voice. "Boys. Sit right there and don't move."

JJ grabbed Regan's hood and Shelby's, and yanked them apart.

Shelby kicked like a crazy person, and JJ gave her a shake. "Stop that, or I'll put you in cuffs."

"She hit me first," Shelby burst into tears. "She hurt me."

"Oh, please," Niko muttered. "Lie much?" He and Brayden were sitting on the path with a lot of space between them.

Regan stood still and, after a second, realized JJ was in her cop uniform. She wore her big belt with the gun and other stuff on it. The badge shone on her black jacket.

No, no, no. Regan stiffened in dismay. If she got arrested, Papá would send her away for sure.

Oh, honestly, JJ thought. Shouldn't a Halloween event be fight-free?

"Regan. You want to tell me why you're fighting?"

Regan looked down and shook her head, mouth compressed in a stubborn line.

JJ looked at the blonde Regan had been tussling with. "What about you? What's your name?"

The child's tears had dried up, probably because JJ hadn't been impressed. "Shelby Berman. That horrible girl started it. She hit me."

"Did not," Regan muttered.

What a mess. JJ looked at the big bruiser who'd kicked Regan—from behind, the little shit. "And you? What's your name?"

Maybe a year older than Regan, the blond, blue-eyed boy was heavier and taller. His expression was ugly. There was a streak of mean there. From his bull-like scowl, she wouldn't get any answers from him.

"I'm Brayden Kearns, and my dad'll be super-pissed if you don't let me go."

"My boss'll be super-pissed if I do." JJ turned to the last two children.

The slender boy who'd yanked Brayden away from Regan was staring at the ground. Chevy, one of the local handymen stood behind him. From the resemblance, his father.

Another girl—the one who'd walked beside Regan in the parade—waited off to one side, crying and shaking.

"Does anyone want to tell me what the fight was about, or should we walk to the police station and call your parents?" No one looked happy with that solution, and JJ almost grinned.

"Well?" JJ eyed the boy who sat at his father's feet. He was casting worried looks at Regan. "What's your name?"

"Niko, ma'am. Niko Chavdarov." He straightened his shoulders. Straightforward brown eyes met hers. "I don't know what it was about. I ran over when I saw Brayden kick Regan."

"You're lying," Shelby burst out. "That new girl hit me in the face—right in my eye."

And a sweet punch it'd been. Okay, then, the station it was. Gabe would expect documentation, and bullies weren't something that people turned a blind eye to. Not any longer.

Regan had some scratches that needed to be cleaned too. JJ studied the people who'd gathered and recognized two. "Guzman, Tucker, could I deputize you two to help escort this lot to the station?"

***

Cazador scowled as he finished charting for his last patient. Next town event, he needed to have his assistants working. There'd been a constant flow of people coming into the clinic. Drunks falling down. Two fistfights. A minor car accident outside town.

Dammit. He'd hoped to spend the evening with Regan, watching her trick-or-treat and enjoy the games.

His phone rang. Gabe's name was on the display. "What's up, 'mano?"

"Bro, if you're free, can you join me in the station?"

Caz blinked. Had there been an accident in the temp lock-up? "On my way."

After grabbing his medical bag, he entered the lobby. Two children were being escorted out of the building by their parents. Behind the reception desk in full vampire costume, Regina grinned. "Doc. Go on in."

Caz eyed her bloody fangs. "I hope you're not smiling at children with that mouth."

Her grin widened.

Giving her a wide berth, Caz could only think that Gabe was wise not to allow the receptionist any firearms.

As he reached the station door, Chevy and his son, Niko, came out with Delaney. "Hey, Doc."

Caz stiffened. "Aren't you supposed to be at the haunted house? Where's Regan?"

When both children stepped behind the handyman, Chevy half-grinned. "Regan's all right. She's inside with your brother. I'll let her explain, yeah?"

Caz eyed the children's dirt-streaked clothing and muddy hair. Delaney's face was bruised. Niko had a split lip. Regan—how would Regan look? A cold trickle of worry ran down his spine. Only Chevy's statement that his girl was all right kept Caz from tearing into the police station. Instead, he crouched and held out both his hands. "Come here, you two."

After a second, they both came forward. He gave them a quick visual for blood, ran his hands over legs and arms, pressed on ribs and spines. "Niko's knee is sore, Chevy. Keep an eye on that, please."

Chevy gave an affirmative grunt.

"Delaney, have your grandmother help you with an ice pack on your chin. It'll take some of the soreness and swelling out."

She whispered, "Yes, sir."

As Chevy herded them out, Caz went into the police station, noted the bullpen was empty, and headed for Gabe's office. "Gabe?"

"He went out the back for a minute." JJ came out of the chief's office, and Regan stepped out from behind her.

His little girl. Bleeding. His heart stopped.

"Mija." Caz skidded to a stop in front of her, his bag landing on the floor. Kneeling, he did a quick assessment. The blood on her face—fingernail scratch marks. There was dirt, but thankfully no blood, on her clothing. He ran his hands down her arms and legs, watching her face, looking for any hint of pain. Feeling for swelling.

"I'm fine, Papá. It's no big."

"You're bleeding, and bleeding is big." No, he shouldn't say that. Shouldn't make an injury into something that would leave her afraid. He tried to channel Mako's nonchalance about injuries: *Broken bone—here's a splint. Laceration—let me show you how to stitch it up.*

No, he couldn't. Not with his little girl.

"Well,"—he forced a smile—"it's big for a new father."

He felt her muscles relax slightly.

JJ gave him a half-smile of support.

He opened his bag. "Let's get those scratches cleaned up while you two tell me what happened." He shot JJ a look that said she'd be telling him everything. Like who the fuck had scratched his girl.

Ten minutes later, he had his girl doctored and had heard the story.

Bullies. She'd been picked on by bullies.

In an even voice, JJ had presented both sides of the brawl as related by the five children involved. Either Regan started a fight, or Regan jumped in to help her friend from having her flashlight taken.

JJ quite obviously believed Regan.

So did Caz. A growl slid out of him, and he saw his girl stiffen.

Her gaze dropped. "Are you...mad...at me?"

He pulled her into his arms. She'd been hurt, and he hadn't been there. When she relaxed and actually cuddled closer, everything inside him went soft. "Sorry, mija, I'm not angry. Not at you. I don't like bullies."

"Me, neither." Her little head rested against his shoulder—and gave a firm nod.

"I don't want you to fight, but sometimes you have no choice. I'm proud of you, Regan." He kissed the top of her head.

"You are?"

Her head popped up, almost clipping him in the chin, and he saw JJ's quick smile.

"I am."

"Even though I got in a fight?"

"Hell, your pa's been in more fights than all of the rest of us combined." Bull walked in the back door. "At least, you don't have any knives."

Dios. If Bull continued, Regan would end up slicing up her classmates next time she got angry. "Bull, this is not the—"

"Knives?" Regan stared at him. "You fight with knives?"

"There will be no knives in school," Gabe said firmly. Stepping inside, he nailed Bull in the shoulder. "Dumbass."

"Right." Bull grinned at Regan. "No knives in school, little bit."

As Gabe walked over, he told Caz, "So far, the parents have decided the children have had enough repercussions from the fight. Shelby and Brayden's parents have been warned that their children's bullying habits won't be tolerated. I've spoken to Principal Jones who'll be watching for it at school."

Caz frowned. "I don't remember having a Shelby or Brayden as patients."

"You probably haven't," Gabe said. "They live up at the resort."

"Niko called them resort rejects." Regan's little snicker made him smile.

"Are you going to arrest me, Uncle Gabe?" She looked at him with big brown eyes and bit her lip.

"Nope. Protecting someone from bullies isn't against the law"—laughter lit Gabe's eyes—"or your pa would've been locked up for years."

"Why am I not surprised?" JJ snorted. "Let me guess. Cazador would see someone getting picked on and jump in."

"Or an animal," Bull interjected. "He was death on someone hurting animals. Still is, actually."

"Of course," JJ said. "And his brothers would wade in beside him, right?"

When Bull grinned, Gabe laughed and admitted, "Still do, actually."

"Oh, honestly." Officer Jenner tapped the badge on her jacket. "You, Chief, are the *law*."

Her gorgeous turquoise eyes shot to Caz—and didn't she look adorable all pissed off? "You, Doc, are a *father*. That means setting out limits on when to fight and when not to fight."

To hell with limits. Caz held his brave-as-fuck daughter out so he could look into her face. "Bullying other children will get you in trouble, mija. Saving them? That's what we do."

JJ rolled her eyes, but Caz saw the way her lips curved up. The softness in her gaze when she looked at his girl.

He wasn't the only one who was proud of Regan.

CHAPTER THIRTEEN

*H*ave a plan. Have a backup plan for when the first plan goes to *shit.* - Common Sense

The little white ball zipped past Regan's paddle, and she shouted in outrage. "Da—darn!"

On the other side of the Ping-Pong table, her opponent did a victory dance, and Regan had to laugh. Delaney was really funny. And fun, too.

After Halloween, they'd decided they were BFFs. This Sunday, since Delaney's mom had to work, she'd asked Regan over to her grandparents' house. They'd played with Mr. Hudson's dogs and helped Mrs. Hudson cook and watched *Beauty and the Beast*.

Delaney had taught her how to play Ping-Pong. Although Regan hadn't won a game, it was still really fun.

"Kids, y'all should start picking up. Cazador should be on the way, and Giselle will be home soon." Mrs. Hudson's voice came from the kitchen into the back room.

"Okay, Grams," Delaney shouted back.

"Is Giselle your mom's name?" Regan asked. "It's pretty."

"Uh-huh. Gramps says she's as pretty as her name." Delaney's mouth turned down for a second. "Although she says Daddy dumped her for a redhead."

Dumped her. Like a divorce? "That sucks."

"Yeah. Daddy gave his secretary Mom's place in the company an' everything. It made Mom really mad." Delaney heaved a sigh, then smiled at Regan. "Having you here was awesome. Everything's more fun with another kid, you know?"

"I know." Kneeling, Regan put the paddles into the box on the low shelf. "At Papá's, it's all grownups and no kids at all. Feels weird, right? At least you have dogs here. We only have chickens... though it's chill getting eggs."

Delaney shrugged. "The dogs are Gramp's. Mom won't let me have any pets at our house. She says we're not home enough, but I think it's cuz she doesn't like dogs or cats."

Regan pulled in a breath of sadness. Mom hadn't liked pets, either. "I think there might be a cat living somewhere near our place. I heard it meowing last night."

"A neighbor's kitty?"

"We don't have any neighbors." There weren't *any* other houses on their side of the lake. But if there weren't any houses, how did the cat get fed? It was awful cold outside. There was still snow in patches. Was the kitty going to *freeze*? "How do you—"

The front door opened, and Delaney's mom came in. Regan had seen her a couple of times when she'd picked up Delaney at school. Like her daughter, she had straight blonde hair and light skin. Her boobs were big—seemed like they'd get in the way of everything.

Regan hoped she didn't grow up and get boobs like that.

"Delaney, are you ready to go?" She looked at Regan with a stiff smile. "Who's this?"

Regan scrambled to her feet. "I'm Regan."

Delaney covered the Ping-Pong table with a bright cloth.

"She's the new girl in my class at school. I walked with her in the parade and—"

"Delaney, what have I told you about how to introduce people?"

"Sorry. Um..." Delaney looked down at the floor. "Mom, this is Regan. Regan, this is my mother, Giselle Washik."

"Does Regan have a last name?" When Giselle made a *you're-so-dumb* sound, Delaney kind of shrank a little.

Regan frowned. Delaney was great at drawing and so funny, but not good at remembering names or things. Shouldn't her mom know that?

"We don't use last names a lot at school." Regan dug her fingernails into her palms to make herself stay polite. "My last name is Ramirez. My father is Cazador Ramirez."

"Cazador." The woman's eyes sharpened. "Mom didn't mention you were friends with Caz's daughter. Neither did you."

"Um, maybe because she hasn't been living with him very long." Delaney shot Regan a strange look.

"You live with him. Out...somewhere. The chief lives there, too? And Bull?" the mother asked.

"I guess." Regan shook her head. "It's a bunch of houses in the middle of the woods. Uncle Gabe and Bull are there and Audrey. And JJ, too."

"JJ?"

"She's the new police officer," Delaney said.

Giselle's eyes narrowed. "She's living with her boss and Caz? *Really.*" Her lips closed over the word like she had a Popsicle. "Is this JJ skinny? A redhead with tangled hair?"

"I think her hair's pretty." Skinny didn't sound right, exactly, either. But JJ didn't have big boobs like Delaney's mom, so maybe that made her skinny? Regan took a step back. "I'll get my coat and wait for Papá."

"No need to wait. I'll take you home and save your dad the trip. Delaney, get your coat."

Saying no wouldn't be polite, would it? Regan stared at the woman. Audrey said once that the men didn't ever invite people over. This was bad.

Giselle turned to Delaney's grandmother. "Mom, I'm taking Regan home. Thanks for—"

"You are? Well...that's nice of you, dear." Mrs. Hudson sounded surprised, then she smiled at Regan. "Where do you live?"

Regan's mouth dropped open. "Um. I don't know."

"What do you mean you don't know?" Under the hard sound in Giselle's voice, Regan felt her stomach begin to twist.

"I..."

"She's the new girl, Mom." Delaney stepped up beside Regan. "It took me a long time to know where we live, and we live in town."

Giselle glared.

The dogs outside started to bark.

"I guess it doesn't matter," Mrs. Hudson said lightly. "That must be your father, Regan."

Regan's feet wanted to take her running out the door, but she wasn't five. She made herself cross the room to pick up her coat and use the words that Papá had told her to say. "Thank you for letting me come over and play with Delaney, Mrs. Hudson."

"It was a pleasure, child." Mrs. Hudson waved her hand toward the door. "Off you go, now."

Released, Regan ran out the door.

Papá stood beside the car, and Giselle stood right in front of him. She was smiling real wide and sticking her big chest out. Like Mom had done when she had a new man around.

Regan scowled, her body getting cold even though she'd put on her coat.

"I was going to bring your sweet little girl home—she had so much fun playing with my baby—but she wasn't sure where you lived."

"I'm glad she had a good time." Papá smiled at Giselle, spotted Regan, and held out his hand. "Mija."

Giselle moved closer. "Why don't you come in and have a cup of—"

Regan ran over, took his hand—and squeezed his fingers hard. Twice.

"Ah. We do need to leave now." Nodding at Giselle, Papá walked with Regan around the car and opened the door for her. As she hurried to put her seatbelt on—so they could leave right away—he winked at her and closed the door.

"Please tell your mother thank you for hosting the children," he said to Delaney's mother and got into the car. It was still running, and he backed it up.

Regan waved at Delaney—and Papá did too—and then they were gone.

That had been weird. Regan played with the zipper on her jacket. "Papá. Um—"

"Just ask, mija. I don't bite. I was more than ready to leave."

He wasn't mad about her signal to get away...only he sounded kind of mad. "She—Delaney's mom—"

"Giselle."

"Yeah, her. She wanted to bring me home only I didn't know where we lived."

"Thank fuck," he muttered.

"Huh?"

He laughed, and it sounded like his mad was all gone. "You have such big eyes."

Regan frowned, and then she figured it out. "You don't want her to know where we live?"

"It's complicated."

Paying attention this time, she watched as they passed Uncle Bull's place—the roadhouse—and turned down Main Street where Papa's clinic was. The car turned left—there was the haunted house at the B&B—and they were on the road that went toward the lake.

"It's like this, mija. Mako, the man who raised your uncles and me, didn't like people. We lived in a wilderness and only went to town a few times a year. After we grew up and left, he was too alone, so we talked him into moving to Rescue. Although he made some friends, he still didn't trust most people. We bought up most of the land on that side of the lake to make sure no one could live near him. That's why the Hermitage is so isolated."

"Oh." The only houses around were on the other side of the lake. "But he's not there anymore."

"True enough." Papá's brows pulled together. "Although it's not a huge secret, most people don't know exactly where we live. Your Uncle Gabe is a cop, Uncle Bull owns a bar, and I'm the medical person in town. None of us wants people who might want something or be angry coming to the house. Does that make sense?"

"Uncle Bull kicks people out of the bar, an' they get mad." Regan considered a bit and nodded. "You don't want them or bad guys, like dopers or murderers, or people who are sick coming to our house."

"Exactly. If a person is too ill to wait for the clinic to open, they need to call for an ambulance." He took her hand and squeezed it. "Home is our private place. Safe from work and other people. "

Regan scrunched her mouth up as she thought. Maybe Giselle wasn't a murderer, but she wasn't very nice, and she acted like Mom had when she was chasing after some guy. Giselle didn't need to come to Papá's house, even if she was Delaney's mother.

"If someone asks where you live, tell them they need to call me. Or your uncles."

"Aye, aye, sir." It was what Bull and Papá said to Uncle Gabe sometimes. She giggled at Papá's snort.

"You know everyone's numbers, sí?"

"Yeah." She'd already known Papá's cell number. Her uncles made her memorize theirs and had her say back the numbers whenever. Like Uncle Gabe'd point at her. *"You got hurt and the ambulance can't get Caz on his phone. What number do you give them, Regan?"* She'd shout out the number, real fast, and he'd grin and toss her a quarter. Uncle Bull did the same thing, and would high-five her and give her cookies. Audrey and JJ started doing it with their numbers—Audrey gave her comic books, and JJ had gummy bears.

She knew everybody's phone numbers really good now.

Smiling, she looked out the window, seeing blue flashes of the lake through the trees, and then Papá slowed. The entrance to their little road was hard to see. He turned left onto the road. As he drove, she realized the road curved back toward the lake—like they didn't want anyone to know there was a road on this side of the lake.

Mako must've been kinda sneaky.

And, hey, now she knew how to get home.

CHAPTER FOURTEEN

A lie gets halfway around the world before the truth has a chance to get its pants on. - Winston Churchill

Monday night, on his long couch, feet up on the coffee table, Caz wasn't paying much attention to the movie on his big-screen TV. Regan was curled up, her head on his thigh, half-asleep. JJ was tucked against his other side, warm and soft, with his arm over her shoulders.

He'd never been so content in his life.

Getting JJ over here again hadn't been easy. When he and Regan had asked JJ to join them for supper and a movie, she'd returned a firm no...even though the war in her eyes had been obvious. But he'd called in the big guns, and his daughter had rolled over JJ's objections like a Bradley tank.

Taking advantage of JJ's soft heart had been a tactically sound plan and incredibly fun to watch in execution.

Unable to resist, Caz rubbed his cheek against her curly red hair. Silky and fine.

Her scent was sweetly woodsy with a hint of spice, a fragrance so light he wanted to get closer to breathe her in.

Wanted to get closer to do...everything.

Tilting her head slightly, she gave him a narrow-eyed look even as a flush pinkened her cheeks. Was that from desire or anger?

When her nipples formed hard little peaks beneath her blue thermal shirt, he had his answer...as well as a throbbing semi-erection within his jeans.

She didn't have big breasts—not even close—and probably didn't think she needed a bra, which, physically speaking, she didn't. He'd noticed the bra disappeared when she was at home. Did she have any clue how tantalizing that faint jiggle and her small nipples were? Of all the places a man's mind could go?

He rather doubted it.

Supper had been a pleasure—good food, laughter, and easy conversation. Regan had been full of school stories, and JJ was wonderful at drawing the girl out. He and JJ had added in tidbits of their days, reminding him of Mako's decree that each boy provide a summary of the day.

JJ had been as relaxed as he'd ever seen her. In fact, she'd been the one to suggest popcorn to go with the movie. The bowl now sat on the coffee table, emptied down to the last few unpopped kernels.

With a sigh, Caz realized the movie credits were scrolling on the TV screen. Regan was only half-awake, occasionally blinking.

Caz used the remote to turn the TV off and low music on. "Good movie."

JJ chuckled. "It was, although the LEO was incredibly unprofessional."

"Gabe has the same reaction to cop movies." Caz rubbed his thumb over her shoulder. "It sounds like you're settling nicely into the job, princesa."

"I am." JJ smiled. "Gabe sent me out to deal with two neighbors in a dispute. He said if he'd shown up, it'd probably turn into a fight."

"He's a smart cop to see how well you work with riled-up people. We both appreciate your ability to soothe everyone down." If she hadn't already had a career, he'd have tried to talk her into the medical field. "Rescue will need that talent of yours even more during the winter."

Delight filled her eyes. It mattered to her, being useful. Needed. And accepted by the town. Sure, everyone wanted to be liked, but it appeared, for JJ, that was a bigger deal. She'd told him that her fellow officers back in Nevada had been sexist. Had stopped backing her up. But, he had a feeling there was more to the story.

With his inability to tolerate puzzles, Gabe probably knew. But asking the chief of police about his officer would be inappropriate.

Caz would wait for answers until JJ was willing to share... although it seemed that might take a while. Some women—people, he should say—would spill every private detail of their life at the drop of a hat.

JJ wasn't one of them.

The thought of her being hurt, emotionally or physically, bothered the hell out of him. He'd never met anyone like her, such a mixture of tenderhearted and tough, friendly and reserved.

Ah well, he had time. He wasn't going anywhere and neither was she. What with Regan in the picture, he needed to move slowly.

But move he would.

Said daughter yawned widely, and her head rose. "JJ?"

"Yes, sweetie?"

Regan's lips tipped up at the endearment. Then she sat up and snuggled against him so she could look at JJ. "Um, me and Delaney wondered about...she said she heard you shouldn't be living here. Cuz it wasn't right or something. But she didn't know why it wasn't right, and I don't know either."

Caz stiffened. Oh...hell.

Each of Regan's words hit JJ with a small stinging pain like sharp hail from an unexpected storm.

Someone knew she was living at the Hermitage and had interpreted it in the worst possible way. Didn't this sound an awful lot like Weiler? There, the gossip had started with disparaging female officers in general. After Nash's lies, the rumors about her had grown ugly—that she was breaking up marriages and relationships, stealing their men, and sleeping her way to the top. Considering she'd never gotten a promotion, that last lie seemed rather stupid.

"Good officers have to risk their lives to cover for her inadequate skills." That falsehood had hurt the worst. So not true.

She realized she hadn't answered Regan. That Caz was watching her. Waiting for her. She had no clue what to say.

She sat up, edging away from him, and immediately missed the feeling of his muscular arm around her.

"Regan." Caz drew Regan's attention. "For people to live together in families, towns, or cities means we need guidelines on how to get along. Some are straightforward. You shouldn't kill others, lie, cheat, or steal. Nearly every place and time period agree...so we made them laws. Sí?"

"Well, yeah."

"Other so-called rules vary, depending on what year it is, the trends, where you live on the planet, what religion you're into, and even whose voices are loudest in your location."

Regan wrinkled her nose. "Huh?"

"In Sacramento, would anyone notice if you had a single woman living in the apartment next door to a man?"

Regan snorted. "Mom was single, and we lived next to guys all the time. So did everybody."

"Exactly." Caz touched his daughter's nose with a fingertip. "But some people think if *their* religion has a rule or if *they* grew up with a rule, everyone else has to do the same. That's how we get crazy ideas like girls shouldn't show any skin, but boys can go shirtless. Or that women shouldn't live next to men or shouldn't live close to their boss—even when there aren't any other places to live."

"That's stupid."

"It is." Caz glanced at JJ.

She shook herself mentally. Regan's question should've been hers to answer, and she'd been a coward.

"When Gabe hired me, there weren't any rentals at all—because it was tourist season. I'll be moving to one of Dante's rentals one of these days."

Although Gabe had told her she should just stay put.

Regan's face fell. "No, I don't want you to leave."

JJ felt her heart simply melt. She didn't want to leave either. The evening had been so wonderful, all of them cooking and cleaning up and enjoying a movie together. Regan was adorable and Caz... How rare was it to simply enjoy a man's company? Whatever he did, he seemed to have fun, and he didn't try to escape any of the kitchen chores. He'd turned washing dishes into a team activity.

A sexy one. Every time he touched her—gripping her hips to move her out of his way or hand-feeding her a bite of cheese—the heat in the room had risen another degree. Or when he'd laughed at something she'd said and given her a kiss. The simple, swift kiss had left her feeling as if lightning had zinged through her.

When he nuzzled her hair a couple of minutes ago, her lust-o-meter rose right into the danger zone.

No lust, Jayden Linnea Jenner. No.

"Can't you stay here, JJ?" Regan asked.

JJ reached across his chest to touch her hair. "I wouldn't go far —just to a cabin on the other side of the lake. When I'm there, I hope you'll come and visit me."

Regan brightened. "Okay. I will."

"Good." She met Caz's dark gaze and saw his concern. For her. For her reputation.

JJ's stomach tightened as she thought about rumors and mean-spirited people. In Weiler, her reputation had been ruined so very easily.

Rescue was far smaller. It wouldn't take much.

CHAPTER FIFTEEN

*Y*ou've only got three choices in life: Give up, give in, or give it all
you've got. - Unknown

The next night, as the slamming of Regan's bedroom door echoed
through the house, Caz shook his head. Through the house? Dios,
they'd probably heard that sound in Rescue.

Had Crystal possessed such a temper? He had no idea. He
barely remembered the woman or their drunken hookup.

It could be Regan had inherited *Caz's* hot temperament. The
poor kid.

Huffing a half-irritated, half-pained laugh, Caz dropped into a
living room chair and scrubbed his hands over his face. "That did
not go well."

This parenting stuff was tricky. How had Mako made it look
so easy? Hell, the sarge'd had to contend with four street-hard-
ened kids.

Then again, the cabin where they'd been raised was
surrounded by wilderness. No outside access. No school or teachers. No conflicting opinions. No outside peer pressure.

No witnesses. If he'd drowned all four of them, no one would've known.

The sarge had probably been tempted, especially since the four of them had fought...a lot. Caz had started more than a few brawls, especially when Gabe got bossy. Hawk was slower to anger, but once he lost his temper, it was *gone*—and he got dangerous. Bull rarely got angry, but just a blow from him could do damage. As children, they'd fought because they were strangers. Later, they'd brawl for the sheer fun of it.

Truly, it was a wonder the sarge hadn't simply executed them.

Caz didn't have four headstrong boys. He had one little girl. Just one. Surely, he could manage to be a decent parent.

Yes, she had a mouth on her when she didn't get her own way. In a way, that was a compliment. It was a sign she'd begun to trust him. Hopefully, after three weeks, she was beginning to believe he wouldn't toss her back into foster care.

He knew how pervasive that worry could be.

When Mako had taken them in, Bull and Gabe hadn't been anxious, but Caz and Hawk were sure the sarge would get bored or irritated with them. That he'd dump them. They'd needed a year or so to believe Mako wouldn't give up on them—that the man had never given up on anything. That he actually gave a damn about the kids no one had wanted.

At that point, Caz's behavior had gotten worse—because he wasn't terrified. Because he'd been able to be a normal kid. *Thank you, Mako.*

Feeling more secure, Regan was starting to behave like a normal little girl.

Dios help him.

Hearing voices outside, Caz grabbed a jacket. A snowstorm might cool off his temper, and some time alone would let Regan's temper settle. He'd give her half an hour before trying again to get the story from her.

Because he knew full well she hadn't vandalized any books. The girl loved books almost as much as Gabe's little librarian did.

"Yo, bro. Your kid has some lungs on her." Next door on the covered deck of Mako's cabin, Bull sprawled in a chair with Gabe sitting next to him. Steam rose from the mug Bull held.

"You out to enjoy the balmy weather?" Caz pulled on his coat and crossed through the rapidly mounting snow.

Gabe gestured to a night sky filled with white flakes. "First real snowstorm of the season."

A tradition, in fact—watching the first winter storm.

Bull disappeared inside. By the time Caz had climbed the steps and taken a chair, his brother was back out with a mug of hot chocolate. "Here. Join us."

Caz took a sip. Chocolate well laced with Kahlúa. "Nice. Thanks, 'mano."

"The girl all right?" Gabe frowned at Caz's house. Regan's shades were pulled, but light streamed around the edges.

"She's fine, although the doorframe might be the worse for wear." Caz looked up to see two expectant gazes on him. "You two are as nosy as Regina and Irene. Or Tucker and Guzman."

With a sound of pain, Bull slapped a big hand over his chest. "Such sharp words. I'm wounded."

Caz snorted. "If the blade fits..."

"Hey, first niece and all that. Brief us, bro." Gabe made a *gimme* gesture with his fingers.

"It's like this. Regan came home from—"

When JJ stepped out of the door, Caz could almost hear his heart saying *there she is.*

A sense of rightness filled him.

JJ hesitated. "Sorry. I heard voices and had to check. Police paranoia."

"I hear you on that," Gabe muttered.

When she started to head back in, Bull beat Caz to saying, "Stay, JJ. We're celebrating the first real storm."

"You're not interrupting, if that's what you think, princesa." Caz motioned to the chair next to him. "Join us."

"Oh. Okay, I'd like that." She stepped back inside long enough to get a coat and then settled into the chair beside Caz.

Beside him, yes. This was where she belonged.

"Now tell us what happened with Regan." Bull glanced at JJ. "The munchkin yelled at him and is holed up in her bedroom. Slammed her door so loud we heard it out here."

"Uh-oh." JJ cast a worried look at Caz.

"Maybe you should institute Mako's rules on temper tantrums." Gabe grinned at JJ. "The sarge said the cabin was too small for pissed-off men. Yelling, fighting, bickering—whatever—had to go outside."

"Men?" JJ asked.

Bull took a sip of his drink. "Mmm. The rule went into effect a couple of months after we arrived. I was a man of nine. Gabe was ten."

"Oh God." JJ looked at Caz. "And you were eight?"

He nodded. "Dios, I hated being the youngest and the littlest."

"Bro, you're still the youngest and littlest," Bull pointed out and laughed as he leaned sideways to evade Caz's backhand.

"You were only eight, and he sent you outside every time you lost your temper?" She looked horrified. "In Alaska?"

Gabe fingered the top of his ear. "Got frostbite more than once till I figured out that punching someone in winter was a real bad idea."

"He really told you to go outside into the snow?"

"Told us?" Caz snorted. "More like grabbed us by the collar and pitched us out the door into the snowbank."

"B-but...the cold." Her eyes were wide.

"Coats and boots would get pitched out next." Bull grinned.

Gabe shook his head. "Somewhere around January, we realized

he'd deliberately have us shovel snow into that spot. I'm surprised he didn't draw a bulls-eye on it."

In the dark night, a figure crossed the inner compound.

"There's my woman." Gabe raised his voice. "Goldilocks, did you finish your work?"

"Research is done and sent off. I'm *free*." Bundled in a coat, Audrey climbed the steps.

Leaning forward, Gabe grabbed her hand and yanked her onto his lap. "Come and be my blanket, sweetness."

"Gabe!"

Caz grinned. She still turned red when Gabe did shit like that. What would JJ do if Caz set her in his lap?

JJ turned to Caz. "I want you to know, if you try throwing Regan out into the snow, I'll shoot you myself."

Roaring with laughter, Bull pointed a warning finger at Caz. "I hear she's a dead shot."

"She is." Gabe grinned at his officer. "But it's all right, JJ. Caz has the softest heart of all of us. I don't think you need to worry."

"Oh." She eyed Caz, not convinced. And he loved that she was so concerned for his little girl.

"I wouldn't do that to my daughter. No." The thought was outrageous, actually. "Circumstances were different with Mako. The sarge...didn't do well with small spaces filled with yelling people, even if the people were merely boys. How long we remained outside was up to us, and honestly, being dumped in a snowbank usually ended a fight right away. Although Gabe stewed longer than his...smarter...brothers."

Gabe growled under his breath. "You'll pay for that one."

Knowing he was giving himself away to his brothers—and not caring—Caz took JJ's hand and squeezed. "You have a tender heart and a protective one. My girl is the richer for knowing you."

Like Audrey, JJ had an adorable flush.

All the grownups were outside. Regan could hear them—not what they were saying, but the sound of her uncles' and Papá's voices. Sometimes Audrey and JJ. Having fun.

Without her.

Probably laughing about her.

Squished way down in the beanbag chair, Regan cuddled her stuffed cat and cried. Papá was mean and nasty and didn't love her anymore. He never had.

After a while, her tears dried, and she snuffled. And started thinking.

Maybe she'd been a stupidhead.

She set the cat on her knees so they could talk. "See, Mrs. Wilner told Papá that Brayden and Shelby said I ripped pages out of books, and there are books that are all messed up. And Papá asked me if I knew anything about it."

Regan scowled. "I didn't do it. I know Brayden and Shelby did. Just to get me in trouble."

Now Papá hated her.

Only, he hadn't yelled at her. He hadn't said she'd done it, either. He'd just asked if she knew anything about how it had happened, and she'd run into her room and slammed the door like a big baby.

Would he throw her out? Hugging the cat to her, she leaned her forehead against her knees. Not Papá. He wouldn't. If she said she was sorry and wanted to talk, he'd listen. Maybe he'd even believe her?

She rubbed her chest where it kinda hurt. He might. He liked her a little. "I'm his mija," she told the cat.

Yeah, she'd been a stupidhead.

Feeling better, she got up and left the room. After work, JJ had brought over sugar cookies, and she and Regan frosted them. With colored frosting and sprinkles and everything.

JJ likes me. Maybe she could get JJ to arrest the resort buttheads. Set a trap or something. Standing in the dark kitchen, she ate a cookie and stared out at the darkness. Snow swirled past the window, and the wind made loud *whishing* sounds.

In her fluffy slippers, she padded to her room and climbed into the beanbag chair, turning so she could watch the falling snow in the window over her head and eat another cookie.

A scraping-screeching sound made her jump. A tree? Only there were no trees between the house and the dirt road. She'd asked Papá why the forest wasn't close. He'd ruffled her head—she really liked when he did that cuz it meant he was in a great mood—and he said if anyone got this far, they already knew the houses were here, so the sarge had gone for a clear field of fire.

Whatever that meant. Probably making sure there wasn't a forest fire.

The noise wasn't from a branch or anything. She rolled out of the chair and looked out the window. This one had a metal grill on the outside so no bear could climb in the window.

Uncle Bull said the bears were sleeping in caves right now, until next spring. Still...

The sound came again. Longer.

Her eyes widened. That was a kitty. A sad kitty. The one she'd heard before. But it was snowing now. The cat would die out there. Regan put her face close to the window to look out. The snow was getting deeper.

Against the white-covered ground, something dark moved away.

She should get Papá.

But if she did, the cat would be gone. She could barely see it now.

It might come if Regan went out there. She hesitated. It was awful dark outside—and the Halloween flashlight in her jacket was dead.

But...wait. Papá had put a flashlight in her nightstand in case the electricity went out, although he said her nightlights'd come on too. "It's nice to know you have light, right, mija?"

A stab of guilt hit her. He was so nice. He acted like...like a real dad.

Another *meow* sounded. She pulled open the drawer, grabbed the flashlight, and ran down the hall into the garage. After shoving her feet into boots, she yanked on her puffy red jacket, and went out the garage's side door, which was outside her bedroom window. It was a strange house, since the part that looked out on the road was boring. In cities, the street side was the pretty one. In the Hermitage, all the big windows and fancy stuff faced into the "compound" and toward the lake.

Stopping in the snow right outside the door, she scolded herself, because she forgot to check first. Bull said to never step outside without letting her eyes adjust to the dark and doing a quick look outside first. *"Be able to see and know what you're walking into."*

She squinted against the wind. In the dark and covered with snow, everything looked different.

"Kitty?" she whispered.

No meow. But as she walked farther, she saw tracks. Little paws kind of tracks. She checked them with her flashlight. Uncle Gabe had showed her and JJ and Audrey how to tell dog and cat tracks apart. Kitties didn't have claw marks and the heel dent should look like a blobby "m". She'd told Uncle Gabe the "m" looked like the fat lettering kids spray-painted on buildings in the city. He'd laughed.

It was easy to get her uncles and Papá to laugh.

She bit her lip and glanced at the cabin. The grownups wouldn't laugh about her being outside in the dark. Even foster homes had rules about that.

But...the cat.

She'd hurry. Trudging forward, she followed the tracks and out onto the snow-covered flat road where her light shone off the tall reflectors. The road curved, but the tracks went straight and across the ditch and right into the forest.

Her hand was shaking, making the flashlight jump. It was so cold, and jammies weren't as warm as jeans. She pulled her mittens out of the pockets and put them on, then broke into a half run. She went past trees and bushes, and everything was so dark.

There wasn't as much snow under the trees, and sometimes she had to search for the tracks after a bare spot. "Kitty? Kitty, want to come home with me? There's food."

The tracks disappeared into a bunch of bushes, ones she couldn't get through. Shivering, Regan called the cat again. "Kitty." Only the wind was so loud, would it even hear her?

No tracks. No kitty. Giving up, she turned around and saw only trees. Trees everywhere. Okay, she'd follow her own tracks back home. But...her footprints got fainter. No, it was getting darker in the forest. The trees seemed to be moving closer.

With horror, she lifted the flashlight and turned it toward herself. The bulb was just a dim yellow.

And then it went out completely.

Having left the men talking on Mako's deck, JJ had gone up to her rooms and changed into pajamas for bed. She grinned at herself in the bathroom mirror. Why did she have the feeling she'd be dreaming about being tossed out into a snowbank for fighting?

First Sergeant Mako had been quite a hardass.

A loud clanging made her jump. It came from the inner compound, and just the sound was urgent. Frightening. Still in her pajamas, she stepped out on the upstairs deck.

Caz stood at the patio grill, ringing the big bell that stood off to one side. Huh, she'd always thought it was just a kind of yard art.

"Yo, what's wrong, bro?" Bull called, probably from his deck that she couldn't see from her balcony.

"Regan isn't in the house. The door in the garage is unlocked, her coat and boots are gone. She left tracks but they're fading fast. We need to find her."

JJ's heart sank as she looked into the dark night. The wind-whipped snow was falling heavily, muffling sound, and decreasing visibility.

"You got it. Meet you outside your garage." Bull disappeared.

Gabe was on his own deck, talking to Audrey and pointing to Caz's house. Maybe asking Audrey to stay in Caz's cabin in case Regan returned.

JJ yanked on a thermal shirt, a fleece overshirt, then cold weather clothing, grateful that Lillian had made her buy the serious stuff. She grabbed a flashlight as well as Mako's small emergency pack. Gabe had given the backpack to her and explained everything in it.

Downstairs, she ran out through the garage. Someone had turned on floodlights outside, illuminating the thickly falling snow. Outside the pools of light, night reigned.

Two of the guys were already following tracks. Bull and Caz. Why hadn't they waited for her?

Oh, duh, they wouldn't know she was joining them. Stretching her legs, she moved faster. The powdery snow was piling up quickly. Deeply. A tremor ran through her. Regan was so little.

"Hey," she called.

Both men turned.

Before they could speak, she said, "Tell me what you need me to do as we keep moving."

"Thank you, JJ." Caz touched her arm in a gesture of gratitude.

"Let's go." Bull surged forward, his flashlight pointing where small footprints had made a path. As Caz had said, snow had already partially filled in the tracks.

JJ followed the men, turning every now and then to look behind her, fixing markers in her head. It was frightening how quickly the lighted houses disappeared in the dark and the whipping snow.

When they reached the smoother road, they broke into a jog. On the other side of the snow-filled roadside ditch were pole-mounted solar lights that marked the edge of their private airplane runway. The glow from those lights was barely visible. Damn.

She glanced behind her again. "Gabe isn't coming to search?"

Caz followed her gaze. "He's getting his snow machine out of the outbuilding and gassed up. We should have been more prepared."

"The sarge'd be pissed we got caught with our pants down," Bull said.

As they reached the end of the cleared land, the road turned, and the tracks continued straight into the dense forest. Not good. In the trees, the patchy snow and bare ground made footprints difficult to see.

Bull roared, "Regan. Regan, shout if you can hear me!"

The wind whipped the sound of his voice away.

Caz led, stopping to snap branches at intervals to mark their trail. The tracks went deeper into the woods, on and on. JJ shivered and pulled her coat tighter. The thought of the child out here...alone...was appalling.

What had Regan been thinking?

At a wide, bare space of frozen ground, the tracks disappeared.

Face tight with worry, Caz snapped several more branches to mark the way back out. "Bull, check for tracks to the right, I'll go straight, JJ, head left. As soon as you reach snow, circle clockwise and see if you can cross her trail. If you reach these broken branches, you've come full circle. Stop and wait. If you find tracks, shout and mark the spot with three branches in a teepee. Don't forget to mark your back trail."

He wrenched off three long branches, handed them to her, then hesitated. "You're not used to snow...maybe—"

"I got this." She slapped his shoulder and headed left... although his concern sent a sweet warmth through her.

She was out of sight of their flashlights, all too soon. Past the small circle of her light, the trees were ominous black sentinels. Bushes filled in gaps between the trees as she trudged through the snow, circling the windswept area. She stopped every few paces to run her flashlight over the snowy areas before moving on.

It was so cold. The air bit at her lungs, stung her cheeks, and she shivered. If she was cold, little Regan must be freezing. Fear washed over JJ. If they didn't find Regan soon, the little girl might not survive. She'd helped search for children in the desert. Two hadn't made it.

This was so much worse.

Urgency bit at her tired feet. *Move faster.*

The high whine of a snowmobile sounded. Gabe was on the road.

Wait, what was that? She bent forward, and her light showed a shadow—a depression in the snow. A footprint. "Here!" she shouted. "Tracks are here."

The way the sound of her voice echoed off the trees, even if the men heard her, they'd be unable to get a good direction.

She wouldn't wait. Moving away from the footprint a couple of steps, she pushed the three branches into the snow and used the stringy smaller limbs to secure one to another. There was her teepee marker.

Grabbing a bunch of dead branches from the bushes, she returned to the trail and laid the branches on top of the snow in a straight line to mark the beginning of the path.

Then she followed the tracks, dragging one foot at intervals to deepen the path she was leaving behind her, snapping any branches close enough to reach. Hurrying and dragging and snapping. Her breath came hard, and she felt the trickle of sweat down her back.

"Regan!" She kept going, slowing to search for the small footsteps past bare patches. Leaving branches to mark those spots.

"Regan!"

A high-pitched shout made her stop. Hope rose. She almost abandoned the trail to follow the sound, but another shout changed her mind. The sound was bouncing off the tree trunks. Impossible to get a good direction. "Stay where you are, Regan. I'm coming. Stay put!"

Farther and farther. *Don't be stupid and get lost.* Drag a foot in the snow. Break a branch.

God, she was tired. And so damn cold. No little girl should be out in this. How cold was Regan?

Her flashlight caught something—bright red. A jacket.

"Regan." Tears filled JJ's eyes, and she almost tripped.

"JJ!" Regan flew forward, wrapped one arm around JJ, and burrowed against her.

Putting the flashlight down, JJ hugged her back. "It's okay. You're found. It's okay."

"I was so scared. I'm so cold."

A high meow sounded, and a brown furry head appeared in the neck of Regan's coat. From inside the coat.

"That's a cat." *Well, duh, JJ, state the obvious.*

"I heard him, and I followed him so I could rescue him, but I couldn't catch up. But when my flashlight went away, he came back for me."

JJ could barely understand the words with Regan's teeth chattering so hard. But...a cat. Of course, the child had gone after it. Caz would have a fit.

Except, how could he? He'd have done the very same thing.

Smiling, JJ knelt, opened her pack, and dug out the emergency blanket. The kid had on boots, mittens, and a jacket, but her pajama bottoms looked soaked through. "I'm going to wrap this around you. Can you walk? I'm not sure I can carry you and the cat and still juggle the flashlight."

Regan's pointed chin went up although JJ could feel the shivers coursing through her body. "I can walk."

The child had a hood on her jacket. And the cat was probably keeping her core temperature up, which was good for both of them. "Can you feel your feet? Wiggle your toes?"

"Uh-huh. But my fingers are..."

Of course. JJ grabbed the small gel hand warmers and flexed the disc as Gabe had shown her. As they activated, she tucked one into each mitten. They were supposed to get warm in a couple of minutes. "That'll help."

Rising, JJ pulled in a breath. "Time to get out of here. Hang onto the cat, but if he gets too heavy, I'll carry him. We're going to walk side-by-side"—even though that would be harder—"so we don't lose each other. Just tell me to stop if you need a break. Right?"

"'K." Regan was shivering so hard that JJ's heart broke. But shivering was better than not shivering.

JJ started off, gripping a fistful of the girl's jacket in one hand, her flashlight in the other. She'd done a good job of dragging one foot. The track she'd left was clear—here, at least.

Was that a light? She froze, blinked the snow from her eyelashes. "Yes!"

A light bobbed in the forest. No, two lights, coming fast.

"Regan! JJ!" Caz's shout was clear, followed by Bull's booming yell.

Regan let out a squeak, then a loud, "Papá!"

"Here! We're here!" JJ whipped her flashlight in a circle and forced herself to stay at a pace Regan could manage.

A flashlight blinded her for a second, and then the men were there.

"Dios, Regan!" Caz squeezed JJ's shoulder in unspoken gratitude and scooped up his daughter.

"Don't squish the cat," JJ yelled, hoping he'd hear before one of them got scratched.

"Cat. You have a..." The torrent of Spanish that followed was incomprehensible.

Bull was laughing as he wrapped an arm around JJ for a quick hug. "Good job, JJ. Bro, let's head back. I can hear the girl's teeth chattering from here. We'll take turns carrying her."

"Lead on," Caz said.

JJ was cold and exhausted...and couldn't stop smiling.

His house was finally quiet. As his family made their way to their own homes, Caz closed the deck door and walked back into the living area.

Once out of the forest, Regan had gone with Gabe on the snow machine back to the house while Caz had stuffed the cat down his own jacket for the walk back. They'd arrived as Audrey was helping Regan out of a warm bath. With the cat and girl reunited, hot chocolate and tea had to be drunk, and stories had to be told. Everyone watched to make sure she was past the dangers of hypothermia.

It was a miracle kids were so resilient.

After Caz had tucked her in, JJ read her a story while he thanked his family and saw them out.

Footsteps came down the hallway. JJ.

"Is she asleep?" Caz asked.

"Not quite. She wants you to come in to say goodnight. Again." JJ's brows drew down. "She's pretty worried about you being angry. You're not going to yell at her, are you?"

"No. Tomorrow we'll talk about what she did wrong and what she did right." Caz smiled. "At least she remembered what I'd told her about hikers staying put if lost." However, she hadn't taken her emergency bag, or told anyone where she was going, and had left the house after... "It's going to be difficult not to yell."

"If you yell at her, I'll yell at *you*," JJ warned—and she wasn't joking.

The cop had a definite soft spot for Regan. Caz was smiling as he walked down the hall.

Regan's bedroom was dark, lit only by the nightlights. In the quiet house, he could hear the patter of wind-whipped snow against the windows and the slow purr of a very happy stray cat.

"Papá." Regan's eyes opened, and she tried to sit up. "I'm sorry, Papá. Are you mad at me?"

"No, mija. I told you that I'm not angry." He smiled at her. "Did you think of a name for the cat?"

"He's Sirius."

"Good name." His girl had fallen in love with the Harry Potter universe. Caz stroked her hair then ran his hand down the long-haired brown tabby's back. It was scrawny, the fur was dull. Recent rations had been poor, it seemed.

"I'm sorry." Regan's eyes, so big and brown, pleaded. "I should have—"

"Shhh. We'll talk it all over tomorrow."

"You...you won't make me leave?"

Dios, she was worried about that? "Absolutely not."

He tucked a lock of hair behind her ear. "I didn't know I had a daughter, or I would have come for you before, Regan. You're mine now, and...and I love you, mija." Yes. There was the truth. "And I will never stop."

"You do? Really?"

How had he not realized how much he cared?

Or told her? Mako— none of them—were the types to go around saying such things. But, that was his family's shortcoming. He'd been an idiot not to realize his little girl needed to hear how he felt. "Yes, I love you very much."

Her fragile shoulders were still tensed.

"You're my girl, and this is your home." He smiled slightly, remembering what Mako had said when he'd taken them out of the foster home. *"If you come with me, I'll raise you till you can stand on your own two feet."*

"Regan, you'll live here until you're all grown up and ready to head off to college or your own place or get married. Until you're ready to try your wings. And right here with me will *always* be where you can return when you need to."

There, that was what she'd needed to hear. Her body went slack, and she sighed as if holding herself tense had taken all her strength.

Then the cat butted her hand, as if to remind her she had more than one problem.

Before she could worry about that, too, Caz chuckled. "Yes, Sirius may stay. You're in charge of food, water, the litter box, and any messes he makes." He eyed the long hair, white ruff, and bushy tail. Looked like it had some forest cat DNA. "And brushing all that fur, as well."

"Really?" Her eyes were wide, her breathing almost stopped, and then her eyes lit with happiness.

"Really." Caz bent down to kiss her cheek. "Now sleep, *mi tesoro*. You won't have school tomorrow—the roads will be closed —so you can sleep late."

"Oh..." She flung her arms around his neck. "I love you, too, Papá. Thank you for finding me. For coming after me."

He hugged her, breathing in the soft scent of clean little girl. His little girl. "I will always come and find you. That's what fathers do."

As he walked out of the room, he couldn't remember why he'd run so hard and long from loving someone.

CHAPTER SIXTEEN

T*he real lover is the man who can thrill you by kissing your forehead.* - Marilyn Monroe

Unable to settle yet, JJ picked up the living room. Then she washed the mugs and glasses. Then she tidied the kitchen. Because she couldn't get herself to leave. Little Regan had almost died.

The knowledge was impossible to deal with.

A sound made her look up. Caz walked from the hallway into the kitchen, pulling off his heavy flannel shirt. He probably didn't even realize she was still there, and now she'd have to...

The entire front of his T-shirt was shredded and covered in blood. She gasped.

His head jerked up. "Princesa, I didn't realize—"

"What did you *do*? How badly are you hurt?"

"It's just a few scratches. I'll certainly never put a cat inside my coat again." He half-smiled. "I tripped over a log, and he panicked."

Her head spun as she stared at the blood. Sucking in a hard

breath, she forced the emotions away. "I can't believe you didn't clean those immediately. *Doc.*"

Caz shrugged. "There were more important things to do. Making sure Regan was all right and not hypothermic. Settling everyone down."

"Shirt off. Let's see how bad it is." She used her LEO voice.

As he shrugged, obviously deciding not to rile her further, she realized he didn't play macho games. It was just another reason she liked him so much.

He pulled off his shirt.

She winced at the sight of long scratch marks and relaxed. "It's not as bad as I thought. They're not too deep. Where's your first-aid kit?"

"I'll get it." Shirtless, he headed for the hallway.

And wow. The man was incredibly...male. The finely sculpted musculature of his back was captivating.

He pulled the first-aid kit from a cupboard in the hall and headed back...and she was still staring.

His chest was broad with small, dark nipples. The scratches ran across his ribs. Lean ribs.

"Here you go." When he handed her the kit, the muscles of his pectorals and biceps bunched and rippled.

"Thanks."

The line of his jeans went across a ridged abdomen.

He cleared his throat, and she jerked her gaze up. Laughter lightened his dark eyes.

"Right." Turning on the water, she took the washcloth he handed her and cleaned the scratches. Applied antibiotic ointment. Applied Band-Aids to the worst spots.

Rather than watching her hands, he was studying her face.

"Done." She started to step back.

He touched her cheek. "Thank you, JJ. For the first aid. For finding Regan. For caring for her."

"She almost *d-died*." JJ's eyes, her nose, her face started to burn, and she swallowed against the thickness in her throat.

"Ah, princesa," he murmured and curved his hand around her nape, tucking her head against his shoulder. And she needed to be held so much she ached with it.

As if he knew, he pulled her closer. "It's over. Everyone is safe."

Wrapping her arms around him, she pressed her face against his shoulder—and cried.

Not trying to shush her, he simply held her, making soft comforting sounds, and let her cry herself out.

Oh God. Still hiccupping with sobs, she felt like a fool. She'd bawled all over him. Why had she done that? But she had. She lifted her head and met his eyes. "I'm sorry. I don't even know why—"

"Fear." Arm still around her waist, he stroked her hair in a gentle caress. "Fear for Regan, for all of us. Exhaustion, too." He chuckled. "And frustration, because we can't take it out on her by yelling."

She laughed, realizing belatedly that she was still flattened against his bare chest, her hands pressed against his back. All hard muscles covered by taut, velvety skin. She tried to pull back. "You're hurt."

"I'll be far more hurt if you move away." Then he froze and shook his head. "Forgive me, I keep forgetting myself."

How could he not, considering the way she was behaving? "You're not the only one acting inappropriately." She rubbed her cheek against his warm skin, inhaling the faint scent of soap, of clean sweat.

He could have died out there. If they hadn't found Regan, he wouldn't have stopped looking for her. None of them would. Her years in law enforcement had taught her that life could be violent. Brutal. And end far too soon.

She tipped her head back, running her fingers through his

thick black hair, seeing his eyes darken with heat. Going up on tiptoes, she pressed her lips against his.

When he hesitated, she started to pull back. "Sorry, I—"

His arms tightened around her, and he pulled her up against his body and kissed her. Totally, thoroughly, wonderfully kissed her, sending desire flooding through her veins.

Yes, this was what she wanted. To celebrate life. With Cazador.

He lifted his head, his breath warm against her lips, and she felt his erection against her stomach. His brows drew together. "Princesa, perhaps we should stop before..."

"No, we're not stopping." Belatedly, she remembered what the bartender had said, so long ago. About his rules. "But just for tonight. That's it."

He studied her face then smiled. "Sí. But this is not the place." Stepping back, he took her hand and led her up the stairs to his bedroom.

Once inside his room, she saw the bed.

The bed. Nash's cold voice filled her head. *You're worthless in bed. What kind of a woman can't get off?* She'd forgotten, hadn't she?

Everything in her wanted to make love, to kiss and caress and take Cazador inside her. To feel the wonder of being so very intimate with someone she...she cared about. A lot. However, although she'd be content with the closeness of making love, someone like Caz wouldn't consider that enough. He'd want her to get off. And then they'd both feel bad.

As he turned the lock on the bedroom door, she shook her head. "Caz." Her voice cracked as if she were a boy hitting puberty. "I...this isn't going to work. I'm sorry. I should go home." She took a step toward the door before she realized he hadn't let go of her hand.

In fact, he squeezed her fingers before bringing them up to his mouth. "Your fingers are cold, princesa," he murmured, moving closer, so she had to look up at him. He tugged her hair, then kissed her slowly, making her toes curl.

Her fears thinned like mist on the water.

Until he raised his head.

"You may always leave if you need to, mamita. But I would like to know why. And since I cannot read your mind, you will have to talk to me." He pulled her to the bed and sat beside her, his arm behind her back.

What could she say? She stared down at her lap until he touched her cheek, turning her head so she had to look at him. The room was dim, easing her embarrassment.

"Downstairs, you wanted to continue." His eyes were dark, perceptive. "What changed?"

God, how humiliating. But...okay, if she explained, it would be done. And she'd promised herself that she was done with dishonesty in the bedroom. In relationships. "I did want to, but then I remembered that you might be unhappy when I don't...when I can't get off. Not with a guy."

"Is there a reason why?" His head tilted slightly. "No, let me rephrase. Can you get off on your own?"

Had he seriously asked her that?

He had. Feeling her cheeks heat, she nodded. Once when diving into a pool, her swimsuit top had come untied—and off. She'd climbed out of the water—and had seen everyone pointing to her bare breasts. She could still feel the sting of embarrassment.

She felt like that now.

Hand still cupping her chin, he rubbed his thumb over her lower lip. "Does that mean you need more going on than just a dick inside you?"

Her attempt to move back was halted when he curled his fingers in her hair, taking a firm grip. "No, Jayden, we are talking, not retreating." His voice was firm.

Retreating? She stilled. She wasn't a coward. She could do this. But when her gaze met his, she couldn't think of what to say next.

He never seemed to have trouble finding words. "This is good information to have. Oral sex, fingers, toys? Which is your favorite?"

Oral sex, totally oral sex. She blushed red. This talking about fucking was impossible. Could she just disappear somehow? *Honesty, JJ.* "Oral sex, but it's okay. I know how guys feel about it and, well, I don't want you to do something you think is gross."

His brows drew together. "Someone told you that men don't like giving oral sex?"

"Uh, yes."

"Who told you this? Your mamá?"

"God, no." She suppressed a snort. Mom hadn't discussed sex. Ever. "My ex-boyfriend. He, um, started to do it a few times and made gagging sounds and said that's how guys feel."

"Hmm. Time for a detour..."

"What?" A detour in the discussion of how she got off? She'd totally go for that.

"Why did you and the *cabrón* break up?"

Or not. "You're sure nosy."

His lips quirked as if he'd almost laughed. "Verdad. True. Answer me, please?"

"He was another officer at the police station. When we started dating, he was really nice, but then..." She frowned. "He started criticizing everything I did. He even lied about how I performed my job. Eventually"—*after far too long*—"I broke up with him."

"Good for you." Caz's thumb swept over her lips again, sending tingles down through her. "Mamita, use logic. If the man is that dishonest about work, would he not lie about sex as well?"

Nash had...lied?

She must have looked shocked, since Caz chuckled. "JJ, how experienced are you?"

"Not very. Before Nash, there were a couple of guys. Short-term, not boyfriends. I didn't have time for men, not with Mom sick. After that, I had the academy and learning to be a police officer."

"And so you believed what this Nash said." He shook his head. "To the truth, then. Any gender can be selfish. Some women don't enjoy giving blowjobs, no?"

"I guess." Actually, she rather enjoyed them.

Although she hadn't said a word, his eyes warmed. "A person has the right to say no to things they don't enjoy. But there should be a balance. Must be a balance." He rose and stalked across the room, and she stared. He was angry—for her. That was just...heartwarming.

Caz turned to face her, his gaze direct. "Not all men hate giving oral sex. Your Nash should have said *he* didn't like it, and if he wanted blowjobs from you, he should have offered something you enjoyed as much. Especially since women usually need more than a cock pumping away. God knows we males would get irritable if you ignored our dicks the way some men ignore your clits."

She stared at him in disbelief. How could he talk about sex so...bluntly?

Okay, okay, she'd think about the idea of balance later. Bottom line, Nash had lied—and she'd believed him.

Even worse, she'd been a fool, giving Nash whatever he wanted without receiving anything in return. "I always thought of myself as being into equality. I mean, look at what I do for a living. How could I have been so blind? Such a wuss?"

"Controlling assholes are stealth attackers, snipping away pieces until your self-esteem is reduced to nothing." Caz sat back down beside her and put a hard arm around her waist. "Let me correct what Nash said. *He* didn't like giving oral sex. Overall, I think more men enjoy it than dislike it, but I don't discuss sex with others. It's not something my family does."

It was reassuring to know he wouldn't talk about her to Gabe or Bull. But, now she wanted to know... "Um..."

His swift grin said he knew exactly what she was wondering. "I love going down on a woman. I love the taste, the smell, using my lips, my tongue, and my fingers."

She shivered as her whole lower half turned into a molten pool of desire.

His masculine chuckle ran over her nerves like warm hand. "Look at those wide eyes. Yes, we are going to fuck. But I think we need to shut off that pendejo's whispers in your head, princesa."

How did he know she'd heard Nash's voice?

"So. You are going to trust me." His smile took on a wicked edge. "I am going to take away your sight, yes, and then..." He pulled her thermal shirt over her head and off, laughing at her squeak of surprise.

His gaze swept over her and heated. "I love how often you go without a bra."

"You... Wait... You know when I'm braless?"

"I am a man. Of course, I know." His palms covered her small breasts, his thumbs on her nipples, feather light touches, before he took her mouth again, his hands still on her breasts. The combination sent heat-lightning streaking through her.

"Tonight is simply for fun. For pleasure. I will enjoy you until I can no longer wait and must be inside you. If you get off, fine. If not, that's all right, too. Same for me. Tonight, our only task is to savor each other's bodies, sí?" His nonchalant shrug was very Hispanic. He wouldn't pressure her to get off, to perform.

The bundle of anxiety inside her relaxed. "Okay. Yes."

Leaning forward, she kissed his shoulder, his neck. "Anything else?"

"Most certainly," he murmured and pulled her to her feet. "You will let me be in charge of this session, my inexperienced one. I'll tell you what I like, what I want you to do. Until I speak, you will lie perfectly still and stay perfectly quiet."

"But..."

"No. Those are the rules. This time." He'd undone her jeans. With a swift tug, he pulled everything down, off her legs, and helped her step out. "On your back, Officer, or I will find your police handcuffs."

She frowned. "That's not even funny."

His eyes danced. "If you won't share yours, Gabe has a set."

"Oh my God. That's just wrong."

"We'll try it some night." Before she could answer him, he flattened her on the bed, stepped back, and studied her. "Hmm." Picking up her shirt, he folded it and laid it over her eyes.

"You're not going to tie it?" Her attempt at sarcasm came out breathy instead.

"No need since you aren't going to move. At all. No touching me, no wiggling or squirming. No speaking, no breathing hard, no moaning or groaning."

"What?"

"You heard me, mamita. This is my time to play. You may have an equal amount of time with the next round." He curled her fingers around the headboard's fancy ironwork. "Don't let go until I tell you to."

Don't move. Don't speak. She couldn't even see what he was doing.

Every nerve on her skin came alive in anticipation. Where would he touch her?

The nightstand drawer was opened. Closed. The mattress dipped as he settled beside her. His kiss was warm and gentle, and each breath brought her his dark, spicy scent.

He ran a finger teasingly over her cheek, down her neck. The air was cool. His finger was warm, stroking across her upper chest. Her nipples tightened to hard, aching points, and she arched her back for more.

"You will not move, mamita. Not a muscle."

Her mouth opened, and he reminded her, "No speaking. No sounds. This is my time, and I am a demanding man."

As she tried to relax her muscles, to stay still, his finger circled one breast then the other. Spiraling around, palming, kneading. His thumbnail scraped over her nipple, making her gasp at the magnificent pleasure.

He played with her, so unhurriedly, even as he talked to her in his rich Spanish-accented voice. "Such pretty breasts. See how the bottom is softer than the top. How tight they're getting. I like this pink color."

With warm fingers, he tugged on a nipple, rolling it, pulling it. "They get longer, harder." His mouth closed over the throbbing peak, his tongue lashing it, circling. "Mmm, even redder. Let's see..." He sucked gently then harder. "Yes, there's a pretty rosy color. Ah, I should make them match."

He moved to her other breast. "Freckles. I love the little freckles along here." His lips grazed over the tops of her breasts.

Her head spun with the amazing sensations, the way he played. Shouldn't she give him something back? Move or moan. No. She'd been ordered to stay still and quiet. But that meant she had nothing to distract her from the sensations playing over her body. Nothing to do but feel.

His lips moved down—and he blew a raspberry on her stomach. The sound, vibrations startled her, and she yelped and then giggled.

He kissed her and chided sternly, "No sounds, cariño. You were bad, so you will have to suffer."

She wanted to yank the cloth from her eyes so she could see, but no, she had to just lie still, tell her body not to move despite the surging anticipation, despite the way her skin felt too tight, too sensitive. The way her pussy throbbed for attention.

He put his hand over her mound, and a finger slid inside her— oh, she was slick—and then his tongue licked around one nipple.

His mouth closed. Sucked. "Take your punishment silently, mamita," he cautioned.

His teeth tightened on her nipple in a light bite. The stinging sensation turned into a heavy, slow wave of pleasure that shook her, rocked her. Her lips tightened over the gasp, and she held so very still—and every touch on her body grew even more exciting.

"Very good." He chuckled. "It's good you enjoy being bit since it's something I like to do."

Oh. My. God. Her nipple burned and throbbed—and was begging for more.

He moved to the other breast—making them match—before sliding down. His lips were warm on her belly. "So soft. I like softness here very much." His lips touched her mound. "Plump and begging for my lips."

His voice anchored her, stabilized her in the deep waters of desire.

"Open your legs wide for me, *querida*. Only move your legs."

She spread her legs a few inches and got a light slap on her thigh that made her jump. And burned right to her pussy.

"Stubborn woman. Wider."

She wanted to tell him he was bossy, to frown at him, to divert him from seeing her or looking at her down there. Another teasing slap derailed her thoughts, and she opened her legs.

"Now there's a pretty sight." He settled between her legs. His hands ran over her thigh to soothe the sting, and then he pressed her legs even farther apart. Exposing everything.

Before she could worry, he spoke, his darkly resonant words soothing her even as his fingers excited her. "Such a pretty color, and so slick. I grow even harder when I see how wet and ready you are for me. Sí, my dick is demanding to be inside you, but the rest of me wants to play right here for a few hours or so."

Hours? She wasn't going to survive more than a few minutes.

His fingers drew her apart, sliding over her folds, and she felt his warm breath on her mound. On her clit. His tongue ran over the sensitive nub in small circles, and the exquisite sensation was like nothing else.

"Mmm, you taste like sin, mamita."

All of her nerves had melted right down to her pussy. Everything ached and begged for more.

He gave her more, his tongue even more wicked than his voice, his fingers keeping her open, then pressing inside her, curving up to rub inside as his tongue lashed the outside. Trapping her clit between two devastating forces.

The sensations increased, thickening, overwhelming, and he never relented, moving only slightly up or down, one side or the other.

Everything inside her gathered, every muscle turning rigid as he paused, paused, and then his lips closed over her clit, and he sucked, even as he pressed down on it with his tongue, rubbing directly on top.

Like a ship in a tsunami, her world spun out of control as the huge waves of pleasure rolled through her and over her, drowning her in sensation. *Don't scream, don't scream.*

His fingers inside her kept it going, drawing out every last ripple until she was a quivering mess, heart thudding wildly, gasping for breath.

"There now." He was on top of her, laughing slightly. "You are incredibly beautiful when you come." He kissed her, slow and gentle, then harder, propping himself up on her right side while his free hand roved over her damp body.

"You may put your arms around me...for a minute, I think."

As she released the headboard, her fingers were stiff. But her hands were happy as she hugged him and marveled at the rock-hard muscles of his shoulders, his deltoids. "I—"

"No, you may not talk."

In a silent request, she patted the shirt that still lay over her eyes.

His low laugh made everything deep inside her quiver. "No, it will remain also. Until I'm inside you, when I get there."

Wasn't that going to happen now?

"I haven't yet gotten enough of the way you taste." His teeth nipped at her ear lobe, and goosebumps raced up her arms. "I just wanted to give you a chance to get your breath."

He curled her fingers back around the headboard's scrollwork, kissed her lightly, and moved down.

The second time his shy woman orgasmed had been even more satisfying than the first. He hadn't lied; he never lied. JJ truly *was* gorgeous when she climaxed. The way a flush rolled upward from her nipples to her cheeks, deepening her color, was enthralling.

He wanted to see her eyes. But she was a worrier. Just from the little she'd said, the asshole boyfriend had left her insecure of her beauty, her scent, her taste. Left her anxious about what to say, how to give back in order to please a man.

So Caz had removed her ability to do anything—eliminating the option of failure—and Dios, she had responded beautifully.

As she lay limp except for after-orgasm quivering, he pulled off his jeans and suited up. Settling between her thighs, he lifted her knees. "I'd like to feel your legs around me. Can you do that for me?"

She did. Her inner thighs were like warm silk pressing against him. He froze for a moment, fighting himself for control.

"Hands on my shoulders." As she obeyed, he removed the shirt from over her eyes.

Blinking, she focused on his face. Her eyes had turned the blue of the center of the hottest fire.

Holding her gaze, he stroked her cheek, feeling the connection between them. The desire. It was disconcerting how much he wanted her, physically and emotionally. "Are you ready for me, JJ?"

Her lips formed the word although no sound escaped. *"Please."*

Fisting his dick, he positioned it at her entrance. She was very wet—and so very beautiful. Testing, he slid in an inch and saw her pupils dilate.

Her fingers dug into his shoulders.

"You're tight, mamita, and Dios, you feel good."

The tiny crease between her brows said he should go slowly. She was too tight—this time. But that tightness forced him to hold onto his control with everything he had. As he moved in and out in small thrusts, she enclosed him in heat. "You feel magnificent."

Not enough. She needed words to counteract the poison that Nash had fed her. "You're like a hot fist around me, slick and so amazing that I have to fight not to simply pound into you like a virgin boy."

An almost inaudible gurgle of laughter escaped her. Her eyes lit with happiness. She was a generous, giving woman. A responsive one.

Slowly, excruciatingly slowly, he worked his way in. Her nipples were hard points against his chest as he penetrated her fully, taking and making her his own.

Mine. Such an anachronistic sentiment—and one he felt to his depths. *Mine.*

"Hang on to me, mi princesa. The time for slow is over."

When her hips lifted, he almost smiled. Could she be more perfect?

His first hard thrust sent heat searing through his cock. His balls. Then he was pounding into her, feeling her soften around him, under him. Her arms curled around his neck, holding on.

When a flush ran over her cheeks, he rubbed his chin against her temple, smiling. Because she was aroused again. How could he resist taking her with him this time?

Changing position, he moved higher, his pelvis slightly above hers so he could grind downward against her clit with every thrust. She stiffened as if he'd hit her with an electrical charge, and her core tightened around him. "Mmm, mamacita, that's good."

"Oh, oh…" Her eyes glazed with need.

She was simply beautiful.

His balls drew up tightly. The heat was an urgent mass at the base of his spine. Yet he held out—pounding hard, twisting slightly to tease her clit.

Her fingers became claws, biting sharply into his shoulders. Her legs tightened around him.

"Time to come, mi pequeña poli," he murmured and bit the sweet curve between her neck and shoulder.

Her head tipped back, and she gave a tiny, high cry. He held her, feeling the sensations take her.

"So fucking beautiful." Her cunt was still rippling around him as he gave in to his own needs, driving in with short fast thrusts. He was deep, deep inside her as heat poured out of him in the most satisfying pleasure he knew.

For a moment, he let himself collapse onto her soft body, before lifting his weight off. As he looked down into her shining eyes, her scent, her taste, her very self were imprinting on his heart.

JJ woke just before dawn. For a moment, she didn't know where she was, feared she was back in Nash's apartment. But a breath brought her the fragrance of snow and sharp tang of evergreens from the barely open window. Moving her head, she drew in the scent of Caz's clean spicy-lime aftershave…and of musky sex.

Lots of sex, Lord help her. Her vibrator had never gotten her off so many times—let alone that hard. She'd had three orgasms with just the first round. *Three.* What was the proper etiquette for receiving that much pleasure? Was she supposed to send a thank you note?

After the first time, they'd slept, cuddling like spoons, both of them exhausted.

He'd woken her around two am. Drowsily, she'd felt him move away, heard something crinkle, before he'd snuggled back up behind her. His right arm beneath her curled up so he could cup her breast. So nice, she'd thought sleepily. And then his thick, rigid cock pressed at her entrance for only a second before sliding in. She stiffened. Shocked.

"Don't move, princesa," he'd murmured in her ear. He cupped his left hand over her pussy, finding her clit. Working his magic as his unmoving shaft throbbed inside her.

God, she was approaching the pinnacle, ready to come. And then her brain had woken up. Worries flooded in, and she'd tensed. He'd laughed, low and masculine. He started thrusting, big and heavy inside her, even as he continued stroking her clit. Her brain didn't have a chance against his control over her body. A few minutes later, she climaxed so hard her heart almost stopped. He'd followed, his arms tightening around her, and she'd never felt so wanted.

Then they'd slept again. All night.

She breathed softly, listening. The wind had died down, and the world was quiet.

Lying still, she savored the feeling of his heavy arm over her waist, his warm breath ruffling her hair, his chest against her back. In a harsh world, he was safety and comfort, laughter and compassion.

Yes, she liked him. For more than his lethal sexy body and gorgeous face—although, *yum*.

For more than the sensually decadent way he made love—although, again, *yum*.

No, what was messing with her plan to keep her distance was his personality. How caring he was with everyone—her, Regan, his patients. His subtle sense of humor. His ability to talk about stuff that had her stammering with embarrassment. His straightforward honesty. The way he teased his brothers. Even his annoying protectiveness.

Oh, she liked him far too much. More than liked him, if she had to admit it. And that was simply impossible.

Although gaining a daughter had slowed down his hookups with women, he'd undoubtedly go back to being a player once his life settled down.

What did that mean for her?

She sighed. It meant the man would shatter her heart. Because she didn't have the willpower to give him up even though she knew there'd be an ending.

Everything in life came to an end. She'd learned that the hard way, over and over and over.

With Cazador, their time would end sooner rather than later. Maybe even after this night. They wouldn't halt because of an accident, illness, or disaster. He'd simply shift from watching her with heat in his eyes to seeing her as a friend.

That would hurt so, so much.

But she could deal.

Okay, then.

She would indulge if he wanted to continue. Although it'd have to be a very quiet, secret fling. He had his daughter to consider. As a LEO, she had her reputation to consider.

When he called it quits, as she knew he would, she'd cry, pick up the pieces of her heart, and go on.

Because that's what a woman did.

CHAPTER SEVENTEEN

W*ho dares, wins. Who sweats, wins, Who plans, wins.* ~ Lieutenant Colonel Sir Archibald David Stirling, Founder of the SAS

"This is the last of them." On Wednesday, the day after the snow-storm, Regan handed Uncle Gabe her stack of dishes. He was scraping off the uneaten food for the chickens. She bet the hens would really like the crunchy taco shells and meat.

"Thanks. Good job, Regan." Finishing, he handed the dirty plates to Audrey to put them into the dishwasher.

Regan looked around for another job. Uncle Bull was wiping down the table. Papá and JJ had put the leftovers away and were getting drinks for everyone.

"Mija, can you carry these to the coffee table?" Papá asked.

"Sure." She grinned and took two glasses. Why was it so much more fun to help here than in the foster homes? Maybe because everybody liked each other? Or because even when they were grumpy, no one was mean. Nobody hit her or called her bad names or sweared at her.

This afternoon, she was supposed to do homework...but fell asleep. Papá just laughed and said that running around in the snow made people tired.

They'd done a lot of running around today. She'd helped fix up the snowmobiles. No, that wasn't right. In Alaska, they called them snow machines. Alaska people were weird, sometimes.

As she set the drinks down, Uncle Bull took a seat at one end of the sectional—his favorite spot. Gabe and Audrey sat on the other end.

"JJ." Sitting in the middle, Papá patted the cushion beside him. "Sit here."

As JJ sat down, she smiled at him, kinda soft, almost like how Audrey smiled at Uncle Gabe.

"You, too, mija." He took Regan's hand and pulled her down on his other side.

"Are we going to sing?" Regan bounced a little. Papá had let her play the drum for a couple of songs last time.

"Later, sí." Papá nodded at Uncle Gabe. "Over to you, viejo."

"Regan, when we were growing up, sometimes one of us boys had a problem." Uncle Gabe's mouth twisted kinda funny. "We had lots of problems, actually. But if we couldn't fix a situation on our own, the sarge made us all talk it over to figure out what to do."

Uncle Bull raised his pointer finger. "When planning a mission, the first step is to gather intelligence."

Why were they all looking at her? She shrank closer to Papá.

He put his arm around her, pulling her against his side. "I told them about the books getting ripped up at school."

Gabe nodded. "Tell us what you know, Regan."

Were they going to throw her out now? Her heart felt like it had feet and was trying to run right out of her chest. With hard boots. "I...I didn't do it."

Audrey made a pfffting sound. "No one thinks you did, honey. You love books too much to hurt them."

Leaning forward, JJ reached around Papá to take Regan's hand. "Somebody damaged those books and said it was you. That's not right." JJ's eyes narrowed. "And they shouldn't get away with it."

Sometimes Regan forgot JJ and Uncle Gabe were cops.

After JJ squeezed her hand and sat back, Regan looked up at Papá. Did he—

He kissed the top of her head, and her heart stopped running and went all squishy instead. He believed her.

"Who told the teacher it was you?" JJ asked. "And what did they say?"

Regan looked around. Audrey had a pen and paper so she could take notes. Uncle Bull was leaning forward and so was Uncle Gabe. Mission planning. How chill was this?

"Mrs. Wilner didn't tell me who, but"—Regan stopped to think, to say it right—"she said they saw me tearing pages out of the books. Only they couldn't have, cuz I *didn't*."

Uncle Gabe's face got a pissed-off look, but his voice got even softer. " 'They' indicates there were more than one involved and that Mrs. Wilner knows who the liars are."

Audrey tapped her pen on the pad. "Did you see the books that were damaged, Regan? Can you describe them?"

"Uh-huh. They were the new ones Mrs. Wilner got in. Still in the box—she hadn't even put them on the shelves yet. They were all shiny and pretty." Then the teacher had shown her one of the messed-up books, the pages all raggedy and ripped. It kinda felt like a little kid had gotten kicked. Did books hurt?

"Shiny." Audrey patted Uncle Gabe's arm. "I'd guess the books are hardbound with glossy covers."

"Glossy?" Uncle Gabe grinned at JJ. "Bet those hold fingerprints."

Papá frowned. "You'd need to obtain the culprits' prints. Getting permission to fingerprint a minor might be problematic."

Fingerprints. Like Shelby or Brayden would've left their prints on the books? Cuz she knew it was those two stupidheads.

"I hate to say it, but you're right." JJ scowled then smiled. "Wait. What if we—the police department—make it plain we're not keeping the prints? The matching could be"—she smirked —"an exercise for the students."

Not exactly sure what JJ meant, Regan looked up at Papá who was grinning. Audrey clapped her hands. Her uncles were laughing.

All right, then. Whatever it was sounded okay to her. Regan settled back against Papá.

They all believed her.

CHAPTER EIGHTEEN

*A*t 70 years old, if I could give my younger self one piece of advice, it would be to use the words 'fuck off' much more frequently. - Helen Mirren

On the Friday after the snowstorm, JJ stood in Regan's schoolroom for grades three, four, and five. The room was a visual blast of color. Creamy yellow walls boasted bright artwork projects. Another wall had a turquoise bulletin board. The colors of the brilliant rainbow arching over the computer corner were matched by the chairs below. A dark green rug marked out the reading corner. To counteract the decreasing sunlight, the teacher had created a summer wonderland.

Seated at the table, Niko, one of Regan's buddies, was labeling a page with the last student's name.

As JJ waited, she stretched, feeling a low ache in her lower half and a few sore muscles, as well...all from the unfamiliar activity. Because that one-night-only had turned into...more. For the past three nights, since the snowstorm on Tuesday, she'd been in Caz's bed. In his arms. Making love over and over.

And then getting up way early to go home before Regan rose. Although she had an escort. Because Caz insisted. *"It's dark out there, mi corazón. I will walk with you."*

She would've thought waking up with him would be awkward. Instead, it was...wonderful. With everything he did, from making love to holding her in his arms all night, he made her feel cherished. Each morning, it was harder to leave him. This morning, he'd pulled her close and bent down for a long kiss and—

"Officer?"

She blinked and looked down to see Niko holding up the paper he'd been working on. "Sorry. Daydreaming."

When he grinned, she ruffled his hair. "Thank you for your help, Niko." He'd volunteered to label each paper with the finger-printed child's name.

"Sure."

JJ taped the final paper to the wall and stepped back to admire the thirteen sets of enlarged fingerprints. Each print was big enough to clearly show loops, whorls, and arches.

Finished with his job, Niko had joined the others at a table where Gabe was demonstrating how to dust for fingerprints.

Mrs. Wilner walked over to the table. "Chief MacNair, can you dust these books for prints?"

She set down two hardbounds with glossy covers. Each had a noticeable gap where pages had been torn out.

"Of course, Mrs. Wilner," Gabe said politely. "It would be my pleasure."

Regan, standing with the other students, gave JJ a hopeful look.

JJ smiled back in reassurance, even as her heart hurt. Damn, this needed to work.

"Got some nice clear prints here." After the images of the fingerprints from the book covers were enlarged and printed out, Gabe handed out copies to several groups. "Team one and team two, see if you can match this print. We'll call the owner: Perp Number One."

That got a bunch of grins.

Two more groups got a print from Perp Number Two.

Joining JJ, Mrs. Wilner asked in a low tone, "I wasn't thinking when you proposed this, but my fingerprints and those of the publishing company and shipping people would be on those books, too."

"Yes." JJ watched Gabe explaining how to match the minutiae. "Gabe is dusting only the little prints. A child's hand is noticeably smaller than an adult's."

"Oh." Mrs. Wilner examined her own fingers and glanced at the children. "I hadn't thought of that."

"We got one!" The little girl on Team Two waved the paper excitedly. "It matches!"

"Good job. Let's see if we all agree." JJ walked over. As the students gathered around, she used a pointer to show how the various crossovers, bifurcations, ridges, and islands in the perp print and the student's print matched up.

After everyone agreed it was a match, she handed out tiny badges to the members of Team Two.

When Team Four matched their print against one of the students, Gabe confirmed the finding with the class, congratulated the team, and gave them badges, too.

There—both criminals had been identified. JJ hoped Regan felt better now.

Sitting at her desk, Regan tried to keep from cheering. On each side of her, Delaney and Niko weren't even trying to hide their grins.

Regan wanted a badge, too, but her team hadn't won the contest.

Uncle Gabe and JJ were so chill, like super-cops or something, and Regan's classmates were all interested. So was Mrs. Wilner. Principal Jones had even come to watch.

"This is one of the ways we gather evidence from a crime scene," Uncle Gabe told everyone. "Now that we've done the work, if you were the police, who would you want to talk to about the damage to the books?"

"Shelby!" Team Two shouted, all together.

"Brayden!" Team Four joined in.

"Yeah, Shelby and Brayden said Regan did it, and *they* were the ones who ripped out the pages. They're dirty liars," Delaney yelled, louder than Regan had ever heard her.

Shelby's face turned really red, and Brayden's was too, only he was glaring around at everybody.

Delaney was right—they were dirty liars. And bullies and mean.

"I think we'd better have that talk." Principal Jones motioned to Brayden and Shelby. When he led them out, all the kids who'd been picked on cheered.

"We didn't even have to beat them up and get suspended for fighting." Niko high-fived Regan.

Grinning, Regan looked around. The other kids were smiling at her like they were glad she wasn't in trouble. She was happy she wasn't in trouble—or suspended for fighting.

Sometimes, maybe, there were other ways to fix stuff besides using her fists. Like how the uncles, and Papá and JJ and Audrey had sat down and talked and planned. Together.

Cuz that's what Mako taught them to do.

A happy shiver ran through her. She was part of Mako's family now, too.

The fingerprinting "presentation" had gone better than JJ could have imagined. Not that Caz had been happy to hear the two brats had definitely set up his daughter. Hell, she and Gabe barely managed to keep him from driving to the resort to yell at the parents. Or worse. They'd been able to tell the doc that Principal Jones had already scheduled a discussion with the two children and their parents. Thankfully, the doc had a full waiting room and hadn't been able to indulge his temper any longer.

She had to admit Caz's anger on behalf of his little girl was heartwarming. Even being a police officer, her father would've reacted the same way.

Yet a pissed-off, knife-carrying father with a history of killing people was a bit of a concern. She grinned. She and Gabe planned to keep Caz far, far away from those parents and kids.

After doing a batch of paperwork in the station—and fortifying herself with more coffee—JJ headed out, waving as she went past the reception desk.

"Stay warm, Officer," Regina called.

As JJ hit the street, she was smiling. It was great to feel part of everything and that she was making a difference. Helping. The station was already becoming a second home.

Walking down Main Street, she stared at the high heaps of snow pushed to one side by the snowplow. Some piles were as tall as she was. If she were a kid, she'd totally be making snow caves. Maybe Regan and her friends would like some help?

Alaska sure was different.

The day after the snowstorm, Gabe decreed that the Alaska newbies must learn basic maintenance. Audrey, Regan, and JJ got to help fix up the Hermitage's half-dozen snow machines. During the lessons in the outbuilding, the three guys had regaled them with humorous—and horrifying—tales of riding disasters. Breaking through the ice, avalanches, running into trees or barbed wire fences, frostbitten hands and feet, overturning on an incline, losing control on ice. Her mental list of dangers had run right off the page...and then they'd all gone out riding.

Dangerous or not, she loved riding snow machines.

It appeared all the business owners—the ones still here—were open today. People she talked to had shrugged off the storm, saying it was just a taste of what was to come. Snow season didn't really get going until December. This was only the beginning of November, God help her.

Yet she loved everything about the Alaska winter. The snow machines. Doing snow-chores—checking windows, water lines, and roofs, clearing paths, making sure the chickens' water hadn't frozen. The Hermitage evenings with a roomful of people, laughter, good food, a fun movie, and of course, singing.

Mako had made a strange and wonderful family.

Shaking her head, she popped into Dante's Market.

"Yo, it's my girl copper," Dante called. "How's it going out there?"

"Good, actually." She leaned on the front counter and smiled at the old Okie who'd been in Alaska for decades without losing his accent. "Seems like everyone who's survived a winter or two is pretty much fine—except for an older man who started having chest pains when he was trying to shovel a path to his car. A couple of power lines went down along with a ton of tree branches."

He nodded. "I helped Jones rebuild his shed that collapsed under the snow. Fool principal didn't give the roof enough of a slant. How'd our newer people do?"

"Mostly fender-benders and cars that slid off the road. There are some newcomers who aren't used to driving in the snow." She shook her head. "One guy was driving on bald tires and wondering why he had no traction."

Dante tugged at his beard and gave her an inquiring look. "And you? Nevada isn't known for snowstorms."

She grinned. "Caz coached me." He'd driven her SUV to the roadhouse. Bull had cleared the parking lot, leaving heaping mounds of snow around the sides. "He made me drive around the roadhouse parking lot, deliberately fishtailing and skidding. My car left a lot of dents in the snow piles around the sides before I figured out how snow affects traction and how to deal with it." On the way back, she'd driven up and down Main Street to get a feel for snow on pavement.

Caz was an amazing teacher. Patient...and very thorough.

"Good." Dante chuckled. "I put my truck into a ditch the first year I was here. Twice."

Thank God for Caz. Putting Rescue's patrol car into a ditch would be totally humiliating. "Now I just have to watch out for the other drivers."

"True, true. But our newbies around here will learn to drive—and to stock up, too." He waved his hand at the market shelves. "Notice how my stock of canned goods and toilet paper has gone down?"

"Huh." Last night when they'd started cooking at Mako's, Caz had shown her the immense pantry. A huge—filled—freezer took the end. The shelves were filled with commercial and home-canned goods, canisters of beans and noodles, freeze-dried foods. And lots and lots of toilet paper.

She eyed Dante's shelves. "Are you going to run out of supplies? Should we institute rationing?"

"Nah, it's all good. I'm just waiting for my part-time lads who have younger backs to haul stock out of the back room." He winked. "Like all Alaskans, I make sure I'm prepared for the long haul. Just in case."

"Good enough." She headed back out into the cold. The temperature had dropped low enough to steal her breath as she checked in with the rest of the local businesses. No break-ins, no problems.

At least in these quiet months before skiing season started, she'd have time to learn to be an effective LEO during winter.

As she started to cross to the municipal building, a moose sauntered across Main Street and moseyed down the hill toward the lake. *Damn.* Okay, maybe she had more to learn than she'd thought.

In her pocket, her cell rang out shrilly. She pulled it out. A brawl at the roadhouse with a request for help. Odd that Bull hadn't put a stop to it. No, come to think of it, Bull and Gabe were out in the boondocks somewhere. An elderly couple, having lost power in the storm, had been using candles—and ended up with a cabin fire. Gabe had drafted Bull to help make repairs.

No Bull at the roadhouse. No backup from Gabe. As tension tightened her belly, JJ jumped in the patrol car, headed the few blocks to the roadhouse, and strode inside.

Three guys, obviously intoxicated, were fully engaged in a fist-fight. A fourth man knelt on the floor near the corner, hunched over his stomach. Shards of glass and broken chairs littered the floor. Two waitresses stood off to one side. Near them, Felix was sporting a purpling bruise along his jaw and leaning on the bar. He'd obviously tried to intercede and failed.

Up to her, then.

"Rescue Police. Break it up." At her loud shout, the three brawlers looked over, hesitated, and re-engaged.

Assholes.

One guy landed on a chair, shattered it, and charged back into the fight.

"Shit," she muttered and calculated her approach. The big bearded one was the most aggressive. The smallest guy was getting the crap beat out of him. The third was a total slugger. Okay, then.

"One more time. *Police! Stop now!*" She moved forward, pepper spray in one hand. Yanking the collar of the little guy, she threw him across the room and sprayed the biggest aggressor.

His howl of pain shouldn't have pleased her. But it did.

She waited a second to see if the third guy would be smart and stand down. When he swung at her, she hosed him down, too, and retreated rapidly from the pepper-filled air.

Sorry, Bull. The restaurant would need to be aired out. Considering the mess of glass and broken furniture, the place would be closed for a bit anyway.

"JJ, look out!" a waitress screamed.

Before JJ could turn, someone tackled her from behind. She landed hard on her shoulder. The man punched her in the forehead. Hard. Pain burst in her face, and she went dizzy for a second.

"Fucking bitch cop!" It was the guy who'd been sitting in the corner. He punched her again.

Her cheek exploded with pain.

And training took over. She slammed her fist into the side of his face, rocking him sideways, then twisted to the other side and swung her leg up sideways in front of him. Her ankle clotheslined his throat and knocked him off of her. Rolling to her feet, she yanked out her stun gun and shut him down.

Goddamn testosterone-poisoned males. Using handcuffs and zip-ties, she secured all four men. Wrists *and* ankles—because she was in a seriously bad mood. And hurting.

After sitting heavily on a chair, she turned to the wide-eyed wait staff. "Hey, Ophelia, can you get me an ice pack, please, and get Felix one, too?"

"You bet. Coming right up," the tiny brown-skinned waitress called and hurried into the kitchen.

"You're my hero, Officer JJ." Felix cast her a smile and sat down heavily at a table.

A sound from outside drew her attention. Gabe's truck skidded to a halt in the snowy parking lot followed by Bull's. The cavalry had arrived. She hadn't called for it—but she had backup anyway, and how amazing was that.

Useful, too. It would've been tricky to haul four perps to the station.

As she rose to give her report, she realized blood was running down her face and dripping onto her jacket. With careful fingers, she touched her face. Damn, that hurt. *Ow.*

When Caz saw JJ's bloodstained face, fury filled him until it felt as if his head would explode. "What happened? Who...? Tell me. I will kill whoever did this to you."

"Just a bar brawl, Doc." She was holding a blood-soaked piece of gauze to her cheek. "No big deal. It's all part of the job."

"To hell with your job. You have blood all over you." His anger grew, filling the room. She could have been badly hurt. Could have died. Like Carmen. "You will not go back to that job, a job where you have to fight."

"Excuse me?" Her mouth thinned into a line. "My business, not yours."

He moved forward, putting them face-to-face. "Being a cop isn't safe, isn't a place for—"

"If you say woman, I'll flatten you the same way I did them."

Them? She'd faced more than one? Every thought in his head disintegrated. He gripped her shoulders hard. "Where was Gabe? Where was your backup?"

Her fist in his gut knocked him back a step.

"Forget it. I'll bandage myself up." Turning, she walked away.

She'd almost made to the door before he got himself under control and could speak in an even voice. "JJ, stop."

She stopped, but didn't turn. Obviously trying to decide.

Dios, he was an idiot. "Forgive me, please. I was out of line."

Stepping between her and the door, he held his hands up in

surrender. One side of her face was swollen and bruised. Her forehead was gashed. The cut on her cheek was even worse.

Her opponent must have worn rings. His temper flared up so hot, he took a moment to leash it again. "What I said was wrong. Come, let me get you stitched up."

He'd already sutured her face once. How often would she get hurt? How badly? *Control, Ramirez.*

Taking a seat on the exam table, she eyed him. "How do you manage to stay in the medical field if you get this upset at seeing an injured woman?"

She had no idea of what she meant to him, did she?

"It is why a medical person avoids ministering to family. Caring for family and friends clouds judgment." Her startled expression broke his heart, and he touched her uninjured cheek with his fingertips. "Yes, I care for you, mi—Officer Jenner."

She stared at him and then shook her head slightly. Rejecting his words.

As he washed his hands, gloved up and opened the sterile dressing pack, cleaned, glued, and sutured, she remained silent.

He cupped her uninjured cheek. "Talk to me, JJ."

"What is there to say? All this overprotectiveness is because you've lost people, isn't it? Your mom and sister. Your Carmen."

A momentary hope that she understood swept through him. "Sí. And I can't protect you. Not with the job you have."

"You know, that's what Nash said. That he didn't want me to get hurt. That I wasn't good enough to protect myself. That I needed to quit being a police officer...so he'd be comfortable."

"I didn't mean—" Caz stopped, seeing the snare he'd walked into.

She shoved his hand away and hopped off the table.

"Thanks for the repair job, Doc. As for the rest, you don't get to go there. You won't make me less than I am." Her eyes were the blue-green of the Holgate Glacier—and held even less warmth.

Turning, she walked out of the exam room.

Before Caz could follow, he heard voices in the hallway.

"Hey, JJ." It was Audrey's voice.

"What are you two doing in here? Are you hurt?"

"No, we were upstairs in the library. Gabe told us to come and get you. Are you all right?"

"Some batch of vile bull-pizzles hit you, did they?" Lillian's English accent was very sharp. "My dears, let us go to my place. I have a lovely Corsican rosé calling out for someone to drink it."

"My shift isn't over yet," JJ protested.

"Jayden Jenner, you have been injured," Lillian said firmly.

"But..."

"Gabe said to take you home. That anyone who takes on four-to-one odds gets to leave work early." Audrey's voice rose. "Four to one—what were you thinking?"

"I'd say she was thinking she's quite competent at her job," Lillian said.

Four to one. She'd taken on four men and won? Caz closed his eyes, pride in her skills battling the rage of worry.

"Well, all right. I'd love a drink, actually," JJ was saying. "Thank you. I appreciate it."

"No thanks, love. We'll have marvelous gossip to accompany our wine."

Caz leaned against the exam table as the clinic door closed behind the women. On their way to a drink, a retelling of the fight, and congratulating JJ on a job well done.

Because that was what friends did.

They didn't lose their tempers and demand a person retreat to a safer job, a safer world. Friends didn't do that. Family didn't do that. Lovers didn't do that.

Gabe wouldn't quit if Audrey told him to. He'd listen. He'd be extra careful. He wouldn't quit.

If there was an epidemic, Caz wouldn't leave the job, even if his woman demanded he stay safe. He'd listen, he'd take precautions, and he'd do the job he was born to do.

Caz cleaned up the exam room, disposing of the blood soaked gauze.

JJ's blood.

All the logic in the world wouldn't remove his need to see her safe.

CHAPTER NINETEEN

E *very normal man must be tempted, at times, to spit on his hands, hoist the black flag, and begin slitting throats.* -HL Mencken

"Dios, is there something in the water around here?" Regan's father muttered as they walked along the riverbank. On top of the snow.

Regan looked up, tripped, and Papá caught her arm to keep her from falling. Walking sure was different in snowshoes.

"Use your poles, mija," he reminded.

"Uh-huh." She forged forward, remembering to keep her feet farther apart. Snowshoes were wider than shoes. "What about the water?"

"It means..." He frowned, probably trying not to swear, cuz he was kinda grumpy right now.

She grinned up at him. His hair was all dark, and his eyes were dark, and his skin was brown, even though there hadn't been any sun in the last few days.

His eyes narrowed. "Why are you smiling?"

"I look like you." That sounded awful dorky. "I mean, I'm smiling cuz the sun is shining, and it's all sparkly out here."

He shook his head, grinned, and tugged her stocking cap down over her eyes.

Giggling, she pushed it back. "What about the water?"

"It's a saying. And applies since I heard you got into a fight at school."

She scowled. "You talked to Mrs. Wilner." Concentrating on her feet, Regan worked her way around a half-buried tree trunk. "What did you mean: *is there something in the water around here?*"

"JJ broke up a bar fight on Friday—against four drunks."

Regan stopped so fast she stumbled, and he caught her again. JJ hadn't come over all weekend or on Monday, either, even though it'd been Veterans Day and no school. "Was she hurt? Is she okay?"

Papá's mouth tipped up at the corners, but his eyes didn't smile. "She's all right. Got a bit bruised."

He tapped her nose. "*Is there something in the water* is a saying that means: is there some strange drug people are drinking that makes people act oddly? In this case, what's making all the women around here into MMA fighters?"

Regan snorted. He was so funny. "Not MMA. I only hit Shelby once." And kicked her once. And hit Brayden a couple of times.

"Uh-*huh*." He didn't believe her.

She scowled at him.

After brushing the snow off of a fallen tree, he sat down. She tried to sit beside him, but the trunk was so high, her butt wouldn't reach.

He lifted her and sat her on the log. "Picking you up is like grabbing a marshmallow."

She patted her puffy red jacket. Audrey said she and JJ had picked it out because it was one of her favorite colors—and that the color was beautiful on her. She really liked it.

The next time she looked up, his smile was gone. "What, Papá?"

"The fighting, mija. We need to talk about the fighting."

"The resort buttheads are..." She stared out at the lake. It was so covered with snow she couldn't tell it was a lake. "They're mean. To me, Niko and Delaney, an' some of the third-graders. Why do they pick on littler kids? That's like cheating."

"Sí, it is." He put his arm around her, pulling her up against him, and it made her feel good inside, that he still liked her even if he was pissed off.

He gave her a little squeeze. "People pick on other people because they think it'll make them feel better about themselves. They believe saying someone is ugly or clumsy will make them look better. Feel prettier or better."

"That's stupid."

"It is. They haven't figured out that you have to be happy with who you are. If they spent less time trying to pick on other people and more time improving themselves, they'd be nicer and more content."

"Yeah, that'd be the day."

"So, let's talk about improving you, instead." When she looked up, his eyes were laughing at her.

"I'm good. Better than they are."

"Ah, but we're not talking about them. Let's talk about the fighting, Regan. Is it working for you? Aside from that one second when you hit someone, how does punching those resort bullies make your life better?"

"Huh?" Make her life better?

"Think, mija. If something doesn't improve your life, why do it?"

She looked away and saw a humungous bird fly over the snow.

"That's a bald eagle. See the white head?" Papá smiled and tugged at her hair. "Tell me about your first fights. How old you were and why you first hit someone."

She dared a quick glance up. No, he still wasn't really mad. "Uh...I was little, like first grade, and there was all this Christmas stuff, and I didn't know anybody, and—"

"Wait, if it was Christmas, why didn't you know anyone? Weren't you in school all that semester?"

"Nah, I'd only been there a week. I was the new girl." Her shoulders slumped. "I'm always the new girl."

"Why?"

"Mom." The weight sat on her chest, heavier than her coat, than her clothes. She'd hated Mom sometimes. So why did she miss her so bad? "She got in trouble and got sent to jail, so I got stuck in foster care and got sent to a new school."

"Ah." He sighed. "If you were always the new girl, it must have happened a lot?"

She forgot he didn't know how Mom was. Had been. "Sometimes she was in jail. Or she'd find a guy, and we'd move in with him so...new school. Or she didn't like the city we were in, or she lost her job. Or we'd go to San Diego cuz she wanted to be warmer in the winter."

Papá looked mad for a minute, then he kissed her head, right on top of her stocking hat. "You were always moving and always the new girl. The other kids were mean?"

"Sometimes." She tugged on the fingers of her gloves. "Mostly. I'm littler. And brown. That makes me easier to pick on, you know."

"I do know. I had that problem...and boys probably fight more than girls."

Papá got into fights when he was a kid. That's what the uncles had said. "I never used a knife on anybody."

He busted out laughing. "You win, mija. Fists are safer, yes. So, you get into fights because you're little and new and think you need to push back hard?"

She nodded.

"All right. Only this is your home, and we're not planning to move. You won't be the new girl much longer, and these children will be your classmates for a long time. Do you want to fight them for years?"

Oh. She pushed closer to him, looking at the forest, the cabins on the other side of the lake. Years. That was like a long time. "What should I do? Won't they keep picking on me?"

Caz's heart almost broke. "Mija, there will always be bullies. The trick is to not give in and to try to avoid violence." Not something he'd been good at when he was her age. Nevertheless, he'd learned.

The memory of the last Rescue town picnic came to mind, the pleasure of holding a knife to a mouthy pendejo's throat, and he shrugged. *Mostly learned.*

"Always stand tall, look them in the eyes. Sound strong. I think you're already good at this, yes?"

That won him a tiny smile.

"After that, it depends. Walking away and ignoring them is the easiest solution. Make sure your teacher knows they're trying to push you around."

Regan made a face.

"Telling Mrs. Wilner isn't being a tattletale, Regan. If bullies get away with their behavior, they'll go on and hurt other children, little ones. The teacher needs to put a stop to it."

She nodded. "But the teacher isn't always there, and our aide's been sick."

"Sí. You can try talking. Shutting them down by facing up to them. Don't let them feel good about their crappy behavior. Saying things like: 'I don't know why you said that to me, but I don't care.' 'Thanks for letting me know.' Roll your eyes and walk away. If you make them feel stupid—without going so far as to start a fight—they will not want to continue."

"Oh. I get it. Nobody likes feeling dumb."

"Exactly. Also, bullies are cowards. If several of you stand together, they won't take you on. If you see someone being harassed, go to them. Have an understanding with your friends that you'll hang together against the assh—ah, the bullies."

Regan looked down. "That's why I got in the last fight. Shelby and Brayden were pulling Delaney's hair, and I yelled at them, and I pushed Shelby to make her move away."

The surge of pride was unstoppable. He couldn't keep from grinning. Dios, he was a terrible father. He'd probably ruin this child. Somehow, he needed to show her the balance. "We will make a bargain, you and I. If you start a fight without a good reason, you'll get in trouble at school and at home, too. If the bullies are only being rude, you shouldn't hit them or shove them. However, if they are pushing or hurting you or your friends, if they have made it physical, then—although you might get in trouble at school—you won't be in trouble with me."

He couldn't protect her. The feeling of helplessness made him shake. "Maybe you shouldn't go to school. You could—"

"Papá, I want to go to school." She patted his arm, comforting *him*. "Delaney is there. And Niko."

She was making friends. Widening her world. He couldn't keep her in a safe box and expect her to grow. "But—"

"I can handle the resort buttheads." Her shoulders were back. Chin up. Fuck, he was proud of her. She leaned into him. "If they were grownup, I'd need you."

Her facing off against an adult? The thought was horrifying. She was just a mite, so tiny and thin and—

The realization hit him like a blow.

He'd been even smaller when the druggie killed his mom and sister. Even younger.

All these years, he'd blamed himself for not stopping the bastard, yet as he looked at Regan, at her size, he knew there was no way he could have won that fight. He'd been a child. The pain was sharp, an abscess opening and draining so it could heal.

Folding both arms around her, he gave her a hard hug. "So, staying in school it is. I trust you to try for the middle path, yes?"

"I will, Papá."

"Good. Then let's head back. I think there's a pizza in the freezer. Pepperoni?"

Her delighted bounce was his reward.

As they walked toward the Hermitage, he saw the light in Mako's cabin. Upstairs where JJ lived.

Someone else he wanted to keep in a nice safe space—and who had shown how she felt about it.

He missed her, more than he'd have dreamed possible. She was working late today, but tomorrow...tomorrow it would be time to have a talk.

CHAPTER TWENTY

*N*egotiate—*and keep your weapon loaded. Otherwise, your diplomacy'll be a doormat for some asshole's feet.* - First Sergeant Michael "Mako" Tyne

JJ scowled at the light coming from the windows. Morning, already? She hadn't had any sleep, dammit. Again. Her bed was too cold. Too lonely. Dammit, she missed Caz more than she'd ever thought possible. The stupid, hard-headed dumbass male.

At least she had today—Wednesday—off since she'd worked extra over the weekend. Growling under her breath, she pulled the pillow over her head and tried to go back to sleep.

Around noon, she gave up and built a fire in the wood stove, had breakfast, then sat in the living room and worked on her crochet project—a dark red-and-black scarf for Regan.

No matter how annoyed Caz was, he'd let Regan have the scarf. Although he might not accept the matching larger one JJ'd crocheted for him.

Aaand, now she was grumpy again. After donning winter gear, she went out for a long hike in the snow, hoping the peace of the white-covered land would seep into her soul.

Once back, she worked on her grocery list, adding more items so she didn't feel as if she was the only unprepared person at the Hermitage. This survival stuff seemed to be contagious.

In that spirit, she settled down beside the toasty-warm wood stove and watched *The Martian* on her laptop. Best sci-fi survivalist movie ever, right?

Once it finished, she added potatoes to her list and was totally revved up to make a grocery run into town.

After a quick shower, she dried off and grimaced at her reflection in the mirror. There were ugly sutures in her forehead, and a red line where Caz had glued the slice over her cheekbone. At least, the swelling along her jaw had gone down; however, the bruising had turned a putrid-looking yellow-green. *Ugh.*

Unexpected sympathy for the doc welled inside her. Considering her appearance now, she must've looked an unholy mess when she walked into his clinic.

Avoiding the sore spots, she brushed her curly hair and looked at herself in the mirror. Bruises, gashes. Dark circles under her eyes. Sadness in the downturn of her mouth. She'd been avoiding Caz. Both him and Regan.

Who would have thought she'd miss them so much?

Little Regan had stolen her heart. All those giggles and courage and enthusiasm. Burning with brightness.

And Caz. God, she missed him. He had become her best friend. No, be honest, she felt more than friendship. Some was physical. When she was near him, there was an underlying sizzle as if her body was revved up and waiting for his touch. Some was simply...caring for a man. For him. A whole lot.

But even without the male-female stuff, she simply liked him. Liked being with him, working with him, talking to him. He was honest, kind, compassionate, and strong. He had a moral code and would stick to it.

He'd acted like her ex, yes, but for different reasons. Nash had wanted her to quit the force because he couldn't tolerate her being better than he was. Because he wanted to control her.

Caz simply wanted her to be safe.

His past had given him cause to react like that. She understood—really, she did—and it hurt to know what he'd gone through. What he'd lost.

Yet it was pretty obvious he wasn't going to accept who she was. What she did.

Knowing his past and his issues wasn't going to change her decision about what she did for a living. She wasn't going to give up the career she loved. No one would do that to her.

Hell, she loved the job even when she got hurt. Being a LEO was who she was.

She was...could have fallen for him. She'd so wanted to give him what he needed to be happy. But she couldn't. Not in this. It wasn't fair of him to think she would.

Dammit. Her heart ached because the truth was she needed to stay away from him.

With a sigh, she dressed and glanced out the window. Just after five and already night. Somehow, the darkness matched her mood.

Dante's would only be open for a little while longer. Coat on, she grabbed her purse and the grocery list.

Downstairs in the hallway to the garage, she heard noises from the big workout room. A glance through the doorway brought her to a halt.

Caz was working the tall canvas punching bag that hung on chains from a ceiling beam. Punch, punch, punch, dance back, roundhouse to head height, come down solid, punch, punch, punch, sidekick to where the opponent's knee might be. Each blow hit the bag with a solid sound she had to appreciate.

In leggings and a T-shirt, Regan stood to one side, watching. Fascinated.

Well, yeah.

God, the man looked deadly. Barefoot. Black sweatpants. A black sleeveless shirt was darker across the chest and back where he'd sweated through the material. His biceps, triceps, and delts were pumped-up—and looked harder than granite.

Made her want to touch. Just...touch.

He started punching the bag so fast she almost didn't see his fists move.

Her mouth went dry.

From the stories Gabe had shared, he and his brothers enjoyed brawling. And they all won at various times. Gabe through technique and good strategy, the son named Hawk through sheer berserk never-give-up. Bull overpowered his opponents with size and weight.

With Caz? Apparently, Caz was so fast and skillful his punches never missed, and his opponents rarely managed to get in a return blow. To top it off, if he got too annoyed, he'd pull a knife.

JJ spotted his boots and sure enough, he had a knife sheathed inside each. Well, as an officer of the law, all she could say was she was glad he was on the side of good.

Stepping away from the bag, Caz lowered his hands. "Like that, mija. Your turn."

As Regan took his place, Caz reached for a towel and saw JJ.

Shit. Why was she standing in the doorway, staring like a dumbass? She took a step back and—

"JJ." Just the sound of her name in his oh-so-masculine voice made her stomach quiver.

"Sorry, I—"

"JJ!" Tearing across the room, Regan hit like a bullet and wrapped her arms around JJ. "Where've you been? Are you mad at me? Did I do something wrong?"

Oh...double-shit. Appalled, JJ looked over at Caz who seemed equally startled.

Dammit, she'd been thoughtless to disappear without a word

to Regan. Kids were always sure they were the cause of whatever disaster occurred—from being evicted to divorces to getting abused by a parent. A kid simply *knew* it was her fault.

JJ bent to hug Regan hard. "I'm absolutely not mad at you, and you haven't done anything wrong."

The little girl's eyes brimmed with tears. "Are you sure? I didn't mean to make you come out in the cold to look for me or—"

"You went to save a kitty." JJ gave Regan another squeeze. "I'd have done the very same thing. And to hike out in the cold and the dark? That's pretty brave in my book."

A glance showed that Father Caz was frowning at her. *Oops.* "Of course, next time you'll tell someone before you leave, right? Take a grownup with you."

Regan nodded vigorously. "And take my emergency bag."

"Good. You saved a precious life and learned what to do better next time. Sounds like a win to me."

As Regan held on even more tightly, guilt stabbed JJ in the heart. She hadn't meant to hurt the girl.

Caz rubbed his neck and gave JJ a wry smile that said he felt the same way.

"I take it you're having fighting lessons?" JJ asked Regan. "Have you learned anything useful?"

With the resilience of youth, Regan jumped to the new topic. "Totally. How to make a fist and not break my thumb, how to punch, how to get away from someone grabbing me."

"Those are great things to know. Only...I thought you weren't supposed to be fighting." JJ threw an accusing look at Caz.

"No jumping to conclusions, Officer Jenner." Caz's lips quirked. "Mija, tell JJ what we agreed upon."

"If someone is mean, I'll walk away or use my words and, for sure, tell a grownup. But if they get...phyis—no, physical, then I fight back, cuz Papá says there's diplomacy an' then there's being a doormat, and I'm not a doormat."

Now, that diplomacy versus doormat sounded like a quote from the first sergeant. JJ carefully didn't smile. "That sounds like a well-thought-out response. Very nice."

"I know, right?" Regan grinned. "And if I hit someone, I should do it right."

Imagining the school turning into a war zone, JJ narrowed her eyes at Caz.

Although he smiled, his jaw was determined. He believed in Regan's walking away, but if anyone laid a hand on his girl, he'd ensure she could destroy them.

Stroking a hand down Regan's soft brown hair, JJ met his eyes. And nodded.

Caz heard a door slam at the front of Mako's house—the deck side.

"Regan, Caz, are you guys in here?" Audrey called.

"In the training room," Caz yelled back.

Audrey appeared in the doorway, blonde hair tucked up under a stocking cap, cheeks pink from the cold. "There you are. Regan, did you still want to bake a cake with me?"

"I..." Regan bit her lip, looked at the punching bag, then at him. At JJ.

"Go ahead, mija." He ruffled her hair. "Maybe JJ will have supper with us tonight and stay for a movie. We can cook her something special."

JJ stiffened at his below-the-belt scheme. He pressed his lips together to keep from smiling.

"Yes!" Regan grabbed JJ's hand. "Please, please, please?"

There was not a person in the world who could resist those puppy-dog eyes. JJ tried. "I...um, I should..." And lost. "Sure. I'd love a movie night."

The look she shot him should have fried his balls.

"Excellent. Let's go then, my girl. You can take some of the cake back to your house for dessert." Audrey's speculative look at Caz meant Gabe would be hearing about the tension. She pointed a finger at JJ. "Thanksgiving is next week—big dinner. You will be there, woman, or I'll sic your boss on you."

"Um." The uncertainty in JJ's eyes broke his heart. He'd caused that, damn him.

As the two left the room, she took a step toward the door.

Caz caught her arm. "No, princesa. We need to talk."

"No, no, we do not." Using the same technique he'd been teaching Regan, she jerked her wrist from his grip. "That was unfair, using Regan to get your way."

"Were you playing fair to disappear from our lives without any explanation?" he asked mildly.

"Don't give me that bullshit. You know why I'm avoiding you."

"Because you're a coward?"

Her face flushed such a deep red her freckles disappeared. "I'm no coward." She shoved him back a step. "Isn't that the problem, *Doc*? That I'm not willing to sit on the sidelines of life so you can be comfortable?"

That was exactly the humbling conclusion he'd reached. She wasn't the coward—he was.

Although an apology was on his tongue, he didn't speak.

Right now, she was revved for a fight, no matter what he said, partly from her tension and frustration. Partly from biology. In avoiding him, she'd had no exercise or martial arts workouts for several days now, and she normally worked out every day. Fighters needed to fight— which was why he and his brothers would indulge in a roaring melee now and then. Mako had never sat out a brawl.

"So I can be comfortable?" Caz gave her the same smirk he'd often used to goad Hawk in a fight. JJ wasn't the only one who needed a down-and-dirty sparring session. "Sí, I'd be more comfortable if you were an accountant. You're always in my clinic because you get hurt. Maybe you're accident-prone?"

Her hands closed into fists. She dropped her purse, yanked off her coat. Her boots and socks followed.

Then she punched him right in the belly.

As pain exploded in his gut, he jerked back. *"Fuck."* That'd hurt a hell of a lot more than he'd been expecting. The woman knew how to punch.

Hands raised, she danced lightly on her toes. Ready for more.

"Very nice, princesa." He rubbed his gut. "Taunting you into a fight might have been a bad idea."

"Taunting?" Her narrow jaw firmed as she realized she'd been set up. But rather than backing off, she started to circle him. She wanted this fight as much as he did.

He eyed her. She moved like a boxer, but from her stance, he'd guess her preference lay in a hard-kicking offshoot of tae kwan do or Muay Thai. Or a mixture.

He smiled. This should be fun. "No crippling."

"Done." Her fist popped out at him again, and this time, he moved enough to avoid it. She blocked his return punch. Spinning, she tried to kick his leg out from under him. He stepped out of the way, and they traded a flurry of punches and kicks, most blocked or avoided enough to take the force from them.

She was grinning, her temper gone.

His face probably held the same expression.

She was damn good. His training—years and years, starting with Mako—and added strength meant he'd probably win in an all-out fight, but she was no pushover. In a real fight, he'd have to work for a victory.

"You're good, Officer Jenner. Damn good." He barely avoided catching a kick to his groin and tsked at her. "No crippling, remember?"

"Broken bones are crippling." She waggled her eyebrows. "Smashed balls are merely agonizing. Or so I hear."

They spun, trading blows, grunting when something got through.

"What's the matter, Doc? Trouble keeping up with a woman?" She jabbed right, then left, her footwork a thing of beauty.

He contrived a look of worry. "Perhaps I am getting slow in my old age?"

"Yes, I'm sure I see gray in your hair. You're past thirty, right?"

His roundhouse—carefully pulled—thumped her ribs, and he followed with a punch to the chin that she barely avoided. "Thirty-one, sí. And you...little one?"

That earned him a front-kick to his thigh, hard enough to be grateful she hadn't aimed at his balls. Not that he'd have let that kind of kick past him.

"Twenty-seven." She growled at his skeptical look. "The freckles make me look younger than I am."

They did, as did the tousled hair.

"Remember not to hit me too hard," she snapped. "I might break, you know."

Redheads were known for having hot tempers. But hers was fading already. Perhaps because they were both sweating and breathing hard.

"I will be careful of you, my delicate flower," he promised and nailed her with a harder punch to her belly. To let her know in the most obvious way that he was being sarcastic.

Her breath huffed out, and she punched him back, her fist grazing off his jaw.

They were both going to have some painful bruises.

Time to call it quits.

"I worry, JJ." He caught her upraised leg, tossed her onto her butt, and grinned when she regained her feet faster than he'd expected. "I'm sorry I overreacted after your fight. Gabe said you took out four assholes damn fast. He's proud of you."

"He is?" When her expression brightened, his heart took a slow slide. That someone so marvelously competent should feel insecure was due to that asshole Nash.

If looked at with the same lens, Caz's overprotectiveness was just as insulting.

He was an idiot. "I apologize for what I said. I would never want you to quit a job that fulfills you."

When her hands lowered, he stepped in fast, grabbed her around the waist, and dropped with her onto the mats. Before she could recover, he moved on top of her. Ignoring her fisted hands, he bracketed her face and took her lips in a long, coaxing kiss.

Her hands curled around his wrists, pushed.

Not willing.

But when he started to move off, she went soft beneath him and slid her arms around his neck. "Caz."

"What do I need to do to earn your forgiveness, mamita?" He kissed her stubborn pointed chin, the freckles on her cheeks, her soft lips.

"It's okay." Her fingers tightened in his hair as she nibbled on his jaw. "I know you have a problem with women getting hurt."

With *women*? He'd tried to clarify what he felt for her in the clinic. Apparently, she hadn't believed him. "JJ, I hate to see someone I care about getting hurt."

Her breathing stopped for a second. "No."

"Sí. I care for you, mamita."

Her turquoise eyes gleamed with tears. "This isn't like you. You go through women like a hot knife through butter."

"I did, yes. My rules *used* to be: one night only and never someone from Rescue." Caz felt the barriers that had protected his heart being swept away like autumn leaves in the wind. "Neither of those rules seems to apply to you."

Her breathing stopped again.

He couldn't keep his heart safe. No longer. Because he wanted more from her than a one night hookup. He paused. She'd been lied to in the past. Hurt. *Be clear.* "I don't know what will happen between us in the future, mi princesa, but I would like to see where this leads."

"What about Regan? If we...if..."

That she would worry about his little girl turned him into a marshmallow. "Yes. It seems her mother was...indiscriminate in her men, and Regan has seen more than a child should. Nonetheless, we will be honest with her."

"No. She's still settling in, and we don't know where we're going with this. Maybe we can be friends and have"—JJ smiled slightly—"covert sex. Then she won't be hurt when you..."

When he broke off the relationship? That wasn't going to happen. This woman was going to be part of his life. Part of his and Regan's lives.

She felt right in a way that no one had, ever.

"All right, mi corazón." My heart—yes, that was how he felt. But if JJ would feel more comfortable at a slower pace with no expectations, then that was what they would do. The blunt words would be spoken soon enough. "Friends with covert benefits. For now."

"Okay." Her lips tipped up. "Um...since we're both already sweaty, want to get even more so?"

Despite her insecurity after Nash, she was still brave enough to say what she wanted. Was it any wonder he was falling for this woman?

"Look at you. Initiating sex. Very nice." He kissed her. Slowly. Tenderly.

When he lifted his head, her voice came out husky. "And?"

"I've always thought a fight should end amicably." He lowered his mouth to an inch from hers. "Very amicably."

This time, the kiss was deeper, more suggestive, and he was harder than a rock before they were done. However, there were practicalities to consider. "Do you happen to have condoms in your bedroom, mamita?"

"No. But I carry a couple in my purse over there." She flushed slightly. "I wanted to be like the guys."

"Like the guys, hmm? I should check and see if I can tell your girl parts from boy parts." Chuckling, he reached out a hand, snagged her purse, and handed it to her.

Still lying on her back on the mat, she propped the purse on her chest and pulled out her wallet.

After locking the door, he pulled off his shirt, then, ignoring her gasp, stripped off her jeans and briefs.

Down on his stomach between her thighs, he pulled her legs over his shoulders. Exertion had left her scent deeper than before. She smelled shower clean with a hint of sweat and tantalizing arousal. And she tasted like the ocean, heady and primal.

When he licked over her, she dropped her purse.

Now, didn't that make a man feel powerful? "I found the girl parts, I think." Smiling, he applied some effort to see if he could keep his woman from picking the purse back up.

As he used his fingers, tongue, and lips, her obvious pleasure hummed through him like a song. The lovely quiver of her thighs on each side of his head guided him, as did the clenching of her pussy around his fingers, the hitch in her breathing. So lovely.

He also felt when her brain restarted. How her body grew tense again. Ah, she was delightful.

Before she could begin to worry, he lowered her legs. Rising to his knees, he took her hands, pulled her to a sitting position, and plucked the half-crushed condom packet from her fist. After setting it on the mat, he pulled her sweater over her head.

She stared at him, obviously unsure why he'd stopped.

"Mmm, no bra." He played with her enchantingly small, firm breasts. Her nipples were so sensitive, she squirmed when he pulled and rolled them between his fingers. It was tempting to flatten her out on the mats and simply take her.

Too straightforward. She was a thinker, a worrier, and needed the gift of being relieved of those worries. Something he would very much enjoy doing.

He walked to the other side of the room and returned with the big exercise ball Gabe had bought for Audrey.

. . .

JJ stared at the gray rubber ball—it stood as high as Caz's knees. "What are you doing, Caz?"

"Come. Sit." He pulled her up, sat her on the ball, and smiled. "Lie back."

He arranged her body so she lay with her back and head on the ball and her legs holding her butt off the ground. "Am I going to do ab crunches or something?"

His grin flashed before he shook his head. "This position isn't exactly right."

"What?"

As he pushed her, the ball rolled beneath her until the cold rubber was beneath her low back and her unsupported head now hung down toward the mat.

"What *are* you doing?" She arched her back, flattening her hands on the mat, making a bridge to keep from sliding off the ball onto her head.

"Perfect." A low masculine chuckle sounded as he knelt between her legs—and she suddenly remembered she wasn't wearing any clothing. "Keep your balance, JJ, or you'll roll off."

"I won't roll off." After all, her hands were on the floor on one side. On the other side of the ball, her feet kept it from moving.

His warning became clear when he lifted her legs up and over his shoulders, resting a hand on her stomach. Holding her in place. His mouth came down on her pussy, lips teasing her clit, tongue flicking over it as he slowly slid a finger inside her.

Oh, God. The pleasure sizzling through her was so intense she wiggled. The ball shifted and started to roll under her, and she squeaked.

"Stay still, mamita." He didn't slow at all. His fingers thrust in and out, moving faster as he sucked lightly on her clit, rubbing the nub with his tongue. His mouth was hot and wet. The fingers inside her intensified every sensation until she needed to squirm—only she mustn't. Her muscles tensed, keeping her still and on the ball, as the pleasure simmered in every nerve in her body.

He paused for a second, blowing air over her sensitive clit, before engulfing it in warmth, using his tongue on one side, then the other. The needy pressure inside her grew. She tightened around his fingers.

It built and built until an overwhelming storm of sensation rolled over her. So much *pleasure*. Wave after wave swept through her. Her back arched farther, her hips bucked. She lost her balance and started to roll sideways. "Help!"

Laughing, he gripped her hips and held the ball steady. Pulling her up to a sitting position, he hugged her. "I love watching you climax."

She was still breathing hard, flushed, naked. And his words made her feel...wonderful.

His kiss was hard and possessive, then he kissed each sensitive nipple, making her quiver.

He rose. "Stand up for a moment, mi princesa."

After removing his sweatpants, he picked up the condom and sheathed himself. After pushing the ball into the corner, he sat on it, positioned far enough forward on the ball that his testicles dangled, big and heavy. Rising from trimmed black hair, his thick erection was rock-hard.

She stared, unable to look away.

"Come here, mamita."

There? She pulled in a breath and walked over.

"Turn around and sit down on me, very slowly. Legs outside of mine." Guiding her so her back was to him, he held her hip with one hand and his cock with the other.

Her pussy was still throbbing, every muscle relaxed, and she didn't have any words to argue. He'd made her come. Just like that.

His cock hit her entrance and slid inside slowly as he eased her down onto him. He felt huge, hot, filling her completely. "*God.*"

His chuckle was rough and dark. He was in, tight and deep inside her. Her legs were outside his, and as he parted his knees, she was opened completely.

The mirrors around the room showed...everything. Her tangled hair, her nipples peaked tightly, her mound and pussy.

"We'll play a bit, *sí*? I want to feel your hands on me." Leaning her forward, he took her hands and cupped them around his heavy testicles, showing her how to stroke and tug ever so gently. "Mmm, that's perfect, *mi princesa.*"

He grew harder inside her—and oh, she loved knowing what he liked and touching him like this. She was getting even wetter.

When he set his hand on her pussy, she sucked in an audible breath at the burst of pleasure. "I said '*we'd* play', didn't I?" he reminded as his finger circled her.

She met his eyes in the mirror, and he smiled. The slow slide of his finger over the sensitive ball of nerves sent heat streaking through her. And need. The intensity always ratcheted so much higher when he was deep and hard inside her.

For a wonderful time, they...played. Just touching. Exploring. He teased her breasts, never abandoning her clit. She explored his balls and the sensitive place where his shaft entered her.

Her need to come kept rising as the pressure inside her gathered more tightly. She squirmed.

"I need to move," she begged and couldn't believe the whining sound came from her. But...it was all right. Because this was Cazador. "Please, please, please?"

"You had only to say, *mamita.*" He nipped and kissed her shoulder, sending goosebumps down her arms. "Let's do this without falling off, yes?" He slid backward on the exercise ball until his weight was balanced in the center. Her toes barely touched the floor.

"Lean forward, put your hands on my thighs, and rock back

and forth. Just small movements." He tightened his hand over her breast, making her moan at the added sensation.

His hand was dark against her untanned skin. His other hand was between her legs, a hot pressure over her clit. So wonderful.

"Mamita. Move."

"Right, right." How in the world could she do anything when every thought disappeared with his touch? Leaning forward, she lifted her hips until he slid slightly out, then she dropped back. She went faster the second time. When the ball added an extra bounce, shoving him wonderfully deep inside her, her toes curled. "*Yes.*"

"That's it. Keep going." He punctuated his order by pinching her nipple, sending zings of pleasure down to her pussy.

Slowly, she rocked. Bounced. His hard hands on her pussy and breast kept her from going too far, from losing him, but, damn, it felt amazing. The place where his shaft hit grew increasingly sensitive, making his touch on her clit even more...*more.*

So much pleasure. She leaned farther forward. His shaft rubbed another spot. *God.* Oh there. *There.* The sensations kept heightening. Rocking frantically, she clenched around the hard penetration inside her.

More, more, more. Her whole lower half tightened for an infinite, ultimate moment then released in huge, mind-blowing waves of pleasure. "Oh, oh, oh." She gripped his hard thighs, her head tilting back, and the fireball of orgasm crashed over her. Through her.

Before she had recovered, he pulled out. Moving off the ball, he positioned her on her hands and knees on the mat, and knelt behind her, leaned forward, and entered her from behind in one swift thrust. One wonderful thrust. She contracted around him in little bursts of exquisite sensation.

With a carnal growl, he pulled out then started to hammer her, hard. Every thick penetration was more and more pleasurable, and then his hands gripped her hips as he pressed deep and came with a low groan.

Head hanging down, she gasped for air. Her arms were shaking, her insides trembling. The man was going to kill her. "I don't think that was what the ball was designed for."

"Exercise is exercise." With a low hum of pleasure, he ground his groin against her, setting off happy post-orgasmic quivers deep inside her.

His arm under her stomach held her up as he nibbled on her shoulder and then sighed and pulled out.

As he rose, she flopped over onto the mat and stared up at him. "You're a crazy man."

"Eh, so judgmental." He made a tsking sound as he headed for the bathroom to dispose of the condom.

When he returned, he joined her on the mat, pulling her over and on top of him. "Yes. I want you here."

That was how she felt, too. Bare, skin-to-skin. Touching him, breathing him in, hearing the slow thud of his heart under her ear...it completed something inside her.

His hand slowly stroked over her hair, down her back. "I missed you, mamacita. For more than just sex."

"Me, too," she whispered, rubbing her cheek against his damp skin.

After a while, she tilted her head. Mamacita, mamita—Spanish words sprinkled his English. Propping herself up on her forearms, she looked down at him.

Thick black hair, eyes the color of the darkest chocolate, the strong, clean jawline, the lips—so perfectly formed and so devastating on her body, the mouth that was already starting to smile.

"Question, please."

His eyes glinted with amusement. "Ask away."

"You've lived in the States all your life. Why does your accent come and go, and why do you swear in Spanish and all that?"

His expression went serious as he studied her face. "My father brought my mother here from Mexico. When I was two, he was killed—an industrial accident at work—and she stopped trying to learn English. We spoke only Spanish at home. When she was murdered, I was still struggling to learn English. On the streets, I ran with Mexican gangs. When Mako took me in at eight, I spoke mostly Spanish."

On the streets as a seven-year-old. Her heart wrenched. It was a wonder he survived. "You learned, obviously."

"I did. By the time I was eighteen, my English had no accent. Being homeschooled in the back of beyond, I didn't run into much prejudice until I enlisted. Then...well, there was a bigoted sergeant who had the IQ and attitude of a rutting moose and a lieutenant who wasn't much better. Since it was what they expected to hear from me, I gave them an accent."

She stared at the sardonic twist of his lips. "You deliberately provoked the bigots. Why am I not surprised?"

A Latino shrug was her answer. "As a Spanish-speaking, Special Forces medic, I was often sent to South America, and now, I still visit Mexico as a medical volunteer. My accent never had a chance to disappear."

The subtext was clear; he wasn't interested in losing his tie to his heritage.

But he did it by volunteering in deadly countries. That was so like him, wasn't it? "I guess you'd better start teaching Spanish to Regan, hmm? And me."

His arms tightened around her, his gaze warming until she almost melted.

God, she loved him.

CHAPTER TWENTY-ONE

G unfight Rule #1 Bring a gun. Preferably, bring at least two guns. Bring all of your friends who have guns. - Unknown

On Thursday, Bull stood in his second-story downtown office and studied the map of Rescue that nearly covered one wall. All of Mako's acquisitions were marked with red pins. Each of the properties Bull had sold also had a green pin. Leased businesses held yellow pins. There were still too damned many places with only red pins.

But they were making progress. A real estate broker was interested in setting up downstairs. A married couple had finally finished the new pizza place remodel. Talk about making his day.

As he walked back to his big mahogany desk, he heard the downstairs door open and shut, then Caz called, "Bull, do you have a few minutes?"

"Sure. C'mon up."

Footsteps on the stairs indicated another person with Caz. Lighter weight. Probably female.

Caz escorted JJ into the office.

JJ, hmm. All LEO, her hair was braided back tightly, clothes spotless, jacket open to show her uniform shirt. No wonder Gabe was pleased with her.

"JJ, good to see you." Bull motioned to the couch and chairs by the window that overlooked Main Street.

Caz drew her over to the couch and sat beside her.

"You look cold. I just made a pot of coffee." As Bull poured and delivered drinks, he tried not to frown. Their body language spoke of more than casual sex—looked more like intimacy and caring—and those emotions were worrisome. He wasn't sure he trusted this woman—any woman—with his brother. Audrey had been enough of a problem, but, at least her expressions displayed every emotion she felt.

As she'd shown all too well at the poker table, JJ could conceal everything she was thinking.

Bull sat down in a chair across from them. "What brings you to my office?"

"Did Gabe tell you about what happened to me in Nevada?" JJ asked. She could be blunt when needed. He liked that about her. Really, he did like her. Just, maybe, not with Caz.

"He mentioned you'd been harassed."

"It was, perhaps, a bit more than that." JJ told him—and Caz —about the police station in Weiler. Typical harassment for the first years, then how things had changed with a new chief of police. And how badly her life had gone downhill after breaking up with a fellow officer.

Her face was unreadable—she'd donned her poker mask—and her voice stayed even. But the hand wrapped around Caz's had white-knuckled fingers. The past few years had been brutal for her, more than she was willing to show them.

Anger roused in him. He glanced at his visibly pissed-off brother. Caz had never been much of a one for hiding emotions, and abuse against women was one of his hot buttons.

But Caz was letting JJ lead this talk, so Bull took a sip of his coffee and asked, "Are you going to sue them? Sounds like you have a case."

She sighed. "I don't want their money, and I don't want to muck about with lawyers. I just wanted to leave it all in the past, you know?"

"I can understand that. But...?" Bull motioned with a tell-me-more gesture.

"But what about the next female officer? Since the administration and officers got away with that behavior toward me, won't it be even worse for future females—as well as female citizens? I don't think an all-male police station is healthy for the community, especially a station that is prone to abusive behavior toward females."

Her reasoning was correct. "I agree. What do you want to do?"

"I thought you might have some ideas, 'mano." Caz motioned with his coffee cup toward Bull's desk. "You play in the business and legal worlds."

"Let me think for a minute." Bull considered. Her station was city police, not state police or feds with all their checks and balances. Since the police chief in Weiler was a Barlow, going up the ladder to complain wouldn't work. However...a Chief of Police was usually appointed by a mayor and council. That might be a vulnerable link.

"There were other female officers who had problems?" Bull asked.

"Yes. I know two personally who left because they couldn't stand the harassment."

Bull rose and walked across to his desk. "Give me names and contact information. Along with your training officer's information. Let me see what I can do."

Caz grinned and pulled JJ to her feet. "Help her set the Weiler police station to rights and I'll work on keeping your freezer filled."

"Damn, you're on." Bull grinned at JJ's confused look.

The doc was the best hunter of the four of them. Sure, Bull would've helped JJ no matter what, but if Caz wanted to sweeten the pot, no way would Bull turn that down.

He ushered them out of his office. "I'll get back to you when I have a plan."

Two hours later, he had a good grasp of the story.

He'd called JJ's training officer, the one who'd recommended her to Gabe. Turned out Mako'd been Gene's drill sergeant way back when, and he'd been at Mako's funeral. Hearing the retired officer talking about the bright young woman he'd worked with, how she'd taken hold, and how she'd been stabbed in the back by the very people who should have been on her side...it had pissed Bull off.

The harassment, the discrimination, ignoring rules and regs because she was female. Slander. It had all pissed him off.

It'd been touching to hear Gene get choked up when he said she'd called him from Alaska to thank him for his training, his friendship—and for sending her to Rescue.

Well, the people in Rescue knew how to value her. And, after talking with Gene, Bull had a better understanding of JJ.

Bull shook his head. They'd all been unattached when Mako died. Then Gabe had found Audrey. Caz had gained a daughter and now JJ.

Hawk was still single. And although he had a bottomless well of love he could offer a woman, that well had been capped off with unbreakable cement. There would be no family for Hawk.

Probably not for Bull either. He'd tried, fuck knew. Unfortunately, Gabe was right when he'd said women were manipulative, and an open, honest person like Bull would get exploited every time. Married twice, been burned twice.

Bull's mouth tightened. Gabe wasn't wrong.

He let out a breath and shoved the bitterness away. He had a family. Four brothers. Two potential sisters-in-law. And a fantastic niece. Good enough for any man.

Right now, he had a lovely bit of vengeance to accomplish for Caz's woman.

Unfortunately, he couldn't do more than set this into motion. But he had enough to hand over to the lawyers. More than enough.

Yeah, Nash and the other Barlows who infested the Weiler police station were in for a world of hurt.

CHAPTER TWENTY-TWO

H*ome is the nicest word there is.* ~ Laura Ingalls Wilder

Tuesday evening, with the cat prowling around his feet, Caz gathered supper's leftovers to empty into the latched chicken-scrap canister on the deck. The sound of Regan and JJ's laughter from the living room area made him smile. It had been almost a week since he and JJ had enjoyed makeup sex in Mako's gym.

JJ had missed Regan as much as Regan had missed JJ, and the last few days had been healing. Did JJ realize how important she was to them?

Earlier, she'd left him a text that she wouldn't be over tonight. That he and Regan should have a father-daughter night together. Was she worrying about becoming part of their family?

Regan wasn't about to let her off the hook. And after they cooked the spaghetti dish Bull had taught her, Regan charged over to JJ's to beg her to eat with them. To tell her all the food was ready so if JJ was tired, she wouldn't have to do anything. Caz grinned. Could anyone with a heart resist a little girl wanting to show off her new skill?

Certainly not JJ.

As he dumped the leftovers in the chicken can, his gaze caught on the brilliant light show going on in the night sky. The two cheechakos—newbies to Alaska—shouldn't miss this show.

He opened the door and called, "Pause your movie, grab a coat and shoes, and come outside."

A minute later, still pulling on coats, JJ and Regan walked out.

"Is something wrong?" JJ asked. "Do I need a weapon?"

"No, Officer Jenner. Look." He pointed to the sky and watched their eyes widen.

"Is that war?" Regan asked in a whisper. "It's not fireworks."

That his little girl would think first of war was a terrible reflection on the state of the world. Caz shook his head then tugged on her hair. "No, mija, that's called the aurora borealis. The northern lights."

JJ let out an awe-filled sound, and he put his arm around her. Yes, right here was where she belonged.

Sirius had followed them out of the house and meowed impatiently.

Caz snorted. "He's thinking, 'stupid humans, staring up at the sky'."

Giggling, Regan picked the cat up and returned to staring at the rippling curtains of greenish-white light. "What makes it that color?"

Such a curious and clever mind. Years ago, he'd asked Mako the same question. "A wind from the sun throws particles at Earth. This is what happens when those particles bounce off the oxygen and nitrogen—way up high, maybe fifty miles or so."

"Huh."

He grinned. "Or some people think it's the dancing spirits of the dead."

"I'm going with that explanation," JJ murmured.

He grinned.

As a breeze came across the snow-covered lake, Regan's hair flew into her eyes. As she tried to comb it back with her un-cat-impeded hand, she gave a huff of annoyance. And looked over at JJ's French-braided hair.

Helping his daughter pull her hair back, Caz frowned. He might know his way around a woman's body, but fixing hair? Not a skill in his toolbox. He'd have to learn.

JJ noticed the direction of Regan's look and the tangled strands in Caz's hand. "Long hair is troublesome, isn't it? Would you like me to French braid your hair? Maybe tomorrow before school?"

Regan's mouth dropped open. "Really?"

"Sure. Run on over after your breakfast. It'll be fun."

The happiness in Regan's face was like the sun coming out.

As they turned to go back inside, a low drone sounded with the distinctive buzz of a Cessna 185 flying low. Approaching.

The bush plane circled the Hermitage. It was obviously preparing to land.

Caz hurried into the house, to the garage, and used the master controller to flip on the Hermitage's floodlights that illuminated their private road. Regan and JJ crowded beside him as he walked out to watch.

The pilot made a quick pass, probably checking the windsock and snow gauge, then the plane descended in a neat line between the solar LED pole lights that marked the runway beside the road.

"It landed on the snow." Regan's voice was filled with wonder.

"The plane has skis on the bottom," Caz told her.

A door slammed, and Gabe stepped out of his cabin in boots and coat. Bull was still at the roadhouse, or he'd be out here, too.

Hawk was home.

. . .

JJ studied the plane then Caz's broad smile. "Would this be your pilot brother?"

"Yes, that's Hawk's plane." Caz took Regan's mittened hand. "He's come home for Thanksgiving—and it's about time. Let's go greet him."

JJ hung back. "You go on and—"

"Come, princesa." Caz tucked a hand behind her back, guiding her forward. They walked down the cleared road nearly to Gabe's house then tromped through the deeper snow to where the Cessna sat, pinging in the cold night air.

The door opened, and a man appeared, pulling on a jacket. Using the door to balance, he lowered himself carefully onto the small metal step and down.

"What the hell?" Caz muttered under his breath. He put Regan's hand into JJ's and hurried forward. "Hawk. How badly are you hurt?"

"Fucking-A, don't shit your pants. I'm fine." The man's voice was rougher than a truck load of gravel.

"Don't bullshit me, 'mano." The doc blocked Hawk's path. "Where?"

"Sliced-up leg, couple busted ribs—all on the left."

"Sucks to be you." Gabe joined the men. "It'll hurt, but can you get your arms over our shoulders?"

Hawk didn't answer, just complied. The glaring floodlights showed how his face tightened with pain.

Caz glanced at JJ and Regan. "Can you two get coffee and soup started at Mako's?"

Hawk shook his head. "My place—"

"Your place will take time to warm up. You'll sleep downstairs at Mako's tonight," Gabe said.

Hawk shot him a glare, but nodded.

JJ almost smiled. Caz had mentioned that Gabe had been the boss of the boys in foster care—and ever since.

"C'mon, Regan," JJ said. "Let's go cook."

As she guided Regan through the snow, she heard Hawk's low growl. "A female and a kid? Here? What the fuck?"

JJ set her jaw. He didn't have to like her, but he'd better be nice to Regan.

By the time she heard them enter the garage, JJ had a can of beef and barley soup simmering on the stove, coffee poured—and had given Regan a mug of hot chocolate.

Murmurs and low swearing drifted down the hallway. It appeared Hawk needed help getting his snow-covered boots off, and he wasn't appreciative. At all.

A glimmer of sympathy ran through her. She felt the same way about accepting help, especially if she was tired and hurting.

Being in pain, the guy didn't need strangers around. She'd serve their coffee and head up to her rooms or take Regan to Caz's.

She looked over to see the men help Hawk into the living area.

"Regan, can you take this in and put it on the coffee table, please?" She handed the girl a tray with the dishes, silverware, and coffee fixings.

JJ followed with the pot of soup and the coffee pot. "Here you go, guys."

Face dead white, Hawk was leaning back on the sectional, legs stretched out in front of him. In vivid contrast to Caz's dark coloring and sharply chiseled, clean-shaven gorgeousness, this man had sandy-colored hair, steel-blue eyes, and a short beard. His tanned fair skin was marred by a white scar that ran across his forehead, and a thicker one down his left cheek. Rather than Caz's rippling panther-like musculature, Hawk was bulky with muscle.

He wasn't as nice as Caz either. When he looked at JJ and Regan, the blast of animosity was palpable.

Well.

Regan shouldn't be subjected to the jerk. "Caz, I'm going to take Regan back to your cabin. It's a school night."

After glancing between his brother and his daughter, the doc's mouth tightened. "That would be helpful, mi princesa. Thank you."

He curled his arm around Regan. "Mija, can you go with JJ and let her help you get ready for bed?"

Regan bit her lip, looked at Hawk, and went up on tiptoe to whisper in Caz's ear, "Is he *really* my uncle?"

CHAPTER TWENTY-THREE

A prerequisite to empathy is simply paying attention to the person in pain. - Daniel Goleman

It was the day before Thanksgiving. Starting tomorrow, Regan would have four days without school. No *school.* How chill was that!

She stuffed the last bite of breakfast into her mouth, grabbed the pretty scrunchies that Miss Lillian had given her, and ran outside. JJ's cabin was next door; she didn't need a jacket for that.

Although, friggers, the cold was major. She grinned as she dashed across Mako's deck. *Friggers* was her new word since Mrs. Wilner and Papá didn't like her saying *fuck.*

She trotted into the house, through the humongous room, headed for the stairs, and stopped short. A guy was sleeping on the giant couch. He had a couple of blankets over him.

It was the new uncle. Hawk. Chill name, but... She stared at him. Papá and her other two uncles were pretty hot. Women were always doing flirty stuff around them, especially around Uncle Bull. All touchy and everything.

Girls might not go for this guy as much. His face was messed up—like scarred over his forehead and the side of his face. And he had a beard, only it wasn't neat and perfect like Uncle Bull's. It was ragged. He looked mean, and he had a ton of tattoos, all over his arms.

His eyes opened.

Frozen in place, she swallowed hard as he slowly sat up, never looking away from her.

"Finished staring?" The nasty growly sound he made was like when Papá dragged Sirius out of the fish guts.

She nodded.

"Then get the hell out of here."

"She's here to see me." JJ was there, suddenly, and her arm around Regan was like the most wonderful thing in the world. "And I live upstairs."

JJ took Regan to the stairs and whispered, "Go on up, sweetie. I'll be there in a second."

Heart pounding, Regan fled up the stairs and could hear JJ using her super-cold cop voice. "I don't know what your damage is, but stop acting like an asshole. She's only nine years old. Are you the only one of Mako's sons who didn't learn you're supposed to protect the children?"

Regan could feel her ears making a roaring sound, the kind that said she should run away and hide before a grownup got mean.

Only what if he hurt JJ? He was really big. What if JJ needed help? Regan stood frozen in the center of JJ's living room, stuck between actions, unable to move.

When JJ walked in, Regan let out a squeak and ran over.

"Hey, hey, hey, you're okay, sweetheart." JJ hugged her.

Like a baby, Regan started to cry. "I thought he'd hit you."

. . .

"I thought he'd hit you." The high little voice from upstairs was far too clear. As was her crying.

Leaning forward on the sectional, Hawk dropped his head into his hands. *Fuck. Way to screw up, dumbass.* He'd made Caz's kid cry. *Great start to coming home, buddy.*

Christ, he hurt. His leg felt as if a wolf was gnawing on it like a tasty bone, chomping from calf to thigh and back. With every move he made, his ribs exploded in agony.

He had good reasons for being in a shit mood, dammit, and having the kid stare at him as if he was a horror-movie monster hadn't helped.

Guilt hunched his shoulders. How many excuses for his shit behavior could he make? The woman was right. Hell, he'd scared a little kid. Yeah, being looked at like a freak burned—always had—but didn't mean he should be an asshole.

The sarge would've tossed him into a snowbank.

With a grunt of pain, Hawk managed to get to his feet. Gabe had told him to wait for help this morning, but fuck that. He'd take himself off to his cabin if it killed him.

Everyone would be better off without seeing his face or enduring his bad temper.

Early Wednesday evening in his living room, Caz took a sip of beer and swirled it around in his mouth, savoring the bite. He glanced over at Bull who sat in the big overstuffed chair. "This is for spring?"

"Yeah." Bull'd brought bottles from his brewery in Anchorage. It was a tradition for him to use his brothers as taste-testers. "The amount of hops seemed appropriate. I save the malt-heavy ones for fall or winter."

"I like it." Drinking more, Caz moved his sock-clad feet toward the wood stove that radiated warmth. The chunk of firewood he'd added crackled loudly as it burned. "It's better than the one you did last year. That one tasted like cat piss."

Bull gave a gut-busting laugh. "Thanks, bro. Unfortunately, my customers agreed. That one is history."

Caz eyed his brother. "When I went by, Hawk didn't even open the damn door. He said Gabe'd fed him, you changed his dressings, and he didn't need anything-the-fuck-else."

Bull ran his hand over his shaved scalp—something he did when he was troubled. "Yeah, he's in asshole-mode. He let me in long enough to help with the bandages and kicked me out."

Caz scowled. "Everything look all right?"

"No signs of infection. I told him you'd see him tomorrow, like it or not." Bull snorted. "He's worse than a hibernating bear when he comes home wounded."

"Papá." Followed by Sirius, Regan came out of her bedroom with several papers. The teacher had assigned the children to write about the snowstorm. "I'm all done."

"Homework, hmm?" Bull held out his hand. "Can I see?"

Without a second thought, Regan gave him her work and leaned against his knee as he read.

Caz smiled. The Bull could win over anyone and anything quicker than anyone Caz had met—even a wary little girl from a foster home.

It was good to see her settling in, finding her place in the family.

"Interesting. I like the way you broke down what you did right and what you'd do better next time. Sounds like the way the sarge debriefed our missions." Bull ruffled her hair. "You're as smart as your dad."

Regan beamed. "Are you going to eat supper with us, Uncle Bull? I can help cook."

"Sure, little bit. I'd like that. I'll teach you to make chicken parmesan." He glanced at Caz. "Anyone else coming? Hawk or JJ?"

"Just you." Caz half-grinned. "Guess we're just not very popular."

Regan's stricken expression wiped his smile away. "Mija?"

"I'm sorry, sorry, sorry! It's my fault." Her eyes puddled with tears. "Hawk doesn't like me an' maybe JJ doesn't anymore, too, cuz I messed up, and she was mad at him, and he might've hit her."

What the hell? Caz pulled Regan closer and ran his hands up and down her arms. "Who might have hit her?"

"Mr. Hawk. Cuz I stared at him, and he told me to get the hell out of there, and JJ came down and got me and called him an asshole."

Hawk swore at Regan? Anger flaring like a wind-whipped bonfire, Caz bit back the curses he couldn't say with his daughter there.

"Regan, I—" Bull stopped and glanced at Caz for permission to step in.

Just as well. Caz gave him a short nod, relieved that he had time to finish fighting his temper down. Wrapping his arms around Regan, he set her on his lap.

Bull leaned forward. "Little bit, I'm sure JJ isn't mad at you. She's a cop, and keeping people in line is what they do, right?"

"Oh." Regan bit her lip. "I guess I didn't think of that."

"As for Hawk. I know why you stared—all those scars and tats." Bull shook his head. "Everybody stares, but it bothers Hawk."

Regan looked down at her lap. "I shouldn't've stared."

And Hawk shouldn't have sworn at her. But it might help if she understood him a little better. Caz gave her a comforting squeeze. "You know how you feel about always being the new girl?"

Her mouth twisted unhappily. "Uh-huh."

"Kids stare at you, like you're different and not one of them."

Caz knew the ugly feeling. It would probably bother Regan even more than it had him. "And you hate it, sí?"

"Yeah," she whispered.

"Because you hate it, do you get grouchy with the kids who're staring at you? Maybe get rude to them?"

Her nod was reluctant. "Mr. Hawk got grumpy. Like I do."

His daughter had the courage to face the truth; she made him so proud.

"Sí."

"He's also hurting, Regan." Bull set his forearms on his thighs.

"Huh?"

"His helicopter went down in a bad place, and his left leg got all ripped up, from here to here"—Bull ran his finger from his calf to above his knee—"and his ribs are broken. Whenever he moves, it probably feels like someone is punching him in the side."

Actually, as Caz knew from unhappy experience, the pain was more like someone shoving a knife between the bones. But close enough.

Regan's eyes were wide. "Is he gonna be okay?"

"He'll heal. But pain makes people cranky, and we all have things that set us off when we're cranky." Bull shook his head. "Or even when we're not."

Caz winced. He had his own hot buttons. Like last summer when some damn Patriot Zealots had called him racist names and then shoved a woman. They might've pissed him off, but after the fight, he'd been in a fine mood.

Not a story he'd share with his little warrior.

"I guess I got things that make me mad." Regan tugged on her hair and watched Bull carefully. "What are your things?" Her wary expression indicated she didn't want to blunder into upsetting Bull the same way she had with Hawk.

Regan had a wise soul.

Bull came across as a friendly, approachable person, but that surface friendliness covered a very guarded interior. No one escaped being orphaned, living on the streets, or being in combat without some emotional damage.

They had all suffered. Bull just hid his wounds better than his brothers did.

"It's a good question, mija." Caz looked at Bull.

Well, hell. Bull barely kept himself from scowling...because Caz obviously wasn't going to bail him out.

Two pairs of brown eyes were focused on Bull.

Biting back a quick, easy answer, he considered. His worried little niece wanted the truth—and Mako hadn't raised them to take the easy route.

He rolled the cold bottle of beer between his palms. He knew full well what shit riled him up. The good news was that Regan would never be the cause. The bad news was she'd undoubtedly see him behaving badly someday. At least if he answered her question, she'd know why.

"I'm pretty even-tempered." He ran a hand over his goatee and gave her a rueful smile. "But I do get angry sometimes. You know how they tell you kids that your body is your own, and strangers shouldn't touch you? "

Regan nodded.

It was excellent that children learned that these days. "Well, sometimes adults get over-friendly with other adults, and I don't like being handled if I haven't given someone permission."

The kid looked confused for only a second. "You mean those women who're always grabbing you?"

"Exactly." He was fucking tired of it, in fact. Why a woman thought she could run her hands over him when she'd slap a guy for doing the same thing to her, he'd never know.

When he'd been a young, horny SEAL, he'd mostly enjoyed being lusted after. For the first year or two. Then, not so much. Later, not at all. Especially after he'd heard a woman tell her friends, "*I don't care if he's smart or stupid or anything. Just look at the guy. If his dick compares to the rest of him, I'm good.*"

Over the years, he'd heard variations on the same theme—and grown increasingly disgusted.

His father's girlfriend had said that kind of shit about his father. Had hung all over Dad until he'd given in. Had been the reason that the car...

Mouth tight, Bull gave himself a shake to escape the waking nightmare.

Regan watched him with an unhappy gaze. "Okay, Uncle Bull. I won't touch you unless you say."

Dammit. Way to scare the baby. Bull huffed. "Little bit, you're family. You have my permission anytime, anywhere." He opened his arms.

The smile and hug he got melted his heart.

Before he could fall into a morass of sentiment, he straightened. "You know, if you go fetch us a couple of eggs, we could make a cake for dessert. Chocolate, right?"

She gave a happy squeak. "Chocolate cake?"

"Why not?" Bull averted his gaze from his brother's annoyed stare. Health professionals like Caz were all about salads and low-fat foods. Poor bastards.

"Two eggs coming up." Regan grabbed her coat and was out the door.

Caz leaned back in his chair and chuckled. "You realize the smell of chocolate cake will probably drift over to Hawk's deck."

"Yep." As it happened, chocolate cake was Hawk's favorite dessert. And even in the dead of winter, Hawk would sit outside and watch the stars or the northern lights. "Everything I said to Regan was true—but it doesn't mean we'll let him get away with being an asshole to a little girl."

"No. I intend to visit him later tonight. We will talk." Caz's mouth was set in a firm line, and Bull felt a touch of sympathy for

Hawk. Unlike Gabe, Caz rarely lectured his brothers, but when the doc took one of them to task, he never lost.

As Regan trotted across the deck, the fluffy cat appeared and did a whirlwind pounce on Regan's boots before skittering away.

At the infectious sound of little girl giggles, Bull grinned and then gave Caz a commiserative look. "She's smart, charming, and sweet. Add in those eyes and that face, and guys will be flocking to her before she even hits her teens. Bro, you are so screwed."

"Dios, I know."

Bull rolled his beer between his palms and smiled slowly. "You realize any young man interested in her will run a gauntlet of uncles. Hell, even Hawk will be on board for that kind of fun."

And if any guy dared to mess with little Regan, Bull would rip the asshole apart like a ragdoll.

Later that night, after Regan had gone to bed, Caz let himself out of the house and crossed to Hawk's cabin. At the deck door, he could see his brother sitting on a dark leather armchair in front of his glass-fronted woodstove. No beer, no book, just staring into the flames.

Pity slid through Caz, fraying his anger. He tapped on the sliding glass door, waited a second, and let himself in. No point in waiting for an invite that'd probably never come.

Glancing over, Hawk didn't speak.

Caz opened the fridge, pulled out a couple of beers, opened them, and took a seat in the matching oversized chair. There were only two chairs in Hawk's living area—that said a lot, didn't it?

Even with Hawk's minimalist preferences, the room felt unfinished. Unlike Caz's cabin with glossy cherry wood furniture, oriental carpets, and light upholstery, this rustic-style room had rough-finished dark beams, reclaimed wood for the tables. Dark.

No pillows, no carpets. Hawk had never indulged himself with anything soft.

He could break a brother's heart.

Caz held a beer out.

Face unreadable, Hawk took it, drank some, and set the bottle down.

They sat for a few minutes, watching the fire.

"She's yours, huh?" Hawk's steely eyes were hard, his tone almost belligerent.

Caz smiled slightly. "She looks like me, yes?"

After a long pause, Hawk sighed. "Yeah. Fuck. I never figured on kids here."

Caz got it. His brother'd never planned on children for any of them. Because the pilot who could dance a plane through turbulent winds, the sniper who could traverse any land was the same one who rejected any change in his personal life. He'd always wanted his home and family to stay the same.

"Hearing I had a daughter came as a shock to me, too."

"You keeping her?" The edge in Hawk's voice told how he felt.

"Sí." Caz ran a finger through the moisture on his bottle. "Her mamá is dead, and there is no one else. I took her from a foster home. Should I have left her there?"

Hawk's experience with foster homes had been ugly. His jaw tightened. "No."

"Regan is only nine, 'mano, and her mother wasn't a good one." Caz softened his voice. "She's had no stability. No one who truly loved her. I can give her that."

"A kid will mess up your chance of fucking every female in the state."

Caz chuckled. "True enough. However, with JJ, I lost my interest in other women."

Hawk's hand tightened on the bottle.

"I intend to keep her, too."

The look Caz got held anger. "Maybe we should just open the damn doors and let everybody in."

Caz crouched in front of the woodstove and put in another chunk of firewood. The wood sat for a second on the sullenly glowing coals before bursting into flames. "The sarge didn't like people. Wanted to stay as far from them as possible."

"Smart man."

"Yet he ended up with four children. He changed our lives." Caz straightened.

Silence.

"And we changed his. Read his letter to us again, Hawk." Caz waited a second, then laid a hand on Hawk's shoulder. Reminding his brother that he was loved. "Our family has grown by one little girl. Someday also, a tough cop with a big heart. Can I ask you to be nice to them, 'mano?"

The muscles under Caz's hand tightened before Hawk exhaled. "Yeah. Sorry. I was...outta line with your kid."

There it was, the apology and promise he'd known Hawk would give. Caz squeezed his shoulder. "*Our* kid...Uncle Hawk."

CHAPTER TWENTY-FOUR

R*eputation is an idle and most false imposition, oft got without merit, and lost without deserving.* ~ Act II, Scene III, *Othello,* Shakespeare

At Mako's cabin on Thanksgiving, after nibbling on salmon pate and crackers, Bull had declared the turkey ready, and everyone had helped carry platters and dishes to the big dining room table.

Caz shook his head in amazement. The amount of food there would induce terror into anyone who worried about calories. Bull had made the traditional turkey, mashed potatoes, alder smoked reindeer sausage dressing, and gravy. Then they'd all added a few of their Alaskan favorites. Stuffed moose hearts. High bush cranberry sauce made with cranberries they'd picked this fall. The goose he'd had in the freezer had been turned into nigliq soup, one of his favorites.

Lillian had been invited, but the motherly Brit was hosting her own dinner for a batch of family-less men like Tucker and Guzman. She and Dante would stop by later for drinks and desserts. In anticipation of their visit, pies and sweets lined the counter in the kitchen.

Caz smiled as everyone settled around the big table. All seven. His family.

As the oldest son, Gabe had given in to pressure and taken the head of the table. They all felt the sarge's loss, but this was right. Death happened. Change happened.

Why had Caz been arrogant enough to think he could prevent it? Could keep people from getting sick, from being in accidents or burglaries or explosions? As Regan leaned over to whisper to JJ, Caz smiled. Hell, he couldn't even keep his loved ones out of snowstorms.

Rather than fighting the inevitable, he would simply appreciate and cherish his loved ones for as long as he could.

Bending, he kissed the top of Regan's head.

She looked up at him, nose wrinkled in a quizzical expression. "What was that for?"

"Because I remembered how much I love you."

"Oh. Okay." She leaned into him and whispered, "I love you, too."

JJ was watching, her expression tender.

Caz touched her cheek, to give her the sentiment silently because neither of them had said the words yet. Maybe her heart would hear.

Gabe cleared his throat and lifted his glass of wine. "To Mako. We miss you, Sarge."

Everyone touched their glasses together in a myriad of clinking and then sipped. Regan was beaming because she had a wine glass, too, although it was filled with apple juice.

Picking up the turkey platter, Gabe held it for Audrey. She took a slice, and he took one, then started it on its way. That was the signal for everyone to do the same. Caz took turns with JJ in helping Regan get food.

Observing Mako's protocol for meals, they went around the

table, telling about their highs and lows since the last time they'd gathered.

Bull was having trouble keeping chefs. Rescue didn't have enough social life for the city-raised bachelors.

Gabe and JJ had tangled with a couple of PZs, found the men had outstanding warrants in Anchorage, and sent them away to spend the winter in a nice warm jail. The two cops were so pleased, and everyone had laughed.

Audrey, who balanced running the library with being an internet researcher, had been digging up information on grizzly bear attacks for a thriller writer. She rolled her eyes and told them, "It's not a good dinnertime subject."

Seeing Regan's wide eyes, Caz diverted the conversation with his own offering. "I'm collecting a list of people with medical and first-aid training. Kenai Peninsula didn't have many fires this year, but it's getting drier. We need to be prepared."

As his brothers nodded, he caught JJ and Audrey exchanging grins. Audrey added, "Boy Scouts are taught 'Be Prepared', but Mako's sons take that a dozen steps further."

"True enough." Caz looked across the table. "Hawk, what've you been up to?"

Hawk gave him an annoyed stare. He'd undoubtedly hoped they'd overlook him—as if.

Everybody waited.

With an irritated grunt, Hawk said, "I was working for the government with my last job—the one where I got hurt. But the contract is finished, and I'm done."

Gabe eyed him and interpreted, "You're home for good."

"So it seems."

Grinning, Gabe and Bull gave a hooyah—the SEAL's battle cry. Caz met Hawk's gaze and lifted his glass.

Although Hawk's expression didn't change, his gaze softened.

Time to let him off the hook. Caz smiled down at his daughter. "How about you, mija? Do you have anything to say?"

"Uh-huh." She set her fork down and pulled in a breath. "Uncle Bull?"

"Yes, little mite." Bull lowered his fork, giving her all his attention.

"Will you teach me to make turkey and dressing an' gravy and potatoes?"

"You bet. You'll be my official junior sous chef."

Regan's grin became even wider with the congratulations from around the table. Bull seemed pleased, as well, probably because Regan jumped into everything wholeheartedly. She would be an asset in the kitchen.

Hawk didn't speak, although Caz'd been pleased to see him give his semi-smile at Regan. It'd take a hard heart not to smile, and Hawk's heart wasn't hard—far from it. When Caz had complained about his brother's behavior, Mako pointed out that, oftentimes, injured animals were aggressive to hide their vulnerability. Hawk's bad temper covered soul-deep wounds. Someday, perhaps, his brother would heal.

But it meant that Hawk didn't like change, especially with home and family. He could, eventually, be won over. Sometimes.

Audrey had succeeded, probably because she'd saved Gabe's life. Then the clever librarian had found Hawk's favorite authors and started bringing him books from the library.

JJ, though? Getting her and Hawk to accept each other? God help him.

Regan was still awful full. After Miss Lillian and Mr. Dante arrived, everyone sat around, talking and having dessert. The pumpkin pie was pretty good, but cherry pie *slayed*.

Now, she sat on the couch beside Miss Lillian—no, beside *Grammy*. Since Miss Lillian didn't have any kids, she'd said Mako's sons were hers now and that made her Regan's grandmother.

A grandmother. How chill was that? Back when Regan was a baby, they'd lived with Mom's mom. But that grandmother died, and Regan didn't remember her hardly at all.

Having Miss Lillian instead was...really okay. Grammy'd been an actress in England, and when she got upset, she said Shakespeare stuff like *scurvy varlet*. Way more dope than calling someone a stupid butthead.

This afternoon, she'd listened to Regan's speech for tomorrow's winter festival and said it was great. A *real* actress liked her speech. Regan had grinned, like, really big.

The deck door opened, and Uncle Gabe and Uncle Bull came inside, all dressed for cold weather.

"Why are you wearing glow sticks?" Regan pointed to the bright red glow bracelets circling their coat sleeves.

"The night has come." Uncle Bull motioned to the window and the darkness outside. His voice got even deeper. "We wear the red light so you can see your doom approaching."

A chill ran down her spine, and Regan edged closer to Papá.

He put his arm around her. "What doom?"

"Foolish inhabitants of the Hermitage," Uncle Gabe folded his arms over his chest. His face looked mean. "Killer Bull and I need a cave for the winter. We will take the Hermitage for our own."

Papá's lips twitched in that way that showed he was trying not to laugh. He gave her a squeeze before he stood up and crossed his arms over his own chest. His face turned mean, too. "You can't have the Hermitage. *We* live here."

Bull's laugh was scary. "Not for long. We're taking Mako's cabin—and will kill everyone in our way."

Regan shivered, but maybe she wasn't really, *really* scared. Not when Papá turned and winked at her. JJ had her hand over her mouth, and her eyes were all crinkled up. Audrey was biting her lip.

Grammy leaned over and whispered, "It's all in fun, my sweet.

Mako's sons grew up playing games and today, they're going to let us play, too."

Well, okay. Regan jumped to her feet and crossed her arms over her chest. "You can't have our place."

There, she was going to play, too.

Papá grinned down before he told Uncle Gabe, "The brave people here will defend the Hermitage to the death, but it will be your death. This is *war*."

Bull nodded. "*War*."

Uncle Gabe pointed to Hawk. "As the noncombatant, you're judge. Yell out when someone is put out of action."

Hawk looked like he'd rather fight, too, but he nodded.

Then Gabe scowled at Papá and nodded. "*War*."

Outside, Papá had sent everyone to different places—the "likely approaches"—and said to stockpile grenades. He whispered to her, "That means make up extra snowballs to throw from your hiding place."

Foster care had taught her a lot about hiding, and she found a dark place to scrunch under at Mr. Hawk's deck.

Where were the others?

JJ had wrapped a black scarf around her head and was hard to see. She was behind the chicken coop.

Audrey's light hair showed up real good where she was hiding behind Papá's cabin.

Miss Lillian had pulled her hood up to hide her white hair, and she'd taken one side of Mako's house with Mr. Dante on the other.

Not hiding, Mr. Hawk sat on Mako's deck. Papá said if Gabe and Bull made it onto the deck, they won.

No way. Regan shook her head. Her team was the good guys. They wouldn't lose. She'd make sure of that.

As she patted together snowballs—grenades—she saw a

glimmer in the darkness. It disappeared. Edging out of her hiding place, she stood up a little.

There. Uncle Gabe had burrowed into the deep snow so his glow stick couldn't be seen. Farther away, another glow stick moved. Uncle Bull.

A snowball sailed across the compound toward Uncle Bull, but it landed short. Two more followed. Still short. It was a really long way. Too far.

Uncle Bull threw—awful hard—and a shriek rang out.

"Right arm out of action, Audrey," Hawk announced.

"What?" Audrey yelled back.

"You can only use your left arm now," Bull explained in a loud voice. "Too bad for you, champ."

"Well, eff-it-all." Audrey's blonde hair disappeared back behind the deck.

Hands over her mouth to keep the giggles from escaping, Regan crouched down, making like a mouse. Bull had sure thrown that snowball a long way. She'd have to wait till the bad guys got closer.

They did. Taking turns running forward and then disappearing into snow banks and behind stuff.

Papá stepped out from behind the gazebo—when had he gotten over there?—and threw a grenade at Uncle Gabe from behind.

Only Uncle Gabe must have heard it. He turned and smacked the snowball away with his arm.

"Gabe's left arm is out of action," Hawk yelled. And Uncle Gabe dove behind the grill, and she couldn't see him at all.

Uncle Bull charged toward Mako's cabin. He was *fast.*

Audrey's snowballs were totally missing. Standing, Regan threw and missed and missed and then hit his leg. Even as he was falling, JJ jumped out from behind the chicken coop and her snowball got Bull in the right shoulder.

Regan was giggling, because he was pretending so good. Like he was really hurt. He even moaned.

Hawk called, "Bull, loss of right leg and left arm. A third hit anywhere will kill you from blood loss alone."

"Shit, bro, seriously?" came from Bull's snowbank. And Regan giggled harder.

Picking up her next grenade, she stepped out—and a snowball smacked into her left shoulder. Cold snow flew up into her face, and she shrieked.

"Regan, left shoulder is gone," Hawk yelled.

Not using her left arm—because that was part of the game— she moved back farther. And scowled, because now the bad guys knew where she was.

Papá said in a fight a person had to keep moving. She needed a new spot.

The deck had an overhang in front of the trellis stuff that kept animals out from under it. A big drift had piled in front of it. She pushed her grenades in front of her and crawled along the bare earth, hiding behind the high snowbank.

Crawling on one arm was *hard*.

On the other side of the deck, she flattened the snow in a little window in front of her so she could look out.

Uncle Bull was moving, creeping with his unhurt leg and one arm. He was awful sneaky the way he dragged his other arm through the snow so the glow stick was covered.

Regan stood up and threw and hit him right in the back.

"Bull, you're dead," Mr. Hawk called. And he looked right at her and made a kind of salute with two fingers.

Grinning, she dropped back down—and then a snowball hit right over her head.

Uncle Gabe was *good*.

The good guys had won and everyone had returned inside to "conduct an after action debriefing". In other words, to replay all the highlights of the battle. JJ grinned. She hadn't had so much fun in forever. The fighting had reminded her of being in paintball tourneys with Dad. So long ago.

She wiggled into a more comfortable place on the sectional—and off the bruised shoulder she'd banged against the chicken coop when jumping out of harm's way. Caz put his arm around her and...okay, it felt good to be claimed in that way.

"You guys grew up doing this?" she asked. Mako's sons were impressively skilled at war. At stealth. Bull was damned good. Gabe—well, she'd caught glimpses of Gabe only a few times.

She'd never seen Caz at all.

"At least once a week in various forms." Caz chuckled. "Forest battles, a team assault on a fixed target, attacking a moving threat. Different weaponry, different obstacles."

"Whenever dealing with energetic boys got to him, Mako'd revert to drill sergeant mode and send us off on some exhausting scenario." Bull nodded at Lillian and Dante. "Excellent takedown there at the end."

JJ lifted her glass in agreement. The older couple had been amazing. Gabe had almost reached the deck, but the snow had been packed down, and he'd lost his cover. So he charged.

Caz had lunged up from behind him, knocked the chief down, and rolled out of the way. Lillian and Dante—and JJ—slaughtered Gabe with a barrage of snowballs. The two people might be older, but they were dead shots.

Lillian was such a blast. The Brit brushed her clothes off with regal nonchalance and walked over to the groaning, dying Gabe. "*Woe, destruction, ruin, and decay; The worst is death, and death will have his day.*"

She'd nudged him with a boot, smiled, and called, "Come along, my team. Let us celebrate our victory with tea and biscuits."

Not that hot chocolate and second desserts had settled people down that much, especially Regan. The girl was still vibrating with adrenaline. She'd done so well—definitely her father's daughter.

"A good battle, all around." JJ looked down at Regan who'd curled up beside her. "You, my girl, can be on my team any time."

The way her face lit up could melt the hardest heart.

"Time for something other than fighting. Someone needs to unwind a bit." Bull grinned at Regan, rose, and took two instruments off the racks along the wall. His guitar and... He handed a violin to Hawk who sat a couple of feet down the sectional from Regan.

"There's a plan." After grabbing his guitar, Gabe handed Caz the drum.

Tucking the violin under his chin, Hawk drew the bow over the strings. The guys worked for a minute, getting the instruments into tune, then he played a quick introduction to John Denver's "Country Roads".

As the singing started, JJ joined in.

But Regan didn't. JJ frowned. The girl had taken to singing with the men like a duck to water. Why was she quiet now?

She was staring at Hawk.

"Regan," JJ murmured a warning, even as Hawk frowned at Regan.

She didn't notice his scowl, just slid down the sectional to right beside him. "That sounds like someone singing, only better." Her eyes were wide. She wasn't looking at Hawk, but the violin. "That *slays*."

Even as the singing faltered and stopped, Hawk's scowl slowly disappeared as he stared at Regan. "You like the violin?"

"I never heard anything like that." The plea in the big brown eyes was heartrending. "Can I learn?"

"Jesus." Hawk stared at her for a long moment. "Uh...yeah. Sure."

A second later, the big bad Hawk showed even he wasn't invulnerable to Regan's happy glow. Because the man almost smiled.

Needing a moment of quiet in all the chatter, JJ ran upstairs. Pulling on her slippers, she stepped outside onto her tiny balcony into the darkness. The air was so cold and clean, she pulled breath after breath into her lungs.

As her eyes adjusted, she saw the light from the windows glinting off softly falling snow. Again. Nevada got a few dustings of snow, but nothing like this. Alaska was an entire world of snow —and everything changed with it. Cars had to be plugged in at night. Going outside involved a whole ritual of donning coat, boots, gloves, scarf, and hat. And sometimes sunglasses. The sun on snow could be blinding.

But the nights...oh, they were glorious. If clear, huge stars would sparkle in an immense black bowl of sky. If the moon was out, the world looked as if the gods had spread glitter on every surface. If clouded over, the darkness was amazing.

Or there were the northern lights.

She pulled in another breath. The singing drifted upstairs to her and out into the night. Into the cold silence. An owl across the snow-covered lake gave a hoot.

Such a lonely sound.

She wasn't lonely, though. Not any longer.

On the evenings she didn't work, she joined Caz and Regan for supper, homework, and reading or a movie. Sometimes, the gang would gather at Mako's cabin. Every night, she and Caz would be together, then she'd discreetly sneak out well before Regan's rising. Although he frowned on the secrecy, he was letting JJ have her way. For now.

As long as she was in his bed every night.

She shook her head. Just the thought of him warmed her. The memory of how his hands felt on her body, of his kisses. Of him inside her, so thick and hard. The way his grip on her would tighten right before he came. His wicked sense of humor—like getting her to the point of orgasm—and reminding her to be quiet because Regan was asleep downstairs.

Trying to hold in her cries totally intensified her orgasm.

He knew that, the jerk.

Making love with him was always different. Sometimes intense, sometimes she felt so out of control it was almost terrifying, sometimes sex was simply fun. He was open about everything —what he liked, how he wanted her to touch him, what he enjoyed about her body, what he liked doing to her. It was freeing to share what she preferred...although he usually already knew.

He could read her so easily.

Had he been able to tell how much she loved him?

Smiling, JJ headed inside, shaking the snow out of her hair. He cared for her. He'd said so, and she was beginning to believe it. But there was no need to rush into anything. They had time.

Downstairs, she veered over to the kitchen to put the dessert leftovers away and do the final cleanup. Everyone was still over in the living area on the sectional, and she smiled as a song ended and everyone tossed out suggestions for the next. Even Regan.

Lillian walked around the island with coffee cups.

Regan followed with a few plates, and JJ stepped back to let her put the load into the dishwasher. None of the guys had dishwashers in their cabins, but since their family meals in this cabin generated so many dishes, they'd overruled the tech-phobic sergeant and installed one here.

Regan put the last dish in. "Done."

"Very good, dear." Lillian added her cups to the top rack. "I like your hair. Did JJ do it?"

"Uh-huh." Regan patted her French braids, miraculously intact despite the snowball fight.

"You can tell JJ's an expert," Lillian said.

"You can?" Regan snatched a cookie before JJ could put the lid on the container. They grinned at each other.

"Long hair is easy to braid. Short hair, now, that's tricky." Lillian ran her hand through her chin-length silver-white hair. "I never did master the art."

JJ chuckled. "I had incentive. I learned the painful way that if hair gets in your eyes, you'll lose fights. My only choices were to either cut my hair really short or keep it braided back."

Regan's eyes were big. "Police sure get in a lot of fights."

JJ laughed. "That was actually in a boxing class. Although, Rescue does seem to have a lot of brawling."

"We do. Too much alcohol. Too many obstreperous Patriot Zealots." Lillian's gaze met JJ's. "Small towns are prone to bickering—and *rumors*, as well." The slight emphasis had as much impact as a shout.

"All towns are filled with chatter," JJ said cautiously.

"Of course." Lillian smiled at Regan. "Child, would you please let Dante know that we need to be on our way?"

"Sure." Delighted to be asked for help, Regan trotted around the island and crossed to the living area.

"Rumors, Lillian?" Stomach churning with dread, JJ leaned against a counter and waited.

"I dislike listening to gossipmongers, but I thought you should be aware." Lillian kept her voice low.

"Of what exactly? What is being said?"

"The worst is speculation that you're sleeping with all the men at the Hermitage. One story says you had sex with Gabriel to get the job as his officer."

Shock silenced JJ completely.

"The buzz is that you did the same thing in your Nevada city."

No, no, no. The air had gone icy. With numb fingers, JJ finished snapping the cookie container shut and set it to one side on the counter.

Nash's smear campaign had driven her from Weiler. Now it had followed her here? All she wanted was to be as good a patrol officer and as enmeshed in a community as her father had been. When he died, she'd lost the sense of belonging to something bigger than herself.

She just wished to help. To fit in. Why was it so hard?

Even if she protested against the gossip, no one would believe her. Most people believed the worst of someone, especially of a woman in a nontraditional career.

"I see." JJ swallowed. "Thank you for telling me. It would've been awful not to know why people were whispering."

"That's what I thought." Lillian's face creased with worry, making her look older. "Combatting gossip is...difficult, but do remember that rumors fade."

"Yes, I'm sure the gossip will die down." She wasn't sure of that at all. In Weiler, her reputation had been utterly destroyed. What if it happened here?

"Well, it's time for Dante and me to get moving." Lillian took her hand. "Come and visit me this week."

"Sure." JJ endeavored to smile. "Thanks, Lillian. Really."

As she followed the older woman toward the living area, JJ came face-to-face with Hawk. He was leaning on the island, beer in hand...and had undoubtedly heard what Lillian had said.

Great. He'd already disliked her, now he probably figured she was slut of the week.

Ignoring his gaze, she walked past.

As she joined the others, Caz put his arm around her.

Her stomach churning from Lillian's news and feeling as if she'd fallen into quicksand, JJ leaned against him. What was she going to do?

Caz's brows drew together. "What's wrong, *mi princesa?*"

"Nothing." *Everything.* "I think I just need some alone time."

He frowned. Because he could undoubtedly tell there was more...but then he gave her a long wonderful engulfing hug and kissed her forehead. "Rest, then. We'll talk tomorrow, *mi corazón.*"

CHAPTER TWENTY-FIVE

The enemy invariably attacks on two occasions: When they're ready or when you're not. ~ Murphy's Laws of Combat Operations

On Friday after Thanksgiving, JJ found Dante behind the counter of his market. "Hi, Dante."

"Afternoon, girlie. How's the cop business?"

She smiled. "The snow cuts down on a lot of problems—and adds others." Was that why the gossip was spreading? People didn't have anything better to do? "I have a question for you."

"Shoot."

"When I got here, we'd talked about my renting a cabin. Is one available?"

"Well, damn, I thought you were settled in at the Hermitage. That's what Gabe told me." His brows drew together in a concerned expression. "Is there a problem with the men?"

Obviously, Lillian hadn't shared with him. JJ's shoulders relaxed slightly. "No. No, not at all. But I don't feel right about continuing to live in Mako's house. I'm not a family member or anything. It would be more appropriate for me to rent somewhere else."

"Trouble is, I got some complaints from customers this season about those old cabins. Too smoky, appliances going wonky, bugs. Some bad shingles with dry rot beneath." As he smoothed his big white beard, she wondered if he played Santa for the local kids. "Anyway, I figured this was a good time to deal with everything, and I hired Chevy and Knox to bring the cabins up to snuff."

She stared at him. "You're saying you don't have anything to rent?"

"Not a one." He considered. "Might could be they'll have one livable in a couple more weeks. Mebbe."

Her anxiety rose. "I see. Is there anywhere else you can think of?"

"Can't think of anywhere. The B&Bs are closed down. No customers, you know, so this is when they go on vacation. One goes to Phoenix until February, the other'll return in January for the ski season."

"Okay, but... Right. Okay." God, what was she going to do? "Can you plan on me booking a cabin when one is ready?"

"Surely I'll do that."

"Thanks, Dante."

As she walked out, frustration and dread filled her. Was Rescue going to be just like Weiler—a place where she'd started to fit in and then been driven out?

She looked up at the sky, noting the day was already growing dark.

Winter was closing in.

That evening, Rescue held its Black Friday festival at the roadhouse.

After last August's popular harvest festival in Lynx Lake Park, the town's residents had wanted a winter gathering, one for just Rescue after the tourists were gone.

Arm around Regan, Caz walked around the overly crowded roadhouse. Perhaps it was time to consider finding a community center. "The place looks great. Your decorating crew did a wonderful job."

Regan beamed up at him. The schoolkids had spent part of the day here—and were considered part of the party crew.

The dividers between the restaurant and bar sections had been removed to create one big room. Silver tinsel glittered from the chandeliers. Twinkling red lights and garlands were strung along the bar, fireplace, and around the windows. A huge fir tree with golden ornaments and lights filled one corner. A wealth of potluck dishes covered the bar top. "Smells good, don't you think?"

Regan sniffed and smiled. "I'm hungry."

"We'll eat as soon as the program is over." The entertainment was homegrown with each class in the school, local singers, and band groups performing. Regan's class had all dressed in red for their short performance.

Last week, Audrey, JJ, and Lillian had taken Regan to Soldotna to shop. When he'd offered to take the day off, Regan had proudly told him it was an *all-woman outing*. From what she'd reported, all three generations had enjoyed a marvelous time.

"Hey, Regan. Over here!" Delaney waved.

"Papá, can I go?"

When his daughter looked up in appeal, Caz grinned. "Our table is right in front. Come and sit with us after your program."

"Thanks, Papá." She cut through the crowd—a little red meteor in search of her buddy.

As the roadhouse filled, Caz wandered through the crowd and caught up with friends. He'd have liked to have JJ with him, but last night, she'd told him she'd be on duty today and wouldn't join them.

He understood the demands of a job; however, he'd felt something was wrong. Her expression last night had been distant. Her stalking cat grace had been missing. Her shoulders had sagged. Worry trickled down his spine.

Possibly, she'd just been tired. She wasn't used to a daylong family gathering, after all. But she'd seemed to enjoy herself right up until the moment she suddenly needed time alone. Perhaps she was missing her mother?

Well, he'd catch up with her later. See if something was worrying her. Have an early night, give her a backrub, and tuck her into bed.

Preferably his bed.

"Caz, how are you?" Sarah from the coffee shop interrupted his thinking. She was seated with her husband, Uriah, who did the coffee shop baking, and her kindergartner, Rachel.

"Good. It's been an interesting month." He smiled at her. "How are you feeling?"

She patted her huge belly. "Only a week or so to go. Beverly says I should do fine."

Uriah frowned. "Can we call if...?"

"I'm pretty sure Beverly has delivered more babies than I have. She's been at this a long time." In her early sixties, Beverly was an excellent midwife. "But if she needs backup, absolutely call me. You both have my cell phone."

"Thanks, Caz." The lines smoothed out of Uriah's face.

Sarah rolled her eyes. "He is such a worrier."

Caz gave Uriah an understanding look. Nothing made a man feel more helpless than watching a woman having a baby.

As he kept moving, he spotted Dante and Lillian sharing a table with Tucker and Guzman near the front.

A back corner of the room was filled with the Patriot Zealots who'd brought their wives and children, as if to remind the town that they had families. It was easy to forget since their children didn't attend school, and their women rarely came to town—and never without the men. As usual, the women were dressed in the typical PZ garb of long skirts, long-sleeved blouses, with hair pulled back tightly. No makeup, no jewelry. Each woman with her children sat next to a man. The men talked. The children and women were silent. Subdued.

Caz growled under his breath. Whenever one of their women visited his clinic, he'd tried to talk to her about her life. Unsuccessfully. Even when alone with him—a health clinic policy he insisted upon—each woman insisted she was fine and was happy at the PZ compound, despite old bruises, scars, and the signs of abuse. He'd never been so frustrated.

Unfortunately, all he could do was let them know he would help, and that Gabe would help. Anytime, anywhere.

It wasn't nearly enough. Yet without reports, witnesses, or complaints, his hands were tied.

On duty, JJ walked through the roadhouse, giving each person a quick assessment for drugs, intoxication, and belligerence. So far, so good.

Gabe had planned to serve as the police presence tonight, but she'd told him she'd do it. If she avoided sharing a table with Caz and the chief, maybe she'd also avoid feeding the gossip.

She had really hoped Lillian was wrong—that there were only a few gossips, and this mess would pass over like a quick rainstorm. That brief period of optimism had cracked quickly. Ever since she'd entered the roadhouse, she'd been treated to sideways glances, open stares, and whispers that increased wherever she went.

Some people didn't even bother to keep their voices low.

"That's her, the female cop," a striking brunette in city clothing was saying to two other women. "She's the one living with all those men. I bet they're pleased to have their own live-in slut."

As nausea twisted JJ's stomach, she moved away, pretending to want some fruit punch. But when she got to the bar where several older women were serving the cherry-colored liquid, one pretended not to see her. The other gave her a scornful stare.

"Could I have a drink, please?" JJ asked politely.

Mouth pressed tight in disapproval, the woman handed over a drink.

I haven't done anything wrong, dammit. "Thank you." Back rigidly straight, JJ held the woman's eyes until the woman looked away.

Lillian had been right. Once again, she was being lied about, treated like filth. Shunned.

Carrying the glass, JJ headed toward the back of the room. Her throat was thick, her heart felt like lead in her chest. The too-short weeks of feeling part of this community made the loss so much worse. She had so wanted to be a meaningful part of the town.

She'd been a fool.

As Mayor Lillian spoke into the mic on the tiny dance stage and welcomed people, the last few stragglers entered the roadhouse.

To JJ's surprise, Hawk limped in, using the walking cane Caz had given him. Face pale and strained, he stepped to the side of the door.

Although still pissed-off at how he'd spoken to Regan, JJ pulled an empty chair away from a table of loud men. She pushed it against the wall at the end of a line of occupied chairs and waited for him to notice. He needed to sit until he got past the pain and could join his family.

At least he had a family.

As he straightened, his gaze landed on her. She motioned to the chair she'd planted her boot on to keep someone from appropriating it then pointed to him. *Yeah, it's for you, stupidhead*...as Regan would say.

He scowled. Nodded.

As he moved toward her, a woman and little boy hurried in. The kid ran right into his wounded leg.

Hawk gave a growl of pain.

Looking up at the man, the child gasped and hid behind his mother. The woman saw Hawk and retreated so fast she almost tripped over her boy.

JJ frowned. That seemed excessive. Admittedly, Hawk's face looked like rough road, but there was no need to act as if they'd seen Leatherface with a chainsaw.

Body a tense line, he watched them flee to the PZ corner, shook his head, and moved toward JJ. He gave her a cold look from eyes the color of steel. "Thanks for the chair," he rasped and sat down very carefully.

Yes, he was hurting. "You didn't drive here, did you?"

He flicked a glance at her. "Don't need my left leg to drive."

No wonder he looked like hell. "But...why?"

"Seems I have a niece. And own part of the town."

True enough.

Caz had told her how, as the town was dying, Mako'd purchased a number of the failing businesses. With the newly opened mountain resort, Rescue was making a comeback. Mako's sons were cherry picking who could purchase or lease the business properties. The guys seemed invested in bringing in good people.

From Hawk's irritated expression, he'd rather have a root canal than have to be part of a community. Yet, here he was.

He sat back as Mrs. Wilner herded her class of third, fourth, and fifth graders out onto the stage. They were leading the singing of historic songs—gold mining tunes, Alaska Native songs, and old Russian songs. The children introduced each song with a bit of its history.

Hawk's expression softened when Regan stepped forward to tell about the deaths from winter during the Klondike Gold Rush.

JJ smiled. Last week, she'd helped Regan make her performance more dramatic. Many of the other children had mumbled or spoken in a monotone. Regan's delivery was clean, clear, and filled with emotion.

"Fucking amazing," Hawk said.

When Regan finished, she looked at her father's wide smile—and her expression lit up. When she checked the back of the room, JJ pumped her arm in the air for victory and got a happy grin.

Hawk gave Regan a thumbs-up, and the girl's smile almost split her face.

"Good for you," JJ said to him.

His face had gone back to being hard and unreadable. "What?"

"You made her whole night."

"Yeah, right." Yet the flash of vulnerability in his pitiless... haunted...gaze was startling.

Reconsidering her impression of him, she gave him a nod.

Behind her, two men entered the room, getting her attention when one said something about the law. She glanced over her shoulder.

Stopping by the wall, a rail-thin, black-bearded man continued talking to his friend. "Yes, I get why you don't want to rock the boat here. But the movement will stall unless there is drastic action. Something to draw the attention of the nation."

The brown-haired man shook his head. "No. That is not the way."

After a second, JJ recognized them. The clean-shaven one was the Zealot leader, the so-called Reverend Parrish and the black-bearded one was Captain Nabera.

Parrish glanced at her, frowned, and his voice dropped. Nabera shot her a cold look before both men turned their attention to the stage.

As JJ leaned back against the wall, Principal Jones drew the school's part of the program to a close. "...and I want to remind you there will be music to enjoy as you eat." He waved to a trio of old-timers with guitars and a banjo.

People started to move around. Without even looking at JJ, Hawk limped over to the table where his brothers and Audrey were sitting, passing Gabe who grinned at him.

Joining JJ against the wall, Gabe listened to the trio for a moment and nodded approval. "They've been practicing."

"They're good. I'm surprised they didn't ask you and your brothers."

"They did, and we're on in about an hour. You should join us."

"No." She took a step away from him. Singing at the house was one thing. In front of people? Oh God no, especially with these rumors.

"That's what Audrey said...at first. She'll be up there with us."

"Chief, just the man I wanted to see." Mrs. Wilner, Regan's teacher, hurried up. Her shaggy hair, narrow face, and pointed nose reminded JJ of a curly-haired dachshund—and the woman was even friendlier.

JJ gave her a smile and started to ease away so the two could talk.

"No, don't leave, Officer. I want you, too."

"Want us for what?" Gabe asked.

"One of my programs during the winter months is to explore careers. Your fingerprinting presentation caught the children's imaginations. I'd like to have you two visit our classroom and explain more of what you do, as well as the process of getting there."

Oh, damn. JJ really wanted to keep a low profile right now, yet the idea was a good one. "Children—girls—have so many more choices now."

"Exactly. How can we get the children to dream if they don't see the end result?" Mrs. Wilner beamed. "So I can pencil you in for—"

"No. That's a bad idea." An attractive blonde with big hair

turned away from a nearby group. Arms crossed over lush breasts, she scowled. "You keep that woman away from our vulnerable children."

JJ almost cringed.

Mrs. Wilner looked confused. "Excuse me? Who in the world are you talking about, Giselle?"

The blonde put her nose in the air. "Whatever that officer and those men do out at their place is their business, but she can stay away from the school."

Gabe growled. "There's nothing going on at the Hermitage. Where the hell did you—"

"Nothing, my ass. We saw her. Making out with the doc right there on the street. Like—"

JJ found a smidgeon of courage and firmed her voice. "Last time I looked, even police officers were allowed to—"

Giselle flipped her hand up, palm out, in the time-honored *talk to the hand.* "Don't speak to me. Or my daughter." Turning, she grabbed the hand of Regan's friend, Delaney, and headed toward the other side of the room.

"That woman." Mrs. Wilner sighed, then looked at JJ and Gabe. "We'll figure something out."

JJ put her hand on her stomach, feeling as if she was going to throw up. Wouldn't that just top off an ugly night?

Expression hard, Gabe was watching the Hermitage table with Bull, Hawk, Audrey, and Caz. The adults, even Hawk, were keeping Regan running with orders. The little girl was eating it up.

"Gabe? I..." When he turned to look at her, she faltered to a stop, because what could she say? She wasn't a slut, but she'd certainly been having sex with Caz. There were no rules against a law enforcement officer having a sex life. Having relationships. Yet, considering the mess in her past, it'd been decidedly unwise.

She bit her lip and felt like crying. Did that mean she needed to go through life without love?

"You didn't do anything wrong. But we do need to address the situation." Gabe's lips curved, but the smile didn't reach his eyes. "Let's talk tomorrow."

"Ah...since I'm off, I figure I'll drive up to Anchorage tonight. Spend a couple of days in the city." Yes, it would be fleeing, yet she needed to think without any distractions.

In Weiler, the disaster affected only her. Here? What would it do to the reputation of the police department? To Caz and his health clinic? And...the most vulnerable of all—to Regan?

Gabe studied her. "All right. We'll talk Monday. We'll figure this out, JJ."

"Sure."

The festival had been *awesome*.

In her bedroom, Regan turned over in bed. Sirius mewed in annoyance before he settled back down against her tummy. Again. Okay, maybe she was moving too much, but she was kinda bouncy.

She'd done good in her part of the program. Everybody said so. Mr. Hawk—Uncle Hawk—had even given her a thumbs-up.

JJ had been working, so she hadn't sat with the uncles, Audrey, and Papá, but she'd been there. Regan grinned into Sirius's fur, remembering how the cop had done a fist pump for Regan. JJ was so chill. And she gave great hugs.

There'd been so much food. A couple of the casserole-things were icky, but there'd been cherry pie and cookies and a ginormous cake with sprinkles. She'd pretended to be a waitress and brought drinks for the grownups, and Uncle Bull said he'd hire her when she was older.

Niko had been there with his family, and his dad had said she could come over and meet his dog.

Regan's smile faded. Delaney's mom hadn't let her sit with

Regan, and Delaney had looked weird before they left. Like she almost wanted to cry.

Well, Regan would talk to her tomorrow and—

"What the fuck were you thinking, bro?" The angry voice came from outside. That was Uncle Gabe. Something crashed, and Regan cringed at the loud grunt. The groan.

Regan sat up. Was he hurt?

"Dios, Gabe. At least tell me what I've done before you punch me."

That was Papá. Uncle Gabe had *hit* him?

"What do you think you've done? Did you not hear the shit they're saying about JJ?"

"JJ? What about JJ?"

Regan crawled out of bed and over to the window. Nothing to see—just the side of Mako's cabin. But she could hear. Real good.

"You and JJ? Ring a bell?" Gabe made a growly sound like a mean dog. "I told you your rep could hurt her. For fuck's sake, they're saying she's doing us all out here."

"*Please.* No one would believe that."

"Except you two were seen locking lips. Jesus, Caz, I thought we had an agreement. Hands off my officer."

Papá didn't say anything for a long time. "That was the plan. It didn't—and won't—work out."

Uncle Gabe made a sarcastic noise. "Bro, no female lasts more than one night with you. She doesn't need your crap."

"There's something between us."

"Are you shitting me? It's serious?"

"Sí."

"Is that why she headed for Anchorage?" Uncle Gabe's voice kept getting louder.

"She what?"

"Yeah, you're really close. I can tell."

"Pinche cabrón." Then there was that sound again—and Regan's stomach got all tight because they were *fighting*.

A groan.

"Next time you want to talk, 'mano, use your words first, not your fists." Papá's boots sounded on the deck. The door to the house opened and closed.

Uncle Gabe was still outside, and she didn't think he was supposed to be using words like that.

Feeling sick, she climbed into bed and buried her face in Sirius's soft fur. What was going on? Uncle Gabe had hit Papá, and Papá had hit back. But why? Something about JJ.

Did Papá want her for a girlfriend?

Regan hands closed into fists. Mom had gone after guys—like a lot—and when she had a new boyfriend, she forgot she had a kid, too. She'd be with the guy all the time, wouldn't come home till she needed clothes.

Apartments were scary at night.

If Papá got a girlfriend, would he forget he had a daughter?

"But JJ likes me," Regan whispered to Sirius. "Doesn't she?"

CHAPTER TWENTY-SIX

The only thing more accurate than incoming enemy fire is incoming friendly fire. - Murphy's Laws of Combat Operations

Papá'd been in a crummy mood on Saturday and Sunday. He'd been looking at his phone a lot, and his face got all hard. An' he was still nice to her, but he wasn't happy at all.

JJ wasn't at her place. On Sunday, Regan had been sitting on Mako's big couch...again...and crying when Uncle Bull came in, and he took her to his roadhouse and taught her how to make cherry pie. He said she'd get him put in jail for child labor—and then laugh. He was kinda crazy.

Last night, Papá got the first Harry Potter movie, and they ate popcorn and watched it, only she kept missing JJ. And not missing JJ.

She hadn't been able to eat any breakfast with her stomach feeling icky. Sirius ate her eggs when Papá went to finish getting dressed.

School had been hard. All day, Delaney kept giving her funny looks but wouldn't talk about it at lunch. Just said her mom was saying bad stuff.

Finally, the bell rang and school was over. Regan walked out with Delaney. "What? Tell me now."

"Mom says that JJ's doing sex with all your uncles and your dad. All of them." Delaney looked sick.

Regan stared. "No, she's not. Well, not Papá. I would've seen." Although JJ had been over a lot. For supper. To watch movies.

"Not if they were doing it after you went to bed," Delaney pointed out as they walked down the dirt sidewalk toward town. "Mom saw your dad kissing Officer Jenner. Right out on the street and everything." Her voice lowered. "Open-mouthed and tongue."

"Ew." That's what Uncle Gabe had said, wasn't it? All of it. And locking lips—that was kissing, right? "I guess she might be his girlfriend. Maybe that'd be okay. She's nice."

"That's what I told Mom. That she's really nice and does your hair and stuff." Delaney nodded fiercely. "But Mom says she's only nice to you to suck up to the doc. When she has him good and tight, she'll make him get rid of you."

Every word struck like the slaps of a hard hand, like the way Mom would hit her if she got in the way. Especially when Mom was flirting with a new boyfriend. That was how grownups were. A new lover meant a kid got forgotten.

Or gotten rid of? The chill that filled Regan was as cold as the muddy snow under her boots.

Maybe JJ didn't even like her, was just being nice so she could hang around with Papá.

"Oh, it's the little stupid girls. The noob and the fatty." Brayden came running up beside Shelby. He shoved Delaney off the path and started to push Regan.

Anger filled her until she couldn't see, and she hit him with all of her strength. Just like Papa and JJ had taught her.

He fell back on his butt, nose gushing blood. "Bitch spic!"

Shelby slapped Regan right across the face. "Leave him alone."

Regan kicked her in the knee and followed with a fist to her belly. "Soft belly, you fucking bitch."

Brayden was up. A hard fist hit Regan's mouth and her cheek, and she screamed and put her head down, ramming him in the chest. He tripped and fell, and she landed on him and kept hitting him.

"Fighting again? What are they teaching you here?" JJ yanked Regan off of Brayden and dumped her in the snow off to one side. Then she grabbed Delaney and Shelby and pushed them apart.

Regan stared. Delaney had jumped into the fight? Her friend's hair was all over the place and scratches ran down her face. Shelby fought like a girl.

"Mr. Jones," JJ called to the principal who'd just left the building. "Can you deal with the older ones? I'll escort Regan and Delaney to town and have the doc look—"

"No!" Regan yelled. "No, you won't."

JJ turned. "What?"

"You just want my Papá for your boyfriend. You're not my friend. You were never my friend, and I hate you." Tears burned her eyes, and everything hurt.

Regan ran toward town.

Stunned into silence, JJ stared after Regan, feeling as if she was the one who'd lost the fight.

Oh, God, she had. She'd lost...everything. To be part of Rescue, to be able to serve them. Lost things she'd only begun to realize she wanted. A man. A family. That little girl who'd fled as if JJ was a monster.

As despair swept through her, JJ bit her cheek to keep from crying. All weekend in Anchorage, she'd been mustering her courage. She'd decided to stay. To outlast the rumors.

Because she had Caz. Almost a family. Caz and Regan were worth fighting for.

But now... She looked down the road. Regan was still running.

Turning, JJ ran her gaze over Delaney...and remembered how the child's mother, Giselle, had been so nasty. But it wasn't the child's fault. "Where is your mother picking you up?"

"Not my mom, but Grams is." Delaney looked as if she'd rather be anywhere but with JJ.

"Are you hurt anywhere?"

"Uh-uh. Shelby just scratched me." Delaney backed down the path.

Who was JJ to stop her? "All right. Make sure your grandmother cleans the scratches and puts an antibiotic ointment on them." JJ made a shooing motion and the child ran toward town.

Escaping. Fleeing.

JJ's shoulders sagged. It appeared that was what she herself needed to do.

She and Caz weren't really in a relationship, but they were in... something. He'd undoubtedly heard the rumors about her, but, knowing Caz, she doubted he'd care, except for how they might affect her.

Every beat of her heart spread the pain deeper. For him, she would've stayed and tried to weather the storm. Would have ignored the name-calling and ugliness, but this mess involved more than just the two of them.

Regan mustn't get swept into the sewer along with JJ. Even if JJ tried to explain what was happening, the child was too young to understand about vindictive gossip. About lying.

"*I hate you.*" The words hurt so much. JJ pulled in a breath as she climbed into the patrol car and headed out of town. She'd heard mothers talk about the pain of hearing "I hate you" from their children. But, at least they'd had a solid foundation of love first. JJ and Regan had only a budding friendship. Which was now shattered past all repair.

If JJ told him, Caz would undoubtedly talk with his daughter, but JJ had seen her face. It was more than a shallow anger. If Caz wanted JJ, and Regan stayed obstinate, then... What would happen?

Leaning her head on the steering wheel, JJ fought for control.

Regan had suffered enough. Had lost a mother. Even now, she wasn't confident about where she fit in her father's life. Of his love. Nothing should be allowed to mess up her world. Putting Caz in the middle, forcing him to choose sides between a lover and a daughter, would be wrong. In fact, it would be less painful for him if he never knew how Regan felt.

JJ would simply leave.

Leave her female friends—Audrey, Lillian, Regina, Sarah. Her eyes started to burn with tears.

Lose the boss she liked and respected. Who considered her a skilled LEO.

Leave Cazador. A tear ran down her cheek. He wouldn't understand—and she couldn't explain. If he hated her for running, then...at least he wouldn't mourn her loss. That would be best for him and for Regan.

Unable to move, to drive, she buried her head in her hands and cried.

Caz was at a loss for what to do. Regan had been sullen and snarky from the moment she joined him in the clinic until he tucked her in. Undoubtedly the fight at school had something to do with it, but...this seemed like more.

Damned if he knew what.

He felt as if he was failing JJ and Regan. But, after talking with Lillian and Sarah and Regina, at least he knew what was being said in town.

Gabe had been right—it was ugly. He needed to talk with JJ.

He'd wanted to all weekend, but she'd disappeared. Gone to

Anchorage. And had ghosted him. With each call and text she'd ignored, his anger had grown.

Now, she was back. He'd have gone over earlier, but Regan hadn't been in a place where he felt comfortable leaving her alone, not even if he was next door.

So, he'd waited. After checking that she was asleep, he walked to Mako's cabin and upstairs to JJ's. He knocked.

"Who is it?"

"Caz."

"Not receiving tonight, sorry. Whatever it is, I'll see you tomorrow."

His temper flared. "Tonight."

When she didn't open the door, his jaw tightened. Outwaiting his prey had never been a problem for him. After a minute, he knocked again.

And again.

And again.

"Fucking hell." The stomping across the room said his quarry was moving. The door was yanked open. Her hair was a tangle of curls, her eyes red, and the lids swollen. Her face flushed with annoyance.

Of course. Those fucking rumors. His own anger slid down a notch. "JJ, I know the gossip is upsetting you."

Her shoulders sagged. "I'm sorry. I should have come to the door. I just didn't want to deal with the mess tonight. I planned to talk with you tomorrow."

The leaden tone was so unlike her. He reached for her hand.

She stepped back, out of reach. "Caz, this isn't a good time."

Of course it wasn't. She wasn't someone who easily shared her problems. And her reaction wasn't rage as Gabe's had been. Caz fingered the sore spot on his jaw—his brother still had a good right punch. "The buzz will die down, JJ. What they're saying is ugly, but new gossip will replace it soon enough."

"I don't think so." She shook her head. "This is what

happened to me before, in Weiler, and it didn't die down. Nash kept feeding it—and then it fed on itself. If I so much as talked with any officer, a girlfriend or wife would be sure I was coming on to him."

"Dios," Caz muttered. "No wonder you left."

"I did." She pulled in a hard breath. "And I'll be leaving here."

He heard the words, but they took a moment to impact. Then it felt as if a grenade had taken out his heart. "Say that again."

"I'm sorry, but we're done. Not that we were anything more than fuck buddies, but—"

The anger returned. "We were more than that. I care for you, and you know it. We can outlast the gossip. And if we're together, then the rumors will—"

She shook her head, and sorrow filled her gaze. "I...can't. You don't understand and...I'm leaving and that's all there is to say."

"Just like that? No talk, no trying to work it out. You're just leaving?" Caz narrowed his eyes.

"Yes."

Her tone left no recourse, no room for argument, none for the comfort he wanted to give. "Because of rumors and nasty talk, you'll give up everything we might have had?"

The sorrow disappeared under a cool indifferent mask. "That's right."

Disappointment and loss tasted like ash in his mouth. He held her gaze. "You told me you weren't a coward. What happened?"

Turning, he walked toward the stairs, hoping against hope that she'd call him back. He reached the first step and turned...only to see the door closing. He heard the lock turn.

She'd shut him out completely, physically, mentally, emotionally.

An ache filled his chest until he bent his head against the pain. Dammit, JJ. Pulling in a breath, he went down the rest of the stairs and out into the dark night.

CHAPTER TWENTY-SEVEN

Success in life is the ability to move from one mistake to another without losing enthusiasm. - Winston Churchill

Tuesday evening at home, Bull sat on his sectional, made notes on a recipe he wanted to modify, and kept an eye on Regan's work. Caz had to stay at the clinic until an ambulance took a patient off his hands. Bull had volunteered to child-sit.

Regan was sitting on the floor and using the coffee table as a desk. She was concentrating so fiercely on knotting a paracord bracelet he was surprised steam didn't come from her ears. She'd jumped into working on the craft so quickly, he knew she had other things on her mind. Was stewing over something. Maybe over the fight at school that'd left her face bruised?

She finished another knot and looked up.

"Good," Bull told her. "Now, pull the cord as tight as possible and slide it up."

Lower lip between her teeth—she really was damn cute—she kept going. The girl had the kind of determination that they looked for in SEALs. This little mite would never go belly up and whine she just couldn't do it. She'd stay the course.

As if she felt him watching her, she looked up. "Papá said you guys used to fight. When you were my age."

Bull grinned. "Yeah, we did. A lot."

"You're a lot bigger than Papá. Did you hurt him?"

Huh, he had a feeling she'd hold a grudge if he said yes. "Nope. Well, we all got some blows in. But winning? I think it was pretty equal."

Her little nose wrinkled in an expression of disbelief, and he laughed. Fuck, she was a cutie.

"Seriously. I'm bigger, and I won that way. Now, Gabe was actually a better fighter—he can think when he fights—so he won a lot. Caz—your daddy—he's so damn fast that no one could even hit him. And Hawk, well, when he got into it, I'm not sure he even felt us hit him.

Yeah, Hawk was scary that way. "A lot of time when I was pounding on one, Gabe'd grab the other and do a sneak attack from the rear." Bull shook his head. In spite of those childhood lessons, he still had trouble checking his six. Just wasn't in his personality to anticipate attacks from the rear—in fighting or in business.

A soft tap-tap came from the deck side door, and Hawk limped in. Silently. Seeing Regan, he stopped short, his mouth tightening.

Bull jerked his head toward the kitchen. "Got a pale ale you might like. Bring me one, too."

Brow furrowed, Regan watched Hawk walk into the kitchen. "I can go. I'm big enough to stay by myself."

Bull shook his head. "Nope. You can stay here and finish, then we'll see what we want to cook for supper. It's time you learned a new meal to prepare, don't you think?"

She nodded enthusiastically.

Being left alone didn't bother her—her independence made

him think she'd had to fend for herself too fucking much. Yet, she hadn't been taught the basics of cooking. She could microwave a meal from a can, but hadn't known how to prepare anything more difficult than a fried egg. He was finding it an honor and joy to teach her kitchen skills.

Hawk handed him a beer, sat down as far from Regan as he could get, then patted the sofa. "New?"

"Yeah. The armchairs and couch I had before didn't let me stretch out enough." The U-shaped sectional was long enough to surround both the television area and the woodstove in the corner —and to let a big man sprawl in comfort on a lazy Sunday morning. He'd gone with a combination of studded brown leather and softer-than-shit beige cushions. It went well with the room's brown and cream colors. "I didn't want anything fancy."

"It's nice." Regan shifted positions on the hardwood floor. "Although you should get a rug."

"You're spoiled, girl," Bull said. Caz had Oriental carpets here and there. Dark reds, florals.

Yeah, it was obvious only a male lived in Bull's cabin. Actually, Audrey was the only woman to have seen his place. Well, Bull wasn't much interested in changing that, either. When he visited his restaurant and brewery in Anchorage, he'd spend the night with a woman friend. Like him, she had no interest in anything romantic.

Leaning back with his beer, he studied his brother. "What's up?"

Hawk was clean—hell, he'd always loved his showers—but his hair and beard hadn't been trimmed anytime in the recent past. His eyes were tired. Haunted.

Bull shook his head. Like too many combat vets, he had times when the past violence was more present than...the present. Times where nightmares dragged any chance of sleep away. It'd been a while since he'd been covered in blood and guts. His brother's experience was far more recent.

Hawk shrugged. "Walls closing in."

"I hear you. Welcome to winter." He smiled at Regan who was singing to herself as she made the knots. When he hummed a harmony to her tune, her expression lit.

Hawk's face softened for a moment before he caught himself.

Bull glanced out the window at Gabe's cabin next door. The lights were on. "Maybe we should gather everyone at Mako's. The kid might as well learn to cook for half-a-dozen as two."

"Not tonight." At Bull's raised eyebrows, Hawk went into an elaborate explanation—for him. "Gabe's looking to rip someone a new one."

That didn't sound like Gabe. "Did a Patriot Zealot annoy him?"

"No. Caz did." Hawk took another sip of his beer. "JJ gave notice."

"What the fuck?" But Bull knew why. Gossip and bars went together like salt and pepper. When bartending at the roadhouse, he'd heard the shit people were saying about Officer Jenner. Just went to show that assholes flourished in small towns as well as cities. But, damn, he hadn't thought she'd let it drive her away.

Unless maybe she and Caz had a fight?

"What's that mean?" The high voice reminded him there was a kid in the room. "Gave notice. What's it mean?"

Hawk looked away. He probably figured he'd used his quota of words for the day.

Thanks, bro. "Means JJ told Gabe that she's quitting and won't work for him any longer."

After a flash of satisfaction, Regan went pale. "But what will she do?"

"Find another job. Somewhere else." *Dammit.* He wasn't blind. Caz loved the woman. And Gabe needed her as his officer. He glanced at Hawk. "When's her last day?"

"Usual. Two weeks."

Bull turned to Regan. "It's considered polite to work for a

couple of weeks after you tell an employer you're quitting. It gives them time to hire someone else."

A crease formed between her brown eyebrows. "She'll work for Uncle Gabe for two more weeks and then...she'll just *leave?*" The last word was said with almost desperation.

"Afraid so. She's a police officer. If she doesn't work at the Rescue Police Department, then she has no other job to take."

Regan's eyes filled with tears. "I didn't want her to leave. I didn't *mean* it." Dropping the paracord, she fled into the bathroom. The door slammed behind her.

"Fuck," Hawk muttered.

"Agreed." Bull took a long pull of his beer. "A bit of a guilty conscience there?"

Hawk's gaze was on the hallway where the bathroom was. "Bet she heard the gossip."

"Schools. Of course she did." Bull winced, thinking about it. "The two bullies who pick on her and her bestie probably rubbed her nose in it...and she overreacted."

"You think? She seems pretty sweet."

"She is. She's also got Caz's temper."

Hawk's gray-blue eyes lit with amusement. After a second, he frowned. "Bullies?"

"Yeah." Bull's lips twitched. "I'm sure you noticed the bruises on her face?"

"Hard to miss."

"Apparently, some bigger boy pushed her friend down. Regan flattened the asshole."

A corner of Hawk's mouth lifted. "Good."

"Stay for supper, bro. The kid's gonna be messed up, especially if she had something to do with JJ wanting to leave."

Hawk's glance at the bathroom door held sympathy. Bull knew Hawk'd had the hardest time of any of them with anger management. As a kid, when he lost his temper, he went berserk —and doled out a lot of damage. After breaking Gabe's nose, he'd run away. Had planned to stay out in the wilderness and die.

They'd tracked him, got him back, and then Mako'd called his buddy, a kid psychologist, to help. Dr. Grayson had stayed for a week at the cabin. Gabe hadn't held a grudge—none of them did. They'd all had fucked-up childhoods, had all spent time on the streets. Hawk's past, though, was the stuff of nightmares. Because the monsters had been his parents.

Hawk was still watching the hallway.

Finally, Regan came out, eyes all red.

Hawk glanced at Bull. Nodded. And asked Regan, "What're you cooking for supper?"

Uncle Hawk was still awful scary, but he was kinda nice, too. Regan had helped Uncle Bull make pulled-pork sandwiches.

Hawk had even helped, getting lettuce, radishes, and stuff from the greenhouse. As he cut it all up for a salad, he didn't talk hardly at all, and when he did, his voice still sounded mean, like scraping a knife over a rock.

At least neither uncle said anything about Regan bawling her head off in the bathroom. JJ would've thought that was a plus. The thought of JJ had Regan's lip quivering again.

"So, little bit, did anything interesting happen today in school?" Bull handed her a brownie with tons of chocolate frosting.

"Uh." Stalling, she licked the frosting off her fingers. The scary uncle wouldn't want to hear about a kid's day.

Leaning back in his chair, Hawk lifted his eyebrows. At her.

"Um. Kinda? After school, a moose came down the hill— between the kids walking home and the school. Some of the resort stupidheads were, like, all scared and trying to get past it to get back inside. It got upset." She half-grinned and admitted, "I got scared, too, but I wasn't stupid. The teacher—Mr. Hayes—

yelled to try to get kids to get away, but no one paid any attention.

"Surprised the moose didn't stomp one of them," Bull muttered to Hawk before saying to Regan, "Trudging through the snow makes moose irritable. You remember what to do when you see one?"

She nodded. Everybody except Hawk had given her a moose lecture. Even Audrey, cuz she said people laughed at her for messing up. Being laughed at was bad. "Back away and give it space. Run behind a tree if it charges. I tried to tell the other kids that, but no one listened to me."

"Use command voice," Hawk said.

"Huh?"

He straightened, his blue gaze on her. "Sometimes I take injured people to the hospital. In my plane."

She must have looked stupid, cuz Bull said, "If roads get closed, bush pilots will fly sick people to the city hospitals. Hawk helps out now and then."

"Oh. That's chill."

Hawk took a drink. "Did it a lot when I was young. But people don't listen when they're hurting or scared."

It took her a second to catch on. He'd been young, and people didn't listen to him. "What'd you do?"

"Mako taught me in command voice. Nobody ignores a drill sergeant." He motioned for her to stand up.

She slid off her chair.

"Stand tall. Suck air into your belly. Push your stomach down and get more air in. Yell—and push out each word from your gut. Deep voice, one word orders."

She frowned. "What's that mean? One word."

"Not shut-up, but: *Shut. Up.*" He pointed at her. "Do it."

Her face heated. Yell in front of them? Still, the lesson started with Mako—and Mako was special. She hauled in air.

"Suck it down into your gut," Hawk reminded. "Works best if you're in front of them. Face-to-face."

Yeah, shouting at someone's back wouldn't work good. She tried again, filled her belly, and blasted out, "Shut. Up." Her eyes widened. "Friggers, I sound different."

Bull grinned. "Nice job."

"Practice it." Hawk's eyes were serious. "Practice till you can bark out commands even if you're scared enough to piss yourself. Because that's when you'll need it."

"Hooyah." Bull pointed at the deck door. "Go yell at the patio grill for a few minutes. I want to be able to hear you in here."

She bounced on her toes, headed for the door, and spun. "Thank you, Uncle Hawk."

A corner of his mouth tipped up, and he did that kinda half salute.

CHAPTER TWENTY-EIGHT

T*here are very few personal problems that cannot be solved through a suitable application of high explosives.* - Scott Adams

In his favorite armchair, Caz stared into the flames dancing behind the glass door of his red cast-iron stove. Winter was closing in, and the heat coming from the stove was comforting.

Not as comforting as it would be to have JJ leaning against him, sharing the evening. But the woman he'd come to think of as his had avoided him since their angry words on Monday.

This was Friday and the last day of November. She'd be gone in a little over ten days.

After losing his temper and calling her a coward, he'd backed off. He wasn't the kind of man to browbeat a woman into doing something his way, overriding her concerns or wishes for her own life.

Well, that and he'd really thought she'd take time to overcome her instinct to run and then talk with him. Instead, she'd given Gabe her notice. Gabe was furious with them both. But Gabe... wasn't the problem.

Dammit. Caz ran his hand through his hair. He and JJ needed to talk and figure this out. Somehow.

Because he wasn't sure what to do. If he didn't have any obligations, he'd find work wherever she would be happy. Not a problem.

But he had Mako's mission. Bring Rescue back to life. It was a deathbed wish that Caz was archaic enough to find binding. The task required all four sons working together.

He had his brothers, who not only needed him pulling his weight with Rescue, but also in the family. Gabe was doing pretty well now. Bull, not so much. Although he never let anyone think he had problems, there were days when his drawn face and the dark look in his eyes showed he still suffered from PTSD. Even aside from being captured once, the SEAL had been involved in some ugly action.

And Hawk. Although home, he was messed up. Unlike the rest, he had nothing solid from his childhood to build upon. He needed them all to balance him out until he found himself again.

Finally, and most important, Regan needed stability. She was making a place for herself here, in the family with her uncles, in Rescue with Lillian who insisted on being Grammy, with Audrey who shared her joy of books. With her buddies, Niko and Delaney.

And with JJ. Caz picked up his bottle of water and took a sip. She hadn't even been over to see Regan. Irritation rose within him. It was difficult to forgive her for abandoning Regan as quickly as she had him.

Although, Regan hadn't asked about her. Caz frowned. In fact, his girl had gone from every other sentence of "JJ says..." to never mentioning her.

That was odd.

Even more odd was that tenderhearted JJ hadn't asked him to explain her leaving or arrange to say goodbye to Regan.

His eyes narrowed. In the conversation on Monday, JJ hadn't even *mentioned* Regan.

He raised his head to look toward Regan's bedroom. She'd been very, very quiet for the past couple of days. Not sullen, but damned unhappy. She hadn't wanted to talk with him about it.

Two silent females. Neither of whom was mentioning the other. What were the chances of that?

When JJ had scolded Regan in the past, Regan behaved like a typical child. A brief sulk, then back to normal with no hard feelings. She was much like him in that way. When Regan had yelled or snarked at JJ, the cop quietly corrected the disrespect. And was usually amused more than anything.

But...what if Regan had heard the gossip? Dios, he'd been an idiot. Of course she had. Small schools were rife with rumors. If Gabe had heard about Caz and JJ making out in public, so had Regan.

How would his little girl react to that?

She had adored JJ and wanted her around all the time. But, with the gossip, would she feel threatened instead?

His hot-tempered girl might well have taken JJ on. If Regan had been upset, JJ wouldn't have argued. She'd have thought she should leave. She'd run from Rescue, from Caz, and she'd never put the blame on a child.

Yes, it must be something like that.

Caz winced. He'd called JJ a coward. All right, tomorrow, he'd tackle one female and then the other. Neither would escape a conversation with him, and he'd get to the bottom of this.

He rose and walked down the hall, needing to check on his little girl one more time. As he started to open the door, his shoulder slammed into the doorframe. For a moment, he felt drunk.

No, the earth was moving. In the kitchen, the dishware clanked. The fireplace tools rattled.

Earthquake.

Dropping to one knee, he looked toward the bed.

With a squeak of panic, she was clutching her pillow.

"Stay put, Regan. It's an earthquake."

The second the shakes stopped, he ran across the room to her bed. It'd been a mild quake. The power hadn't even gone out.

"Mija? Are you all right?"

Face pale, she sat up in the bed. "Sirius ran away."

Caz glanced around and finally checked under the bed. The wild-eyed feline stared back without moving. "He's all right—just scared. He needs awhile to unwind."

Dios, so do I. Sitting beside Regan, he pulled her close.

She laid her head on his chest. "We had quakes in Sacramento, but little ones. This one bounced me up and down."

"Yes, it did." A couple of books had fallen to the floor. Pictures were askew. Nothing looked broken.

"How come there're quakes?"

"Ah. Because the ground way down deep is two big slabs of rock." He put his left palm partly over his right hand. "When those slabs move against each other, everything shakes until they get back into balance."

"Oh."

"Do you know what to do in case of a quake?"

"Um. Drop?"

"Good. Drop to the floor, crawl away from anything that might land on you or anything like windows that might break. Best is if you hide under a table and hang onto it or curl up and put your arms over your head. Don't try to run anywhere." He frowned. "We get a lot of earthquakes in Alaska, so...it's another situational awareness thing. Assess rooms and know where you'll be safe. Where would you be safe in here?"

He felt her relax as she turned her attention from the scary earthquake to what she could do next time. She really was amazing.

"Um. Under the desk?

"Good. If you're in bed, stay put, put a pillow over your head, and hang onto the headboard. Since animals scratch and bite, we let them hide on their own, sí?"

"Oh." She nodded solemnly. "Sirius was a lot more scared of the earthquake than the blizzard."

Smart cat.

"Okay, mija. I need to make sure everyone else is all right."

She made no protest, but she was still wired up. Sleep wouldn't come for a long while.

"I'll leave the lights on, and you can read until I come back. Then we'll share some hot chocolate."

She nodded. "'Kay."

"Brave girl." He kissed her cheek, then headed out, donning boots and coat. The inner compound lights were on.

Gabe was on Bull's deck, already checking on people. Typical cop. He spotted Caz. "Everything good, bro?"

"We're fine," Caz called. "I'll pop over to Mako's."

"Good. I got Hawk and Bull."

When Caz reached Mako's deck, JJ was just coming out. Her boots and coat were on. "Oh. I was just heading over to see if you and Regan were okay."

Gabe wasn't the only cop in the Hermitage. "We're good. Everything all right over here?"

"Only a few things were knocked over. That was quite a shake." She saw Gabe moving from Bull's house to Hawk's. "Looks like you have things handled. I'll go back in."

"Wait." In the bright floodlights, he could see her swollen, reddened eyes. The dark circles beneath. She was hurting as much as he was. As Regan was. "We need to talk."

She shook her head. "No. We don't." There was an audible quaver in her voice.

He was done with bullshit. "I know what's going on, and we are going to talk. Now." He snagged her wrist.

"Cazador." She tried to brace her feet as he pulled her off the deck. "Dammit, stop it or I'll hurt you."

Curiosity engaged, he looked over his shoulder. "You think you'd win?"

"Maybe not"—she glared at him—"but you'd be in no shape to want to talk."

"Caz, do you need—" Gabe stopped mid-sentence and eyed Caz. Then he scowled and turned to JJ. "You need help, JJ?"

It seemed Gabe was still angry about losing his officer. "You should answer him, princesa."

"If I ask him for help, what happens?" Her gaze was wary.

Law enforcement officers with soft hearts had an exploitable vulnerability. "Then you will get to watch a fight before we have our talk."

"Damn you," she muttered, and her glare held enough heat to melt the snow from Lynx Lake. "No, Gabe. I'm good."

"All right then." Before turning away, Gabe shot Caz a warning look...followed by a slight nod. The chief was pissed off at losing his officer. The brother, however, hoped Caz would work things out with his love.

JJ let Caz lead her to his cabin. Once inside, he could see how she'd tensed. How she was closing off.

To keep from hurting Regan.

After tugging off her coat, he gripped her upper arms. Pushing her was the wrong way to have a discussion. Try a better approach. "I know you're trying to cause the least amount of hurt —I see that, princesa."

Her eyes reddened before she looked away. "Talking isn't going to fix anything, Caz."

"That is possible, sí. First, I'm sorry I implied you're a coward. You're not." He cupped her cheek, wanting nothing more than to pull her into his arms. Instead, he waited until she looked at him. "But, JJ, life doesn't exist without pain. Breaking up hurts, losing someone hurts, being angry with someone hurts."

She nodded. Her expression was unreadable. Her poker face.

"If problems remain unspoken, if anger isn't dealt with, then hurt can linger. Can leave open wounds in the soul. I would ask, please, that we speak of what is happening and let the emotions air—no matter how uncomfortable—so healing can occur."

She stared at him, and he saw the moment she understood.

"For Regan." Her eyes closed for a moment as she pulled in a slow breath—and nodded.

Taking her hand, he led her to the living area and seated her in an armchair. Unable to help himself, he kissed the top of her head before heading down the hall.

He tapped on Regan's door. "I want to see you in the living room now, please."

"Coming, Papá."

By the time he reached the living room, she'd joined him. As they walked across the room, she caught sight of JJ and stopped with a jerk. Her face went blank.

This wasn't going to be easy, was it? He took her hand and led her to the couch across from the woodstove. "Sit there, mija."

"Caz, I don't know." JJ was shaking her head.

"I do know. And I will begin." Somehow. He wasn't particularly diplomatic when his emotions were involved. Mako had taught them to speak bluntly and honestly. He paced in front of the stove. "I am very happy to have a daughter. I love you very much, Regan."

She looked up at him and dropped her gaze back to her hands.

"I was hoping to have a woman to love as well. It was looking good. I need to know what happened."

JJ shook her head, her gaze on Regan who hadn't looked up. "Caz, I don't think—"

He held up his hand. "A Mako rule is that a person be allowed his say"—he smiled briefly—"or fists fly."

She frowned, but settled back.

"I'm not sure why there is a separation between the two of

you. Perhaps because of the gossip about JJ? Does that have something to do with it? Regan?"

Regan bit her lip...and nodded.

JJ's heart sank. Caz was wrong. This hashing-out discussion was too much to ask of a child, especially one who'd barely come to live with him. She started to rise.

Caz shot her a look that had her settling back. Regan *was* his daughter. JJ would have to respect that.

"Tell me what you heard, Regan."

The girl shook her head.

Caz sighed. "This is a problem for all three of us, so we are going to be very honest with each other. Even when feelings might get hurt. Even when things are hard to say."

And he waited.

JJ wanted so badly to take the little girl into her arms. *Damn you, Cazador.*

"I heard..." Regan's big brown eyes met JJ's and looked away. "That JJ's doing sex with my uncles and you, Papá."

"Ah. That's a very good start." His smooth, comforting voice was the one she'd fallen for at their first meeting. "JJ, can you give her the truth?"

What? JJ stared at him. He wanted her to tell his daughter *all* the truth?

He nodded.

Okay, fine. Not fine. Shaking inside, JJ pulled in a breath. "I've never done anything with your uncles." *Oh God.* "But I am—was— having sex with your father."

Regan blinked and then looked at Caz.

"Yes. JJ was spending the nights after you went to bed." Caz rubbed his neck. "We should have told you. That was our mistake, and I'm sorry for it, mija—that you found out from others rather than from us."

JJ expected Regan to shout, to do anything other than nod.

"What else did you hear?" Caz asked gently.

"Delaney's mom said that"—Regan's lip quivered—"that JJ's only nice to me cuz she wants you for her boyfriend, and then she'll make you get rid of me."

The words were so soft that JJ barely heard them. "What?" The meaning became clear, and rage filled her. She jumped to her feet. "*What?*"

"I'm sorry, I didn't—"

"No. That's just...just, no." JJ realized she was looming over the child like a crazy person and dropped down beside her. Hugged the little girl. "No, no, I would *never*... Yes, I care for your daddy, but oh, God, Regan, you're totally part of him. You're so special to me—I would never want you to leave."

Regan sagged against her, and the child was crying so hard that her words tangled together. "I'm sorry, JJ. I'm sorry I was mean to you and don't be mad at me. Don't go, please don't go."

"Honey..."

Regan lifted her head. Her dark brown eyes were so much like Caz's. Tears poured down her face. "Please?"

JJ sighed and gathered her closer. "I'm not mad, sweetheart. I never was. But people will talk and—"

"They will talk." Caz was smiling slightly, but his jaw was tight. "But, if you think about it, slandering someone is a form of bullying, no? Will you teach Regan that she should run away from bullies?"

The words were a slap to the face, to her pride, to everything she was.

JJ's spine straightened, and a second later, she laid her cheek against the top of Regan's head. The girl who was brave enough to stand up to her schoolyard bullies. Could JJ do less?

No. I will not teach her to run from the bastards in the world. No. "You're right. Let them talk. I'm staying."

Caz's eyes softened. "That's what I thought."

He sat on the couch and put his arms around them both.

JJ felt her hopes rising and tried to put a curb on them. What if Regan changed her mind? She should have a chance to think. "Sweetheart, are you sure you're all right with me and your father being together? I—"

Caz gave her a frown.

And Regan tore out of her arms and ran down the hall to her room.

JJ's heart dropped. "I knew it."

To her surprise, Regan ran back just as fast. She climbed back into the space between JJ and Caz as if it was her right, then pushed a folded up piece of paper into JJ's hand. "I made this for you."

Although her arms didn't want to release the little girl, JJ sat up and unfolded the paper. And stared.

Caz leaned over to see.

The crayon drawing was of three figures—a man with dark brown hair, a child with longer brown hair. And a female—still no curves, JJ noticed wryly—with short red hair. The child stood in the middle. All three were holding hands.

Beneath was careful printing: *"Papa and I love you, JJ. You should live with us in our house. Please don't leave."*

A brown splotch appeared on the paper, and JJ realized tears were running down her face.

"No," Regan wailed. "Don't cry." She flung her little arms around JJ.

The welling up of love almost choked the words away. "I love you, too, Regan. I love you."

After Caz tucked his daughter into bed, JJ read her a story, which Caz figured had turned into two. Not a bad plan since his girls needed to spend time together. He'd like to claim that females were overly emotional but—he rubbed his chest—his own heart felt as if it'd taken a battering.

Dios, he was proud of them. Regan, who had moved past jealousy and insecurity into honesty. JJ, who would have left to give Regan more security—and now would take on the town to provide a good example. They were astounding.

He was very lucky to have them in his life.

Laughing softly, JJ came into the living room and plopped onto the couch beside him.

"What's funny?" He handed her the glass of cabernet he'd poured and took a sip of his own.

She gulped down a big swallow and made a contented sound as she leaned against him. "Your daughter—who is not yet even a teenager—told me I should spend the night with Papá. In his bedroom. Your daughter, Doc Ramirez, is pimping for you."

"Not a doctor," he reminded and rose, pulling her up beside him. "We should do what our resident matchmaker says. I wouldn't want to make her angry. I've heard she has a bad temper."

"Like her father before her." JJ was laughing as he took her hand and tugged her up the stairs. To his room.

To his bed. Where she belonged.

He and Regan would be sure she didn't stray again.

To that end, he painstakingly slowly stripped off JJ's clothes and used his lips and hands to bring her to her first climax.

And, as long as he was about it, a second one, too.

Coming down from the mind-blowing orgasm, JJ panted for air. Her heart was going too fast, like a high-speed car chase. "You're trying to kill me."

As Caz moved up her body, his dark eyes filled with laughter—and heat. "No, mamita. As a medical professional, I assure you that what I have done—and will do next—should bring you no harm."

Her eyes rounded. *Will do next?*

Caz stripped, sheathed himself, then got the cushions from the loveseat in the corner. After stacking them on the bed off to one side, he added a bed pillow. To her surprise, he lay down beside her and pulled her up and over him. On her knees, she straddled him, his cock directly beneath her pussy.

"Why did you make a stack of cushions?" She looked at the pile on the other side of the bed. "And why am I on top of you?"

"Me? I am taking a well-earned break from my labors."

She shook her head. "That innocent look doesn't work."

"Not with an experienced police officer, no." He chuckled and his hands moved over her breasts, teasing the nipples, tugging and pinching until she was squirming on the hard dick beneath her pussy. The cock she needed so badly inside her.

"You want"—her voice came out husky—"me to do the work?"

"Exactly." He slid a hand under her ass and lifted her up slightly, using his other hand to position his cock at her entrance.

Slowly, she lowered herself onto him. Down and down. He seemed bigger in this position. So big. The flood of pleasure was incredible.

Her eyes burned slightly, because she'd thought this would never happen again.

His gaze softened, and he touched her cheek lightly. "I missed you, too."

He pulled her down for a long kiss, one that melted her heart.

And then she finished taking him inside.

"You feel amazing. Slick and hot." With a tight grip on her hips, he smiled at her wickedly. "Move for me, mamacita."

Just what she wanted to do. She used the muscles of her thighs to rise slightly, seeing his pupils dilate.

His gaze on her was hot. Taking her hands, he guided her

palms up and down her breasts, making her rub herself until her nipples were rigid peaks.

"Nice. Now, let's see how hard you can work." He pulled her forward and set her hands against his shoulders to brace her weight. Gripping her hips, he pulled her slowly up off his cock and slammed her down.

"Oh, God." She'd already come twice, but somehow the feeling was rising within her again with his firm hands on her, his thick cock inside, the sudden penetration.

"Repeat that movement, if you would," he said in a mild tone, although his hands never eased their hold.

"Right, right." She leaned forward, moving slow, then pushed herself back onto his cock. Amazing. Forward and back. She tried to go slow, but urgency was beating inside her, her clit was starting to throb. Faster and faster, she slammed against him.

When he reached down to rub her clit every time she rose up, the pressure grew. Her body clenched around the thick impalement.

"Oh...oh, I have to..."

"Let it go, mamita," he murmured. His other hand covered her breast, pinching the nipple. The sensation was a glorious burst of pain—and set everything off. Like the grand finale of a fireworks, pleasure bombarded her in mind-bending explosions.

Her attempts to move up and down turned into completely uncoordinated squirming as she came, drowning in sensation.

He was laughing as he rolled and positioned her on the stack of pillows, face to the mattress, hips high in the air.

Before she could speak, he settled between her calves, and with one shockingly hard thrust, penetrated her completely.

"Caz!"

"I had a nice rest, thank you." He squeezed her buttocks. "Now I will enjoy my woman."

. . .

Enjoy her he did. *Finally.* Since the first taste of his woman this evening, Caz had been fighting for control. Now, he hammered into her, hard and fast. Around his dick, her muscles gave small post orgasmic twitches.

Being JJ, she was trying to push back on him to increase his pleasure. He'd never known anyone more giving.

Slowly, heat rose at the base of his spine and moved into his groin. His balls drew up, the sensations magnificent. Over and over, he buried his length as deep as he could go. The urgency became unbearable until finally, as brilliant pleasure shook him, he emptied himself into her. Gave himself to her.

Running his hands over her back, he stayed on his knees, caught in the beauty of the moment. The softness of her skin. The flush on her face. The slight smile on her face.

As his heart began to slow, he wrapped his arms around her, pulled her off the mound of cushions, and laid her on the mattress.

"Stay there for a moment." He stroked her hair, and then went into the bathroom to deal with details. In the future, perhaps those details could go away.

When he returned, he lay down beside her, pulled her into his arms, and savored the feel of her warm body against his. Damn, but he wanted to be inside her again.

"Caz." She snuggled closer, rubbing her cheek on his chest. "About earlier. I'm sorry. I should have told you Regan was upset."

"You did what you thought was right, mi corazón." He stroked her back, pleased to feel the tension gone from her muscles. A fretter, his woman was.

"I guess I just... I'm still worried about Regan," she said as if to confirm his knowledge.

"Tell me."

"She has enough trouble at school without having me in her life. In your life."

JJ wasn't wrong. There would undoubtedly be problems. "I

understand. It's true that if someone says something rude about you, she will probably plant a fist in their face." He chuckled. "Genes breed true, apparently."

"That isn't funny. She—"

"JJ, she will have any number of difficulties in the future. That's life. Some trouble will undoubtedly come because of the gossip about you."

She made an unhappy sound.

"Let's weigh this out. On one hand, she has a woman who loves her, whom she adores. A role model. Someone who teaches her how a woman can be strong, shops with her, and fixes her hair. She's never had that kind of attention, never been a treasured child."

"How could anyone not love Regan? That's just wrong."

"Yes." Caz hugged her. So very sweet. "But she's a survivor. Years ago, Mako explained how exercise rips the muscles, and the tiny tears force the muscles to grow. That applies to living, as well. Pain forces us to grow."

"I don't want her in pain, dammit." JJ started to sit up.

He gripped her arms, holding her until she looked at him. "She won't be alone. If there is trouble, Regan will learn how a family holds together and defends each member. And she will be stronger for it, because that's what a family is."

JJ stared down at him, a caring man, as compassionate as he was strong and responsible. He'd lost his mother and sister, survived a horrible foster home...and had become part of an incredible family.

I want a family.

She hadn't realized she'd spoken the words aloud until she saw the creases at the corners of his eyes deepen. "Mamita, you have a family if you'd only look at what is before you. Accept us."

She stared at him.

He caressed her cheek. "Te amo, mamita. I love you."

The words she'd been waiting a lifetime to hear. "You... I love you, too." As joy flooded her heart, tears blurred her vision. She choked on a laugh. "But you knew that, didn't you?"

His smile answered her.

CHAPTER TWENTY-NINE

T*he faster you finish the fight, the less shot up you will get. -* Unknown

JJ inched a little closer to the woodstove the following afternoon. The temperature had dropped, and damn, it was cold. The mug of tomato soup she was sipping warmed her hands. And her heart, as well. Noticing she was chilled, Caz had made the soup—and Regan had insisted on carrying it to her.

She swallowed hard...because she'd missed them so very much last week.

Through the window, she watched them. They were both wearing their new matching red-and-black scarves. When she'd brought her gifts over, Regan had stared at the scarf like she'd never received a present before, then put it on and worn it in the house all day.

Caz's dark eyes had gone all soft, and when she'd given him his, he'd kissed her.

JJ sighed. She could live on his kisses.

The two were taking scraps to the chickens and collecting eggs. JJ grinned as Regan nailed Caz with a snowball.

He put the can of scraps down, swung an arm around Regan, and dumped her on her butt in a pile of snow.

There was a lot of squirming and shrieking—and the little girl was giggling so hard she almost couldn't get out of the snow. Hands on his hips, Caz was laughing.

God, she loved them.

Thankfully, her cell rang before she could get too maudlin. She pulled it out of her pocket. It was Gene from Weiler. Smiling, she took the call. "Hey, training officer. How are you?"

"Good. I'm damned good." His rough voice was loud and cheerful. "And so are you. Did you see the news? Those lawyers you and the other female officers sent were damn effective."

JJ straightened. Bull had mentioned the lawyers had prepared a case. "Really? What happened?"

Gene laughed, long and hard. "It seems like the mayor and city council aren't real happy about a potential lawsuit and have been stirring things up. To avoid corruption charges, the Chief of Police resigned Friday—and Captain Barlow and Lieutenant Nash Barlow followed him out the door."

"Oh, God, seriously?"

"Yep. The new chief plans to look real damn hard at what's been going on, will be recruiting to bring more diversity into the department, and the deterrents for harassment will get some teeth. The guy came up through the ranks in San Francisco, and, as it happens, he has two sisters who are LEOs."

As Gene chatted about what he'd heard, warmth crept through her. She'd hoped that the bluff of a lawsuit would work.

If it hadn't...if she'd had to take the bastards to court, Caz and his brothers would've been there at her side. She wouldn't have been alone. And didn't that feel good?

"So, how is it living in Alaska?" Gene asked. "I saw you had snow."

"Oh, God, do we have snow." Laughing, she started to tell him about all the ways Alaska was different from Nevada.

CHAPTER THIRTY

W*hen all else fails, gain fire superiority, move toward the path of the enemy guns, and destroy everything in your path.* ~ Unknown

On Monday morning, JJ parked her car and walked toward the coffee shop. Even though it was overcast and cold, she couldn't stop smiling. It was so, so good to be back in Caz's arms every night. For the last three nights, he'd made love to her as if she'd been gone for months. Or maybe all the sex was to celebrate surviving an earthquake.

Admittedly, the quake hadn't been that big a deal, not even in town. Short days and cold nights meant most of the populace had been inside, many in bed, when the shaking happened. A couple of people had fallen. No power lines were down.

She'd better get used to quakes, since this was her home now.

And how cool was that?

Her spirits soared even higher because...Caz *loved* her. And so did Regan.

Her step had a decided bounce as she crossed the sidewalk.

Inside, the coffee shop was crowded with people caffeinating up before work. JJ joined the line at the counter, pleased to fall back into her routine.

The weekend had been a healing one. She, Caz, and Regan had spent a lot of time together, just doing simple things that somehow created the strongest bonds.

Later, she'd gone over to Gabe's cabin.

After collecting a big hug from Audrey, JJ apologized to Gabe and asked to withdraw her resignation. The chief's expression had stayed totally hardass for a terrifying few seconds before he laughed and said he was damn pleased. He'd been afraid he'd have to beat the hell out of Caz—and those knives were a real problem.

What with Audrey snickering in the kitchen, all JJ could do was laugh.

She'd spent Saturday wondering whether to defend herself against the reputation-destroying rumors, then realized the answer lay with one question: What example did she want to give Regan? So on Sunday, she'd spoken with several Rescue residents —the ones who had an ear to the ground.

She huffed a laugh. In Weiler, informants had kept her apprised of problems in her precinct. In Rescue? Well, small town gossip was simply a different kind of information gathering.

As the line moved forward, Sarah, behind the counter, spotted her and raised a hand with a welcoming smile.

The door opened with a blast of cold air. Chevy entered with his partner, Knox.

Knox nodded with a respectful smile. "Officer."

Acceptance was a lovely feeling.

The queue was slow, but JJ didn't mind. The hissing, grinding, and rumbles of the coffee making were pleasant, and she was perfectly happy listening to Chevy and Knox debate the merits of cinnamon buns over donuts.

Until she heard a whisper, a sneering sound.

Stiffening, she turned to look.

Giselle and another women sat in a window booth. Snatches of the conversation were audible. "...Hermitage...officer...fucking...slut."

Oh God. JJ's shoulders hunched before she straightened up. She hadn't planned on tackling the gossip in such a crowded venue, but here she was.

Guess it's time to be a good role model for a little girl.

She stepped out of the line and moved close enough to the booth to confirm Giselle really was spewing lies about JJ. Again.

JJ sighed. The people she'd talked with on Sunday had offered opinions as to Giselle's motivation. Apparently the woman had been chasing Caz since she moved to town—and Caz wasn't interested.

"Excuse me, Giselle." JJ made her voice loud enough to be heard by anyone who cared to listen. She was done with whispers. "You're going around telling everyone I had sex with all the men at the Hermitage, and I only got my job because I screwed the Chief of Police. Neither of which is true. So why are you doing this?"

Every conversation in the room went silent.

Face bright red, Giselle turned—and realized JJ'd blocked any chance of getting out of the booth. She tried to sneer. "I don't know what you're talking about. I don't even know you."

"You're right. We *don't* know each other, so I don't understand why you've spread this bullshit about me. And yes, it was you. I asked people who started this gossip, and everyone pointed at *you*." JJ paused. "What did I do to you that you'd be so nasty?"

Giselle looked around the room like cornered prey. "It's not—"

"The Chief of Police loves Audrey, and they live together. Were you trying to break them up by telling lies about me?"

Gasps came from a few people. And...*oh shit*...Gabe stood up from a booth near the back. Face hard, he crossed his arms over his chest.

But, he had a right to be angry. If the chief and Audrey hadn't been in a solid relationship, this kind of malicious gossip could have truly done some damage.

Everyone loved Audrey and Gabe. Which meant Giselle was in trouble, and she knew it. Her mouth dropped open. "No! I would never. Audrey's a great person. And the chief—" Giselle's hands went up.

"As it happens, I have a relationship with Cazador, and you're saying I screwed his brothers. Seriously?" JJ leaned forward. Intimidation 101. "Are you trying to cause problems between the brothers, then?"

Now Caz stood up. He and Gabe had obviously been having their morning coffee together. Caz looked at Giselle without any expression whatsoever.

Giselle's face went white. "Oh, fuck! I'm sorry!" She turned to JJ. "I'm *sorry*, okay? I...I'll tell people I was wrong. Completely wrong."

JJ wanted to punch her.

No. Police officer, remember? With an effort, she nodded. "All right. You fix it, and we'll call it even."

As JJ stepped back, Giselle slid out of the booth, pushed past the line, and fled the building.

JJ closed her eyes, her nerves jangling. Damn, she'd rather be in a fistfight than deal with stuff like this.

Caz chuckled as he joined her. "You're a holy terror when you get going, Officer Jenner." His expression held both pride and laughter, and then he tilted his head toward the people lined up at the counter. "Listen."

What? Tense, JJ listened.

"...some officer we got," Knox was saying to Sarah. "She's like a knife, you know, the way she cut that woman right down to size."

"A knife?" Chevy let out a loud laugh. "Now don't that just make sense? The doc loves sharp blades—no wonder he fell for her."

JJ snorted. "You Rescue people are crazy."

"And wrong." A wicked glint in his eyes, Caz leaned down to whisper in her ear, "Since I'm the man, I'm supposed to be the blade. *You* are the sheath."

There were no words. She punched him in the shoulder. Hard.

"Gabe, my blade hit me," he whined loudly.

As the entire coffee shop burst into laughter, Caz politely offered her an arm and walked with her out of the shop. Grinning, Gabe followed.

On the sidewalk, JJ leaned against Caz. Honestly, she'd been in shootouts that'd left her less shaken. "I take it you two heard everything?"

His warm hand curved over the back of her neck, massaging the knotted muscles. "Sí. Very nicely handled. You faced the enemy, disarmed her, and accepted her surrender with grace."

"Agreed," Gabe said. "See you at the station."

She stared after him as he crossed the street.

A man and woman came out of the coffee shop. The woman smiled. "Officer."

"Ma'am." The man nodded politely.

JJ exhaled slowly. *Well, okay then.*

"Let's go." Caz nodded toward the municipal building. "We both have work to do. For our town."

Yes.

A few minutes later, after collecting a long warm kiss from Caz in the clinic, she joined Gabe in the station.

"Officer. Look." With a wide smile, he viciously ripped her resignation into tiny pieces. "Don't do it again."

"No, sir. Of course not, sir." Shaking her head, she settled down at her desk. Both of Mako's sons were a bit crazy.

As she started on her paperwork, she heard the chief making a phone call. "Hey, Bull, JJ's staying. Yes, officially as of today. Sorry, bro. I win the pot."

Win the pot? Catching on, she stomped into the chief's office and scowled at him. "You made bets?"

"Heard that, did you?" Damned if he didn't laugh. "We were all betting you'd see reason."

See reason, my ass. "More like you bet on how successful your brother's persuasive talents would be."

"Ah, well, we all know he's effective. The bet was for how quickly he could work his magic."

JJ eyed reports and papers piled on the desk...and wondered how the papers would look strewn all over the floor.

"Whoa." He held up his hands and said hastily, "Welcome to the family, JJ. We're all very pleased with our brother's choice."

So...instead of being mad, she walked out of his office in a haze of happiness. Because the truth was clear in his voice.

Mako's sons were pleased she and Caz would be together.

Two hours later, she parked the patrol car in front of the station and started a quick foot patrol down Main Street.

As she walked past the coffee shop, Sarah saw her. With one hand on her pregnant belly, Sarah picked up a coffee cup and waggled it in invitation.

Someone wanted to hash over the scene with Giselle.

And God, she totally needed coffee. Laughing, JJ nodded and turned toward the door.

Boom.

As the entire street shook crazily, JJ staggered and fell to her knees. It felt like she was on a roller coaster—only the entire world was on the same ride. With a yell, she grabbed the street-light and clung with all her might.

The upheaval didn't *stop*.

Over the roaring came the sounds of screaming, of breaking glass, thuds of things falling, and shouting. A car alarm went off.

And it lasted...and lasted...and lasted.

"Nooo!" Regan cowered under her school desk as everything shook. Roaring filled the room, like a train roaring outside. The building was groaning and screeching. Everyone was screaming. The lights went off.

As the floor bucked, dropping and rising, and the desk banged on her shoulder, she screamed, too.

In the windows, the blinds swung like crazy. As her desk slid across the room, she hung onto it, sliding too, slamming into other desks and chairs. Books, backpacks, and crayons were flung to the floor. With a shriek of metal, the window frame twisted and glass flew everywhere.

Then...it stopped.

Regan choked on sobs, her throat sore, and her face wet. *Papá, I want Papá. Papá and JJ.*

Why didn't Mrs. Wilner tell them what to do?

No, the teacher wasn't even in here. She'd gone to the admin building to get more poster paper for the art project. She'd be back in a second. She *would.*

Sunlight came through the window, dust sparkling in the air. Most of the kids were crying, but some got to their feet.

Regan pulled in a breath and tried to stand.

What was that sound?

A low grinding roar came from outside, getting louder and louder. Snapping and scraping and creaking... Something smashed into their one-room building from the side—and Regan went flying. She hit the floor hard, and pain blasted across her side.

It hurt so bad.

As she curled into a ball, the walls and ceiling shrieked and *moved.* One corner crumbled inward. Stuff scraped past the broken windows, flinging rocks, dirt, snow, and tree branches inside. And everything, even the building, was moving.

Regan clung to a desk, feeling the room grind over the ground outside and then tilt upward like a block ready to roll downhill. As the ceiling buckled inward, rocks and snow buried the building and covered the windows. The room went black.

The screaming of the children went on and on.

Earthquake. Another earthquake. Dear God.

Knees throbbing from landing on cement, JJ used the street-light to regain her feet. The quake was done. Hopefully.

JJ spun toward the coffee shop.

Sarah. Pregnant.

Through the shattered window, she saw Uriah reach his wife and help her to her feet. Glass was everywhere, and Sarah was bleeding, but alert. Alive.

"Take her to the clinic, Uriah," JJ shouted, and he lifted a hand in acknowledgement.

She turned in a circle. Devastation everywhere. Broken windows, fallen trees, signs, power lines. Previously parked cars were scattered across the street, but the snow banks had kept the vehicles from hitting the stores. There was buckling on the road and sidewalks.

Where to start? Caz, Gabe, the town.

Regan.

Her priorities and her heart agreed. She called to Uriah, "Tell Caz I'm checking on the school."

"Yes!" Uriah shouted back. He and Sarah's girl was in kinder-garten. "Please. Now!"

JJ dashed for the patrol car.

The short drive was a nightmare. She fishtailed around a

downed tree, bumped across the warping in the road, skidded to a stop...and stared at the nightmare scene.

What had been a circle of portable schoolrooms was a moonscape. A torrential mass of snow, rocks, and trees had torn loose from the slope above and plunged downhill.

The buildings were gone.

"No." Anguish filled her. She jumped out of the car. "No!"

Wait. Downslope and to the left were battered buildings—three classrooms and the bigger administration building. They'd been shoved off their foundations and away from the fan-shaped slide. Four buildings total. Where was the fifth?

From the rooms, children poured out, tripping and falling on the uneven ground. Small children. Older children. None were Regan's age. *No, no, no.*

Almost unheard under the grinding and groaning noise of the biggest part of the slide came sounds. Yelling, screaming. So very faint. From within the slide itself?

She yanked out her phone. There was no service. She tried her radio—no answer from dispatch. From Regina. It would take time to pull things together.

She had no time.

The principal limped out, his dangling left arm obviously broken. With his other arm, he assisted a young teacher. Blood covered her shoulder. Two older children were helping Mr. Hayes. Like chicks around a hen, the littlest children surrounded an overweight, older woman who was half-dragging a groggy younger woman away from the slide. The last teacher emerged, blood streaming from her head. She staggered as she tried to count the children around her.

No help. None of them could help her. *Dammit.*

JJ called to the principal, "Jones, get your students out of this area. Keep the kids with you—and get me help. One classroom is buried, but I can hear them. Get help!"

"Buried." He stumbled as he stared at the devastation then

shook his head. Straightening, he started snapping orders. Two of the older children were sent off together, racing toward town as he mustered the rest and counted heads. After a few questions, he headed back into the admin building with two middle-schoolers. More staff must still be in there.

JJ hesitated and shook her head. They'd have to handle it. She had her own job to do.

Mouth dry, she moved closer to the slide, searching for the missing portable classroom. Too very, very portable. The rocks and trees groaned, and a separate, small slide started on the far side.

As the noisy children and adults headed toward downtown, she could hear the faint screaming again. From the biggest part of the slide. The kids weren't dead. God help them, they weren't dead. *Regan, hang in there.*

Fighting back panic, JJ moved toward the area where the hill used to drop away. The slope had been filled with the debris.

Where was the yelling the loudest?

She crouched, pulled her flashlight from her duty belt, and pointed it at the waist-high mass. *There.* Beneath a tangle of trees, snow, and rocks, the light reflected off metal and glass. The building must be crumbled up like tinfoil. But the children were wailing.

How could they still be alive? She moved the flashlight back and forth and saw a massive fallen western hemlock. The trunk was propping up all the torn-up trees, rocks, and snow. The classroom was somewhere beneath it.

A rumble sounded as another aftershock hit. The slide moved a few inches, and the screaming increased.

Terror ran up JJ's spine. If the slide let loose, the tree holding the overlying mass would be dislodged—and the portable would flatten like a pancake. She couldn't wait. With the disasters in town, help might not arrive in time.

She could see part of the classroom. Could she get to it? The snarled jumble of trees, snow, and rocks had created a lightless hole, a kind of tunnel. There was no guarantee she could reach the building.

No choice.

Moving the patrol car, she backed it to the closest spot and gathered gear.

She'd have to crawl under the mess and around whatever might be in the way. What if the doors or windows were blocked? How could she get into the building? *Chainsaw.*

There would be injured. *Emergency kit.*

Might need to drag someone out. *Blanket.*

She might get turned around in the darkness. *Guide rope.* Hands shaking from fear and adrenaline, she tied a rope to the car's tow bar and walked to the place she'd enter.

Kneeling, she shone the light down into the dark opening and cringed at the nightmarish tunnel-like path to the classroom. Branches protruded along the sides and down from the top. Jagged edges poked upward. It would be like crawling through a bramble patch of trees.

It might not be big enough to squeeze through. She could see one horrendously tight spot that might require squirming rather than crawling. If she got stuck... The jacket and duty belt had to go. After shucking off her jacket, she locked it and her duty belt in the patrol car.

The free end of the rope went around her wrist. Oh, God, she'd always been slightly claustrophobic. *Breathe. No choice.* She crawled into the terrifying hole. From over her head, snow and dirt trickled down. There were gaps in the tangled limbs beneath her. *Don't even think about it collapsing.* She moved forward a foot. Another. She pulled the rope along with her. It would be a guide for the children.

Or a locator for everyone's bodies, including hers.

Every time the mass over her head, beneath her, or around her groaned with a low shuddering rumble, she froze. The high voice in her head shrieked: *Go back, go back. Wait for help. Don't be stupid.*

She went on.

The space narrowed. Branches caught at her clothing, ripped her hair. Her heart pounded. Fear-sweat soaked her uniform shirt.

CHAPTER THIRTY-ONE

F *ailure is not falling down but refusing to get up.* - Chinese proverb

Regan woke to screams and...darkness. A nightmare of darkness. Why was the floor crooked? Kids were yelling, crying, screaming. *Kids. School.* That had been an earthquake. The building had moved.

Panic filled her so full she couldn't breathe. She had to get *out*. She rose and toppled over, falling into a chair, a desk. Sharp things ripped into her hands and knees. She couldn't *see*.

Sobbing and little screams escaped her. *No.* She wasn't a baby. But there wasn't enough air, and she couldn't *see*. Gasping, she stopped.

In her head, she could hear Papá. He'd talked about getting lost. *"Fear makes you stupid. Stop and think, mija, before you act."*

I'm lost, Papá. I need you. Holding really still, she drew in a small breath then a bigger one.

And...she saw a tiny hint of light that flickered, and maybe that was a window, so her coat might still be hanging by the door.

Cuz she always used the loop on the neckband to go over the hook.

The floor was tilted like a mountain. She crawled up the slant, banging on the desks, bumping into another kid who screamed. Broken glass sliced her hands, her knees—sharp, burning pain. *Owwwwww.*

Tears poured down her cheeks, but she kept going.

"*SEALs don't quit,*" Bull said when he talked about him and Gabe in training. He told her most guys rang a bell to say they couldn't hack it. The ones who didn't quit got to be SEALs.

"*Medics don't give up,*" Papá said when she'd asked him about a scar on his arm. He got shot carrying a soldier away from the fighting.

"*Men might have more muscles, but women are stronger in other ways,*" JJ said. "*We do what needs to be done—and we don't quit.*"

Crying from pain and fear, Regan kept crawling.

She found the wall by running into it, and her head exploded with pain. "Fuck!"

Everything hurt. As she felt along the wall, her sliced-up hands burned. That was the door. Carefully, she stood. Coats were scattered on the floor, some still on hooks. Hardly breathing, she felt each one until she found the puffy one with a furry hood. Hers. And there in the pocket was her flashlight from the Halloween parade.

After the snowstorm, Papá had put in new batteries. Would it work? Holding her breath, she turned it on.

Everyone went silent—and she could hear the groaning and creaking of the room itself. Her hand shook so hard the light zigzagged around the room.

Her breathing stopped. Across the room, the ceiling hung down, and that side of the room had scrunched inward. The busted, sagging windows there showed only darkness. Stones and snow trickled in.

She turned. Behind her, the tiny window in the door was

broken, and she could see only more rocks and snow outside. But she'd seen a light outside, right? Where? The window past the door was completely blocked by a huge tree trunk jammed against it.

Heart hammering, she put the flashlight in her mouth and crawled to the last window. More branches filled the opening. But...did she hear something? A shout from outside?

One of the kids started to cry, another one was screaming.

Too much noise. "Be quiet—I need to—"

They were all screaming, whining, crying. She wanted to sit down and cry, too.

But she was part of Mako's family, and Mako wouldn't give up. His family wouldn't. Papá would come. He'd said he would always come for her.

She fought for control. No crying. Head pressed to the window frame, she listened. Something? A voice? The noise inside drowned it out.

Uncle Hawk's voice sounded in her head, telling her what to do. She sucked in air like he'd said, into her chest, into her stomach, and her shout came out, fierce and loud. "*Shut. Up.*"

They did.

"There might be someone out there. Keep quiet. All of you." She tried to stick her head out the window and couldn't. Too many branches. So she yelled, "Help!"

Someone called back, "Coming. Stay *put*." That voice—that was JJ!

Tears streamed down Regan's face. "We're here."

A light appeared. JJ had a flashlight. It moved closer.

"JJ. I'm here, JJ. I'm here." Her breathing was all wonky, like she'd landed on her belly or something.

"That a girl." JJ sounded normal. The same way she did at breakfast. Or playing cards. "The windows are blocked. I'm going to fire up the chainsaw and cut a hole. So you all need to move away from the window area. Can you do that?"

"Okay. Okay." Everything in Regan wanted JJ in here now. Not later. *Now, now, now.* Her hands were shaking even harder.

JJ'd told them what to do, but the kids crowded around the window—right where they shouldn't be. "Move back."

No one budged, just fought to get closer to the window.

She had to be Uncle Hawk. She pointed the flashlight at the other side of the room. *Pull in air. Short words.* "Move. There." No one moved. She shoved more air down, went for a deep Bull voice. "*Now.*"

The kids staggered, fell, and moved downward to the other wall.

"C'mon." Delaney took Regan's hand.

Ignoring the pain, Regan gripped tight, and they slid and lurched after the others.

"Okay, JJ. We're away," Regan yelled.

"Atta-girl." A second later, there was the sound of tapping, and then a chainsaw roared. About hip-high, a blade appeared and cut a long line toward the floor. JJ tapped on the wall again and cut down another side. Across the top. The bottom. The chainsaw stopped. JJ kicked, and there was an opening.

After shoving the chainsaw through the hole, JJ crawled in, slow and careful, with a flashlight in one hand.

As she stood up, everybody staggered uphill to her, crying and trying to touch her, to hold on. Regan, too.

"Easy, easy." JJ patted shoulders and stroked backs.

"All right now. Her voice changed, and she was really good at Uncle Hawk's command voice. "Listen. *Up.*"

Silence.

"Sit down right where you are." She waited until they did. "How many children were in this room today?"

"Only seven." Delaney kept track of that kind of stuff. It wasn't their usual thirteen since some had gone to relatives for the winter. One was sick at home today.

Regan wished she were, too.

The flashlight flickered over the kids sitting around JJ. "Seven. Good. Where is your teacher?"

Regan's hand hurt too much so she linked arms with Delaney. "Mrs. Wilner's not here. She went to the admin building. Before."

"Okay then." JJ tied a rope around the teacher's big desk and straightened. She pulled in a breath.

Regan's eyes widened. JJ was scared, too.

"I know this is frightening, and you're all hurting," JJ said. "But no matter what, you keep going. Regan, you have the other flashlight. I want you to lead. Remember to listen for me."

Go *first*? Regan shook her head.

"You can do it. I know you can. Just grab the rope and follow it out." With a smile, JJ patted her shoulder. "I'm going to bring up the rear, and my flashlight will help the ones in the middle see where they're going."

JJ pointed to the hole in the wall. "Move 'em out, Regan. Let's go."

Caz had just finished giving a woman directions on how to care for the splint on her broken arm when he heard shouting from the lobby.

"Landslide at the school. A portable classroom got buried."

"The cop needs help."

The school? A cop? Caz ran out of the clinic and into the dimness of the lobby that was lit by the generator-powered emergency lighting.

Two middle-schoolers, a boy and girl, stood panting in front of Regina's reception desk.

Fear shot through Caz. Sarah had said JJ was going to the school. He should have gone there, too. "What happened?"

"The cliff—it's gone. Like a slide or avalanche or something came down, and hit our buildings. And ours got pushed out, but"—the girl paused to pull in a breath—"it buried a building. The three-fives."

The third through fifth graders. Regan's room. A ruthless hand seemed to be squeezing Caz's chest.

The boy added, "Officer JJ said she could hear them. Hurry. Please, please hurry!"

Caz started to move, and a hand closed on his shoulder. Gabe. "'mano, I need to go."

"You will," Gabe said. "JJ has the patrol car there. Let's take what else she'll need."

"You can't even see the classroom," the girl said.

Gabe pointed to Regina. "Get rope and the tackle gear from the station stores. Caz—"

His brain kicked in. "On it." To the right of the clinic door, he'd stocked the cupboard with emergency first-aid gear in case Gabe or anyone else had need. He yanked on his coat, slung two of the emergency packs over his shoulder, and grabbed a stack of blankets.

In the lobby, Gabe had Audrey and Zappa, the gray-haired, hippie gas station owner beside him. "Regina, deal with triage here, draft anyone who knows first aid to the clinic, and send help where it's needed.

"Zappa, you're with Caz." Gabe turned. "Audrey, you're with me."

Finally. With Zappa behind him, Caz ran out the back to his SUV.

At the school, the town's patrol car sat at the edge of the unholy mess of the landslide. JJ wasn't in sight.

"Fuck me," Zappa muttered, looking up the steep hill above where the school had been. "Looks like the quake busted off a ledge or something. Turned that shit into a landslide."

As Gabe's black Jeep pulled up, Caz worked his way closer to the slide. Fear blasted through him. Had JJ tried to help and been buried? "JJ!"

Spotting a rope tied to the patrol car's tow bar, he followed it to where it ran into the rubble. Crouching, he could see a hollow, no, a thin excuse for a tunnel, directly under the tangle of branches, snow, and rocks.

Gabe opened the patrol car. "Her coat and duty belt are here." After locking it back up, Gabe squatted next to him. "Do you—"

Caz held up his hand for silence. "Listen."

High, terrified voices came from under the slide. Along with a calm, firm woman's voice.

Alive. She was alive.

The relief blanked his brain for a second. What about Regan?

After steadying his own voice, Caz called, "JJ. We're here. How can we help?"

"Stay out. There's no room. Seven kids coming out." There was a pause. "Call to Regan. She's leading."

Regan and JJ were alive. Under all that. His whole body shook with fear for them. With the need to scramble in and grab them and save them. The rockslide was still groaning, could give way at any moment.

He cleared his throat. Calm and reassuring. That was what they needed from him right now. "Regan, head for me, mija."

"Papá." The shaking in her voice wrenched at his heart.

"I hear you, mi tesoro. You're almost out." She wasn't. Wasn't close enough at all.

Nothing he could do. Hands fisted, he waited at the entrance. Behind him, Gabe was opening the first-aid kits and assigning Zappa and Audrey to tasks.

From the tunnel came the sounds of other children. Crying, whimpering, protests.

"That's perfect, Regan." JJ's voice drifted out. "There you go. Good job, Delaney."

A second later. "Keep going, Niko, you're past the worst spot. Almost there, kids. The doc is waiting for you."

Caz saw a light, a flashlight bobbing. "Only a bit more. Come on."

It was Regan in the lead. His heart gave a leap.

Then his little girl was there, crawling out, covered in mud and blood. As he pulled her into his arms, she was sweaty, shaking, crying, and *alive*. He barely kept from squeezing the breath out of her. "Are you hurt? Let me look."

"You came for me—you said you would, you always would, and you *did*." She was crying so hard she was choking.

He patted her up and down. Noted the winces. Blood covered her palms, her elbows and arms, her knees. Her face was scraped. A gash on her chin was bleeding.

"I'm okay." She swiped away the tears. "Help JJ."

Gabe was already pulling the next child out. And Zappa another.

"Fuck, I'm so fucking proud of you," Caz murmured, pressing his cheek to the top of her head. With gut-wrenching reluctance, he passed her to Audrey and bent to help another child.

Five, so far. No more came out.

He heard the murmur of sound, a child crying, another,

"JJ," Caz called. "Talk to me."

"There's a narrow place with a hole to cross. Brayden is—I can't get him moving." The carefully controlled tone showed JJ was terrified.

Fuck, so was he.

Gabe knelt to crawl in, and Caz pulled him back and took the flashlight from his hand. "You won't fit, 'mano. This one is mine."

"Dammit." Gabe scowled. Nodded.

"Maybe, I should?" Audrey asked.

Caz shook his head. "They might need more strength than you have, chica. If it's too narrow, I'll come back."

After eyeing the tiny opening, Caz yanked off his coat. Smaller was better. He dropped to his knees and crawled into the barely open gap. He could almost feel the weight over his head. "I'm coming, JJ. Hang tight."

"We are." Her voice had a tremor in it. Fear or hypothermia? Her coat was by the car.

The landslide groaned around him, only kept from moving by the logs and tangled branches. Under his knees, the logs moved an inch. His gut tensed. He crawled forward, expecting to be crushed at any moment.

The way narrowed, curving slightly around a huge tree trunk. Too tight for his shoulders.

There was the boy, just past the curve. The kid was on hands and knees, staring at a black gaping spot in the branches and rocks. Not moving.

"Easy, Brayden." Caz shined the light past the kid and saw Delaney right in front of JJ. The space between the logs and rocks was so narrow JJ couldn't get past the girl to reach the petrified boy.

Caz wouldn't fit through the narrow spot on this side. But, maybe...

He shoved his shoulder up against the tree and stretched an arm out.

Staring into the dark hole, the kid didn't react.

Easy, easy. Any sudden movement and the kid would back out of reach. Caz stretched painfully, not touching the boy until...

His fingers closed around Brayden's wrist. The child jerked, but Caz had a good grip.

Do it fast. If Brayden dropped into that damn hole, there wasn't any leverage to pull him out. Caz yanked him forward and shoved himself backward, making room. The boy hit the tree at the corner with a yelp, but he was past the gap.

Caz pulled the hysterical, crying child close, stroking what he could reach. "It's all right, Brayden. We're going to get out of here now."

If he could manage to crawl backward and drag the boy at the same time. "JJ, you good to follow?"

No answer.

"Officer JJ?" Delaney whispered. Her voice went higher. "JJ?"

Silence.

"JJ?" Hypothermia? Bleeding? He sharpened his voice. "*Officer Jenner*. Stay with me."

"Caz. God." There was an audible shaky breath. "Sorry."

Thank fuck. "If you want a coffee break, princesa, it must wait until we're out. Sorry."

There was a huffed laugh from the toughest woman he'd ever met. "All right then. Let's get this done." JJ's voice was back to normal. "Delaney, go on through. Doc is right in front of you."

The groaning in the mass was increasing. This whole disaster was going to let loose. "Hurry, you two."

Ignoring the branches ripping his shirt and skin, Caz crawled backward, hauling the boy as he went. While shining the light between his legs, he'd line up the next move, move back, and pull the boy after him. Shine, crawl, pull.

The terrified boy wasn't doing anything to help.

"Faster, bro. It's moving." The deep yell was Bull's.

Dios, the tunnel was narrower than it had been. It was closing.

Then there was light. Hands tugged him out. Rolling backward, Caz yanked Brayden out. The poor kid would have bruises on his wrist from Caz's grip.

Delaney had almost caught up to them. Audrey helped her out, and Regan let out a shout of happiness.

With a low roar, the entire mass started to flow again.

"JJ!" Caz dove back in the hole, grabbing JJ's wrists as rocks and snow started to engulf her.

With a bellow of rage, Bull grabbed one big branch and held it up, keeping the opening clear.

Hands gripped Caz's legs, hauling him and JJ out.

And then they were free.

Caz wrapped an arm around her waist as Gabe and Bull hustled them away from the moving, rumbling mass. He turned to look. The big tree that'd held the weight off the schoolroom had been shaken loose. A chill ran up his spine as the last trace of the building disappeared. Crushed completely.

Watching, JJ shuddered and buried her face in Caz's neck. Hot tears dropped onto his skin. "I was so scared," she whispered.

His arms tightened as he put his lips to her ear. "So was I."

A tiny thud struck his side as Regan grabbed him. Clung to them both. She was crying, almost hysterical, as they drew her between them.

The bands around Caz's chest loosened, letting him breathe again. They were both safe.

Behind him, Gabe was assigning children to the cars that had arrived, sending them off to the station and clinic.

A dull roar sounded, making everyone look up. Hawk's ski plane came in for a landing on the snow-covered lake behind the roadhouse. And Caz felt a wave of gratitude and relief. The patients he couldn't treat could get airlifted to the hospital.

Knowing Hawk, he'd get someone to give him a helicopter to use once he got to a city.

"Gabe, make sure the area behind the clinic is clear for a helicopter landing," Caz called.

Gabe raised his hand in acknowledgement and continued moving people out.

"Come, let's get you two back to town." Arms around his girl and his woman, Caz guided them toward the cars. "We have more work to do."

CHAPTER THIRTY-TWO

I f *the patient is screaming, the patient is breathing.* - Murphy's Laws for Combat Medicine

After a time wrapped in a warm blanket and drinking hot fluids, JJ warmed up enough to clean up and apply bandages in the dimly lit station bathroom. The doc had wanted to care for her, but there were far more badly wounded people who needed him.

She donned spare clothing from her locker and managed to pull on her boots. As she rose, every bruise, strained muscle, scrape, and cut yelled in protest. God, she hurt. Yet pain could be set aside.

Unhappily, the terror of being buried alive and the fear of losing the children wasn't as easy to release. Deep inside, she was still shaking.

Thank God for Caz. She'd lost it in the tunnel. He told her she'd gone hypothermic. All she remembered was that everything had gone foggy and darkness had closed around her. His voice—his love and strength—had snapped her out of it and gotten her moving forward.

When he held her afterward, she'd felt the fine tremor in his muscles, heard the strain in his voice. He'd been afraid for her, for them all, yet his voice had never wavered. He'd drawn her out of the tunnel and into the light.

How much more could she love him?

Leaning on the counter, she assessed her condition. *Good enough.* Shaky or not, it was time to get her butt back on the job. Her family—she smiled at the thought—her *family* was doing the same.

Using the patrol car, Gabe was responding to calls.

Audrey was manning the phones with Regina.

The meeting rooms upstairs were open for people needing emergency shelter, and Bull was gathering supplies and food for them. That was Bull—always feeding people.

With his staff and volunteers, Caz was tending to the injured.

In his Cessna, Hawk was transporting people to the Soldotna and Anchorage hospitals, freeing up the air ambulances for the critically injured.

Here goes. JJ slung on the duty belt, attached the keepers to her inner belt, checked her weaponry, and adjusted everything. After grabbing her jacket, she walked out of the station's rooms into the lobby.

The babble of a crowd hit her ears.

Those needing medical care were gathered near the clinic door. A few lay on blankets, others sat on chairs or the floor with relatives and friends to help them.

On the side nearest the police station, volunteers waited to be sent out to help.

JJ headed for the reception desk where Regina handled calls to the station and health clinic. Cell service was out, but the landlines and mobile radio were working. Next to Regina, Audrey fielded calls from the 911 dispatcher.

JJ waited for a pause and asked, "Where do you want me to go?"

Audrey frowned. "Gabe said you should head home. You've already—"

When JJ shook her head no, Regina half-grinned. "Yeah, I didn't think you'd agree. He said he had to try."

The phone rang, and Regina held up a finger as she answered.

"Are you all right?" Audrey asked in a low voice.

"I'm fine." JJ shrugged, winced, and half-grinned. "Mostly. I'll be sore tomorrow." In fact, she'd be lucky to get out of bed at all.

The clinic door opened, and Caz assisted a woman out to join her relatives. He murmured a few instructions on care, smiled at the waiting crowd, and spotted JJ. His brows drew together as he walked over.

Tensing, she waited for him to object—to say she wasn't strong enough, wasn't good enough.

He smiled ruefully. "I hate that you're working when you're exhausted and injured, but you won't rest any more than Gabe would if it were him."

As she stared at him in surprise, he bent down, rubbed his cheek against hers, and kissed her gently. "Do my overprotective heart a favor and be careful, yes?"

"God, I love you," she whispered, only realizing she'd spoken aloud when his eyes darkened.

His hand cupped her cheek. "I love you, too."

She would never, ever, grow tired of hearing that.

After stroking her hair, he straightened. "Take my Subaru. It's got extra rescue and first-aid supplies boxed in the back."

She snorted. "Of course it does." Mako had been a survivalist; his sons hadn't fallen far from the tree.

He handed her the keys, dug in his lab coat pocket, and pulled out a granola bar. Closing her fingers around the bar, he kissed her knuckles and gave her a stern look. "Eat that. There is bottled water in the car. Drink one."

"Yes, Doc." She smiled up at him. "Thanks."

He touched her cheek tenderly then turned and walked to the crowd around the clinic door. "Who's next, Irene?"

The brusque postmistress was in charge of triage. She pointed to a man lying on blankets. "Glass wounds and concussion, I'm guessing. He's complaining of stomach pain, too."

"Let's get him on an exam table." Caz pointed to several people. "You four are now stretcher bearers."

Regan appeared at the clinic door—and held it open for them. She waved at JJ before disappearing after the group.

Regan was helping in the clinic?

JJ fought back the urge to grab the child and tuck her into bed. Hell, that was probably how Caz felt about JJ working right now.

Shaking her head, JJ turned back to the desk and heard Regina saying to Audrey: "I *knew* there was something between her and the doc."

JJ tensed. "I didn't—"

"Disasters are the *best* aphrodisiac. It took a blizzard to get my man to say he loved me." Regina's smile was huge. "This is excellent; you're perfect for him. He needs a woman with guts, one with more depth than a puddle in the street."

"I totally agree," Audrey said.

The two were so openly pleased that JJ could only laugh as her fears dissolved.

"Okay, to work." Regina handed over two pieces of paper. "Here are two calls for help up on Dall Road. While you're there, can you swing by the Patriot Zealot farm and check how they're managing?"

PZs. Oh joy. But weird beliefs or not, they were part of Rescue. This was what she'd trained for, what she could do. Serving. Protecting. "Of course."

"Take Knox with you as your second." Regina turned toward the volunteers. "Hey, Knox, you're up." She waved the lanky man with bushy red hair forward then pointed at JJ.

JJ nodded at the handyman. Today, having another person along would be wonderful.

"You be careful out there." Audrey's worried expression held a friend's concern.

JJ patted her arm. "We will. Thanks."

Crossing the lobby, she smiled at Knox. "If you have a tool box, grab it, and let's go."

With no hesitation at all, he returned her smile and moved forward. "Yes'm."

When they were halfway to the door, Regina called, "Hey, Knox. The girl's already been a hero once today. You drive, eh?"

"Got it. I was at the school. I saw," Knox shouted back. He looked down at JJ. "I handle driving and heavy shit. You handle bossing. Fair division of labor."

"Works for me." It really did. She'd probably fall asleep if she got in a warm car and tried to drive. JJ took a bite of Caz's granola bar. Oats and honey. Boring—and the best thing she'd tasted in forever.

Holding Sissy on her lap, Regan smiled at her father as he wrapped the long cut on the three-year-old's leg. The kid's mom was on a cot in the next room cuz she'd hit her head so hard that she threw up every time she moved.

"There you go, chica." Papá's voice was all smooth and soft and made Regan feel as good as when Sirius purred.

The little kid had settled down when Papá started talking to her. Her face was still wet from crying, but now she was just sucking on her thumb. The ugly place on her leg was cleaned up and glued together, and Papá was wrapping the white stuff around it.

Regan knew about all the different bandages now. After Papá got the glass out of her hands and elbows and knees, Grammy

Lillian had bandaged her and the other kids up. There were the shiny Telfa pads that Papá said wouldn't stick to the scabs, and the plain white wrapping, and the fluffy Kerlix gauze, and the colored wrinkly conform stuff that stuck to itself.

She'd been awful bloody.

But she didn't hurt as much when she kept busy helping Papá. Although Grammy and another lady were working in the clinic, and Miss Irene and a guy were doing tree-somethings in the lobby, there was too much to do.

Papá said he was glad Regan was here to help, too.

"Hey, Doc, we need you. Got a bad one," Irene shouted from the front.

"Dios," Papá muttered. "Mija, can you stay with Sissy until her mamá can watch over her? Maybe have her lie down and take a nap?"

"Sure. I got it."

His smile made her feel great. "You are the best daughter a man could ever want." He kissed the top of her head and went to take care of whoever had come in.

Because that was his job, and he liked his job. Even when it was crazy like this.

Regan liked it, too. Helping. Being part of fixing bad things. She smiled, even though she hurt, because she knew what she was going to be when she grew up.

On the way out of town, JJ and Knox had called in a house fire. Propane tanks and earthquakes didn't mix well.

Another call went in for a downed power line.

Knox turned out to be a great driver, navigating past buckled areas on the gravel road and obstructing boulders, branches, and fallen trees.

Way above them at the end of Dall Road, McNally's could be

seen, perched high on the mountain. "The resort didn't slide off, at least."

Knox followed her gaze. "Bet it's a mess though. Got a lot of display windows. And tourists panic easy."

"Maybe we should—"

"Nope. Look at the bridge up there." He pointed to where the road went over a bridge before switchbacking up the mountain.

JJ's eyes widened. "The far side of the bridge is out."

"Yeah. I'm guessing the bridge's okay but the road around it got fucked up." He shrugged. "Fixing it will take a while since the road crews'll do the big highways first. The Seward and Sterling will be blocked with rockslides and shit."

She shook her head. "It's amazing how dependent all the peninsula's towns are on those roads." There was only one road in and out of Rescue.

"Heh, we have towns where the only way to get there is by boat or plane. It's why we got so many bush pilots in Alaska. Rescue'll be all right."

"We will." Up on the mountain, a helicopter lifted off. Probably one of the resort's tour copters. Just like Hawk and another pilot were ferrying the injured out of Rescue.

After checking the paper Regina had handed her, JJ pointed to a dirt road. "Turn here. It seems this guy has a ham radio, but isn't answering calls. His friend is worried."

"Okay, then." Knox parked in front of an ancient log cabin and jumped out.

JJ followed more slowly, trying not to groan. Breathing through the pain, she studied the building. There was patchy snow and dead brown moss on the wood-shingled roof. No smoke from a stovepipe. Her eyes narrowed as she saw an add-on room had fallen in.

Reaching the door, she rapped on it smartly. "Mr. Rasmussen. This is Officer Jenner with Rescue Police. Harvey wanted us to check on you."

A low groan sounded followed by a faint, "Help!"

With Knox behind her, JJ opened the unlocked door and moved carefully through the mess. Dislodged by the quake, household articles littered the floor—books, a shotgun from the rack over the door, candles, broken lanterns, pictures. "Where are you, sir?"

"Lean-to."

She followed the sound of gasping and opened a door to the add-on room. A cold wind blasted past.

The man lay on his back, pinned beneath a pile of logs.

"Whoa, got yourself in a mess," Knox commented.

"No." Gasp. "Shit."

"Hold on, we'll get you out." JJ glanced at Knox and pointed to the right wall. "Let's pile everything over there."

One, by one, they moved the logs and finally, Knox hefted the last up far enough that JJ could drag Rasmussen out.

Holding his chest, the man groaned. "I was beginning to think I'd never manage to get a full breath again."

JJ put her hand on his shoulder. "Hold up while I do a quick check." She assessed for broken bones, head and spine injury, and before she could do more, he rolled and pushed to his feet.

"I'm good, ma'am." He pulled off his heavy coat and showed the two thick sweaters beneath before gingerly pressing on his ribcage. "Doesn't feel like I busted anything, but damn, I'm gonna hurt for a while."

Knox snorted. "You're lucky to be alive."

"Yeah." Rasmussen motioned to the fallen side of the room. "The asshole who built the lean-to did a shit-poor job. I was dismantling it to rebuild it—and the quake decided to help out."

"Bad timing all right," JJ agreed.

"Yep. Thanks for coming by. I was on the way to freezing to death."

"We should take you back to town to let the doc check you out." JJ led the way into the main room.

Rasmussen shook his head. "A shot of good whiskey and sitting by the stove, I'll be fine."

"Well." The man was moving well enough—and they had another citizen to check on. "All right."

As Rasmussen settled into a chair, she built up the fire in the wood stove while Knox brought in more firewood.

A few minutes later, JJ climbed into the Subaru.

In the driver's seat, Knox was reading Regina's first dispatch note, his lips moving. "What's this word? Pes-tye..." He pointed.

"Pestiferous. *Pest-ih-fer-us*." JJ snorted. "It can mean annoying. Mr. Rasmussen's friend apparently called more than once and nagged enough to annoy Regina."

Knox nodded. "Pestiferous. I like it." Handing JJ the note, he started up the engine and headed out.

As they returned to Dall Road, JJ leaned back in her seat. The pain from her aching muscles and the gashes disappeared under the warm contented feeling. This...this was why she was a police officer. Mr. Rasmussen had needed help, and she'd been there. Her help had made a difference in his life.

Smiling, JJ glanced at Knox. "Do you know the way to the Patriot Zealot property?"

"Sure. Why?"

"It's next on the list."

Knox made a glum noise. "Oh. Fun."

Surrounded by forest, the Patriot Zealot compound was off Dall, down a dirt road, and ended at a metal gate with a small guard hut. Six-foot fencing topped with razor wire enclosed the entire compound. Inside the cleared land of the compound, deer fencing protected the vegetable gardens.

After a glance at the empty guard hut, JJ walked up to the gate. A dirt road ran from the closed gate to a mixture of portable houses and log cabins. In the center of the buildings stood a two-story tower. Although the tower tilted to one side, everything else appeared intact. People milled around the various buildings.

Since entering the compound was liable to get her riddled with bullets, she made a megaphone of her hands. "Hey. Is everyone all right? Do you need help?"

Two men broke away from the crowd and jogged down the rough dirt road toward her.

As they neared, the thin guy with black hair and a beard glared. "What the fuck do you want, cop?"

Ah, this was the one Caz had told her was Captain Nabera.

The other man, the so-called Reverend Parrish, made a calming gesture to his captain and slowed to a walk. "Officer Jenner, I believe?"

She kept her voice calm. "Right. I'm checking on people out this way and stopped to make sure you were all right."

"We are, thank you." Parrish had a richly mesmerizing voice. "Although we do have some injured."

"The Rescue Health Clinic is open. If you have critically injured, you can call either the station or 911 for an airlift to the Soldotna hospital. I have first-aid training if you need assistance now."

Nabera sneered. "Unlike others, *we* are prepared for disasters. We don't need any fucking help."

Parrish gave Nabera another stand-down frown. "Thank you, Officer. Should I assume the Sterling and Seward highways are impassible?"

"I'm afraid so. The quake shook loose more than one avalanche."

"Then we'll bring the injured who need more than first aid to the clinic." Parrish gave her a thin smile. "We've got it covered."

"All right, then." She nodded politely and returned to the car. From what she'd read about militia groups, especially the ones in Alaska, Captain Nabera hadn't lied. The PZs probably *were* well prepared for disasters.

Much like the Hermitage.

The difference was that the guys at the Hermitage were trying their best to help everyone—even the PZ jerks.

Knox let her fume for a minute as he navigated a U-turn and headed back toward Dall Road. "At least they talked to you and were fairly polite."

She shrugged and let her annoyance go. "True, considering I was a woman in a police uniform. I was half-prepared to be shot on sight."

"Eh, Parrish isn't that bad, although I'm not into that conservative religious crap. They're too damned hard on their women. Hell, if I told my sister she belongs in the kitchen, she'd take my head off." He grinned at JJ. "She's a welder down in Juneau."

No wonder he was so accepting of a female LEO. "Good to hear."

"What's next?"

JJ pulled out the next assignment and read off the address. "We're looking for Mrs. Hudson who should've picked up one of the schoolkids, but didn't show. The girl said Mr. Hudson went to Soldotna this morning, and her grandmother is alone."

JJ snorted as she read farther. "The kid said that, after the little quake, Mr. Hudson wanted to stock up. In case of a bigger quake. Regina drew a face with rolling eyes."

Knox laughed. "That's Regina."

When they pulled up to the door of a modular home, JJ saw a car parked under the carport. So the woman was probably home.

The property was nicely kept up. No old vehicles or rusting barrels in the yard. Leafless bushes lined the front in a tidy row. A plastic-covered greenhouse was in the back.

Up on the porch, she went through the usual drill. No answer to her knocking and calling.

Once again, the door wasn't locked. Rural people just didn't lock up, it seemed. Opening the door cautiously, she called, "Rescue Police. I'm coming in to see if you're all right."

"Here." The response was only a whisper of sound.

JJ headed into the kitchen. An elderly woman lay on the floor, face white with pain.

"Ma'am." JJ knelt next to her. "Where are you hurt?"

"Hip." Her head slowly turned toward JJ.

JJ checked—and winced. The woman's right leg was turned out and shorter than the left.

"Busted?" Knox asked.

"Yes. She needs an airlift out. While I finish here, can you call it in and mark out a landing site for the helicopter?" She handed him her radio.

"Can do." Knox stepped outside.

JJ did a quick assessment for other problems. Seemed to be just the hip. As she finished, the woman opened her eyes again. "My granddaughter. I was supposed to fetch her."

"All the children are safe at the police station." JJ grabbed a blanket from the living room, draped it over the woman, and sat down beside her. To keep her company.

The woman gave her a slightly unfocused look before frowning at JJ's badge then her face. "Police woman. My daughter told me about *you*."

Told her...what? Oh. Of course. The gossip.

As Mrs. Hudson's eyes closed, JJ pushed to her feet, feeling... dirty. Unwelcome.

"Helicopter's here." Knox stood in the doorway, obviously having heard. His brows drew together as he frowned at the older woman then JJ. "Gossip and small towns. Damned if I know how that crap about you got started. It's not like you're at the bar every night."

JJ pulled in a breath, emotions roiling. Hurt and anger...and shame. Why did she feel ashamed when she hadn't done anything? *Okay, just give the man a polite explanation.* "Since there was no housing available when I arrived, the chief lent me his father's cabin. His brothers live in the adjacent cabins."

"Ah. So now you're fucking all the guys out there?" Knox snorted.

She couldn't tell what he believed. After all, he'd seen Caz kiss her in the station. Dammit, she was too tired to be tactful. "Listen, if it bothers you, I'll drop you off at the station. I don't—"

"Yeah, that's bullshit, woman." Knox flushed. "I don't care if you fuck the entire Ice Dogs team. You sure do the job better than the last asshole officer. That lying bastard wouldn't've put his life on the line for anyone."

Her mouth dropped open.

"I'm not going anywhere." Jaw set, he crossed his arms over his chest. "Happens that Regina called with two more places to check after this one. We got work to do."

Her eyes burned for a second. God, she was tired. Emotional. A mess. So she simply nodded. "Got it. Thank you, Knox."

Hawk appeared in the open door and limped inside. "Knox, can you and the medic bring in the stretcher?"

"Yep."

As Knox walked out, Hawk glanced at JJ. "If I'd known you were sleeping with everyone at the Hermitage, I'd've come home sooner."

She stared at him.

Humor glinted in his steel-colored eyes, and he almost smiled.

Huffing a laugh, she turned to prepare the woman for leaving.

At well past midnight, Caz began to wonder if he'd have to treat every person in all of Rescue. But when he followed his last patient out into the waiting area, no one waited to see him. Relief swamped him.

A couple of hours before, he'd sent his helpers home. They'd been staggering with exhaustion.

After cleaning up, Caz pulled on fresh clothes and locked the clinic. JJ had left his Subaru in the parking lot. She'd even filled the tank, probably from one of the emergency cans Gabe kept in the station. On the passenger seat, he found a list of the supplies she'd used so he could restock.

Organized and thoughtful. Dios, he adored her.

As Caz drove home, he passed downed power lines and fallen trees that'd been chain-sawed and hauled off the road. At the Hermitage, the ski plane sat on the runway. Hawk was home—probably exhausted and hurting from putting in a damn long day. He'd shoot anyone waking him up now, but Caz would check on him in the morning.

After manually opening the garage door, Caz parked the car inside. And took his first easy breath since the earthquake.

Home.

Silently, he walked down the hallway and pushed Regan's bedroom door open. She'd be asleep. She'd worked her ass off in the clinic until around nine when Bull had swung by and picked her up.

Caz stared at the bed. The *empty* bed. Had Bull taken Regan home with him? But the cabin was toasty warm—obviously, someone had stoked up the woodstove.

Well, no matter how late, he'd go over there to check on her.

And then, he'd see if he could talk his cop into letting him sleep in her bed.

In the main cabin room, he stopped and smiled.

On the carpet in front of the woodstove, two small figures were curled up in a pile of blankets. Regan's dark hair spilled across her pillow. The other girl... Was that Delaney? They were sound asleep with the cat curled between them.

A sense of peace swept through him. His girl was safe.

His amazing daughter.

After the nightmare of the quake, where she'd led the other children out of that nightmare of a tunnel, she'd completely charmed his clinic patients with her mix of humor and compassion. She'd even taken to imitating his calming tone, and Dios, he'd never been so proud. She was a miracle.

In stocking feet, he crossed the room. After tucking the covers closer around the girls, he stroked a hand down Sirius's soft fur and sighed. Every bone in his body felt like lead as he straightened and looked around for his brother. Bull wouldn't have left the children here alone.

"Caz." The whisper drew his attention to the couch.

Sitting up slowly, JJ pushed her hair out of her face.

Now—now his world was complete.

"Hey," she whispered.

"Hey," he whispered back. Taking her hand, he pulled her gently to her feet. "Let's go to bed."

She looked at the children. "I shouldn't stay. I can go home."

"Mamita, this house is where you belong." He didn't release her hand as he took her upstairs and into the bedroom. Rather than turning on lights and running down the solar batteries, he lit a couple of candles. Odd, there wasn't any debris anywhere. "You cleaned up the place?"

"The girls and I did. There wasn't much mess, not compared to the places I visited today. Your cupboards didn't fly open, no bookshelves toppled over. The fridge didn't even move. Did you deliberately make the place earthquake-proof?"

"Of course." He chuckled. "The sarge was a survivalist, remember? The Hermitage is prepared for anything, including earthquakes. Furniture that might topple over is strapped down. Nothing heavy is kept up high to fall down on a person. All our windows have shatterproof film on them. I tell you, that one cost a mint."

"But it worked. One of Bull's windows broke, and it was amazing how the glass broke into chunks, but nothing fell. Like auto windshields."

"Excellent. I pulled more than enough glass out of flesh

today." Including from his girl's arms and legs. "How are you doing?"

"Fine. Just tired."

Considering all the scrapes and gashes and bruises he'd seen on her, he was guessing she felt a bit more than that. But she was here, watching over Regan and Delaney. "Did Bull ask you to babysit?"

"No." She walked over to the window to look out. "Regan heard my car and ran over to ask me to stay with them until you got home."

Contentment warmed his heart as he put his arms around his woman. "I know how she feels. I'm happier when you're here, too."

Hugging him, she whispered the words he needed to hear. "I love you."

A while later, JJ sighed as she lay on Caz, damp skin melding them together. Rubbing her cheek against his chest, she listened to the slowing lub-dub of his heart.

"How are *you* doing?" Although exhausted, she couldn't stop stroking his shoulders, his biceps. The way his velvety skin stretched tightly over rock-hard muscles was an endless fascination. "Whenever I returned to the station, there were more people waiting to see you."

"It was a mess. No one died on my watch, but Hawk and the other pilot were busy ferrying people to the hospitals. Two were so unstable I kept them until an actual air ambulance could show up."

Rescue was incredibly lucky to have Caz. But, from what she'd seen, the people here knew that.

"I don't know if you heard"—he ran his fingers through her

hair—"Sarah went into labor a couple of hours after the quake. She had a little boy."

"Oh, wow." JJ lifted her head. "Is she all right?"

"Both of them are fine. The midwife swung by afterward to get restocked with supplies. Mmm, probably around eleven."

"Everybody had a long day, I guess." A new baby. Nature's miracle. She laid her head down again, loving how his arm tightened around her. "I wonder how long it'll be before things return to normal. Dante's store is a mess. A lot of the stuff on the shelves fell."

"He'll have an earthquake sale and get rid of anything that's dented." Caz made a grumbling noise. "Bull will want help to clean up all the broken glassware at the roadhouse."

"I stopped by there. He's going to need help all right." Then she laughed.

"What?"

"All the cheap drinks kept beside the bar were broken, but Bull had tethered the more expensive bottles of alcohol to the wall."

Caz chuckled. "He's a careful guy."

They all were. And amazingly generous, too. "Did you know he brought in food for the people sheltering in the municipal building?"

"Sí. He stopped in the clinic with sandwiches and sodas for my people. And extra cookies because he'd heard Regan was helping." Caz stroked JJ's back, managing to avoid the cuts and bandages. "Rescue will be all right, although it'll take time to get the power back on everywhere, deal with propane tank problems. Fix windows."

"I sure had no idea earthquakes were a thing around here."

"Well, this was the Kenai's biggest quake in a century or so. The peninsula isn't on the big fault lines, like the ones in the gulf or north of Anchorage. Then again, nowhere in Alaska is truly safe."

She sighed. "Really, there isn't anywhere on Earth that is safe."

"True enough. Which is why a person should live life and celebrate love when it comes." He paused. "I want you to move in here."

"What? Oh, my God, think of the gossip."

"Think of all those people who have been committing the sin of lying about us." He tugged on her hair, his lips curving up. "We should make the rumors a reality and save their souls. Truly, it's our civic duty."

Even as she laughed at his semi-serious tone, she softened.

Move in. He was right. Life was never long enough—and being together was what they all wanted. "Yes, if you're sure, then"—tears prickled the backs of her eyes—"I'd love to live with you and Regan."

"I am absolutely sure," he murmured.

"Wait..." Remembering what Hawk had said earlier, she tilted her head. "If we make the rumors real, does that mean I'll have sex with your brothers?"

A callused hand on each side of her face lifted her head. His dark eyes were implacable. "Absolutely *not.*"

"Oh, well, damn." She snickered—and the stinging swat on her butt only made her laugh harder.

CHAPTER THIRTY-THREE

W*e come into this world head first and go out feet first; in between, it is all a matter of balance.* - Paul Boese

"Popcorn hog," Regan muttered, happily nudging Niko's hand out of the bowl. On her other side, Delaney snickered.

"Shhh, this is the good part," Niko whispered, petting Sirius, who was sprawled half across his lap and half across Regan's. "I love this movie, and you have the greatest TV for it."

Sitting farther down on the sectional, JJ and Audrey grinned.

Since Mom hadn't liked science fiction or fantasy stuff, Regan hadn't seen the Star Wars movies. When JJ found out, she told Papá it was marathon time...although the marathon would last a lot of nights since Papá didn't let Regan watch more than one show or movie a day.

Even better, Papá and the uncles said Regan could invite her besties. Papá had to pick them up and take them home since the guys—especially Uncle Hawk—were weird about having anyone driving up to the Hermitage. But she had her friends here—that's what was important.

On the television screen, Han Solo fired his blaster, and the bounty hunter's head hit the table.

Regan gasped. "Friggers, he nailed him good."

"See?" JJ crowed and bumped her shoulder against Audrey's. "Han totally shot first."

Audrey scowled. "He did not. Han's a good guy."

Regan heard Papá chuckle. He and the uncles were sitting at the kitchen island doing some sort of business paperwork. Or they were supposed to be doing paperwork. She turned.

Papá winked at her. "Han shot first."

"Yeah, totally." Grinning, Regan grabbed another handful of popcorn.

"Oh, darn," Audrey said a few minutes later. "I need to go punch down the bread and get it rising again."

"Not a problem." JJ picked up the remote and paused the movie. "Break time."

"Nooo," Niko groaned. And Regan gave a loud sigh that made Delaney giggle.

JJ only laughed. "Too bad. We'll restart when Audrey gets back."

"S'okay." Niko grinned. "We'll work on the popcorn."

It was why she liked Niko. Not much bothered him; he was a lot like Uncle Bull.

As JJ rose, Delaney raised her hand like she was still in school. "Miss—I mean Officer JJ?"

JJ stopped.

"Um, Grams got home yesterday. I guess people talked to her about stuff, and she's really mad at Mom and wanted me to tell you a message." Delaney turned pink. "And Mom gave me a note for you."

JJ got her cop-face on—all cold and hard—and Delaney edged closer to Regan. Delaney's mom was Giselle, who'd said nasty stuff about JJ. Was JJ going to be mean?

Regan put her arm around Delaney. What should she say?

But then JJ kinda smiled and sat down on the coffee table, so she didn't look big or anything. "Sorry, you took me by surprise."

She took the note Delaney was holding out and read it, and her face got soft. "I think your mama didn't realize how much she loved you. She does now—and she wants me to teach her how to braid your hair like Regan's."

Delaney'd said her mama was being all lovey now. Regan grinned. "Maybe JJ can make our braids match?"

Delaney bounced. "Yes!"

JJ laughed a little, then stopped. "What did your Grams want to tell me?"

"She made me say everything a bunch of times to get it right." Delaney sat up straight. "Grams said, 'Please tell the officer that I apologize for my thoughtless words. I think all of us in Rescue are extremely lucky to have her here.'"

Looking away, JJ blinked fast. Then she said softly, "I'm not sure I remember your grandmother."

"She's Mrs. Hudson," Regan offered.

"Ah, the woman with the broken hip. Is she all right, Delaney?"

Delaney nodded. "Uh-huh. She was in the hospital and the rehab place to learn to walk. She has to use a walker for a while."

"I'm glad she's better. Please tell her thank you, and it's forgiven and forgotten." JJ grinned and wrinkled her nose at Delaney. "Do I need to make you say it a bunch of times?"

Delaney broke into giggles, setting them all off.

"So, Niko, how's school in the new place?" JJ asked.

After almost two weeks off, they'd started back to school yesterday in two houses that'd been bed & breakfasts a long time ago. Uncle Bull told the school they could use the houses until they could fix the portables or get something better. Where their old school and playground had been was covered by the slide.

A lot of the kids wouldn't even go down that road now.

"It's kinda weird. All the middle schoolers are in one house and us in the other one. But I like it," Niko said. "Mrs. Wilner said this is like testing things out so they know what to fix during winter break."

"Sounds smart." JJ tilted her head. "Any more problems with your bullies?"

Regan shook her head. "Brayden wasn't in school."

"He's not coming back." Delaney's mouth tilted up. "His mom was all upset about the earthquake. And Brayden didn't want to come back to school cuz…"

Cuz he proved he was a wussy, like Papá said bullies were.

Regan said aloud, "Cuz he was all upset about the earthquake, too."

"Anyway," Delaney smiled. "They're moving back to Indiana."

Regan grinned. "Good."

"What about Shelby?" JJ asked.

"I think she'll be okay." Niko rubbed Sirius's ears, and the purr got louder. "She was always meaner when Brayden was around."

"Sounds good." JJ patted Regan's knee and stood. "How do you guys feel about nachos for lunch?"

Regan laughed as her friends cheered.

As JJ headed toward the kitchen, Regan felt as if she had little happy bubbles in her chest. Because JJ had moved in, and Niko said that meant she and Papá would get married.

And that meant JJ would be a mamá. *My mamá.*

Sitting in the kitchen, Caz looked up as the children cheered about the food. That was a fine sound.

Across the island from him, Gabe grinned. "Nice to have kids around the place."

"Yeah, it is." Bull plunked down beers in front of Caz and Gabe.

Caz finished reading the profit and loss statement Bull had brought. The company had a name now—Sarge's Investment

Group. Hawk shortened the name to SIG...which was also a nick-name for Sig Sauer firearms. The corporation was doing quite well. Because Mako'd bought properties for very little, SIG was able to offer incentives to new Rescue businesses and still make a profit. "Looks good, 'mano."

Gabe tapped a finger on the document. "What's the next step for the town? Are we going to continue pushing for growth? I'm for that, although the Patriot Zealots might push back."

"Do we give a damn?" Hawk growled.

"The PZs are a problem, and with more than their aversion to the town's growth." Caz frowned. "The women and children I've seen in the clinic have an abnormal number of bruises in various stages of healing."

Gabe's gaze met his. "Knowing you, you pushed."

"Sí. Even when alone, none of the patients"—victims—"will talk to me." It frustrated the hell out of him.

"We're going to have to do something about them, Gabe," Bull said.

"We are. And soon." Gabe's mouth flattened. "I get the impression Parrish's star is waning and Nabera's is on the rise. Trouble is Nabera is a few miles past fanatic and heading straight for crazy."

"Oh good. And here I thought I'd be bored." Hawk's eyes gleamed with cynical amusement.

Bull turned. "You back to stay now, bro?"

"Yeah. Who knows, maybe you'll need a sniper."

"What's a sniper?" Regan put her glass on the island, her inno-cent brown eyes silencing all of them.

Hawk actually looked worried.

"Ah... A sniper is someone who shoots a rifle almost as well as I throw a knife." Caz grinned as relief—and insult—swept over Hawk's face. "What happened to *Star Wars*?"

"Audrey had to go do something with bread, so we're on a break till she gets back." Regan climbed onto the island stool beside Gabe. "When are you going to teach me to throw knives, Papá?"

Throw knives? His *baby*? "You're too young."

There was a husky laugh, and JJ leaned against him. "When, exactly, did you start playing with knives, Cazador?"

His brothers snickered—*pinche pendejos*—because he'd stabbed someone the first time he'd been on the streets. At seven.

"Seems like you fell in love with actually *throwing* knives the day Grayson took yours away and tossed it into a tree," Bull said. "First time we met him, right?"

Gabe's lips curved. "He busted up our fight and disarmed you faster than I thought possible."

"Sí. I'd never seen a knife thrown before. It was..." There had been a stark beauty in how the blade flew through the air, turning over and over. He'd heard the loud thud as it embedded itself into the tree and stuck there, quivering. So very deadly. "It was glorious."

"Who's Grayson?" Regan leaned her forearms on the island. His curious child. No longer quiet or afraid to ask questions.

"Zachary Grayson, a friend of Mako's. When we were kids, he'd visit to see how we were doing," Bull answered.

The psychologist had made periodic trips from Florida to check on them. To do whatever counseling they needed at the time. He'd told them later that he'd been concerned about a paranoid survivalist raising four street kids.

Caz grinned. "The next day, Grayson saw me trying to throw like he had, but my knives just bounced off the trees. He picked one up and showed me that a throwing knife had to balance...and then talked about how a man's life needed balance as well. If I wanted to get where I wanted to go, I must find the balance."

Regan frowned. "Balance in what?"

"In everything, mija." Caz pulled JJ closer. "As a boy, I had to learn to balance anger and peace." He winked at his daughter. "You know that one, sí?"

She grinned back.

"Later, he talked to me about the balance in taking lives...and saving lives."

"Later?" Gabe's eyes narrowed. "Like in another decade? Grayson was who talked you into returning to being a medic?"

And out of being an assassin. "He did. Mako sicced him on me."

Bull snorted a laugh. "Sounds like the sarge."

The sarge's plan had worked...as they usually did.

Caz smiled at his daughter. Like the sarge, he'd be honored to pass to his child the skills he had learned. "After you learn the balance between fighting and walking away, I'll teach you about knives."

Regan gave him a happy nod.

He glanced at JJ. "Do you want to learn, too, mi corazón?"

"Knives? Seriously? No way." Her eyebrows lifted. "I agree with Han. *'Hokey religions and ancient weapons are no match for a good blaster at your side'.* I'll stick to my pistol, thanks."

"That's what I say." Hawk gave a rusty laugh as he nodded his approval of JJ. "Keep this one longer than a night, bro."

"I intend to, 'mano. I will keep her for all the nights." Caz smiled as JJ's laughing eyes met his.

Pulling his love closer, he kissed her once, then again, and whispered, "For forever."

ALSO BY CHERISE SINCLAIR

Masters of the Shadowlands Series

Club Shadowlands
Dark Citadel
Breaking Free
Lean on Me
Make Me, Sir
To Command and Collar
This Is Who I Am
If Only
Show Me, Baby
Servicing the Target
Protecting His Own
Mischief and the Masters
Beneath the Scars
Defiance

Mountain Masters & Dark Haven Series

Master of the Mountain
Simon Says: Mine
Master of the Abyss

Master of the Dark Side
My Liege of Dark Haven
Edge of the Enforcer
Master of Freedom
Master of Solitude
I Will Not Beg

The Wild Hunt Legacy

Hour of the Lion
Winter of the Wolf
Eventide of the Bear
Leap of the Lion

Sons of the Survivalist Series

Not a Hero
Lethal Balance

Standalone Books

The Dom's Dungeon
The Starlight Rite

Lethal Balance
Copyright © 2019 by Cherise Sinclair
ISBN: 978-1-947219-18-2
Published by VanScoy Publishing Group
Cover Art: I'm No Angel Designs
Edited by Red Quill Editing, LLC
Content Editor: Bianca Sommerland
Photographer: Kruse Images & Photography
Cover Model: Craig Gierish